A SIMPLE OPERATION . . .

A professional doesn't ask questions. He just does the job. And considering the money his employer had laid out, Swarse would do the job right.

It was a piece of cake. Put on a white coat and look like you know what you're doing. No one would stop him. He could see the outline of the bed, the form of the patient, the tubes leading from the overhead drip. Blake lay with his eyes closed, the only sound the faint wheeze of his breathing. His arms were outside the covers, palms up.

Swarse lifted the left hand and gently turned it over, finding the rose tattoo. He gave a grunt of satisfaction and let the hand drop. He leaned his weight to the side of the bed until he was firmly balanced, then placed both his hands around the old man's neck, and began to squeeze. . . .

DEEP
GOLD

Arthur Mather

BANTAM BOOKS
TORONTO • NEW YORK • LONDON • SYDNEY • AUCKLAND

DEEP GOLD
A Bantam Book / May 1986

ISBN 0-553-25623-8

Published simultaneously in the United States and Canada

Bantam Books are published by Bantam Books, Inc. Its trade-
mark, consisting of the words "Bantam Books" and the portrayal
of a rooster, is Registered in U.S. Patent and Trademark Office
and in other countries. Marca Registrada. Bantam Books, Inc.,
666 Fifth Avenue, New York, New York 10103.

PRINTED IN THE UNITED STATES OF AMERICA

H   0 9 8 7 6 5 4 3 2 1

DEEP
GOLD

Chapter 1

"Old tart," muttered the man on the bed.

The words were thready and indistinct, more breathed than spoken. He was still unconscious, but his half-open eyes stared with a sightless lack of expression at the white ceiling of the single hospital ward. His age was perhaps sixty to sixty-five, and the operation had left him with a bad pallor. Tubes ran from his nose and arms like disgorged entrails, and a cap of bandages girdled his skull. He had an overlarge nose, and the doctor delicately pushed it to one side as he shone the penlight into the man's eyes.

"Old tart," repeated the patient several more times.

"What did he say?" asked the nurse from the other side of the bed. She leaned forward to make an adjustment to the pillow, and even the discipline of her uniform failed to disguise she was a well-made woman. In her early thirties, very dark, with perhaps Spanish in her blood. The doctor had made a play for her like everyone else, and failed like everyone else. She had a slight accent with an adenoid problem, that gave an attractive huskiness to her voice.

"He said 'old tart,'" murmured the doctor.

"Old tart?"

"Yes. Whatever that's supposed to mean."

The doctor sat back on the bed with a sigh, and flicked off the penlight. He smiled at the nurse, but his eyes took in more than her face. He was fifty, gray, distinguished, and fighting a losing battle with a paunch. "Maybe it's something starting to filter through to his memory already. It's obviously too soon to tell yet, but let's hope so."

He stood up from the bed, and put the penlight in his pocket. The buzz of traffic came faintly through the window. A beam of sunlight found an opening down the side

1

of the blinds and focused on the patient's face, brightening
his sallow complexion.

"Old tart," he croaked again.

"Maybe he's remembering an old flame," suggested
the nurse.

"It certainly doesn't sound like a description of his
mother," said the doctor, grinning. "Or exactly the way
he'd remember an old love affair."

The nurse shrugged, fussing at the sheets, and straight-
ening the bedside cupboard. She knew the doctor was
watching, and it showed in her self-conscious movements
as she ran her fingers gently along the patient's arm.

"I've never seen a tattoo like that before," she murmured, indicating a small, exquisitely designed, black-
and-red rose on the back of the man's left hand.

The doctor nodded absently. "Yes, unusual, isn't it.
It's one of the things I noticed when he first came to see
me."

"I suppose you asked him about it?"

"Of course, but it didn't mean a thing to him. It's
probably been there for years, maybe something he had
done as a young man. But he has no memory at all of
when it was done."

"I don't like tattoos, but it's sort of pretty," she mused.
She lifted her gaze to the doctor. "Is he going to be all
right, Doctor Hodges?"

The doctor nodded confidently. He wished she'd call
him Phillip when they were alone like this, but he knew it
was pointless asking.

"I think he's going to be just fine. It'll take time
before he recovers from the operation, but then we can
start making tests to see if there's been any restoration of
his memory."

Her eyes softened with pity. "It must be weird," she
murmured. "Going through life not remembering. Not
remembering who you are, where you came from, about
your parents, your beginnings, anything at all. Not even
something that happened a few weeks ago."

"Terrible. It made his life a misery."

"I can believe it. I'd hate to have it happen to me."
She began to edge toward the door. "If you've finished

your examination, Doctor, I'm off duty in a few minutes. Do you wish me to leave any special instructions with Nurse Harland?"

He studied the man on the bed for a moment before answering, then he followed her to the door. "That's all right, Honi, I'll speak to her. I think we'll just keep him sedated for the next few days so he can have as much rest as possible." He opened the door, and ushered her through ahead of him. "Care for a cup of coffee before you go?"

She went into the corridor with a shake of her head, and the practiced smile of apology slipped easily into place. "I'd really love to, Doctor, but I'm afraid I have an appointment, and I don't want to be late. Perhaps another time."

She could make a refusal sound as if she would wait breathlessly for a follow-up invitation, but he knew better.

"Sure, some other time." He managed to smile.

"I'll look forward to it," she said.

He knew it would never happen. He stood for a time, appreciating the appeal of her retreating gait, then turned away with a shrug. Sexual fantasies over Nurse Honi Juric were a frustration best put aside; the main thing was she was a hell of a good nurse. If his operation on the so-called John Blake was successful, his name would make all the medical journals. That's what really mattered. If Blake recovered his memory, then he'd be famous. Already there'd been so much publicity he didn't dare contemplate the possibility of failure. And why should he, when it had all gone better than he could have hoped.

The late afternoon traffic was gathering momentum along Columbus Avenue. A sharp late summer breeze had freed New York of its carbon monoxide haze, so Nurse Juric decided to walk. Her red coat was in startling contrast to her former white uniform, her black hair now loose and lustrous in the sun. The parcel swung easily in her hand as she strode briskly to Lincoln Center, then crossed over to the small coffee shop by Sixty-third Street.

The shop was sparse of people, and the large man in the checked coat was waiting for her at the rear. He made the table and all about him seem small by comparison, hunched forward, arms crossed, large balding head pulled deep into his shoulders like a bull ready to charge. Every line in his face expressed a tight watchfulness. His Italian ancestry would have been obvious before he'd lost his hair. He had the whitest skin she'd ever seen, whiter than the patient she tended back at the hospital. She estimated he was about forty-five. He claimed the name Swarse, but she didn't believe him; not that it mattered. She needed the money so badly she wouldn't have cared if he'd said he was Donald Duck.

She sat down, put the parcel on the floor by her feet, and offered a hesitant smile of greeting. She was aware of the same sense of fear from their previous meetings, but she tried to shut it out of her mind. He didn't return her smile, but then he wasn't a man given to the normal pleasantries. He clicked his fingers and brought the waitress scurrying to take his order, delivered in a surprisingly light tone. Then he concentrated on her, massaging his hands together, wintry black eyes never leaving her face.

"I brought the jacket," she said.

He gave an almost imperceptible nod of his head. All his movements were slight, as if as guarded of himself as others.

"Good. The operation on Blake's over?"

"Yes. That's why I called you."

"The doctor pulled it off? He's gonna be okay?"

"It seems so at the moment. It's too early to know if he's going to get his memory back."

"The doctor figures he'll make it?"

"Like I said, it's too soon to tell."

"Do you figure he'll get his memory back?"

She gave a nervous laugh. "How would I know? The doctor's one of the best neurosurgeons in the city. He's the only one who knows." She shrugged. "All I can say is he's confident there's a good chance."

He nodded curtly, took a plastic toothpick from his pocket, and absently mined his teeth. The waitress bustled over with their coffee, but neither made any attempt to drink.

"He's conscious enough to talk to anyone?" he asked.

"No, not properly. He's heavily sedated."

"You mean drugged, that sort of stuff?"

"Yes."

"Too doped to say anything?"

She hesitated, fingers trailing apprehensively over her cup. "Just wanderings," she finally admitted.

"Wanderings? What's that supposed to mean?" he demanded suspiciously.

"Just words."

"What sort of words?" he persisted.

She suppressed a timid giggle. "Old tart."

He stared at her with the stoney expression of a man not amused by someone playing the fool. "Don't play games with me," he growled.

"That's what he said. That's all he said."

"Old tart?"

"Yes, over and over. He wasn't conscious, of course, but the words just kept, well, dribbling out of his mouth."

"What did the doctor say?"

"He didn't know what they meant, he just sort of smiled."

"You too?"

She shuffled about awkwardly on the chair. "Well, I suppose so. It sounded sort of funny. I guess they don't mean anything to anyone except him. Just something that must have come into his head, perhaps that he remembered from his past."

"You said it was too soon yet."

"It is if you're talking about a full recovery. But . . ." She shrugged. "The doctor said it was possible it could have been something he was remembering."

He nodded slowly, and the chair creaked ominously as he sat back from the table. Steam whisped into the air from the hot coffee like a veil between them. The pupils of his eyes seemed to shrink to pinpoints of light.

"I'll have to speak to my, ah, friends about that," he muttered. "But I still want the chance to try and identify him . . . in secret like we agreed before. I figure I might just know him, and I've got good reasons to want to do it in secret."

But he'd never put the reasons into words, and for a moment she hesitated before making a final commitment.

But if she didn't get the money, her parents were stuck in Poland, perhaps forever. Maybe it would help Blake, she rationalized, if this man did know his real identity.

"Well, you have the jacket," she said quickly, pointing to the parcel on the floor.

The corners of his mouth turned with the faintest glimmer of a smile. She suspected it was more pleasure at seeing her squirm than satisfaction.

"Okay. When do you figure is the best time for me to try?"

"Late. I'd wait until after midnight. There shouldn't be many people around the ward then." She gave him the floor and room number, but he made no attempt to write them down. "You can't mistake the room," she added.

"I don't want any foul-ups," he grunted. "I want to be sure I'm looking at the right man."

Her tongue slid apprehensively about her mouth. "Well, he has a tattoo on the back of his left hand. A tattoo of a rose. It's quite unusual. I've never seen one like it before."

He seemed to find some satisfaction in the information, for the cold smile came again. "Good, good," he murmured. "That makes it easier."

"I'm sure you can't mistake the room anyway," she repeated.

"He'll be asleep?"

"Like I said, he's heavily sedated."

"What time are you back at the hospital?"

"I go back on around ten-thirty in the morning."

He fell silent, his brows puckered in concentration. Maybe I've told him too much, she thought, and now I won't get the money. She'd never done anything like this before.

"I'll go for it," he declared suddenly. He reached into his pocket, took out a brown envelope, and dropped it on the table in front of her. "It's all there," he said flatly. "I haven't gone back on the deal we made. You don't have to count it."

She stared warily at the envelope as if it was contaminated with some disease, then cautiously picked it up and turned it over in her hands. It was half what she needed; now if she could just raise the rest.

"It's all there," he muttered, misinterpreting her hesitancy.

She didn't answer, but thrust it quickly into her pocket. He hunched forward toward her, and she felt an uneasy sense of being threatened.

"Anything else to do with Blake," he said, pointing to her pocket. "Anything at all, any phone calls, any messages, anything, and I'll double that. We're in business together now, baby, and I know you'd want to do the best by your partner."

She nodded slowly, wondering how he'd react to a refusal. Was she hooked? Was the real meaning of the envelope in her pocket a partnership contract with this ape? She hadn't thought of it that way before. Maybe her parents were all that mattered, but her hand was trembling when she reached for her cup.

He ignored his own coffee, picked up the parcel, threw some money on the table, and stood to his feet. He seemed to tower above as if it would be so easy for him to crush her.

"I'll be in touch," he said brusquely.

She didn't watch him leave. The coffee was cold, but she drank it anyway, needing to water her parched throat. She sat there a long time, consuming coffee after coffee until sunlight gave way to artificial light, and the traffic along Columbus Avenue to a dazzling headlight tournament. Then she went home, and stayed under the shower for an hour.

It was a piece of cake. Put on a white coat, walk the corridors of the hospital with the confident stride of someone who belongs, who knows what they're doing and where they're going, and no one will challenge you. Only the Juric woman knew his face, knew him as Swarse.

He strode easily to Blake's room, a towel draped over his arm, then went inside and closed the door. He stood motionless in the semidarkness, conscious of the antiseptic odor he always associated with hospitals. The light from the corridor glowed faintly from the bottom of the door,

and through the window was the nighttime shimmer of
New York.

He could see the outline of the bed, the form of the
patient, the tubes connecting to the overhead drip. He
fumbled for the switch, turned on the light, and moved
cautiously to the bed. Blake lay with his eyes closed, the
only sound the faint wheeze of his breathing. His arms
were outside the covers, palms of his hands upward. Swarse
lifted the left hand, and gently turned it over until the
rose tattoo was visible, then he gave a grunt of satisfaction
and let the hand drop back on the bed. He put the towel
down on the bedside cupboard, leaned his weight to the
side of the bed until he was firmly balanced, then placed
both his hands around Blake's throat, and began to squeeze.
To his surprise the man's eyes popped open, and in a
reflex action his hands clawed at Swarse's strangling fingers. The connecting tubes coiled in the air like agitated
snakes, threatening to bring down the overhead drip.

It was unexpected and he bore down harder, tighten-
ing his grip until there was a faint crack, and the man
went limp. He stepped back from the bed, breathing
heavily, softly rubbing his hands together. He was surprised it had taken the man so long to die, and he gave an
irritated shrug of his shoulders. Christ, he hadn't intended
to use so much force, but the man's reaction had taken
him by surprise. Did it matter? The contract put out by
the connection in Australia wanted Blake accidentally dead,
and who was to know he simply hadn't died from the
operation? Such things happened all the time. The prick
of a doctor would just have to live with the fact his patient
hadn't survived, and serve the fucker right. The Australians paid well, and he hoped there'd be other contracts,
for it might mean he could spend a year in the Bahamas
with Ella.

He had the nurse in his pocket now, anything he
asked she had to go with, or he'd drop the word to the
hospital she was on the take, and that'd be the end of her
as a nurse. He retrieved the towel, took one final glance at
the slain man before he flicked off the light, then went
quietly out into the corridor.

Chapter 2

Zarich nursed her along the way she liked. Maybe making it good for her was a way of easing his conscience, but the rewards always cut both ways.

"Don't leave me, don't leave me," she moaned, but he did anyway. He put his mouth to her breast, teasing her softly with his hand, and her heart revved beneath him like a squad car on a fast takeoff.

Then she took over. He couldn't hold her any longer. She was a big girl, bigger than him, and she straddled over, thrusting him down until he was tight in her again, then driving at him with a fierce rhythm. He hadn't figured on losing control, but she was away with a fervor threatening to overwhelm him, so he went with her, not that he could have done anything else anyway. It was just as well she couldn't see the cold detachment in his head; she was concentrating on achieving nothing but mind-blowing orgasm, while he was already framing the first question.

Then she was panting and moaning, breathing obscenities in his ear, and for a brief moment he became part of the cataclysm, then the questions quickly gained ascendancy in his mind again.

They lay side by side on the bed, the sobs in her throat gradually subsiding, her pulse running down until the movement of her breasts returned to normal. It was a nice bedroom, tasteful pictures on the walls, the furniture probably selected from some exclusive shop along Madison where they wouldn't even let you in the door without first examining your credit cards. His ex-wife would have liked it. Maybe one of the reasons she walked out was because he couldn't give her stuff like this. But then Abe had probably bought it for Ella anyway.

"Christ, that was terrific," she finally murmured.

9

"That's good," he said offhandedly.

"You too?"

He shrugged. Why did they always have to ask that? If it was good for her, then it was good for him. He ran his fingers irritably through his sandy hair. He was thirty-two, with a face of crags and crevices that looked as if it had been carved on Mount Rushmore. He wished he could have made six feet—he was only five-eleven—but it didn't stop him from effortlessly scoring with women, a fact he scarcely understood yet accepted as one of those joys nature unaccountably distributes. It had been a joy for Rhonda once, but "no" wasn't a word in his vocabulary, and in the end she said no wife should be expected to live with that sort of constant competition. Could he blame her? But he made it work for him on the job. The Police Department didn't approve, of course, but they looked at his homicide score sheet, and kept their mouths shut. He had a score the envy of every cop in Manhattan, so the brass preferred not to know rather than question his methods.

"Nice room," he observed casually.

She didn't understand the comment, but raised her head from the pillow, and glanced about the room. She was no great looker, but her profile wasn't so bad. He wouldn't have believed how easy it was to pick her up in the bar. She must have a kink for living dangerously, because with Abe paying the bills he'd expect exclusive service, and he wasn't beyond breaking an arm or a leg if he didn't get it.

"Well, I'm glad you like it," she murmured drowsily, trying to snuggle back against him. "Anyhow, who cares about the room with what we've got going here."

"Furniture must have cost a heap," he persisted.

She frowned, lifted herself again, and placed a hand on his chest.

"Forget it, baby. Your furniture's all I'm interested in."

"Did Abe pay for it, Ella?"

She fell silent, her body stilled as if with paralysis. She didn't move for a time, then turned away and reached for her cigarettes on the bedside table. She switched on the lamp, shrugged up into a sitting position, then lit up and blew a cloud of smoke at the ceiling. In the stronger light it was more apparent the way her large breasts drooped badly, with her blond hair hanging like string about her shoulders. She looked older than he remembered.

"Well, did Abe pay for it?" he pressed her.

"Who the hell is Abe?" she bluffed irritably.

He sighed. But then he'd taken her off guard, so maybe it was unfair to expect any clever evasion.

"Abe Liavone."

She stayed cool, taking another drag at her cigarette, but he could almost hear her orgasm-dulled mind trying to shift into top gear.

"What sort of shit is that? I pay for my own furniture, and I don't know any Abe Liavone," she reiterated sullenly.

"I hear differently, Ella," he pressed her. "I *know* about Abe Liavone."

She switched around on her ass, rustling the sheets, and stared down at him with hostility. It always got to him how fast lust could convert to anger.

"You *know*? Then you know wrong, baby." She flicked ash agitatedly about the bed. "Say, what the hell is this? What's it got to do with you anyway?"

"I thought you might be able to tell me a few things about Abe I want to know."

Her eyes narrowed, and she peered down at him through a haze of smoke. "Say, you only told me your name was Ed," she observed with sudden suspicion. "What the hell is your last name?"

"Zarich."

She paused with the cigarette part way to her mouth, then rested her hand back on her drawn-up knees. "Zarich?" She frowned. She contemplated a moment longer, then her eyes widened, and her mouth trembled as if fighting back tears. He figured it was a long time since Ella had cried, and her reaction was more fear than bruised feelings.

"Zarich," she spat at him. "Jesus Christ, you're a cop."

"That's what I do," he said easily, then he spread his hands about the bed. "Apart from this."

He decided against any further pretense, because

throwing her right off balance could trip unguarded words
from her mouth. He was wrong. She'd been easy in the
bar, but she wasn't easy now.

"You bastard," she snarled at him. "You motherfucking
bastard."

"Come on now, Ella, they're not the kind of words
you were using before.'

"You creep, you set me up."

"I'm not setting you up for anything. I'd just like
some information about Abe."

"Go to hell." She flung back the covers, and thrust
herself out of bed. She wasn't a good sight, drooping
breasts flapping with indignation, her broad ass, the texture of her skin like crinkled tissue. He wondered vaguely
how old she really was, then it was all quickly gone into a
handsome purple gown. He sat up in the bed, and soberly
watched her. Her cool was gone now, hands never still,
rummaging in her hair, plucking at her gown.

"I'm on your side, Ella." He tried to calm her.

"The hell you are. Fucking jerk of a cop, get out of
my apartment."

"I'm trying to save you from Abe."

"When I need saving, you're the last prick I'd ask. I
know how to handle Abe."

At least she'd abandoned any pretense of ignorance
about Liavone.

"People who run with hoods like Abe Liavone finish
up dead," he tried to warn her.

"Fuck you, get out," she screamed. "I got rights, I'll
report you, get out, get out."

Maybe he'd come on too strong, and it wasn't going
to work. He shrugged and eased himself off the bed, while
she braced herself against the window, arms crossed, staring angrily at him. He dressed with slow deliberation,
asking no more questions, hoping she might calm down.
The faded denims, the check shirt, the jacket, then pushing his hair into place in the large wall mirror. With a
day's growth of beard he looked more like the guy who
made the heist instead of the arrest.

He tried again. "You owe more to staying alive than
protecting someone like Liavone."

"Fuck off," she threw furiously at him.

He pursed his lips, took a card from his pocket, and placed it by the bedside lamp. "I want you to think about it, Ella," he said. "Do yourself a favor. I've got a hunch a guy like Abe wants exclusive treatment for his money. I figure he wouldn't take kindly to his investment letting herself get picked up like some bar tramp."

She dropped her arms, and for the first time he saw real fear supplant the anger in her face.

"You lousy bastard," she muttered. "You wouldn't do a thing like that?"

He grimaced with mock contrition. "Well, I certainly wouldn't like to, baby, not knowing Abe the way I do." He tapped the card. "You think about it, eh? When you figure it might be safer for you to answer a few questions, just give me a call." He walked to the door, and didn't look back at her until he opened it. She was leaning to the window, hands behind her against the glass, eyes wide, the flush in her face now replaced by a pasty whiteness.

"You . . . you . . . wouldn't?" she gasped.

He capped a hand to his mouth, and blew her a farewell kiss. "It was great, baby. I just know we're going to see a lot more of each other."

There was a cool breeze rustling along Thirty-fourth Street, and he turned the collar of his jacket up around his neck. He felt a little like the way he had as a kid playing in the mud of a Brooklyn backyard, but sometimes there was no other way when you were trying to put away scum such as Liavone. He would give Ella a few days, but he was sure she'd make the call.

It was three in the afternoon when he got back to the station, and there was a message waiting for him.

"Beuso called from upstairs," said Dawkins. "He wants to hear from you as soon as you get in."

Zarich nodded. Beuso didn't know he was running down Liavone, but he might want a report of the Delmenico business. He didn't feel good. There was an emptiness in his stomach he knew wasn't due to hunger, yet why should he get uptight about using women like Ella? Maybe he should marry again. But who? What woman wants a husband who lives and breathes like a hound dog, who picks up a scent and can't stop running, his nose always grubbing in the ground.

"How'd you make out with Liavone's broad?" asked Dawkins snidely.

"It might work," said Zarich blandly.

"You get any answers?"

Dawkins was a small man, with darting eyes and features that looked as if they'd been sharpened by a razor, pointing chin, pointing nose, missing nothing. He knew about Zarich, albeit enviously, and although Zarich outranked him, there was a long association that allowed personal probing. He was a few years older than Zarich, his waistline evidence of a passion for pasta. He was married with three children, and a mortgage, which, he often declared without conviction, was the way life was meant to be.

"Not yet, but it's only a matter of time," said Zarich confidently. He picked up the phone and dialed Beuso. "If she calls and I'm out, take her along easy, Mal. She might want to come and see me here, but tell her I'll set up a meeting place where she might be more . . . comfortable."

Dawkins stuck a cigar into his grinning mouth, and gave a lewd wink. "Understood, Ed," he said. Then he strolled out to his desk, dropped into the chair, and scowled ferociously at the cringing black kid opposite.

Beuso's nasally Southern twang came on the phone.

"Ed, I want you to go over to City Hospital, and talk to a Doctor Hodges," he said.

The name sounded familiar. "I seem to know the name," said Zarich.

"The *Post* ran a story on him the other day. A neurosurgeon who's developed some new brain surgery technique to help people who've lost their memory. I don't know the details, but you might have seen the story."

The connection clicked into place. "That's right, I did see the story. There was a follow-up this morning, something about the guy he was operating on dying."

"Yeah, yeah, that's the one."

"What's the doctor's problem?"

"Well, it's a bit of a sticky one, Ed." Beuso sounded

uncharacteristically hesitant. "He, ah . . . discussed it with me, but he's also talked to some people in high places."

"What's that supposed to mean?"

"I guess . . ." There was hesitancy again. "Just take him along easy, talk to him, see if you can help him out with the problem. We'll talk about it when you get back."

He hung up quickly, and Zarich stared thoughtfully at the phone. Someone was obviously screwing Beuso, and it was being passed on down to him. The *Post* had made quite a human interest story of it, a man without memory who volunteers for a new brain surgery technique, then dies after uttering just two words. He hustled around the office until he located a copy of the newspaper, and reread the story. That was it, "old tart," whatever the hell it was supposed to mean. It sounded intriguing, but why would this Doctor Hodges want to talk to homicide? He'd try and get it over quickly, because he hated to be sidetracked from Liavone.

Hodges was smooth, and cool as a New York sidewalk in midwinter. Clones of Phillip Hodges could be seen any day of the week along Fifth Avenue, or the Upper East Side. Immaculately groomed, distinguished gray hair fashionably cut, flawless well-fed skin, concealed paunch, features arranged with unmistakable superiority. His eyes were slightly contracted behind myopic lens. He looked about fifty, but was so sleek it was difficult to be accurate. His eyes took in Zarich's casual clothes, then he smiled pleasantly, and indicated a chair on the other side of the desk. It was a small office for someone with Hodges' reputation.

"I have an apartment on Madison Avenue," he said at once, as if sensing the anomaly. "But since what we have to discuss concerns the hospital I thought it best if we talk here."

Zarich shrugged complacently. Talk was talk. "I've only had a very vague brief, Doctor. In fact, I've no idea at all why you want to talk to Homicide."

Hodges examined his fingernails, and smiled again. "I don't know if you're aware I'm a neurosurgeon, Lieutenant," he began carefully.

"I read the story in the *Post*," Zarich cut across him.

"Ah, good, that saves considerable explanation. You know something of the man without memory."

"Yes. Is the operation what you want to talk about?"

"Well yes, in a way."

"The story in the *Post* was accurate?"

"Reasonably so. You would have read about John Blake . . . the patient's name?"

"Not in detail. You'll have to fill me in, Doctor."

Hodges paused a moment before continuing. He sat back in the chair and crossed his legs in a slightly contrived attitude of relaxation. "John Blake was an unusual problem, a man we estimated to be in his midsixties. A long time ago, probably when he was a young man, he sustained damage to his brain. A blow, a fall, it's difficult to be sure, but he certainly didn't remember. But it affected what we call the limbic system in the thalmus, a part of the brain we believe enables us to retain memory. John Blake, and let me say that was only a name he invented, because he had no idea of his real identity, in fact he had difficulty retaining any memory at all. Where he came from, his beginnings, anything at all about his past life was a complete blank. Even what happened to him a few weeks ago would have been hard for him to recall."

Zarich stirred impatiently in the chair, and thought about Liavone. He had no idea how what Hodges was telling him connected to Homicide.

"I gathered from the news story you've developed a surgical technique that could correct the problem?"

Hodges made a self-deprecatory motion of his hand. "Well, hopefully, Lieutenant. I was certainly confident enough to try." He sighed. "I won't go into details, but Blake saw an article about the technique, came to see me, and offered to volunteer for the first operation. Or should I say he absolutely insisted."

"Wasn't it dangerous?"

Hodges gave a condescending tilt of his head. "I suppose there's a margin of risk in every operation, Lieutenant."

"But if this was a new technique there must have been more than the usual risk."

"Granted," admitted Hodges. "Believe me, I took great pains to point that out to Blake, but he was adamant. So I carried out a whole series of tests first, then I realized I couldn't have found a more perfect case if I'd scoured the entire country." He shrugged. "So I agreed to go ahead." He indicated a form on the desk. "Of course he signed a clearance document."

"He didn't mind the risk?"

"Lieutenant, this man's affliction had made life a misery for him, I'd guess for something like the last forty years. He couldn't do steady work, he couldn't settle anywhere, he must have had family sometime, somewhere, but it was all blotted out of his mind. He lived in a perpetual fog. I think he didn't believe he had a great deal of life left, and wanting to know who he was became an obsession with him." He grimaced. "I didn't find that hard to understand."

"Something went wrong during the operation?"

"No, it all went perfectly. I was delighted."

"But he died."

"Someone killed him."

Zarich blinked. It was a tactic he might have used himself, a short sharp blow designed to shock.

"You mean here, in the hospital?" he asked in surprise.

"Yes, right in the postoperative ward."

Zarich lapsed into a blank-faced silence. So that was the reason for the phone calls to high places. New Yorkers wouldn't take kindly to the possibility they could be murdered in a ward of City Hospital, and the management would be pulling every string they could get hold of to hush up the killing.

"That sounds incredible," he murmured politely.

"It is incredible. And a disaster."

"How did it happen?"

"I didn't even realize there had been a murder until we decided on a postmortem. When one of the nurses reported no sign of life I came rushing back to the hospital to see him." He shook his head despondently. "I tell you, Lieutenant, I was devastated. Everything had gone so well, but I naturally assumed heart failure. With his age, it's one of those things that can happen. But the postmortem revealed his larynx had been crushed, quite brutally. Someone must have used considerable force. Of course as soon as I realized what had happened, I called the police." He twisted about nervously in the chair. Despite his carefully maintained composure, he was obviously shaken by the recapitulaton. "I can't imagine who would want to kill a harmless, unknown old man like that. It just doesn't make sense. It would have to be a madman."

"They're not usually wandering about the hospital?" asked Zarich blandly.

Hodges looked up, startled. "No, certainly not."

"No one saw anything?"

"No, nothing at all. Whoever did it knew exactly where to find Blake."

"Then we'd have to say it was planned, and not some chance maniac killing. Any idea what time it happened?"

Hodges spread his hands. "We estimate around early morning, say two o'clock or thereabouts. It would be a good time. The hospital quiet, the patients asleep, the nurses relaxed."

"Someone could just wander in like that, and commit a murder?"

"Well, I . . ." Hodges shuffled around in embarrassment, and his face took on a pink hue. "No . . . perhaps . . . well, I suppose someone must have," he admitted.

"You've talked to the hospital management, of course?"

"They're shocked. We all are. You may want to speak to the director later, but as it was my patient they asked me to handle it first." He drew a handkerchief from his pocket, and patted at his brow. There was a nicely monogrammed *H* in the corner of the material. "Lieutenant, both the hospital director and I have . . . ah, spoken to several people about this. I hope the incident can be treated with a certain amount of discretion. This is a good hospital, with an excellent reputation over the years. I don't believe it would be in the city's interests to do anything that would undermine that reputation." He hesitated. "I suppose I'm thinking mainly of the media people. As far as they know, Blake simply died as a result of the operation. They'd have a picnic with us if they knew it was murder." He paused again, shuffling the papers about on the desk, nervously aware of the sudden hardness in Zarich's face.

Zarich shrugged. The poor dead bastard would probably have made Hodges famous; now he was just an unfortunate incident. "That's not up to me, Doctor," he murmured. "Everything will go in my report. What happens after that is obviously up to other people. Of course in the meantime the killing will have to be investigated. We'll want to walk in the victim's shoes."

"Walk in his shoes?"

"Find out everything we can about him. What sort of man he was. Who might possibly want to kill him."

Hodges smiled faintly, and fiddled with his spectacles. "I wish you luck, Lieutenant. I can assure you the man's background is a total blank."

"He must have lived somewhere. Someone must have known him."

"Not to my knowledge."

"You didn't know where he lived?"

"I asked once, but he simply couldn't answer. I wouldn't be surprised if he lived on the streets most of his life. During the few weeks I was doing the tests I found a small apartment for him not far from my office."

"We'll need to look at that."

"Of course."

"And any clothes, any belongings at all."

The doctor nodded in agreement. "You're welcome. But I warn you, there's almost nothing there. I suspect he's always lived in intense poverty."

Zarich rubbed reflectively at his nose. He had a hunch the doctor's anxiety to test out his technique had pushed every other consideration into the background.

"These words I read about, that he spoke after the operation?"

Hodges offered a wan smile. "Ah yes, 'old tart.' The newspaper made quite a mystery of it."

"You gave it to the newspaper?"

"Yes, but then that was before Blake was murdered. I thought it just might mean something to someone, perhaps help us establish Blake's real identity. It was good publicity, but in the light of what happened maybe a mistake."

"Peculiar words. He didn't say anything else?"

"No. You realize he was still unconscious. But he just kept repeating them over and over."

"You think it was something maybe surfacing from his past?"

Hodges shrugged. "It's difficult to know for sure, but yes, highly likely."

"You've no idea what they mean?"

"None whatever. I would like to have had the chance to question him about them."

"Did anyone else hear the words?"

"You think I might have been mistaken, Lieutenant?"

Zarich smiled thinly. "No, I just wondered if anyone else heard them."

"There was a nurse present. Nurse Juric."

"She was attending the patient?"

"Yes, I specially asked for her. She's an excellent nurse."

"She was in the hospital at the time of the murder?"

Hodges paused, and lit up a cigar. To Zarich it seemed more like a ploy to slow down the flow of questions.

"My only vice." The doctor smiled.

Zarich ignored the aside. "The nurse was here?"

"No, she was off duty, and didn't come back on until around ten this morning."

"Then she's here now?"

"Just a moment," said Hodges. He lifted the phone, and pushed the intercom button several times. He waited a second, then spoke very softly. "Honi, would you come in now. The police are here."

He was betrayed by the silky tone of his voice, because Zarich instinctively recognized the inflexion. The doctor had a yen for nurse Juric.

"I thought you'd probably want to see her," explained Hodges. "So I asked that she make herself available."

"I won't keep her long," promised Zarich.

"Just one thing, Lieutenant," warned Hodges. "Nurse Juric has only just found out that Blake was murdered.

Like I did in the beginning, she assumed death was due to heart failure. I only told her the truth half an hour ago."

Zarich reacted with surprise. "Any reason?"

Hodges stared gloomily into space. "As I mentioned before, management and I wanted to keep this terrible business to as few people as possible. At least for now. I knew you'd want to see her, so of course she had to be told. But I'm sure we can rely on her keeping a still tongue."

"How did she take it?"

The doctor mournfully contemplated his cigar. "Very badly," he sighed.

"She saw it as a reflection on herself?"

"No, of course not. She had no reason. But, well, she's used to seeing people die, but not like that."

The door opened, and Zarich understood Hodges' yen when Honi Juric came into the room. It took a connoisseur's eye to see past the uniform and lack of makeup, but she had it all going for her. The hips were too wide, nose too flat, but it didn't matter a damn; the overall effect was a fuse waiting to be lit. She closed the door, moved halfway to the desk, then came to a halt, her feet shuffling nervously about on the floor. Zarich offered a reassuring smile. Maybe it was just him, but it didn't take any brilliant observation to see she was tremendously uptight.

"Honi, this is Lieutenant Zarich," said Hodges.

She tilted her head briefly in acknowledgment, but the tight line of her mouth remained. He would love the chance to soften that line.

"I don't think I can tell you anything, Lieutenant," she said huskily. She sounded as if she had a cold, and there was a faint accent maybe of European origin, but hard to define.

"I think the lieutenant merely wants you to corroborate the words Blake spoke after the operation," Hodges encouraged.

The corners of her mouth relented to a pale smile. "You mean 'old tart,' of course, Doctor?"

"That's right," the doctor replied, smiling.

She shrugged. "He was unconscious, of course, but he just kept saying it over and over again."

"I guess you wouldn't have any more idea what they meant than the doctor," asked Zarich.

She shook her head, trying to concentrate her eyes on him, but they kept sliding away to Hodges for support. "The mind's a strange place, Lieutenant. I'm sure Doctor Hodges has told you that." Zarich could see a slight tremble in her clasped hands. She really was uptight. "I haven't the faintest idea what they mean," she added. "Maybe something from his past like a woman, an experience." The words caught in her throat, and she coughed for a moment. "I don't expect we'll ever know now, not after the terrible way he died."

"You didn't notice anything strange in the ward before you went off duty? Nothing out of the ordinary?"

"No, I left the same time as the doctor. Everything seemed normal,"

Her hands were clasped so tightly it whitened the flesh. She was obviously badly affected by the killing. "I . . . I can't imagine why anyone would want to do such a thing to a lonely old man who probably never harmed anyone in his life."

"Well, I hope we can find out," murmured Zarich.

He fell silent. It wasn't that she was uncooperative, he just had the feeling if she did know anything he'd have to draw it like a tooth.

"Is that all, Doctor?" she inquired of Hodges. "It's a busy time, and . . ."

Hodges glanced to Zarich for confirmation, and he nodded.

"Yes, thank you, Honi," soothed the doctor. He spread his hands in a pleading gesture. "I know I can rely on you not to discuss this with a single soul."

"Of course," she said brusquely. She seemed slightly offended to be asked. Then she nodded briefly to Zarich, and walked rapidly from the office. He answered with a half-smile but she was gone before it touched her. But she left him with an odd feeling, not sensuous but intuitive, the old hound dog instinct of catching a scent even if he didn't know what it meant. He filed it away for future reference.

"If you want to question the night nurse you'll have to wait until later," said Hodges.

Zarich considered a moment. It would probably be another blank, but it could wait for now. "No, I'd like to see the body," asked Zarich.

They went out into the corridor, and through to the elevators. It was a busy time. Scurrying nurses, harassed doctors, people of all ages sitting, standing, slouched to the walls, blank-faced, distracted, painful, fearful, a child whimpering, a woman moaning, the rumble of passing buses, the white flash of bandages, the dark red of coagulated blood, the sharp smell of antiseptic. Hodges led, walking briskly as if threading through an obstacle course, until they reached the comparative calm of the elevators.

Hodges pressed for the basement, and they descended slowly.

"You seem very interested in the words Blake spoke, Lieutenant," said Hodges.

" 'Old tart?' "

"Yes. After all, they're only words dredged from an unconscious man's mind, and surely nothing to do with his murder. Only Nurse Juric and I heard them at the time. Surely they can't have any significance?"

"Well, the whole of New York knows after they appeared in the newspaper."

"Yes, but that was only after he was murdered."

Zarich shrugged. "Then just let's say I find them interesting, Doctor." The elevator slid open, and they stepped out. In contrast to Emergency it was a long empty corridor, an echo chamber for their footsteps. "With someone as totally unknown as Blake, any lead is worth following," added Zarich. "Maybe there's some way those words can help us."

"Of course," murmured Hodges. He made little effort to keep the condescendence out of his voice. Zarich scowled. Come the day some addict mugged the doctor, or broke into his home and blew away a member of his family, then the fucking patronizing tone would change to a scream of rage over incompetent cops.

When they slid the dead man into view, Zarich felt an unaccustomed stir of pity. Detachment over the violence human beings inflicted on each other was a necessity for surviving the hassles of the job, but knowing about Blake made it somehow different. No one to weep for him, even offer a farewell curse. But the white face with the large nose told him nothing. A blank page, as blank as his past. There was a pulpy bruise on the throat as an indication of the crushed larynx. He stood back and ran an experienced eye over the body, hopefully looking for signs. The arms were laid palms down, and he placed an inquiring finger on the rose tattoo.

"I guess you noticed this, Doctor?"

Hodges stepped forward with a quick nod of the head. "Yes, of course. It's unusual, isn't it?"

"You didn't mention it to me."

"No." The doctor absently adjusted his spectacles. "I thought it best to wait until you saw the body."

Zarich raised the hand, and studied the tattoo. "Well, it could give us another lead to establishing identity." He frowned. "Although Christ, it could have been done anywhere. Anytime. It might be possible to trace it through some tattoo studio. Most of these things are done when people are young, so that makes it a long time ago." It sounded like a long shot. He released the hand, and turned to Hodges. "Did he mention it to you?"

"The tattoo was so unusual I think I might have raised the subject myself," said the doctor. He smiled faintly. "I'm not a tattoo man myself, but it is rather different."

"What did he say about it?"

"Of course he had no memory of having it done. I'd agree it was probably done when he was a young man and before the damage to his brain." He gave a sympathetic grimace. "It was rather pathetic. He evidently tried to use it as some form of identity card. You know, showing it to anyone he met, on the chance it might mean something to them."

"And it never did?"

"Not that he remembered anyway. He even carried a small piece of paper in his pocket with the words 'John Blake,' just so he wouldn't forget the name he'd given himself."

Zarich bent forward to make a closer examination of

the tattoo. "I'll get it photographed, and have enlargements made." He spread his hands in a hopeful gesture. "We can circulate it around the country, to studios. Even see if it tallies with anything on our files. We could get lucky."

He fell silent, once more studying the body. It all seemed so pointless. Why would anyone want to kill someone as seemingly harmless as this man? Was it some macabre mistake, or was it possible someone was frightened of what the dead man might remember if the operation succeeded? Could this old man have held such an important secret? It didn't seem logical. Hodges claimed the injury to his brain happened when he was a young man. Jesus, that made it forty years ago at least. Surely it made no sense that a potential killer kept tabs on the man for forty years. That was ridiculous.

It was cold in the room, and he suddenly shivered. Behind him Hodges shuffled about on the floor, and cleared his throat with an impatient rasp.

"I guess that's about all for now," he said.

They left the room, Hodges leading, and once again traversed the echoing corridor.

"I'll be in touch about getting a photographer over, so I'll want the body held for a while," said Zarich. "And I'll want my men to go through the apartment where you had Blake staying before the operation."

"Of course, anything you need, Lieutenant." The doctor hesitated, patting delicately at his mouth. "Ah, will you be needing to interview the hospital director right now?"

They halted at the elevator, and Zarich appraised him with shrewd eyes. He had the feeling the hospital had elected Hodges as fall guy. They were all running scared at the moment, both the hospital and the doctor intent on protecting their reputations. The poor old bastard stretched out on the slab was irrelevant now. The elevator door slid open, and Hodges politely gestured the lieutenant in ahead of him. Zarich waited until the elevator enclosed them before he answered.

"I don't think that's necessary right now," he said drily. He was sure the director could tell him nothing that he hadn't already told Beuso.

"Like I said, we're all hoping your department will be very . . . circumspect about this disastrous affair, Lieutenant," said Hodges uneasily. "That's the one thing I'd like to be able to report back to the director. Believe me, a complete shake-up is being carried out into the hospital's security. Nothing of the kind will ever happen again."

But it has happened, he wanted to say. An unknown man's dead, and nonentities have a right to breathe too. But he merely nodded impassively.

"As I indicated before, Doctor, everything has to go into my report. What happens after that depends on other people."

"Yes, yes of course," muttered Hodges. It wasn't much solace for the doctor, but it was as far as he was prepared to go. He didn't like strings being manipulated above his head by influential fuckers; it made him feel as if he were working in a straitjacket.

"I should have a photographer over here in half an hour, Doctor," he said. "And can you let me have the address and key to Blake's apartment? I want that gone over as soon as possible."

They stepped out of the elevator, and paused by the wall as Hodges took a set of keys from his pocket, carefully detached one, then handed it to Zarich along with a card. "The address is on the card, Lieutenant. Don't forget, anything you want, just ask me. The director has authorized me to give you all possible assistance. Anything you need to know, call me. There's nothing all of us want more than to have this ghastly mess cleared up. Not only for me and the hospital, but for Blake. We owe him that much."

Zarich was sure he meant it about himself and the hospital, but he wasn't so certain about Blake.

"I have a meeting to go to," said Hodges, glancing at his watch. "Is there anything else you need, Lieutenant?"

"I might just prowl around for a while," murmured Zarich. "Take a look at the ward where Blake was killed, and maybe ask a few questions."

"I'll get one of the nurses to go with you."

Zarich shook his head firmly. "No, no need for that. Sometimes it's better if I just look around myself."

Hodges looked slightly hesitant. "Are you sure?"

"Of course, believe me, I'll be fine."

"All right then." The doctor demonstrated his best bedside smile as they shook hands. "Good luck, Lieutenant, for all of us."

"Thank you, Doctor. I'll be in touch."

It told him nothing. There was no secret way into the hospital. No one had seen anything. Someone must have just walked in, maybe posing as one of the hospital staff, killed Blake, and walked out again. It was possible in a large hospital. But motive seemed just as inexplicable as ever.

He saw Honi Juric on the way to the exit, and checked his stride. She was the sort of woman he would have found it difficult to pass without comment at the best of times.

"Good-bye, Lieutenant," she had preempted him, before he had had a chance to speak. She seemed to have an aversion to looking him directly in the eyes, and it bothered him. He caught at her elbow as she began to pass. "Perhaps we could talk about this over a cup of coffee sometime?" he suggested. "Maybe tomorrow?"

He was sure she read innuendo in his voice, an inference he meant more than just talking about Blake's murder. She smiled distantly. There were bloodshot signs of strain in her eyes he hadn't noticed before, as if she'd been crying.

"It might be difficult with the hours I work," she hedged.

"Perhaps I could call you at home?"

"If you *have* to call me, I'd prefer it here at the hospital."

It was an evasive rebuff, but he swallowed it away easily. "I'll do that," he answered.

She turned with a curt nod, and walked rapidly down the corridor,. He shrugged it aside, and stepped out into Columbus Avenue. The city was fogged in a weeping drizzle, and he stood for a minute letting the water trickle down his face. Honi Juric bothered him more than the fact she looked a hell of a good lay, but for other reasons he hadn't quite figured yet. It might be worthwhile having Dawkins check her out.

*   *   *

There were many places he could have gone, but he decided for the bar on Tenth Avenue. It was a source he mined regularly, and sometimes turned up gold. Hodges might fool himself that only a tight-lipped inner circle was aware Blake was murdered, but Zarich knew from experience some fringe-of-the-law character who owed him a favor could have heard of it long before the doctor.

It was a place of dim light and dark shadows, white men and black men, fat and scrawny and in between, all draped silently along the bar, each jealously cossetting his glass, spreading the drinking time. The white shirt of the elderly obese bartender was stark against the gloom, like a warning flag. The floor squeaked beneath his weight, but no one looked at him. Some of them knew who he was, but recognition could be a risky business. He went slowly to the end of the bar, ordered a Scotch, and sipped slowly, speaking to no one. The yellow light formed weird patterns on the wall of bottles behind the bar.

Drinkers moved out, others took their place, some going first to the rest room at the rear. It was like a series of chess moves designed to confuse, until it became impossible to tell who had left, who had stayed.

He drained his glass, and went to the rest room. Small and evil-smelling, with walls of peeling paint, the once white tiles about the urinal stained scummy brown. There were two stalls, shut doors covered with New York graffiti. He unzipped, and began urinating.

"You bin to the hospital for the good of your health, Mr. Zarich?" inquired a soft voice from one of the stalls.

The tone was low and cautious, but Zarich knew who it was. The guy was paying his dues, and wanted Zarich to know it without the risk of a face-to-face meeting.

"You know better than that," said Zarich.

"Man up there got a bad throat, I hear."

"You heard right. He's not breathing anymore."

A gentle chuckle drifted from behind the door. "That's for all of us one day, Mr. Zarich."

Zarich zipped up, but didn't move away from the urinal. "I guess so."

"A real pro did the job on the old man."

"That doesn't make much sense with a harmless old man like him."

"Don' matter if it makes sense or not, that's the way it was. Someone didn't figure he was harmless. The man gotta lot of dough for makin' the hit. Big money, like outa town money, man."

"You know who it was, or why?"

"That's all I'm sayin', Mr. Zarich."

Water gurgled in the pipes along the wall. There was no point in trying to push the informant anymore. That wasn't the way the game was played, and he knew it was all he was going to get. He went out of the rest room, silently through the bar, and back on the street. It was still raining but he was too preoccupied to notice. It made even less sense now. An old man with no memory of his life gets blown away by a high-priced hit man. It brought his mind back to Liavone. He knew the hit man was somewhere in town, and maybe it was time to stop playing games with Ella, and just drag the sonofabitch in, even if he didn't have anything on him.

Chapter 3

"I have to call Sydney in Australia again, baby," said Liavone.

Ella was brushing her lank hair at the dressing table mirror, and her eyes went cautiously to Abe's reflection. She hadn't known him when he was young, but from the mattress on his chest he must have had quite a head of hair once. She'd never seen a man with skin so white. He was sitting on the side of the bed, bare-waisted, a large cigar jutting from the corner of his mouth. Even with the rolls of flesh laying over his belt, he generated physical power. She flushed her tongue over her mouth, and forced a smile.

"I'm beginning to think all you come here for is to make those Australian calls, Abe."

He grinned, and made an obscene gesture with the cigar as he stood up from the bed. "You know better than that, baby. Sydney is business, good business for both of us." He put the cigar back in his mouth, and slipped on his shirt.

She wished he wouldn't smoke those filthy things in the bedroom—it took hours to get rid of the goddam stink—but she wouldn't dare protest. Or ask questions about the Australian calls. He paused at the door, using the cigar as a pointer again.

"Never you mind about the calls, y'hear. Just keep your ears shut an' your body warm until I get back. I might have some news for you when I'm through."

He shut the door loudly behind him, as if to emphasize the point. She placed the brush down shakily on the dressing table, and stared long at her reflection in the mirror. Christ, she was so uptight her stomach felt as if she'd swallowed broken glass. Yet somehow she'd hidden it from him. Maybe it wasn't so difficult when Abe had nothing on his mind but phone calls and screwing. He made love like an ape, no finesse, just using her. At least for a brief moment Zarich had made her feel like a human being again, but Jesus, what a price to pay. That bastard cop. She trembled at the memory of how gullible she'd been, heat flushing into her face. God, she'd been used often enough by creeps like Zarich to know better. Would he really be bastard enough to give her the shaft with Abe? And how would Abe react if he did? She'd seen him ugly several times, and that scared her. She knew he operated on fear, but she never asked him how he made his money. She suspected he was playing around with someone else anyway; there had been those phone calls from a woman leaving a message for a man called Swarse, and when she'd passed it on to Abe he hadn't said a goddam thing. She didn't dare question him, but men were bastards; all they wanted was a hole for their cock.

She mournfully studied her face, punishing herself by creating gargoyle expressions. Christ, she was nearly forty. Zarich had her against the wall, but if Abe pushed her out, what the hell would she do? She brushed again at her hair with quick agitated strokes, trying to contain the surge of panic. She didn't realize he was back in the bedroom until she felt his large hands about her shoulders, and he held her down as she started up from the chair in fear.

"Easy, baby, easy," he soothed her. His face in the mirror squeezed into a puzzled frown. "Don't be so jumpy, I've got good news."

"I . . . I'm sorry, Christ, don't creep up on me like that, Abe." She threw the brush down, feigning anger as a cover, trying not to flinch as he pushed her hair aside and kissed her on the neck.

"Your call didn't take long," she said.

He straightened and grinned at her in the mirror. "The Australians are good to do business with, they don't fuck around, or try to squeeze you. They make a quick deal, then tell you to go earn your money. I've got another job, baby, another easy fat job."

"I'm glad for you, Abe." She tried to smile.

She felt the quiver coming back, and picked up the brush once more to stroke at her hair. He backed away and dropped himself heavily down on the bed, scowling at her lack of enthusiasm.

"You keep brushing like that, and you're gonna finish up bald like me," he sneered.

She stopped with a supreme effort of self-control, and swiveled about to face him. "I'm glad for you, Abe," she repeated with more warmth. "Really glad."

"Come over here," he beckoned. "I've got to go and do this job in a few minutes."

She obeyed, and he sat upright on the bed as she moved the few paces toward him. He circled his hands tight about her ass, and drooled his mouth slowly over her breasts. She tried to respond, gently scratching at his neck.

"You know what I'm figuring, baby," he said in muffled tones. "I've got a lot of dough coming through this Australian connection. Why don't you and I take off on a nice long holiday in a few days? Grab ourselves some time on one of those islands in the Bahamas, just lie around in the sun, and the hell with everyone."

Her fingers tightened about his neck. It was as if someone had handed over a key to unlock her cell door. She played it right, and they could both be out of New York before Zarich knew they'd gone. "That sounds marvelous, darling," she murmured. For Chrissake, let it happen, let it happen, she whispered to herself.

Dawkins draped his portly frame against Zarich's office door, and gestured to the phone. "There was a call from your ex-wife, Ed." He gave a self-satisfied grin. "Maybe you're behind with your alimony payments. And some guy called Musoveld called two or three times in the last hour. Wouldn't leave any message but just kept saying he'd call back."

Zarich received the information blank-faced. Musoveld? The name meant nothing to him. "He didn't say what he wanted?"

"Nope. Only that he wanted to talk to you." He waved vaguely to Zarich's desk. "He left a number for you to call him back. I wrote it down on your pad there."

Zarich shuffled the papers about until he found the number. Rhonda could wait; he knew there was no payments problem. She probably wanted to fill him in on the latest guy she was sleeping with; she had it figured it was a good way of knifing him, but he couldn't have cared less.

"Okay, I'll give him a call," he grunted. He took the address card and key Hodges had given him from his pocket, and held them out to Dawkins. "Mal, get a few men to go to this address, and go over the apartment. A man calling himself John Blake, now dead, used to live there."

"Murdered?"

"Looks that way," answered Zarich vaguely. He didn't like holding out on Dawkins, but this one would have to be cleared with Beuso. Dawkins waited expectantly, then shrugged away the lack of information.

"What are we looking for?"

"Anything that'll help identification. Blake wasn't his real name."

"You want me to go?" he asked in an aggrieved tone.

"No. First get a photographer over to City Hospital to

see a Doctor Hodges. He knews what I want shot. Then I
want you to run a check on a nurse Honi Juric who works
at the hospital. Just tell the hospital management you're
from Homicide, and they'll give you any personal details
you need to get started." He smiled a bleak farewell. "I'd
like that fast, Mal."

Dawkins declined the invitation to leave, his mouth
turned down in sour resentment. "What's the big mystery, Ed? You've kinda left me groping in the dark. Is this
a homicide or not? Have we got a body? A killer? Or what
the hell have we got?"

Zarich mustered an apologetic smile. "I'm sorry, Mal."
He grimaced toward the ceiling. "It's something Beuso's
got going, so ride along with me for now. As soon as I've
got it sorted out, you'll know as much as I do." He
drummed his fingers on the desk, and gave a sardonic
grin. "Which isn't bloody much at the moment, I can tell
you."

As a bid to enlist Dawkin's sympathy it was a failure.
There was no change in the sergeant's resentful attitude,
and he crashed the office door on the way out.

Zarich knew he'd handled it badly. Fuck Beuso. And
Hodges. He'd bring Mal up to date as soon as he'd spoken
to this Musoveld.

Musoveld coughed a lot, and it made conversational
preliminaries difficult. It took time for Zarich to grasp it
was caused more by excitement than clogged bronchial
tubes, even if he did sound like an elderly man.

"Lieutenant, I've been trying to get you for hours,"
he rasped.

"Yes, so I understand, Mr. Musoveld."

"I called City Hospital first, and spoke to some nurse
named Juric this morning. But nothing happened. Jesus
Christ, nothing. Then I called the hospital again, and
some doctor told me I ought to contact you. You get me,
Lieutenant, you get me." The words gushed together in a
medley of crackling phlegm.

"Yes, I get you, Mr. Musoveld," said Zarich patiently.
"Just take your time, take it slowly. We'll both get along
better that way."

There was a short wordless period, the sound of the man's breathing coming like rustling tissue.

"I . . . I read the *Post* story about the man Blake in City Hospital," Musoveld began again. "Shame about him dying after the operation like that, but I've got a feeling I might have known the guy."

Zarich was immediately interested. It didn't seem logical he could get lucky so quickly.

"What makes you think you knew him, Mr. Musoveld?"

"Of course I've never known anyone called Blake, but I understand that wasn't his real name anyway. But for Chrissake, I tell you, Lieutenant, the words 'old tart' took me back over forty years. Yes sir, forty years . . . my God yes."

"That must be going back to the war, Mr. Musoveld?"

"Right, yes, you're right, Lieutenant." Another harsh bout of coughing cut him off in midsentence, and Zarich stirred impatiently in the chair. " 'Old tart,' Mr. Musoveld," he prodded gently.

"Right, right, sorry but it's this bloody bronchitis. Look I was in the Navy during the war, on a PT boat operating out of Darwin in Australia, 'round about . . . oh, 1944. PT Boat five two four. Yes sir. We had a pet name for the boat. Old Tart. That's right, Old Tart. Don't ask me where it came from, but the name stuck. We never called her anything else."

Zarich's interest sharpened. Christ, if there was a connection, then for the first time it made some sense of Blake's words.

"You think Blake could have been one of the crew of the Old Tart?"

"Well, it's hard to be sure, of course, but it's sure as hell possible. Blake was about my age."

Zarich picked up a pen, and wrote PT 524. If Blake had been one of the crew they should be able to identify him through Navy files. Weird that those words should have been the first to surface in Blake, but then like Hodges had said, the mind's a strange place.

" 'Course I was transferred from the Old Tart at the end of '44," added Musoveld. "Bloody lucky, too, seeing as how she vanished in early '45. Lost with all hands."

Zarich threw the pen aside in disgust. "She was sunk?"

"Guess so. No one ever knew what really happened. Just went out on patrol one night, and was never seen again. Jes', I had some good buddies on the Old Tart."

"Then Blake couldn't have been a member of the crew, Mr. Musoveld," declared Zarich pointedly. "Not if it was lost at sea forty years ago."

Another hacking cough forced a pause. "Yeah, yeah, you might be right, Lieutenant, but he could have transferred off the Old Tart after me, maybe before she disappeared."

"You heard about someone else transferring?"

"No, but then I was way on the other side of the Pacific. All I'm saying is it's possible. But man, it sure jogged my memory to read those words."

Zarich retrieved his pen, and tapped it thoughtfully against the desk. Blake's reference to the Old Tart had to mean something, and this was worth following up.

"Could I ask you to look at Blake's body, Mr. Musoveld?"

"Well, sure, but I don't know if it'll do any good. A man can change a lot in forty years."

"I think it's worth a try."

"Okay, okay. Tell you what, Lieutenant, I'm pushing seventy, and I don't get around so easy these days. Why don't you come over to my place, and I'll show you a picture album of mine from the war. I got photographs of me and the crew of the Old Tart. Never know, it could be some help. If this Blake was on her one time, he's sure to be in one of the pictures. Then you could take me along to see the body." He cleared his throat with a rusty crackle. "Haven't seen a dead 'un since the war."

Zarich felt a whiff of a clear and unmistakable scent up the old blood hound nose. "Okay, let's do that," he agreed. He hesitated a moment. "Just one thing, Mr. Musoveld, the dead man has a small tattoo on the back of his left hand. It's a design of a rose, and quite unusual. Does that mean anything to you?"

He waited, listening to the pondering click of Musoveld's tongue.

"Say, I think I do recall something like that about one

of the guys," said Musoveld finally. There was another
hesitant fumbling for memory. "Yeah, yeah, I do. But I
can't put a face or a name on it. Let me think about it
while you're coming over. Maybe it'll come back to me."

"Have you talked about this to anyone else?"

"Well, I mentioned some of it to that Nurse Juric I
was telling you about."

"She told you to call me?"

"No, like I said, she didn't do a thing. Just listened,
and said she'd pass it on. But I could tell by the way she
spoke she thought I was just some crazy old guy. So I
called the doctor, and he gave me your name."

Zarich reflected on that. No matter what she thought,
why didn't she refer Musoveld on to him? "You'd better
give me your address, Mr. Musoveld," he said.

He wrote down a Bleeker Street address in the Village, then glanced at his watch. It was five o'clock. It
would probably take thirty minutes upstairs, and provided
Beuso didn't start playing politics he could be down at
Bleeker by six.

"Say I see you about six, Mr. Musoveld," he suggested.

"That should be okay. Matter of fact I've only just
moved into this place and my daughter's been looking
after the album for me while I get settled in. I'll give her a
call, and I know she'll bring it right over."

"All right then, at six, Mr. Musoveld."

He hung up and stared thoughtfully at the phone. It
sounded promising, and at least it gave him a way in. He
could start checking back with the Navy Department once
he was through with Musoveld. He wasn't optimistic about
Musoveld making an identification; the old guy was right—
forty years could make a hell of a change in someone.

Through the glass he could see Mal briefing the guys,
his face still set in terse lines. Before anything else, he was
going to have to spend a few minutes smoothing Mal's
ruffled feathers.

It was six-fifteen before he parted company with a
traffic snarl, and turned into Bleeker. The street was
crowded with cars and people in temporary flight from the
bonds of earning a living, and it took him another ten

minutes to find a parking space. So he was in no mood for the lack of response to protracted ringing of the bell of Musoveld's apartment, and less compunction about using his authority on the super to open the door for him. If Musoveld had stepped out he couldn't be far because the radio was blaring rock from inside. But the super hadn't seen him coming or going, and the music made Zarich uneasy, for Musoveld sounded long past the rock generation.

He flicked on the light as he stepped inside, and as soon as he saw the wreckage he knew there was more wrong than the rock music. Someone had gone through the tiny room like a whirlwind. He shut the door deliberately on the super's bulging eyes, and went looking for Musoveld. Every room was the same, even the kitchen, cupboard doors gaping, drawers slung hastily to the floor. Whatever someone was looking for, he must have figured himself short on time.

But he had no trouble finding Musoveld, or a man he presumed to be Musoveld. The bath had been filled to the brim and the man was in it fully clothed, eyes staring up at him from beneath the surface. He sat down wearily on the small stool by the bath, and tried to be professionally dispassionate about the pathetic sodden bundle, the wizened blank face, the floating white hair. Then he called the super back for a gagging, bug-eyed identification, learned there was no Mrs. Musoveld, then pushed him back into the hallway again. If he was going to throw up, better there than in the apartment.

Zarich had a strong feeling taking shape that knowing anything about Blake was tantamount to a death sentence. But the murders had no shape, no motivation. Killings always had reasons, a frustrated mugging, a domestic, a gangland execution. He had little doubt it was the same creep who'd killed Blake, but for Chrissake, who sends a high-priced hit man to take out two harmless old men? He shook his head, a puzzled scowl on his face. Maybe killing this man made it a sure connection back to Blake, but how the hell would the murderer have known about Musoveld, or that there was a chance he could identify Blake? Was that what it was all about, some maniac determined Blake's real identity never be known? But why?

He sighed, went back into the living room, located the telephone beneath an upturned chair, and called Dawkins. He was glad he'd taken time to straighten things out with Mal, because the sergeant eagerly absorbed all the details. Then he prowled the apartment while he waited, two people sticking in his craw, and the one uppermost was Liavone. Some hit men leave a trace on their jobs like a fingerprint, and this was so typical of that psychopath's handiwork—he had a thing about carrying out a contract by using brute strength instead of a weapon. Maybe he should have put out a general alert on the sonofabitch in the beginning, but that was something he'd put right as soon as Dawkins arrived.

The other irritation sharing almost equal billing with Liavone was Honi Juric. If she'd heard Musoveld's story, why hadn't she passed it on to him? Or told Musoveld to call him? Had she passed it to someone else, knowing it would cost Musoveld his life? She didn't seem the type, and she hadn't known Blake's death was murder until just before he interviewed her. At least that's what Hodges claimed. He had a mental flashback of that white, uptight face. That lady was going to see him again whether she liked it or not.

He moved into the kitchen, and dolefully surveyed the wreckage again. If he was right about someone killing Musoveld to prevent Blake being identified, then it would have to be the album they were after. If Musoveld's daughter had brought it to him, then it was probably gone.

He was moving back into the living room when he saw the woman standing in the doorway. She was thin and gray, like a tree trying to survive a long drought, no longer capable of bearing fruit. Zarich figured she was somewhere between forty and fifty, and she carried a large book under her arm. Her head moved back and forth in a dazed fashion as she took in the shambles of the room.

"What the hell's been going on here?" she muttered. She stared at Zarich with a glazed lack of comprehension. "Who are you? Where's my father?"

He knew immediately it was the daughter Musoveld had spoken about, the book under her arm, the album.

Well, at least he had that. He moved toward her with a solemn expression of condolence, and the bewilderment in her face switched to alarm. He quickly presented his ID.

"Lieutenant Zarich, Homicide," he said softly.

"You're the policeman my father called about?"

"Yes." He eyed the album clutched in her hand. "There's been a . . ."

"Where's Dad?"

He'd never found an easy way to say it. "I'm sorry, but something very terrible has happened."

She tried to push past him. "What do you mean? Where is he, what terrible thing's happened?"

He grasped her firmly by the arm. "Please, please sit down, Mrs. . . ."

She stared at him, eyes wide. "Eckhart," she muttered.

He held her with one hand, managed to prop one of the chairs into an upright position, and eased her down. Her thin mouth twitched with the effort of finding words. "He's dead isn't he?" she said dully.

He nodded slowly. "I'm afraid he is, Mrs. Eckhart."

"It was a heart attack, wasn't it. My God, I . . ."

"I'm afraid it was murder."

Her eyes filled, but there was no flow of tears. The album slipped from her hand to the floor, and she poked distractedly at her hair. "Christ, I told him he shouldn't come here to live alone," she moaned. "I told him, I told him. We could have worked things out. He and my husband didn't get on, but God, we could have worked something out. He was so lost since my mother died last year." She looked hazily about the room. "Where is he?"

"In the bathroom, but I think it might be best if you don't go in there, Mrs. Eckhart. The janitor identified him. Some of my people'll be here soon. Best leave it to them."

She hesitated as if not sure what he was concealing from her, then nodded woodenly, her eyes flitting about the room. "What was it, some goddam addict trying to beat him up for drug money? He didn't have much."

Zarich bent down and picked up the album. "I'm not too sure at the moment," he said. He ran his hands over the album. It was green-colored, with a faded design of flowers. "But I've a hunch it might have something to do with this. It could be what the person searching the apartment was after."

She looked at him blankly. "His old war album? You must be joking! It's not worth a cent to anyone except him."

"I don't think it was a money thing."

"Then what was it?"

"I'm not sure at the moment." He retrieved another chair and sat down beside her, the album in his lap. "I know this is a terrible shock for you, Mrs. Eckhart, but your father was trying to help me. Maybe that's what cost him his life."

She mournfully shook her head. "I don't understand, Lieutenant. I just don't understand. If it wasn't robbery, it makes no sense to me. Dad didn't have any enemies, everyone liked him." She grimaced. "Except my husband. My God, I wonder how he'll feel when he hears about this? Who would want to kill a harmless old man like Dad?"

Zarich slowly leafed over the pages of the album. He had no intention of taking her through the connection to Blake; it was hard enough trying to explain the murder of one harmless old man, let alone two.

"We'll find out, Mrs. Eckhart," he assured her, with more confidence than he felt.

She hunched silently in the chair, dabbing at her nose with a handkerchief, while he flicked over the pages. Photographs of Musoveld as a young man in Navy uniform. With his family. His wife. All carefully notated beneath each shot. Holding a baby he presumed was Mrs. Eckhart. Of warships, and other Navy men. The port of Darwin in Australia. Then a large picture in excellent condition, obviously taken by a professional photographer, of a crew grouped together on a pier, with a PT boat forming the background. Printed beneath were the words CREW OF THE OLD TART, DARWIN, 1944.

"I'd like to call my husband," whimpered the woman suddenly. "Tell him what happened. See how the sonofa-bitch likes this on his conscience."

He shrugged, and indicated the phone. She picked it up, and took it across with her to the window. He blocked out the sounds of her conversation, and examined the picture carefully, moving his eyes from sailor to sailor. Blake could have been there, but it was impossible to match anyone to the elderly dead face he'd seen in the hospital morgue. One of the heads had been circled with a pen, and he knew from the other photographs it was Musoveld. Christ, it was difficult to relate the smiling young man to the drowned corpse in the bath. He stared long at the picture, vaguely conscious of the venom being injected into the phone behind him.

Was it possible something had happened on the Old Tart all those years ago that had led to two elderly men being viciously killed by a professional hit man? Was it something to do with the chance of Blake recovering his memory? Had the words "Old Tart" been the trigger? But only the doctor and Honi Juric had heard Blake speak the words. Could she have told someone about it before the papers got the story? Was someone so fearful of what Blake might remember he was prepared to kill, and kill again, after all these years? It sounded crazy, but it was the only thread he had. He snapped the album shut in exasperation. The starting point had to be the Navy files. He was sure they'd be able to identify the sailors in the photograph. Hopefully Blake was one of them.

"He's coming over," said Mrs. Eckhart. Grief was gone from her face, replaced by a stoney retribution. Her husband was in for a rough time. She turned to the window, and nodded to the street below. "There's an ambulance pulling up outside," she muttered. "And another car with some men." She looked back at him. "Should I go with them when they take the body?"

He indicated the chair beside him. "Why don't you just wait here for your husband," he said kindly. "We can get all the background details from you later." He motioned with the album. "And I'd like to keep this for a while, if you don't mind? It might just give me a lead on what happened to your father."

She shrugged indifferently. "I suppose you know those pictures are over forty years old."

"I realize that, but I'd still like to keep them for a time." He paused. "Did he ever talk about them, or his experiences in the war?"

She thought a moment, then slowly shook her head. "Not in a long time. I doubt he even looked at them anymore. I was surprised when he asked me to bring them over." She twitched her shoulders. "Until he told me about you, of course."

He heard footsteps on the stairs, and he went across and opened the door. Dawkins was heading the group with his usual energy, taking the steps two and three at a time. The hell with Beuso, this time he'd take Mal right through the entire thing, step by step. It was going to take a lot of digging to find a way through this maze, and he needed someone like Mal to back him up.

Mrs. Eckhart's expression had evolved to bleak accusation by the time they took the body out, and Zarich found himself avoiding her eyes. Maybe it was true her father would still be alive if he hadn't made the phone call, but there was nothing he could have done to prevent the killing.

He put all the procedures in hand on Musoveld, then they went meticulously through the apartment. There was nothing but the bare necessities of an elderly man living alone. Zarich was famished. He had Dawkins put out the general alert for Liavone, then took the sergeant along to the Horn of Plenty on Bleeker, propped the album up on the table, and over a steak and beer told him everything that had happened. He knew Mal would rather have spent dinner time with his family, but he felt a sense of urgency to get it all into the sergeant's head. There was nothing more they could do for Musoveld right now.

Dawkins washed down a mouthful of steak, and grinned wryly. "You think Beuso'll still cover for the doctor?"

"I don't think it's up to Beuso. He's taking the pressure from higher up."

"How's he going to take this thing with Musoveld, I mean if you're right and it ties in with Blake's killing?"

"It'll make any cover more difficult. Musoveld has to connect to Blake. There're too many links. Especially the Old Tart. It all fits."

"You're really running with the scent, aren't you, Ed?"

Zarich chewed silently for a moment, concealing irritation. It was the hound dog thing again. Christ, of course he was running, he was a cop, a good cop, and that meant finding reasons for Blake and Musoveld. "I don't buy two harmless elderly men being taken out by someone like Liavone, if it was him," he scowled. "I want to know why, nail 'em to the wall."

Dawkins gulped again at his beer. "Sure, sure, Ed," he soothed. "I'm with you."

Zarich was immediately contrite. He was too easily aggravated, but it seemed part of his life these days. "I've never seen one quite like this, Mal," he confessed.

"You'll beat it," stated Dawkins confidently. "Beuso knows that. So do I, Ed."

"I wish I felt so sure," grunted Zarich. He glanced across to the doorway at the sound of a girl laughing. She was part of a group, dark-haired, attractive. He hadn't laughed like that in a long time. Maybe he'd seen too many Musovelds.

Dawkins followed Zarich's gaze. "You should get yourself a piece of ass like that, Ed," he murmured.

"Yeah, yeah," Zarich humored him.

"I mean it." He hesitated, then tapped the album. "There's more than this, Ed. Running down scum like Liavone as if your life depended on it." He was encouraged by Zarich's lack of response. "You need a little balance, you know. I don't mean screwing anything that happens by, but something real." He downed his beer self-consciously, as if concerned he'd gone too far.

Zarich shrugged it away. Maybe he was obsessive—just a baying hound dog after all, only running for the blood—and justice had nothing to do with it. Was he trying to get back at someone? His parents for dying so young? The aunt who raised him, all responsibility but no affection? Even when he was giving it to Ella he hadn't felt a thing, hadn't with anyone for a long time. Even with Rhonda, who had sensed it, and in the end it drove her away. He shut it all out. They were thoughts for dark lonely nights, and wouldn't help Blake or Musoveld. He backed off with a careful smile. "So you keep telling me, Mal."

"Give yourself a break," said Dawkins boldly. "Try loving someone."

The sergeant was beginning to sound like a lovelorn columnist, and Zarich put an end to it. He pushed his plate aside, opened the album to the photograph of the Old Tart and crew, and showed it to Dawkins.

"That's the photograph I was telling you about."

"The Old Tart," murmured Dawkins.

"Right." Zarich pointed to the circled head. "That's Musoveld. I want to know who the rest of the crew are. I don't think you'll have any trouble tracing them through Navy Department files in Washington. If we get lucky, one of them will be Blake."

Dawkins studied the picture intently, and slowly shook his head. "It's not going to be easy, Ed. I mean, not knowing Blake's real name. That's a forty-year-old photograph."

"Take all the ID we've got on Blake with you. Photographs of him, of the tattoo, fingerprints."

"Sure, sure." Dawkins knew the social part of the dinner was over, and reluctantly pushed his half-finished steak to one side.

"I want you to move on it quickly, Mal," added Zarich. "Even if it means going to Washington tonight."

Dawkins mournfully bobbed his head. "You think some of the crew might still be around and maybe lined up for what Musoveld got, even though he claimed the Old Tart disappeared with all hands in 1945?"

"I honestly don't know, but I think we should check it fast, just in case it's a possibility." He clasped his hands and rapped them against the table. The girl by the door was still laughing; someone must have told a good joke. "What about Blake's apartment?" he asked.

"A blank. The same as Musoveld's apartment. Nothing. He could have been the invisible man. A few newspapers, some clothes the doctor had given him." He gave a sympathetic grimace. "Some cards with the name 'John Blake' written on them. Poor bastard." He crossed his arms, and leaned to the table. "I had more luck with

Honi Juric. If you had a feeling about her, then maybe you're right, Ed." He took a notebook from his inside pocket, and opened it on the table. "I'm still digging, but as far as her sleeping around, there's nothing. But we opened doors on her bank account through the hospital. This morning she paid in the sum of five thousand dollars in hundred-dollar bills. That was the second entry over a few days for the same amount." His brow wrinkled. "Maybe one for Blake, and one for Musoveld, eh, Ed? Also she has parents in Poland she's been trying to get to America for the last three years. It was a money problem before now. She applied to the hospital for a loan sometime ago, but they turned her down. I gather she's been getting a little desperate about her parents' situation." He tapped his fingers reflectively on the pad. "She doesn't seem to have any close relationships, but I gather it's not from the want of trying on the part of the hospital staff. But we could turn up something later."

Zarich digested the information. It had all the earmarks of a pressure situation. But would she really be desperate enough for money to finger Blake and Musoveld? Be accessory to double murder? He still found it difficult to slot her into that category.

"From what you told me about Musoveld calling her, it's all got to mean something, Ed," concluded Dawkins. "Could be she didn't pass the information on to you, because she was too busy passing it on to Liavone?"

Zarich musingly studied the Old Tart picture. "Perhaps. Musoveld said he figured she thought he was just a crazy old man."

"I don't buy that, not after Blake's murder."

"She didn't know it was murder then. Or at least she claims she didn't know." He shuffled about on the chair, and glanced at his watch. It was eight o'clock. She was probably off duty, but it would be better to catch her at home, where she couldn't use the hospital routine to avoid questions. "I'd say it was time to push her hard. Have you got her home address?"

Dawkins flicked a page, and turned the notebook to him. It was an address on East Twenty-ninth Street. "Tear it out, Ed," suggested Dawkins. "I won't need it right now."

He tore out the page, and slipped it into his pocket. Then he passed the album across to Dawkins. "I'll leave that with you, Mal. Make some calls, get people out of bed if you have to. It might save some lives. Beuso'll pull strings for you if you run into any problems. I'll call Grimley to do some background checking on Musoveld, then I'll go talk to Honi Juric."

Dawkins mournfully consulted his watch. "I'd better call home before I go flying off to Washington."

Zarich gave a perfunctory shrug. He was sorry about Mal's home life, but that's the way it was. It had been like that with him and Rhonda once, only she'd filled in his absences by screwing around. On the way out he glanced at the girl with the infectious laugh. Their eyes met, and almost imperceptibly her expression changed. He knew that look. Maybe that's what he was running away from.

For a moment he thought she wasn't going to ask him inside. She'd sounded reluctant on the security intercom, and now stood with the door just sufficiently ajar to frame her body, eyes alternating between fear and suspicion. She wore a deep red robe that disguised her figure as effectively as her nurse's uniform. He knew he didn't look exactly appetizing; he needed a shave, and his jacket could have used a cleaning.

"I think it's best if we talk inside, Miss Juric," he suggested with polite firmness. He glanced about the hallway. "We can scarcely have a conversation out here."

There was a brief hesitation, then she stepped back warily, and widened the door. In the additional light her face was very white, and her eyes thatched red as if she hadn't slept in a long time.

It was only a small apartment, and he thought immediately of Musoveld's place. Not quite as austere, but still merely furnished with the basic tools for living. There was a photograph of two elderly people on the dresser, and he guessed they were the parents in Poland. She gestured wordlessly to a chair, and he sat down facing her. She was as watchful as a bird preparing to take flight. Maybe she figured he had it in mind to conduct the interview in bed, not that it was a bad idea.

"Would you like a drink, *Lieutenant?*"

She emphasized his rank, as if wanting to stress the official form of the visit.

He made a motion of refusal with his hand. "No thank you, Honi." He slipped easily into her first name, and he saw it register in her eyes. "Something urgent's come up, and I thought we should talk about it."

"I hoped we could do that at the hospital."

"This couldn't wait," he said curtly.

She remained standing, leaning awkwardly to the dresser. Instinctively he knew he had her. It wasn't going to be like grilling some experienced hood, and if he pushed hard, whatever was bugging her would come spilling out.

"I don't think there's anything else I can tell you about John Blake," she murmured hesitantly.

"I understand you had a call this morning from a man called Musoveld. Something to do with information he had about Blake."

She didn't answer at once, her hand theatrically to her head as if prodding her memory. "Musoveld? Let me think now. There's always so much going on at the hospital. Ah, yes, I do believe there was a call. Yes, Musoveld, I remember now."

She might have been a good nurse, but she was a lousy actress. "He had a feeling he might be able to identify Blake?"

"Yes, I think he did make some sort of claim like that. He seemed quite incoherent, and I didn't take much notice. It was obviously a crank call. We . . . we get them sometimes. I'm sure you do too." She tried to smile, red mouth quivering in a white face. "I take it he called you."

"Yes, he did. After he got nowhere with you he spoke to Hodges, and the doctor put him on to me." He fixed her with a hard stare. "Surely anything as important as that was worth passing on to me . . . or the doctor. Any lead is worth following."

"I . . . I didn't want to bother you," she floundered. "I . . . I suppose I was so busy at the time, and like I said,

I . . . I just dismissed it as a crank call. Did . . . did he really have something important?"

The throaty texture of her throat was thickening under pressure. He ignored the question, and nodded to the photograph on the dresser. "I take it they're your parents in Poland. I believe you've been trying to raise money to get them out and bring them to America."

She didn't look at the picture, but her hands went to her throat as if to stifle a sound of alarm. Then she made an effort to recover ground with anger. "You've been prying into my personal affairs, Lieutenant. I resent that. You have no right."

"After Blake, did you get another five thousand for passing on information about Musoveld? About the PT boat called the Old Tart? About the photo album?" he fired at her.

She was so on edge he decided subtlety was only a waste of words. Her mouth popped like a sickening fish, and suddenly she seemed to need the dresser more for support. "I . . . I don't know what you mean," she quavered.

He shook his head wearily. People dig deep holes for themselves, and are always so surprised when they fall in. "You got five thousand for passing on information about Blake. I'd guess about the operation, maybe about him using the words 'Old Tart.' You'd figure Musoveld had to be worth another five thousand."

He was bluffing, but he was sure he could take her. For a moment he thought she was going to fall, but he didn't stir from the chair.

"You're talking crazy," she muttered unsteadily. "I think you'd better go, Lieutenant. I . . . I don't have to answer questions like this."

He leaned forward and rested his elbows on his knees. "Honi, Musoveld's dead. Slaughtered. Pushed down into his bath until he drowned. Even a nurse like you wouldn't have found it a pretty sight. It had to be the same man who killed Blake, and you fingered Musoveld for him."

At last there was no pretense about the quivering hands covering her face.

"Oh no, oh no, oh my God," she moaned. "It couldn't happen again, oh my God, it couldn't."

He let her hang there for a time, then he stood up and took her gently by the arm to a chair. There was a small whisky decanter on the dresser, and he poured her a shot while she slumped in the chair, hands still over her face.

"Poor Momma, poor Poppa," she whispered.

He pried her hands loose, and offered the glass. Her hands trembled so that the whiskey ran in rivulets down her neck and into her gown. The front had fallen open, and he could see the whisky channeling into the division between her breasts. She didn't seem to notice.

"I didn't know he was going to kill them, believe me, I didn't know," she whispered. "I would never have told him about Musoveld if I'd known Blake had been murdered, never, never."

"Told who?" he questioned softly.

"Swarse."

He felt a needle of disappointment, but it was only temporary. He was sure Liavone wouldn't have used his real name. "Swarse?"

"Yes. I didn't know he was a maniac. He told me he just wanted the chance to try and identify Blake. In secret."

"In secret?"

"That's what he said." He had to lean forward to catch her words now.

"You met him after the operation?"

"Yes. That's when he gave me the money."

"What did he ask you?"

"If the operation had worked."

"You said yes."

"Well, I didn't really know, but I said there was a good chance."

"You told him about the words Blake spoke? 'Old Tart?' "

"Yes. He . . . he thought it was a joke at first. Then he said he'd have to make a phone call."

"You got him into the hospital that night?"

"I got him a staff coat, but honest to God I didn't know he was going to kill Blake. I swear I didn't."

Zarich studied her thoughtfully. There it was, the Old Tart again. Every time he heard the PT boat mentioned it seemed to be the linchpin to what happened to Blake and Musoveld. She was crying softly, and he knew he'd broken her; anything he asked she'd answer. He saw her eyes go to the photograph.

"He . . . he found out about them. That I needed money," she said tearfully. "Maybe I needed the money too much. I didn't really want to know what Swarse was up to, just so long as I got the money."

"You know where to contact this Swarse?"

"Only a phone number. I'd just leave a message for him to contact me."

"You know you're an accessory to two murders, Honi."

She closed her eyes, and shook her head. "Poor Momma, poor Poppa," she whispered again.

He watched silently for a time. Maybe she'd been suckered in, but it wouldn't make any difference to the law. He'd lay bets Swarse was Liavone, and he was the one he wanted now. It was going to be tough extracting the name of the hit man's client, but once he had it they were on their way. "I want you to come to the station with me, Honi," he said quietly. "Take a look at some photographic files, and see if you can identify the man you know as Swarse. You cooperate, and maybe . . ." He shrugged. "Well, maybe I might be able to do something for you."

She didn't answer for a time, and he thought she hadn't heard him. Then she put the glass aside, and climbed wearily to her feet. She looked years older than when he'd first seen her at the hospital.

"I'll have to dress," she muttered.

"I'll wait," he said.

The gown had slipped from her body before she left the room. At another time he might have considered it a sexual play, but he figured she was too stunned to know what she was doing.

It was Liavone. Every instinct told him that was the photograph she'd choose, and he couldn't restrain the delicious feeling of finally having that psychotic on ice. It was quiet in the room, empty desks, untended papers, stained coffee cups. New York's nightly banshee wail of a police siren came faintly through the window.

"Do you feel up to making that phone call?" he asked.

She was draped in the chair in an attitude of exhaustion.

"If that's what you want," she said dully.

"Hold it as long as you can. I'm going to put a trace on the call. Just leave a message that you want to see Swarse again."

She nodded silently. He picked up the phone, made arrangements for the trace, then handed it across to her.

"Can you remember the number?"

She shrugged beyond caring. "Yes, I know it."

Huskiness had raddled her voice now, and he hoped she wouldn't give herself away. She paused in the act of dialing, and stared up at him.

"Can you do anything for them?" she whispered.

"For them?"

"For my parents? There are bribes to pay, all sorts of things."

He licked his lips uncertainly. It was a pathetic attempt to do a deal, when she had nothing with which to bargain. She was one of the small fish, easily caught, quickly eaten by the sharks. He'd help if he could, but all he wanted now was Liavone.

"Maybe," he grunted. He nodded to the phone. "Let's see what happens. Does Swarse ever answer the phone?"

"Never. It's always a woman."

He thought at once of Ella. "String it out if you can. Insist that you want to talk to Swarse. Make excuses."

He propped himself against a desk while she made the call. Perhaps he'd given her faint hope, for even in her despondent state she managed well. Insisting she had to talk to Swarse, that it was urgent, until he could even hear the shrill irritation on the other end of the line before the woman hung up.

"She hung up, but she got the message," she answered sullenly.

He picked up the phone, and quickly dialed the trace.

"Did you get it?" he queried urgently.

"Yeah. I'll give you the exact pinpoint in a minute, but it's an apartment building. Number two twenty-five, East Forty-seventh Street."

It was the same building as Ella's apartment. It had to be her. It had to be. "Thanks," he said crisply.

Honi Juric had lapsed back into a comatose state, limbs awry, staring dull-eyed into space. He felt a stir of pity, but nothing could dampen his jubilation. He thought of the times in the past when he'd known Liavone had been the trigger on a killing, but he hadn't been able to prove a thing. Now he had the bastard, and he hoped to Christ it would give him the lead on the Old Tart he needed.

Chapter 4

Kepler Humbert's desk was littered with untended problems. The beef import situation in Japan. The oil licenses in Hong Kong. The transport submissions to the Philippines government. He had allotted various portions of the morning to each, but concentration failed him. Besides, area managers should submit more detailed solution reports, not problems. That was what he paid them for.

He pushed the reports to one side, and glanced about the office. Even the rather grandiose scale of the room, with its antique furniture, Persian rugs, expensive paintings, and magnificent view over Sydney Harbour, failed to provide the usual satisfaction. He wandered to the window, and stood with his hands clasped behind his back. He knew of no office in the world that could match such a stunning view as that provided from the top floor of the Humbert Corporation Building, the tallest structure in the city of Sydney. The bridge alive with swarming traffic, spanning the harbor like a giant skeletal coat hanger. The blue water fretworked with sunlight. Ponderous ocean ships, dancing yachts, scurrying ferries, all criss-crossing the surface with trails of foam. The sweeping curves of the Opera House roof, like sails straining to launch the unique building off Benelong Point and out to sea. The soft violet haze lying over the north shore coastline. It made it all worthwhile.

He had spent forty years building the most powerful and wealthy business organization in Australia, with links right through Southeast Asia. All that time working, planning, scheming, bribing politicians, bending the law, and it seemed inconceivable it could suddenly all be at risk, to be blown away like a puff of smoke as if it had never existed. His life and reputation destroyed. Anything was justified rather than let that happen. Maybe he was sixty-five, an age when most men think of sitting in the sun until they rot, but that was only for idiots. His mind was still sharp, his body scarcely thickened, his hair whitened but still full and healthy. Discipline had retained his looks; certainly there were lines and jowls, but it was not immodest to claim he was still a handsome man. He paid well for his clothes, but then he believed in presenting an immaculate image to the world. He would continue to control his empire while he still had breath. He had in a way enjoyed his role over the years as something of a mystery figure. An American serviceman who had fought in the Pacific area during the war, and spent many furloughs in Australia. Liked what he saw so much he decided to settle in Australia after the war, and go into business. His success had been phenomenal. Competitors wondered at his source of capital, but it took him into mining, real estate, oil, cattle, electronics, a multiheaded giant that devoured everything. It made him feared for his ruthlessness more than respected, but it put politicians in his pocket, community leaders in his debt. He was a bad enemy, and those who wouldn't bend he broke without compunction. It had left him little time for any personal life, an early marriage, fueled by sex, quickly dissolved. There were other ways to compensate.

But he had never faced a situation in all those years that had threatened him with ruin, forced him with all his wealth and power to act like some Mafia godfather. It was an intolerable situation to find himself, but he had no alternative; it simply had to be done. There was no one he could trust, with the exception of Sade, and he didn't dare even take him into his complete confidence. But then that wasn't necessary. Sade would do what he was told like a loyal obedient servant. Ply him with money like an alcoholic with drink, and he was yours forever.

A 747 circled to the north, throwing splinters of sunlight. Perhaps it was the same one that had carried him a month ago on his last trip to the States. He thought about that for a moment. The red button on his desk began to pulsate to indicate Monique had arrived, but she could wait. He was already tiring of her; it was time for a new face, another body. For now his mind was back in New York, on one of those lone night excursions when he went hunting for a woman, not someone with class, but a slut with whom he could wallow. Hiding himself in the dim light of the bar, trying to ignore the drunk pawing him, slobbering words. Then to grasp at the drunk's wrist to push him away, and see that tattoo, the unusual rose design. To feel himself lifted up and transported back forty years like a finger snap. But first of course the denial. Perhaps the uniqueness of that rose design had stuck in a corner of his mind, but surely there had to be more than one person carrying such a tattoo. But it had always been such a source of admiration on the Old Tart, and Donlett had taken immense pride in showing it off. But Donlett was dead, long dead, drowned forty years ago in the Taiwan Straits, yet his dry-throated reaction to the sight of the tattoo had amazed him. That the memory could still get to him, grab at his gut like a sharp stab of gas, the forty years nothing but a superficial protective layer.

There had been no discouraging the drunk, with the tattoo thrust again and again into his face.

"Ever seen anything like that, bud?" the man had drooled. "You tell me, eh, then you tell me who I am." Then the drunk had laughed as if it was some uproarious joke, repeating the question in off-key song to the surrounding bar. "Who am I, won't anyone tell me, who am I?" And the tattoo thrust again and again into his face. "Go on, bud, tell me if you've seen it before."

He hadn't understood any of it, just assumed the man was playing out some drunken fantasy. Yet he'd gone along with the game, buying the man drinks, easing him into the light, so he could search for signs of recognition. Too much time had passed, too many bad things had left their mark on the man's face, but why was he wasting his time, Donlett was dead, he'd kept telling himself. If he'd survived the Taiwan Straits forty years back he would have come forward long ago, told what he knew about the Old Tart, destroyed him so easily. And there had been no sign of recognition from the man, but then he was drunk, and he'd changed a lot himself in forty years. But a long suppressed fear in his belly had pushed him to keep looking at the tattoo, at the drunk's face, listening to the senseless, repetitious song. Now and then the man would turn his head with a certain expression, and he would think, my God, maybe it is Donlett. And there was always the tattoo. How could the sonofabitch possibly have survived falling overboard from the Old Tart? In all the excitement of that long ago day he hadn't even been missed until hours later.

In the end an immaculately dressed middle-aged man had come into the bar, remonstrated the drunk, then taken him forcibly by the arm and dragged him out. But the experience had shaken him. A sleepless night followed, trying to convince himself it was all coincidence, ghosts don't come back, it couldn't possibly have been Donlett. When sleep had finally come, it had been crowded with wartime dreams he hadn't known in years.

In the morning had come sanity, rueful admonitions that he'd allowed his imagination to run riot. For Chrissake, there could be hundreds of people with a similar tattoo, of course Donlett was long dead. Had laughed at himself until he saw the story in the newspaper, and recognized the photograph of the neurosurgeon Hodges as the one who'd taken the drunk from the bar. Then he had read the entire story of the man who had lost his memory, of the planned operation, and realized it wasn't just imagination after all, there was a strong possibility that the drunk was actually Donlett. There was no way he could ever know how he'd survived the Taiwan Straits, but the loss of memory was ample reason why he'd never come forward with what he knew of the Old Tart. But if the operation restored Donlett's memory, then he faced disaster, the horrendous destruction of everything he'd created in Australia. That couldn't be allowed to happen. Any risk, any action was worth taking. That day he spent in his hotel room pacing the floor, trying to think, to think. And, of course, he came to Sade. It was ridiculous, because Sade should have been the first thought to enter his mind. But then it isn't every day one faces a flesh-and-blood nemesis one had imagined was rotting at the bottom of the Taiwan Straits the last forty years. But Sade knew the New York scene, had lived there for five years, and knew people who could solve the problem for him. For the right price, and money was no object. So he'd called Sade to get on the first plane to America, then waited, trying to sedate his fear by strolling through Manhattan, but seeing nothing, his mind seething.

But he'd felt calmer once Sade was there. It was always so easy to brief him, to infer the right words so that Sade knew what action was required, absorbing it all with his bleak, unquestioning face. There was never any need to provide Sade with reasons why a threat should be removed; he was only interested in the size of the payment. So he told him just as much as he needed to know to function. Some people thought it strange he kept an aide like Sade on his staff, but there were times when it was important to have the use of a man with no conscience, and never so much as then. He'd considered it safer not to be in New York when anything happened, but then Sade had never failed him, so he felt quite confident about returning to Australia. He was almost sleeping normally again by the time Sade returned to Australia a few weeks later.

"It's arranged, Mr. Humbert," he'd said in his usual formal manner. "There may be some communication, just to check identity, which I'll bring to you, but it's arranged."

He'd wordlessly written a check, and Sade hadn't even looked at the amount, merely smiled solemnly, and placed it carefully in his pocket. People like Sade made life so simple at times. Yet the following days doubts had still plagued him, that he may have panicked needlessly in New York, that it was after all only circumstantial evidence the man being operated on was Donlett. But that had all vanished when Sade brought him the first communication from New York.

"Old Tart," murmured Sade. Doubtless he'd found the words incongruous, but it hadn't shown on his face. "The man in the hospital keeps repeating the words 'old tart.' Our operative in New York wants instructions."

It had taken a supreme effort to keep the excitement from his face. He'd been right after all. God, to think the sonofabitch had been drifting around for the last forty years like an unexploded bomb waiting to blow him off the face of the earth. Luck had been with him, like it had ever since the days of the Old Tart.

"I think we should proceed as we originally discussed, Sade," he had ordered. He'd made it sound like a board room decision. "And as quickly as possible."

"We have a way in. It can be done quickly."

"I'm not interested in details, I want it done before the man recovers."

"Of course."

Then Sade had left with a deferential tilt of his head, and he'd heard nothing since.

It had made concentration impossible for him over the last few days. He'd canceled all appointments, ignored the calls of the Government Minister looking for crumbs to feed his electorate over the beef deal in Japan. Even the blinking red light indicating Monique was ready to use her imaginative talents was of little interest. But then Monique had become very repetitive of late.

Below on the water a ferry headed inshore to Circular Quay, trailing a white garland about the Opera House. He turned from the window at the buzz of the intercom, and picked up the phone.

"No calls, Megan," he declared brusquely.

"Mr. Sade is here to see you, Mr. Humbert."

A ray of heat seemed to travel up his body, stimulating his heart. "Very well, send him in." He put the phone down, and positioned himself behind the desk as Sade entered the office. He could feel his pulse beating in his fingers gripping the chair. He took a deep breath and forced himself to relax, for he had no doubts Sade had succeeded.

It was impossible to read anything in Sade's face. The man must have decided a long time ago it was safer to live life behind a blank mask. Only the small pale blue eyes seemed to have life, but Humbert had never managed to read their secrets. Maybe it was the perpetual mask that had slowed the marks of time; there was almost a chubby adolescence to his face for a man close to forty. But he was totally bald, with the gait and build of a retired athlete. The dark conservative suits he always wore were an aid to his exaggerated attitude of deference to Humbert. The man was invaluable, and Humbert had used him on what he termed delicate assignments for a long time, yet the irritating formality never changed.

He halted in front of the desk, but made no effort to sit down. "I'm sorry for breaking in without an appointment like this, Mr. Humbert," he murmured politely.

Humbert gave a brusque wave of his hand. There were times he suspected that extreme obsequiousness was a cloak for disdainful superiority.

"That's all right, Sade," he said quickly.

"I thought it important to let you know as soon as possible that the threat in New York no longer exists."

Like his blank expression, the flat nasal voice carried no emotion.

Humbert smiled as thoughts of sleepless nights and lost concentration dissolved in a surge of relief. The end of a nightmare that had come from nowhere now just as quickly eliminated.

"Thank you, Sade. There will be a further expression of my appreciation."

"There'll be a double payment for our operative in New York."

He frowned, then leaned to the desk and cut off the blinking red light. With such good news he felt more like being with Monique than he had in months.

"A double payment?"

"There was the unforeseen threat of the man Musoveld. We discussed it after the last call from New York."

Humbert nodded slowly. He still hadn't succeeded in placing a face to the name, but there was a man who had transferred off the Old Tart in '44. That had been a nasty turn of the screw. Risky enough disposing of one threat, let alone two.

"Of course," he muttered. "The man with the photo album." He glanced sharply at Sade. "That's been resolved as well?"

"I believe so."

He gave a grunt of satisfaction. Maybe the man could have been dangerous, and maybe he had nothing, but there wasn't the slightest possibility he could have allowed such a threat to continue. He was silent for a time, luxuriating in the enormous sense of relief he felt now it was all over. Then he smiled faintly at Sade. "I'm grateful you came here to tell me as soon as you knew, Sade. I'm sure you realize how much it's been on my mind. The second payment is irrelevant, just so long as the job was carried out successfully. But if any other details come forward about Musoveld, I'd like to know, just for my own information."

Sade permitted an icy smile in return. "Certainly, Mr. Humbert." Then he dipped his head, backed off several paces as if taking leave of royalty, then moved silently from the office.

Humbert remained thoughtfully at the desk for a time after Sade had gone. Musoveld? He wished he could recall the man, but did it really matter now the threat no longer existed? No, better to spend time relaxing with Monique.

"I'll be out for a while, Megan," he said over the office intercom.

He passed through the door at the far side of the office, and up the narrow stairs to the small rooftop penthouse. He had no feelings of conscience, but then Sade was always careful not to expose him to any of the unpleasant details. In a way he despised Sade, but what a difficult world it would have been without him.

She was waiting in the pink gown he'd bought her in Singapore, lying back on the couch with the front open, bare legs spread, a glass of what he imagined to be her favorite drink, vodka, in her hand. She was barely twenty-three, blond, and pretty in an obvious way, but had always lacked style. He would have found the aggressive display of pudena stimulating once, but now he found it irritatingly crass. She slid one hand down over her belly, and massaged gently at the hair.

"I thought you'd never come, Kep darlin'," she murmured with an enticing smile. "I've been trying to keep it warm for you, but you're the only one who can do that, baby."

He felt little reaction, but then erection didn't come easily to him these days. She was a hand-me-down from the Minister so anxious about the beef deal, and it had been an erotic three months. For a time he'd believed she was the most inventive woman he'd ever encountered, but it was amazing how quickly it had settled into routine. Even the open legs motion of invitation had palled. She held out her arms, and pouted redly.

"I'm waiting, baby," she crooned. "I've got a little play worked out for us this afternoon, and you're goin' to come in a way that'll take your head clear off your shoulders. Believe me, baby, believe me."

He sighed, and began to slip out of his clothes. He'd been wrong that Sade's news would make him more responsive, because he found her tiresome. This afternoon would be the last time, then he would tell her to go, perhaps with a fur coat as a parting sweetener, for it never paid to make unnecessary enemies. But it was time for a fresh face. She came to help him undress, kissing, teasing, using her hands, but his mind kept drifting away. Musoveld? Yes, he was sure that was the one who'd left the Old Tart in '44. He would have known Donlett then. He searched his mind uneasily for the possibility there may have been others.

Chapter 5

It was as if Zarich had never left Ella's apartment, the same expression of fear and resentment on her face as when he'd last seen her. But this time she was dressed to kill as if expecting someone, face skillfully made up, hair combed out into silky waves, lean body sheathed in a beautiful white dress. She didn't look bad, not bad at all, but he knew it wasn't for him. It reaffirmed his opinion she'd been crazy letting herself get picked up so easily in the bar, because Liavone was obviously keeping her in style. But then maybe she'd been looking for something from him that psychopath couldn't give her.

He had young Greg Walsh with him, tall and round-shouldered as if trying to conceal his gawking height. He would have preferred Dawkins, but what Mal was doing in Washington was important, and this couldn't wait. But he didn't want any suggestion of a stake out that might scare Liavone off the apartment.

She sat apprehensively on the handsome period settee, face screwed into a savage scowl. Maybe she was still burning about the screwing with him, the realization it was only an interlude in the war, and she'd been used. He ignored her, and strolled into the bedroom. There was a partly packed open suitcase on the floor by the window. Everything else was pretty much as he remembered. He returned to the living room, where she was making a shaky attempt to light a cigarette. Walsh stood by the door, his wide eyes taking in the rakish angle of her long legs.

Zarich propped himself casually on the arm of the chair opposite her. It was ten o'clock and maybe he'd been lucky to find her home. She managed to light the cigarette, but the smoke came from her mouth in puffy bursts, as if she was having trouble breathing.

"Thinking of going on a trip, Ella?" he inquired, nodding in the direction of the bedroom.

"You're a shit, Zarich, you know that? Just a shit," she muttered. "You said you'd give me time." She glanced nervously toward the phone. "You've got no right barging in here at this time of night. I've got my rights. You think you can trample over anyone who gets in your way. Go screw yourself. I don't have to answer anything."

"Come on now, Ella," he said, shrugging. "You've got a short memory. You promised to be nice to me."

"I never promised anything about being nice to a sonofabitch like you."

He appraised her appearance very deliberately. "You know, you look very nice, Ella, real nice. You weren't expecting me, so maybe you're expecting Abe."

"Fuck off, you creep."

He glanced at Walsh with an exaggerated sigh, and the young detective returned an uncertain grin. Ella had obviously found some courage since his threat to pass on their time together in bed to Liavone. It wouldn't last.

"I thought we could pick up where we left it before," he suggested. She glanced furiously from him to Walsh and back again, and he knew she'd misinterpreted his remark in sexual terms. Maybe she thought he was asking her to spread her legs for Walsh too.

"The hell we will," she snarled.

"I just want to talk about the phone call you got earlier this evening," he said soothingly.

Her eyes narrowed, and fear won a contest with antagonism in her face. "I might have guessed you bastards were bugging my phone."

"No, this was a phone call from a woman, asking you to pass on an urgent message to a guy named Swarse."

That sucked her wind, bled her of obscenities. "A . . . a message for Swarse?" she faltered. Her hand drooped, and the ash of the cigarette brushed the expensive covering on the settee. She unhooked her legs, and shuffled her feet nervously on the carpet. "I . . . don't know anyone called Swarse," she claimed hesitantly. "I . . . I couldn't make any sense of the call. If it was only a sucker call now I know why."

He leaned forward in an attitude of contrition. "Ella, I'm going to do you the biggest favor of your life," he offered.

She jeered bitterly. "Shit, you're a real joker, Zarich. From what I've heard you wouldn't give your own mother something for nothing. What do I have to give you in return, an arm or a leg?" Her eyes flickered apprehensively to the phone again. Maybe she was expecting a call from Abe?

"I'm just trying to save you from spending the rest of your life in jail," he declared coldly.

She stared at him warily. "What sort of shit is that?

You haven't got anything on me, Zarich. I haven't done anything to expect time like that."

"Try being an accessory to a double murder," he threw at her.

She tried to jeer again, but it dried in her throat. "You'd have trouble making shit like that stick, and you know it," she said defiantly.

"Swarse is Liavone, Ella. I know that, and so do you."

"The hell I did. Since when is calling yourself a different name a crime anyway?"

"Abe killed two people, Ella. A harmless old man at City Hospital, and another elderly man today. I know he got big money for both jobs."

"You're outa your mind."

"No, but you are if you stick with Liavone, Ella. He's going away for life. We've got all the proof we need, and I'd hate to see you go down with him."

He could see he was getting to her, but she wasn't going to crumple like Honi Juric. Ella had been around, learned a long time ago that survival was the name of the game. It was just a matter of edging her toward the direction she had to jump to stay alive, and she'd do it.

"I don't know how Abe makes his money," she said sullenly.

He leaned back in the chair. "You're crazy if you think a jury'll believe that. You take calls for him in the name of Swarse, set things up for him. That makes you one hell of an accessory in my book."

"I take messages, that's all," she blustered.

"Yeah, like messages about making a hit. Does he make calls from here?"

"Sometimes."

"Who does he call?"

She pouted rebelliously. "I never hear any names."

"We can check. I'm trying to help you, Ella."

"He . . . he calls Australia. Sydney," she admitted.

He stared at her. Everything connected to the Old Tart, and the Old Tart connected to Australia. That's where the PT boat had operated during the latter part of the war, where Musoveld had served on her. Christ, was that where the overseas money he'd heard about was coming from? Was it a further indication Blake had been on the Old Tart in Australia?

"You know who he spoke to?" he pressed her.

She hesitated, teeth cutting at her lower lip. "How would I know?"

"He must have said something," Zarich persisted roughly.

"It was to do with some sort of job," she muttered.

"A job?" He could sense her fear growing, loosening her tongue.

"Yeah, someone in Australia was paying him a heap of dough. I don't know what the job was, he never told me anything like that." She stirred in the chair, staring at her hands. "I'm not saying any more until I talk to a lawyer."

"Don't be a fucking idiot," he said furiously. "I'm trying to get you off the hook."

"You don't give a shit about me, Zarich. You just want Abe, and I can go join the fucking bag women out on the street for all you care," she declared shrilly. It was more than Zarich, than Liavone, but a vehement denunciation of a world that had never given her a break.

"You must have some money put away, Ella. You'd play it shrewd."

"I might have."

He gestured toward the bedroom. "You were getting set to run, Ella. Maybe you figured you could get out of town before I put any more pressure on you. It isn't going to work, Ella. You can still use the suitcase, or you can go down with Abe. It's up to you."

He let it sit there for a moment, while she brooded in silence. He was sure when it came to the crunch, she'd decide for Ella.

"I didn't know he was a hit man," she muttered.

He didn't answer. Maybe she didn't want to know, but she'd been around, and must have known Liavone's reputation.

"He said nothing about killing elderly men," she whined.

He still held silence, while young Walsh watched in fascination.

"I can go?" she asked.

"Sure." He tried to lubricate the path for her. "Maybe you're telling the truth, you didn't know what Abe was up to, but he's the one I want."

"Why here? You can pick him up anywhere, you've got ways."

"It's simpler here. Abe has a way of disappearing underground around New York."

There was another period of silence, while he let her find her own way. He didn't believe she was sweating over loyalty, but where her main chance of survival lay.

"What do I have to do?" she asked finally.

"I want him here. Can you contact him?"

"No, he always calls me." She glanced nervously at her watch. "Around about this time of night. Sometimes he comes over, sometimes he doesn't. I was dressed in case we went out to eat."

He figured she was still lying. Maybe Abe was coming, but the packed suitcase and her clothes meant they were getting set to take off together.

"We'll wait," said Zarich flatly. He settled in the chair, and pointed a warning finger. "No changes of mind, Ella. You get one chance, and if you blow it, that's it. You go all the way with Abe, and by Christ I'll make it stick. You understand, baby?"

"Yes, I understand," she muttered. "Stop riding me."

"Just make it good. Pass on the message about Swarse, and don't give him the slightest indication he shouldn't come here," he threatened.

He had it figured she'd decided for survival, but he wasn't going to trust her until Liavone stepped through the door.

They waited another fifteen minutes in silence before the phone rang, and Zarich positioned himself quickly beside Ella, a menacing scowl on his face.

"Make it good," he warned her again.

He knew she would have spat in his face if she thought she could get away with it.

"There's a message for Swarse, Abe," she said after a few preliminaries. "The woman wants to see him urgently." She nodded several times, and Zarich strained to catch

Liavone's words. "That's good," she murmured. "I was hoping you hadn't changed your mind about coming over. Yes I'm just about packed. I feel like seeing you."

The contrived sultry tone of her voice was all the proof he needed that she'd committed herself to survival. She wasn't going down with Abe. She put down the phone, and slunk back in the chair.

"He's coming," she said sullenly. "Now can I go?"

"What did he say about Swarse?"

"He sounded surprised." She looked uncertainly from him to Walsh, then back again. "Now can I go?" she asked again. "I did what you asked."

"I didn't say anything about going yet."

Anger flared in her face. "What the hell's that supposed to mean?"

"Someone's got to open the door for Abe."

"You bastard, you told me . . ."

"That you could go. Sure, but I didn't say when. How's it going to look if I open the door, Ella? Or Walsh here? I don't want any bullets flying around." He gave her a sly grin. "You've gone this far, you may as well stay for the rest of the journey."

She had that much hatred going for him he tensed himself in case it converted to violent action. Her nails were long and well kept, and he figured they could make quite a gash in his face.

"Jesus Christ I should've known," she glowered at him.

"It shouldn't be too hard," he said to sooth her. "Open the door, and we'll take it from there."

She ran her fingers distractedly through her hair. "He'll kill me."

"He'll be on a pension by the time he gets out, if ever. We'll protect you."

"Like shit you will. I'll have to get out of New York."

"You were going anyway, Ella."

He could feel the hatred coming off her body like a heated fan. "You got a woman, Zarich?"

"We're not talking about me, Ella."

"Yeah, I figured not. You couldn't hold one, Zarich. You'd always be horse trading, passing them around, using them awhile, then wondering what sort of price you could get. Anything decent would tell you to piss off."

He turned irritably away, and saw Walsh staring fixedly at the ceiling. Was that really how it was? Fuck her, he wasn't going to let some frayed-out hooker suck him in. He forced a sour grin, and beckoned to Walsh. "Come on, we'll wait in the bedroom, Greg." He backed off from Ella with a warning gesture as Walsh crossed to join him. "Easy does it, Ella."

She didn't answer, didn't even turn her head, just sat slumped in the chair, staring fixedly at her cigarette.

He put the light out, and left the bedroom door just sufficiently ajar to enable him to see into the living room. Walsh positioned himself behind, able to look over his shoulder with his additional height. He took out the .38, checked it, then held it loosely in his hand while Walsh did the same. There was an expectant silence, like the hush before dawn. Occasionally the plumbing gushed in another apartment, but that was all. Ella remained where they'd left her, immobile, as if she'd become part of the chair. She moved only once in twenty minutes, slowly extending her arm to the ash tray on the coffee table to discard her cigarette. He wondered what was going on in her head. Probably a combination of fear of Liavone and hatred for him. The door buzzer sounded three times before she moved, and for an anxious moment he thought he might have to prompt her. He didn't know if she had any real feeling for Liavone, other than a meal ticket, but maybe it was just fear that made her unsteady on her legs when she finally made it to her feet. Zarich didn't give a damn how she felt. All he wanted was the name of the butcher who'd taken out the contract on Blake and Musoveld. And why.

She opened the door, and Liavone came through like a shambling ape in heat, taking her in a grappling embrace. Whatever Abe had read in her tone of voice, he was obviously all fired up and ready to go. Zarich could hear Walsh breathing rapidly behind him, and he passed him a reassuring nudge.

Ella was attempting to break from Abe's grasp and push the door shut at the same time, and Zarich could hear muttered obscenities coming from somewhere around Ella's neck.

"Easy, Abe, easy," she gasped.

Then she managed to break free, and retreated shakily back into the room, pushing at her dress. Liavone looked at her, nonplussed.

"What is it with you, baby?" he demanded thickly. "You sounded like a cat in heat over the phone."

"Don't come on so fast," she protested. She frittered nervously at her hair, and glanced anxiously toward the bedroom.

"Well I figure on some sort of celebration, baby. The Australian thing. paid off and everything's going smooth. It's the Bahamas for you and me." He leered at her. "I didn't expect to find you dressed. What's the matter, are you slowing up?"

Zarich didn't know how long she could go with the pretense without tipping off Liavone. There was a safety margin of space between them, and he moved, the .38 extended, and it abruptly wiped all thoughts of lust from Liavone's mind.

"Freeze, Abe," he snapped. "Right where you are. You're under arrest."

Liavone's head turned in a stupified circuit, from Zarich to Ella, to Walsh, then back to Ella again. "What the fuck is this?" he asked thickly.

"Lieutenant Zarich from Homicide, Liavone."

"I know who you are, Zarich." His hands made uncomprehending gestures. "What the hell are you doing here?" His eyes flicked to the gun. "You've got nothing on me, Lieutenant."

"That's something we can talk about at headquarters, Abe."

"I'm clean, Zarich. You got nothing to pull me in for."

"Honi Juric says differently, Abe."

Liavone made a bad attempt to keep apprehension out of his face. "I . . . I don't now any Honi Juric."

"The nurse, Abe. She had a bad attack of conscience, and told us all about Blake in the hospital, and Musoveld in the Village. We want to know who's paying the bills, Abe."

The hit man seemed to make a physical effort to draw his head into his shoulders, as if to hide from the world. "I tell you I don't know any Honi . . ." he began, then he pulled up short, and his eyes took in Ella again as if for the first time. "You bitch," he said fiercely.

"Easy, Abe," Zarich warned. He nodded brusquely to Walsh. "Let's move him out."

"You motherfucking bitch," declared Abe savagely. "I took you off the street, set you up, then you shaft me with this sonofabitch cop."

Ella didn't look at him, but retreated a few faltering steps, collided with the chair, and almost fell.

"You put me away forever, bitch, you know that. For fucking ever."

"Turn around, Abe," demanded Zarich sharply.

Liavone ignored him, oblivious to everything except his fury at betrayal. He reached into the inside pocket of his jacket. "You lousy bitch," he rasped. "You won't be missed on visiting days."

Ella turned away in sudden panic, blundered into the chair, and sprawled in a tangle of arms and legs to the floor. "Don' kill me, don' kill me," she screamed. "He made me, Abe. . . . I couldn't help it, he made me."

Zarich saw the shape of the gun emerging from Liavone's pocket, and he lined up the .38 on the hoodlum's legs. "Drop it, Abe, drop it," he bawled.

"Jesus Christ," he heard Walsh behind him.

The gun went off so close to his ear he was momentarily stunned, cordite stung his nostrils, his eyes blurred. Vaguely he saw splinters fly from the door as his own shot went wild, then Abe was going down like a felled gorilla, blood fountaining from the side of his head. It was all too late, but he furiously thrust Walsh's gun aside.

"You stupid bastard, I wanted him alive, for Chrissake couldn't you aim for his legs?"

"He was going to kill her, Lieutenant," protested Walsh.

"The hell with her," he bellowed. "The hell with her." He thrust the .38 back into his holster, and stalked across to the prostrate Liavone. Blood was everywhere, on the furniture, the carpet, the walls. He was just as dead as

Blake, as Musoveld, just as silent. He'd followed the scent, and Walsh had wiped it out for him. Perhaps he would never know about the Old Tart now. "For Chrissake," he cried out in frustration. "For Chrissake." He turned on the hapless Walsh. "You asshole gun-happy rookie," he blurted.

Walsh stood like a drooping scarecrow, the gun hanging at his side. "He was going to kill her," he muttered defensively.

Zarich breathed deeply, struggling to regain control. Christ, Beuso would roast him for this. Ella was still on the floor, but up on her elbows, her face drained of color.

"Okay, get on the phone," said Zarich curtly. "Have someone come over here and clean this mess up." He jerked his thumb at the body. "I want people working all night on this creep, right down to the brand of after-shave he used."

Ella finally discovered her voice, although so thin and strained with shock as to be scarcely recognizable. "You lousy sonofabitch Zarich," she whispered. "You lousy shit, you would have let him kill me." She rolled to one side, but staying on the floor as if she lacked the strength to pull herself upright. "You hear me," she shrilled at Walsh. "He would have let him kill me, and not missed a night's sleep. Maybe it'll be your turn next, sonny boy, if you get in the way of him taking someone. Think about it."

Zarich ignored her, jerking his head again toward the phone. "Come on, get on the phone, Greg," he ordered sharply. He looked hesitantly at Ella, then walked over and offered her his hand in assistance. She stared at it as if it was a poison bait, then put her head down on the carpet and began to cry in a way he hadn't thought possible for her.

It was another three hours before he fell into bed. He was out on his feet, and used to a lonely bed by now, but sleep eluded him. The words "Old Tart" kept beating around in his head like a maddening tune one longs to forget. He tried to console himself that Liavone may not even have known who was providing the contract money, but he knew it was only shit, there must have been some contact. But it had to be someone in Australia. Liavone had dialed Sydney direct, so there was going to be no way he could trace the calls. Even the image of Liavone's bloodied body stretched out in Ella's apartment was enough to give him a prickly heat of frustration. But at least he had the Australian connection, because the Old Tart and Australia were beginning to merge as equally important. Was it possible after all that something had happened on the Old Tart forty years ago in Australia to spark off the killing of Blake and Musoveld? Yet according to Musoveld the crew were all dead anyway. It seemed an incredible theory, yet everything he'd learned so far was leading him in that direction. Kangaroos and sunshine were all he knew about Australia, but maybe he should go there. He could work in with the Australian police. Mal would be back from Washington in the morning, and if what he had tallied with Australia, then he'd definitely talk to Beuso about going.

He considered it for a time, then closed his eyes, trying for sleep again. But his mind turned to Rhonda, and then to remembrance of Ella's body. Would he really have let Liavone kill her to keep the hit man alive? He didn't want to believe that about himself, but the moment before Greg fired, maybe it was in his mind. He tried to shut it out, but it stayed with him until he drifted into unconsciousness. Perhaps it was why he slept so badly, and woke late.

He breakfasted hurriedly on coffee, but it was nine-thirty before he made headquarters. A wrangling time with Beuso over Liavone's death didn't improve his temperament, but at least it gave him the opportunity to plant the thought about Australia. So it was ten-thirty before he found a weary, unshaven, but triumphant Dawkins waiting for him in his office.

Dawkins as usual had been very methodical. A transparent overlay had been fixed over the photograph of the Old Tart crew, with a name carefully lettered beneath each individual member. It was an excellent result, and Zarich needed something good to show Beuso after the stinging early morning session.

"The Navy had it all down on computer, Ed," said Dawkins. "So it all came together easy. Just as well I was able to get Beuso to make some calls. The guys didn't appreciate being dragged out of bed."

"Absolutely fantastic, Mal," enthused Zarich, running his eyes along the names. "What about Blake?"

Dawkins placed his finger down on an underlined name beneath a fair-haired smiling boy. "No sweat. The ID I had on Blake worked out, Ed, 'specially the tattoo. That's him there. His real name was Bart Donlett."

Zarich straightened in his chair, and breathed a sigh of relief. At least he had a few things going for him now without Liavone. The PT boat, Australia, and now Blake's real name. "Bart Donlett. That's terrific, Mal. Any next of kin, anyone we can contact?"

"I'm working on it, but I don't think it's going to do us much good, Ed. The guys in the Navy Department really flipped when they found out what I was after."

"How do you mean?"

"Musoveld was right, Ed. Everything he told you about the Old Tart, they confirmed." He opened a folder beside the photograph, and ran his finger down a typed page. "I've got it all documented for you. PT five two four, operated out of the port of Darwin, Australia, through 1944 and early 1945." He tapped his finger at the base of the page. "As Musoveld told you, she disappeared in early April, 1945. Evidently just went out on a routine patrol, and was never heard of again." He stood up by the side of the desk, and pushed the folder across to Zarich. "See, Musoveld was transferred off the PT boat in late '44, so he was leveling with you all along the way." He paused with a wry grin. "But Ed, all these other guys died forty years ago . . . and that includes Donlett, alias Blake. That's what threw the Navy guys. How the hell does a man listed as missing in action in 1945 turn up in a New York hospital for a brain operation forty years later?" He shook his head dolefully. "And then gets himself murdered. That's a screwy one for you, Ed. Figure that out?"

Zarich hunched silently in his chair, and stared with irritable bafflement at the photograph. It was like grabbing at handfuls of sand; everytime he thought he had something, it slipped through his fingers.

"Then they made a mistake," he stated flatly. "It isn't Donlett."

"Well, take it up with them if you like, Ed, but they've got no doubts at all."

"For Chrissake, the body I saw in the hospital was no ghost."

Dawkins scrubbed at his chin with a sound like grating sandpaper. "Well, there was another point. They went back over their records and found something that could explain it, but the Navy makes no guarantees."

"What was that?"

Dawkins leaned across and turned over a page on the file. "Right here, this end piece, Ed. There was a report of an unidentified man being picked up in the Taiwan Straits by a Chinese gunboat soon after the Old Tart vanished. But then no one ever turned up, the war ended, and it was never confirmed, just noted on the records, and apparently forgotten about. It just could have been Donlett." His hand brushed the photograph again. "It could have been any of them, I guess." He paused, with a nonplussed shrug. "Or none of 'em."

Zarich folded his arms, and stared thoughtfully to the outer office. Walsh was standing waiting, feet shuffling nervously on the floor, a report in has hand that probably concerned Liavone. Maybe they'd turned up something on that dead sonofabitch. Perhaps he should ease the pressure on young Walsh; maybe Liavone would have killed Ella.

"That's their explanation," he said tersely.

"It's all they've got, unless you want to start believing in ghosts."

"The hell with that. Hodges didn't operate an any ghost."

"Well, I don't know, Ed. I just don't know. All I can tell you for sure is that they're positive Blake is Donlett."

"Then he had to be the man picked up in the Taiwan Straits, with his memory gone."

"I guess so, but the Navy isn't prepared to go on the record with it."

Zarich picked up the photograph again in exasperation. He had nothing but elusive shadows or hunches, and he wanted facts. He stared at the long-dead smiling faces, Froman, Andrews, Berger, Ensign Winberg, the captain, Jay Schuman. They told him nothing. He had to accept the Navy identification, back the theory Donlett was the man picked up in the Taiwan Straits. What alternative did he have?

"Then in some way the poor bastard must have found his way back to the States, and wandered around in a mental fog for the last forty years," he murmured softly. "That's the way it must have happened."

"Yet the Old Tart was the first thing to filter back into his mind after the operation. From what Honi Juric told me the words 'Old Tart' seemed to act like some sort of trigger for Liavone's client. What the hell was so important about a PT boat that vanished forty years ago to cost Donlett his life? And Musoveld?"

"Find that out, and you get the sixty-four thousand dollars, no questions asked," shrugged Dawkins. He sighed, and stretched his mouth in a wide yawn. "Maybe some of the others in the crew survived. There were about ten of them."

"You mean they're all wandering around the country with lost memories?" said Zarich with heavy sarcasm.

"Anything's possible the way this is coming together, Ed. Maybe we'll never know."

Zarich didn't believe that, never accepted it about any case. He was sucked in deep with wanting to know, and there was no way he was going to let go now.

"I'm dead, Ed," murmured Dawkins. "I've got to get some shut-eye, or I'll fall over."

"Okay, sure," said Zarich quickly. He thumbed over the report. "Is there anything else here I should know, Mal?"

Dawkins levered himself off the side of the desk, and blearily pawed over the pages. "Oh, one important item that could tell us something. Navy records show Donlett married an Australian girl in Sydney in 1944. Anyway I've put a call through to the Australian police to see if they can trace her. Shouldn't be difficult if she's still alive. At least they didn't think so. They said they can work through their marriage records, things like that. They promised fast action, so let's see if they're up to their word."

Zarich grinned appreciatively at the sergeant. "That's great work, Mal, just great. You really put this together."

Dawkins stifled another yawn. "I'm bloody lucky to be still standing on my feet, let alone anything else," he grunted. "Let's hope it gets us somewhere."

He drooped to the desk, arms slackly supporting him, while Zarich silently scanned through the item on Donlett's wife. It was the last thing he needed to convince himself of the necessity of going to Australia. "The way this is shaping up, I might go to Australia, Mal," he said quietly.

Dawkins blinked through his fatigue. "Australia?"

"That's right." He closed the folder, and thoughtfully shuffled the photograph about in his hands. "I've got a feeling that's where all the answers are." He tapped his forefinger gently against his nose, and gave a craggy grin. "Call it the old hound dog instinct if you like, but everything points to Australia. For sure Liavone got his contract from Australia. That's where the Old Tart was during the war. And with an ounce of luck Donlett's wife." He shook his head firmly. "Something happened there in 1945. Don't ask me what, because I haven't got the faintest idea right now, but I'm not going to find out sitting on my ass here in New York. I'll let it settle for a few days until I've got everything in, then I'll take it to Beuso."

"I'll carry your bags," grinned Dawkins wearily.

"I don't think Beuso'll buy a double berth. He'll start quoting budget figures to me. Besides, I want you here, Mal." He rapped his hand against the photograph. "I want the relatives of these guys traced. Brothers, sisters, parents, if they're still alive. Talk to them, but nice and easy. Maybe all they can tell you is these guys were reported missing in action forty years ago, and that's the end of it. But I still think it needs to be done."

"You think what I said could be true? Some of these guys might have survived like Donlett?"

Zarich gave a doubtful shake of his head. "Anything's possible I guess. But why wouldn't they have come forward long ago? I made a joke of it before, but they couldn't all be suffering from loss of memory. No, my

guess would be they went down with the Old Tart, but
Donlett saw something on that PT boat which is a hell of a
threat to someone." He smiled ruefully. "I've been asking
myself questions like that ever since Beuso sent me to
City Hospital. You go home and get some sleep, Mal.
We'll talk about it later."

Dawkins pushed himself away from the desk, and
slouched to the door. "Well, don't go tangling with any
kangaroos," he muttered.

"Say hello to Alison for me," said Zarich affably.

"Sure thing." He went out the door with a vague
backward wave of his hand, and a nod to Walsh in passing.

Zarich watched the departing sergeant, aware that
Walsh was preparing himself as if for a run over hot coals.
Mal was the best; he wouldn't make the mistake of not
taking him into his complete confidence again. He settled
back in his chair, and gestured Walsh inside.

He spent time collating it all, Dawkins' Washington
report and anything he'd turned up on the relatives of the
crew, all the information about Donlett and the operations
of the Old Tart in Darwin during the war, plus the little
that Walsh had uncovered on Liavone. But he needed
confirmation from the Australian police on Donlett's wife
before he could take it all to Beuso, and after five days
he'd still heard nothing.

He rang Rhonda several times, but twice no one
answered, and the third time he received a busy signal,
which was a sign she'd taken it off the hook. He knew
what that meant. He tried to make himself believe he
merely wanted to say hello to his ex-wife, but he knew it
wasn't as simple as that. He shouldn't give a shit what a
woman like Ella thought of him, but her scathing words
had stuck in his gullet. Maybe he wanted some sort of
reassurance from someone who at least had loved him
once. So he did some bar hopping late at night, but it was
like following mirages through the desert. He was the
hunter; that was the reality; it was mother, father, and
lover to him.

He felt a sense of relief when Mal told him that
although the Australian police had run into problems, it

was all confirmed—they'd found Donlett's wife alive but under another name, for she'd remarried years ago. He sent it all to Beuso with a recommendation he follow it to Australia, then waited impatiently all morning until he finally got the call. He'd even donned a suit and tie as if to mark a special occasion.

Captain Beuso was as spare and disciplined as his office. He had a neatness thing which extended beyond his personal appearance to everything he touched. He was fifty with Lebanese good looks, black hair flecked with gray, and the tight expression of a banker preparing himself to refuse a loan. Dark suit, white shirt, subdued tie, not a hair out of place as if he'd come directly from the cleaners already encased in his clothes. His desk top was almost bare, no clutter, no scraps of paper, just a few essentials like a phone. He'd gone to a good school, and he took care to advertise it in his speech. He took in Zarich's unaccustomed garb with an arid smile and raised eyebrows.

"This must be important to you, Ed," he observed, with a trace of sarcasm.

Zarich shrugged. "It's a hell of an interesting case," he murmured.

The captain paused, and leafed over the report as if to reacquaint himself, but Zarich knew it was only a mannerism. He would have missed nothing. There was little personal relationship between the two men. Beuso was a cop who played strictly by the book, and he might have turned a disapproving eye on Zarich's sexual tactics, but he couldn't challenge his record.

"There's not a great deal on the money paid into Liavone's account presumably for the contract, Ed," he observed in a clipped tone.

"Well, we know it came from Sydney, but it's been so well laundered it's close to impossible to pinpoint the actual individual source."

"Liavone might have been able to help us there."

There was an awkward pause. The harsh exchange over the hit man's death was past, but Beuso was letting him know it hadn't been forgotten.

"The Australian police came through on Donlett's

wife. That's a valuable piece of information. It's good she's alive, she might have something for us."

"She's evidently been remarried the last thirty years."

"I hope her memory's good. It might just be something Donlett told her all those years ago she didn't even consider important at the time."

"I hope to be asking her, of course. I'm sure what happened to Donlett in the hospital, and Musoveld, goes right back to that time in Australia."

It wasn't easy. Beuso went through the report line by line, grilling him on every detail for the next forty-five minutes, until he finally relented with a sign. "I guess I have to agree, Ed," he conceded. "Everything certainly points to Australia. The Old Tart. Sydney as the source of Liavone's contract." He nodded slowly, eyes half closed. "Maybe you're right, Ed . . . you should go to Australia."

"It might be worth playing safe and asking the Australian police to keep an eye on Donlett's ex-wife."

"It's highly unlikely anyone in Australia would know we've traced her. The police in Sydney were asked to keep it under strict security."

"The fuckers who contracted Liavone are there. Leaks are possible. I don't think it's worth the risk, not after what happened to Donlett and Musoveld."

Beuso nodded hesitantly. The captain didn't like taking advice from lower ranks, and Zarich knew there'd only be stubborn resistance if he pushed it. "Okay, you'd better go then, Ed," said Beuso.

"I'm sure that's where we'll find answers, Captain. At least some of the most important ones."

"Did Dawkins get any further with the relatives?"

"Well, as I noted down in the report, he's managed to trace a few of them, but it didn't amount to anything except rouse fading memories." He grimaced. "Just boys who didn't come back from the war. Most of the parents were dead anyway."

Beuso probed musingly at his mouth. "Nothing else?"

"I figure that's about it. The relatives thing is a dead end."

There was a silent pause, while the captain idly flipped the pages.

"Have you heard from Hodges again?" asked Zarich.

Beuso played it like poker. "No."

"It didn't make any of the news services about Blake being murdered. That'll make the hospital happy."

"Yes, I guess it will." Beuso snapped his mouth shut on the subject like a door slamming. "I'll make arrangements ahead with the Sydney police for you. I'm sure they'll cooperate, but it's their territory, and you'll have to work in with them, Ed."

"Sure. They may have a case themselves if it all comes together. But I think we should play it all low key. No publicity. I wouldn't want the people who hired Liavone to know I was in Australia."

"I agree. I'll make sure the Sydney police understand that." He tapped his fingers against Zarich's report. "And I'll have copies of this made and sent on to them as well." He thought for a moment, then smiled as widely as his thin mouth permitted. "Okay, Ed, make your arrangements as soon as you can. Check with Shirley downstairs about your expenses and tickets." He hesitated a moment. "You look great in that suit, Ed. Maybe it's the sort of, ah . . . image you should present for us in Australia. After all, you will be representing the New York police force."

"Up until now I've been using it mainly for funerals and weddings," said Zarich with a grin. "But okay, Captain, I promise not to get around Sydney looking like a bum."

Beuso seemed relieved, as if he'd been expecting some resistance. He stood abruptly to his feet, and thrust out his hand.

"Then have a good trip, Ed, and good luck. Keep me informed as much as you can. They tell me the girls on the beaches around Sydney are fabulous, so don't get sidetracked."

"Only if they can tell me something about the Old Tart," said Zarich coldly. Beuso should know him better than that.

He stayed with the suit over the next few days while his traveling arrangements were finalized, ignoring the cracks around the office about him working part-time as a funeral director. The night before he took off, he went to see Rhonda. She held open the door of her apartment for a quizzical examination, and for a moment he figured she had someone with her. She didn't usually go to bed so early, and he even recalled the pink robe she was still adjusting. She'd frizzed out her red hair since he'd last seen her, and it softened the sharp features so often used on him like a cutting edge. The lines about her pale blue eyes crinkled with amusement.

"Well, look at you," she mocked. "It can't be for me, so they've either moved you up to commissioner, or you've gone to work for a stockbroker."

He shrugged, and with an effort managed an easy grin. He wasn't too sure why he was there, but he'd never let her see there was still yearning deep inside. He tried to peer past her into the apartment.

"I'm going out of the country for a time, so I just thought I'd say good-bye."

"That's nice," she murmured, with a trace of sarcasm. "Where are you headed?"

"Australia."

Her eyebrows arched in surprise. "Australia? Well now, that's quite an assignment, hunter."

The name had started out as a gag, and he hated it. "I just thought I'd see you were fixed okay," he said awkwardly.

"I'm fixed. The checks keep coming."

"Maybe a cup of coffee."

She fixed him with a derisive stare. "You're not figuring on a farewell fuck are you, Ed?" she jeered.

It was an attempt to wound, and he should have left right then, but she stood to one side and pushed the door wide.

"I'm not in a coffee mood," she muttered.

Her actions said yes, her words no, and he failed to understand, but he went inside anyway. Nothing had changed. She liked the security of static things; that's one reason she could never take his unpredictable life-style. She stood with her back to the closed door, an unreadable smile on her face.

"You can't stay, hunter."

"Don't call me that."

"You liked it once."

Had he? It must have been pretense. Maybe, stupidly, a farewell fuck was what he really had in the back of his mind. He had no reason to imagine she'd be the slightest agreeable.

"Mal said you called me."

"It was nothing."

"It must have been something."

"No, I . . ." She shrugged. "Nothing."

The door to the bedroom abruptly opened to a young naked man. He looked only about nineteen, but as cool as hell. An erection jutted from his crotch like a ludicrous pointing finger. He took in Zarich with an irritated glance, then turned to Rhonda.

"Come on, baby, get rid of this guy." He pushed down on the erection with his fingers, and grinned lewdly. "You got the damn thing up, and it's not going to go down without you."

Even Rhonda had the grace to be angrily embarrassed. Perhaps her invitation was to let him know the guy was there, but she would have done it with more subtle style than this. She swiftly crossed the floor, placed her hand on the boy's chest, and shoved him firmly back into the bedroom. "Patience darling, patience. Just wait in there a moment."

"Listen, don't give me any smart-ass-bitch treatment. There's better stuff out on the street, baby." He grasped a handful of her hair, and pushed her back. "Say, isn't this the cop husband you told me about?"

"Let go," said Zarich coldly.

"What you goin' to do, cop? Shoot me? Arrest me?"

But he let go anyway when he saw the look on Zarich's face, then she pushed again until he was back in the room. "For Chrissake, Mike, will you just wait. I won't be long."

"Well okay," grunted the boy sullenly. "But get rid of the creep."

She closed the door, patted at her hair, and uttered a breathless laugh. "Little boys get too impatient sometimes," she said awkwardly. "But you've got to admit he's some stud. Could you get it up like that, Ed? I can't remember."

He felt more sad than angry. Had he really left her with that much bitterness?

"I've seen what you wanted me to see, so I may as well go," he said woodenly.

"So he's young, what of it," she said defensively. "What about some of the school girls you were screwing on the side?"

He sighed. It hadn't been like that, but it was pointless buying into an argument. He knew it was a mistake to have come. "I'm just glad we never had any kids," he said.

"Kids? For Chrissake, you were never around long enough to make me pregnant."

He moved to the door, anxious to be gone now. He nodded to the bedroom. "You think that's the best way to spend your alimony checks?"

He knew that would get to her.

"The day hasn't come I have to pay for it," she flared.

He opened the door, and stepped out into the hall. He wouldn't see her again. She was still quite lovely, but it was ugly to see the vehemence he could inspire in her face.

"I'll spend my money any damn way I please," she added furiously.

There was an angry knot in his stomach, but he'd fall down before he let it show in his face. "Take care," he said. His insouciance only fueled her rage.

"I hope you get run down by a fucking kangaroo," she screamed after him.

Chapter 6

Humbert had selected his own residence with the same care and attention to detail as any other business deal. It was a magnificent site overlooking Sydney Harbour from the suburb of Point Piper. A terraced garden ran down from the rear of the house to a free-form swimming pool, then a stretch of immaculate lawn to where the cliff dropped to the sea. Steps led down to a small private pier with a tethered white yacht, set free only six or seven times a year. Occasionally during summer a few carefully selected guests used the pool, but he rarely gave parties, and then only from political necessity.

He sat at the large windows, looking out to where the water shimmered with the night lights of Sydney. It lacked the height of his office view, but he preferred it in a way, especially at night. Darkness concealed the sores that festered in any large city. It was a time of night when he liked to be alone, savor his scotch, let a Beethoven sonata accompany his mood. He was safe. He had to admit there had been occasional anxious moments in the forty years since the Old Tart, relatives that might have recognized him, now all safely dead, but nothing to equal the trauma of finding Donlett alive. But it was all behind him now. He even wondered if he'd rewarded Sade sufficiently, because the man had done a magnificent job. He would think about it, and maybe add another sweetener. He glanced at his watch. There was a new girl coming to see him at eleven o'clock, and that was always a cause for anticipation.

He frowned at the sound of the door bell, then went through the hall to answer. He hoped there was no change of plans with the girl, especially after the recommendation he had been given about her.

It was Sade. "I was just thinking about you," he murmured pleasantly. Even his instinctive dislike of Sade was tempered tonight.

"I'm sorry to bother you at night like this, Mr. Humbert, but it's important, and I don't like discussing problems on the telephone."

He hesitated, then reluctantly invited him inside. He hoped this wasn't going to take long; the girl's arrival time wasn't far away. "But surely we don't have any problems now, Sade," he murmured, as he led the way into the living room. He didn't offer a drink—from experience he knew Sade would refuse, and he was loathe to do anything that may prolong the visit.

As usual, Sade made no attempt at polite preliminaries. "I think it possible we might have been a little premature thinking the New York problem was solved, Mr. Humbert," he stated.

His voice so lacked emotion it was difficult to know if there was a minor problem, or the end of the world. But he felt a slight quiver in his throat as he sat down.

"What exactly do you mean by 'premature'?"

"I've just had a call from our contact in the Sydney police. I'm afraid our operative in New York has been rather careless."

"Careless? What's that supposed to mean?"

"For a start he's got himself killed."

Humbert took a handkerchief from his pocket, patted at his brow, and uttered a short laugh. "Is that all, Sade. Well, perhaps that's not such a bad thing. Safer for us."

"You're probably right, Mr. Humbert," agreed Sade politely. "But he bungled the termination of the second threat. The man called Musoveld."

The quiver in Humbert's gullet gathered momentum. "Bungled?"

"Yes. The man lied to me. There is the matter of the photo album . . . the one he informed us had the pictures of the PT boat called the Old Tart, and crew. You remember?"

"Of course, of course," said Humbert irritably. "But you told me it'd been destroyed."

Sade grittily cleared his throat. "That's what the man lied about, Mr. Humbert. He told me it had been destroyed. Unfortunately, according to Roman, the New York police have the album now."

Humbert put a hand to his throat. He could feel his pulse throbbing beneath his fingers.

"I . . . I'm sorry," continued Sade. "I believed our operative was the best, the very best. A man I could completely trust. Obviously he never found the album. The police did."

Humbert turned to the window to hide what he felt coming into his face. "Jesus Christ," he muttered.

"The New York police are floundering in the dark," added Sade, in the same monotonous tone. "But it does appear they've identified Blake through Navy Department records as a man called Bart Donlett, who served on the Old Tart in Australia during the war." His bland inquiring eyes sought Humbert's face. "The name means something to you, Mr. Humbert?"

Humbert stood to his feet, and walked unsteadily to the window. A ferry slipped across the harbor, the lights giving it the appearance of floating mysteriously in midair. Sade had failed him. He could scarcely believe it.

"Yes," he answered thickly. "It's the man's real name, of course. The identity I asked you to prevent ever being known, Sade."

There was a moment of apologetic silence.

"There's absolutely nothing to connect you, Mr. Humbert," Sade reassured him.

Humbert clenched his hands into tight fists to control his anger. For God's sake, there could be a hundred things to connect him. This moron. This fucking idiot. He could even recall the day that photograph was taken, sweating in the stinking humidity, trying to look like every day was a picnic. The terrible, terrible fact was, he was at risk again.

"Is there anything else?" he asked sullenly.

There was an embarrassed cough as an indication of further troubling news. "There is a New York policeman coming to Australia to continue the investigation into Donlett. A Lieutenant called Ed Zarich."

He turned fiercely to Sade. "For Chrissake, that's all I need. I'm at risk again, Sade, don't you understand that? You may just as well let Donlett and Musoveld live for all the good it's done. My God, my God." He pressed his hands to the window, feeling the coolness of the glass against his sweaty palms. "They know about Donlett and the Old Tart. What was the goddam use."

Even Sade's controlled face registered apprehension. "I'm sorry, but you had to know these things, Mr. Humbert." He paused. "Our operative in New York came with the highest recommendation, Mr. Humbert," he added defensively. "I wouldn't have believed he would lie about the album. It's probably what cost him his life." He hesitated, and the mask slipped back into position. "Shall I go on?"

Humbert stared morosely out across the water. Even the lights of Sydney appeared suddenly dimmed. "What else is there?" he muttered.

"This is all detailed in the report our men received from the New York police. They know of course that the Old Tart operated out of Darwin during the war, and there is of course, ah, Donlett's wife."

The air abruptly sucked through Humbert's teeth made a thin whistling sound. "Are you telling me this Zarich also knows about her?"

"I'm . . . I'm afraid so. The marriage was also in the Navy Department records. Donlett evidently married an Australian girl in 1944." He paused. "But of course you knew about that."

Humbert remained silent, his face still bleakly to the window.

"The New York police requested she be traced by the Sydney police. Our man tried to stall it, but in the end he was forced to let it go through."

"Jesus Christ, they know where she is? They've been in touch with her?"

"I understand so."

"For Chrissake," he muttered furiously. The room fell silent, Sade's eyes hooded with cowed apology.

During the flight back from the States Humbert had fortunately recalled Donlett's Australian marriage. It was an event he'd completely forgotten over the years, because he'd only met her once for a brief few moments when she was a giggling seventeen-year-old girl. But seeing Donlett in New York had regurgitated the memory. So he'd taken the precaution of having Sade trace her, not that he intended to do anything about it, but just as a matter of safety. But now the threat to him seemed to loom larger than ever, and maybe he'd have to do something about her. Would she know anything? Surely Donlett wouldn't have confided in her, but men have loose tongues in bed. But God, it was forty years ago. If she'd known about the Old Tart, surely she would have said something after her husband was reported missing? Christ, just when he felt so safe, was Donlett's wife another ghost out to destroy him? The woman may think she knows nothing, but perhaps the American detective might trigger a forgotten memory. On her own she was harmless, but prodded by this Zarich, anything could happen. He could feel trembling coming back into his hands. The risk was unthinkable. As with Donlett. And Musoveld. And he was conscious of the fact Sade was learning too much. He was as much a hired gun as the man in New York, and he wanted it kept that way.

"I find your description of the New York police as floundering almost funny, Sade," he exclaimed, with bitter sarcasm. "Considering what they know."

Sade offered no defense. "You've postponed any decision about the woman, Mr. Humbert," he murmured instead. "There may be some urgency now. Roman has had her under close surveillance, of course. If it's any comfort, it seems she remembers nothing of importance about the PT boat, or her husband. But of course now . . ." He shrugged.

Humbert covered his trembling with a voice of angry accusation.

"You failed me, Sade."

Sade stared dolefully at the floor without answering.

"You enjoy a very satisfying life-style, Sade," added Humbert.

"I want for very little, Mr. Humbert."

"You are one of the highest, if not *the* highest paid member of this corporation. Do you know that?"

"You've always been very generous."

Humbert thought of the house Sade had bought at Surfers Paradise. He didn't interfere in the man's personal life, but there were macabre appetites behind the blank mask, stories of savagely beaten hookers he'd had to force Roman to suppress.

"I'm sure you want to keep it that way, Sade," he said coolly.

"Of course."

"This threat I face could bring your life-style to a very sudden end."

"I . . . I don't exactly know the form of that threat, but yes, I understand."

"Then I think it would be most fortunate for you if

Donlett's wife wasn't available to be questioned by the New York detective." He paused for emphasis. He could feel air wheezing in his bronchial tubes. He hadn't experienced an attack of stress asthma since Donlett's discovery in New York, and he didn't want another now.

"I'll see it's taken care of," said Sade uneasily.

"Yes, I think that could be in your best interests, Sade," Humbert scowled.

The room lapsed into silence again. The horn of a departing ship came mournfully into the room. He suddenly realized the Beethoven recording had ended.

"I'm really very sorry about New York, Mr. Humbert," murmured Sade.

Humbert retained his expression of disapproval. The unemotional mask made it close to impossible to judge the sincerity of Sade's apology.

"Well, see you correct it," he answered stiffly. "Keep in touch with our man. He's paid well enough, so make sure he sweats on this. We'll want to know every move the New York detective makes. If any problems come up, then we want to be able to stop the sonofabitch in his tracks. Understand?"

Sade nodded silently.

"So keep me informed," added Humbert curtly. "On everything."

He didn't offer to show Sade to the door, but stood with his hands to his back like an aggravated school master dismissing a wayward student, until Sade backed from the room.

He waited for the opening and closing sound of the front door, then he folded wearily into the club chair by the window. He brushed languidly at his hair, and felt dampness on his brow. The unthinkable nightmare had returned with a vengeance, ghosts hovering to destroy him. But he'd fight; he'd always been a fighter.

He heard the door bell, but refused to stir. It was probably the girl, but Sade had ruined any sexual appetite. After a while she went away.

Through the window he could see the ship now, black hull creaming the water, the night glow of the city reflecting in the superstructure. He remembered the Japanese ship coming out of the darkness of the Taiwan Straits like that. There had been times over the years when he'd almost succeeded in forgetting, but it always came back, an unlocked door that could swing open at any moment and make it like yesterday. At such moments the name he'd adopted of Kepler Humbert meant nothing, and he was Jay Schuman again, failed at Columbia, and still without enough clout to finish up as a lieutenant in the Navy commanding the Old Tart. Disillusioned parents reacted in character, his mother by displaying optimistic hope it was another chance for him, his father by asking who he'd cheated to get the rank. The hell with him. Maybe if the old man hadn't been such a failure, his yen for making a buck wouldn't have got him into so much trouble. He wasn't so much a patriot, but the Navy at least gave him a sense of direction he'd never experienced before. He'd enjoyed the Old Tart; even the danger of combat gave him a high like some of the scams he'd got involved in at Columbia. He'd inherited the nickname of the PT boat with no idea of its origin. But it was an old boat, and someone told him she'd had so many refits she was like an old tart who'd seen too many beds. He'd never found out if it was true. That night out on the Taiwan Straits the only thoughts on his mind were to survive the war, and make himself a rich man.

Early April 1945

It had begun in a crummy Darwin bar, a day of the usual heat, flies, and boredom, but at least the saving grace of cold Australian beer. The war had moved to the north, and he wasn't sure why they were still operating out of Darwin.

Carl Yaphank was the last person he expected to see. He hadn't seen Yaphank since their Columbia days together, when they'd run a racehorse scam, except that he'd heard somewhere he was doing time for forgery. You didn't ask a fixer like Carl how he made it from jail to a captain in Naval Intelligence; he just did those sorts of things. It wasn't until after four beers he found out their meeting in Darwin was no coincidence; Yaphank had come all the way from the Philippines looking for him, knew all about his being the captain of the Old Tart. As always, he had a proposition, but even knowing Carl, this one took his breath away. Yaphank had a lean hungry face like a wolf running close to starvation. He'd lived a life of eternal prospecting for the elusive pot of gold, and he was dedicated to finding it, inside or outside the law. It was a commonality that had drawn them together in the old days. Every new plan was always the one to make them fabulously rich, all of them propounded with equal enthusiasm, his lean skinny frame twitching as if he were plugged into an electric circuit. "Cyrano" they'd dubbed him at Columbia, with the long bony nose dominating his face, but he could be so smooth and persuasive after a time you didn't even notice. Certainly not when he was talking about the Japanese hospital ship called the Awa Maru.

"I've got the information all bottled up in Intelligence, so only you and I know about it for now, Jay. It was a lucky break I was the duty officer when the news came through, and I thought to myself, Carl, this one you're going to keep under wraps, and only share with Jay Schuman," he hissed excitedly. He leaned to the table until only a few inches separated their heads. "Man, the ship's there for the taking. My information came straight from the prisoners of war loading her on the Singapore docks, through one of their secret radio sets. She's been guaranteed safe passage by our forces for her return trip to Japan as a hospital ship, but my information says the Japs aren't playing it square." He winked. "They've got cargo on that ship to make us crazy rich, man. Nothing to do with a hospital. She's loaded with gold bullion from the Jap occupied territories. There'll never be another chance like this. She won't be armed and your small boat and crew would be ideal to take her. Think of it, man, rich like you never dreamed."

He couldn't help thinking about it. That sort of wealth made his head spin. "That much gold," he gasped.

"That much," Yaphank assured him.

"I don't know if the crew will buy it," he murmured doubtfully. "I know them pretty well, but I couldn't promise they'd go for anything as crazy as this. Christ, we could all finish up being court martialled, you know that."

"Hell, what's to lose. No one ever got this rich without taking risks. We play it right, and no one will ever know. We've got a couple of weeks before the Awa Maru leaves Singapore. I can keep the information under wraps until then." The long thin jaw was almost touching his face. "It's all ours, man, so go for it. I've got all the details about her route on the way back to Japan, anything you want to know. I figure you might be able to hit her in the Taiwan Straits."

Yaphank had a fast tongue. Watching his skinny body shuffle excitedly about on the chair made Schuman recall how carefully you had to look at his propositions, or you'd end up getting your fingers burned. But he'd never have a better chance to satisfy his yen to be rich. Throw the old man a few bucks, and watch him grovel to pick them up.

"That's a long way for the Old Tart. It'd take a lot of planning, extra provisions, extra fuel. It'd be too risky to stop off anywhere."

"So what? You can do it."

"I still don't know if the crew will go along."

"Talk to 'em. Show me someone who doesn't want to be this rich. Jesus, remember the time at Columbia, man? You could sell 'em. Remember the phoney mining stock you unloaded on the priest in the Bronx." He giggled. "After all, the Japs are the enemy. Christ, we're entitled to some compensation for the bastards dragging us all this way to risk our necks."

Schuman very much doubted if Yaphank ever put himself in a situation where his neck was at risk. But still, where money was concerned, anything was possible with Carl.

"There'll be a split among maybe ten or twelve guys," Schuman warned him.

"So what? There'll be plenty for everyone."

"What happens about you? Do you stay here in Darwin, or go back to the Philippines, and we split later?"

Yaphank hesitated a moment. "I figured I'd come along for the ride," he said, in a more subdued tone. "Of course I'll have to go back to the Philippines first to make sure I keep this thing quiet, but I can make it back here before you leave." He saw the doubt in Schuman's face. "I won't get in the way, Jay. You're the boss on board. Maybe it's my plan, but I don't see why you guys should take all the risks."

Schuman concealed a cynical grin behind a mouthful of beer. Christ, he knew Yaphank. The bastard hated the thought of risking his hide, but he wouldn't trust his own mother. The only reason he wanted in on the action was to make sure no one double-crossed him out of his share. But he couldn't very well keep him out. "If we went for it then okay, but I'm warning you, it wouldn't be any picnic."

Yaphank offered a reassuring gesture. "Understood, man. Perfectly understood. I might be able to help in some way."

Schuman silently considered the plan. Yaphank was a slippery eel, but he'd handled him at Columbia, and he could handle him now. This was big-league stuff, the biggest, and there were huge risks, but Christ the prize. What a life he could have after the war. "If . . . and it's a big if, we get the gold off the Awa Maru, what then?" he asked.

Yaphank grinned, took a crumpled map from his pocket, and spread it out on the table. "I gave this a lot of thought, man, and it's all worked out. Take a look at this." He made a slitting motion across his throat. "But exit the Awa Maru for a start. Like I said, they're the enemy anyway, and if they're not playing it square that's the way it goes. There's a lot of our guys at the bottom of the ocean too."

There were many details to be worked out, and they talked long into the night making plans. Then Schuman went back to his quarters and dreamed of pliant girls and Long Island mansions. And the same sort of dreams proved too much for the crew. After a week of taking them carefully into his confidence they went for it. As Yaphank had said, who doesn't want to be rich, and the Japanese were the enemy. There and then they all decided for their own postwar prosperity.

"It's the Awa Maru, Jay," whispered Ensign Winberg. He didn't have to whisper the sighting report, but excitement had subdued his vocal chords. His youthful pretty boy features glowed in the moonlight, an expression on his face as if he were watching the Second Coming. Pretty or not, Schuman recognized the sound of greed.

He looked out across the waters of the Taiwan Straits, where the approaching ship was lit up like a carousel against the night sky. It had to be the hospital ship, confident of its safe passage guarantee; no one else would carry lights like that in these waters.

"It looks like it," he said brusquely.

In contrast his own voice was coldly efficient, but he was better at hiding his excitement than the ensign. He didn't want the crew fouling up from overenthusiasm.

Winberg kept the binoculars fixed to his eyes. The moon painted a white path like a connecting bridge across the sea to the ship. Schuman held the Old Tart to dead slow, and she rode easy on the flat sea. They couldn't have wished for a better night. It had taken them days to come such a long way, stacked with the extra supplies, and they were already at risk by abandoning their designated patrol route. They'd kept radio silence, answering no calls, and for all he knew they might have been reported missing by now.

Yaphank was hunched silently in a corner of the cockpit, staring out toward the ship as it drew closer, until even without binoculars the hospital ship markings could be plainly seen.

"I can't make out the name," muttered Winberg.

"For Chrissake, who needs a name, it has to be the Awa Maru," said Yaphank scornfully.

The bulk of Berger, the quartermaster, edged up behind Schuman. "Yeah, it has to be the Awa Maru," he echoed.

Schuman saw several heads pop up out of the engine room hatch. Shit, they were only running with a skeleton crew, and he didn't want any slipups when he called for speed.

"Get those guys back, Berger," he ordered harshly. "There'll be plenty for them to look at later."

Berger slid hastily out of the cockpit and trotted rapidly along the deck, and whispered obscenities drifted back until the heads disappeared.

"She's turning away, Jay," warned Winberg suddenly.

Schuman could see it himself and nudged the Old Tart up to half-speed.

"She'll only do sixteen knots," said Yaphank. "You can pick her up any time you like."

Schuman scowled. He wished to Christ that Yaphank had stayed in the chart room as he'd asked. "I know what I'm doing, everything's under control," he replied churlishly.

"Jes', it's just like you said, Jay," whispered Winberg. "Fuck me, it's gonna work, it's really gonna work."

"We'll see," cautioned Schuman. "We've got to board her yet, then we'll find out if it's true about the gold."

"It's true all right," declared Yaphank confidently. "Those prisoners of war in Singapore didn't make any mistake."

"Hell yes, I'm with you, Carl," said Winberg excitedly. "They wouldn't send out a report like that unless they were sure." He turned abruptly to Schuman. "You think they'll put out a radio call when they see us?"

"No, we talked about that. I figure they'll want to keep radio silence as much as we do. If she has got the gold on board the last thing they'd want to do is draw attention to themselves. After all, this is only a PT boat. I'm sure they'll go along first until they see what we're all about."

"The gold'll be there," declared Yaphank firmly.

Schuman had no intention of buying into an argument, for he'd know soon enough now. They had an almost religious fervor in wanting to believe, in craving to be rich. Like him, like the rest of the crew. He could still see the gleam in their eyes when they'd made the decision to go with it. Ferras and Morton in the engine room. Coram on the radio. Martin, Tobaco, Berger, Donlett, Winberg, all with their tongues hanging like a dog anticipating a meal. Kipness, Halmstead sucked in with the same urgency.

He pushed the speed up again and the bow lifted, creaming the water, the sea rushing past with the familiar thrumming sound. The breeze still warm from the heat of the day fanned over his face. The knives prickling at his belly were fiercer than any he'd experienced going into action. At least they knew because of the safe passage guarantee that the Awa Maru wasn't armed. He moved the Old Tart up to top speed, and they braced themselves against the cant of the deck. In spite of her age the PT boat could show her heels on a calm sea, not like in a swell when she bucked and rolled like a rodeo steer.

"Get Martin and Donlett up on the forward machine gun," he shouted to Berger. "I'll circle her a couple of times, and they can throw some tracers across her bow. If they don't get the message, then we'll put a few rounds into the hull."

Berger nodded, turned quickly out of the cockpit, and groped his way carefully forward.

They showed no lights, bolting across the sea like a straining racehorse, overtaking her with ease until they were up close, her bulk towering above them with the nighttime shimmer of a Manhattan office building, giant green crosses painted on the side of the hull, white crosses higher up on the funnel. They could see the name Awa Maru clearly now, forward in large white letters for easy identification. Her captain must have felt bloody safe. The labored thump of her engines mingled with the powerful growl of the Old Tart. He swung parallel for the first sweep, and he could see dark shapes huddled against the railing. He went into it like a fighter pilot circling an enemy bomber for the kill, keeling the Old Tart over in a crazy banking turn, Donlett and Martin clinging to the machine gun for support. He signaled to Berger as he cut close across the freighter's bow, and immediately the machine gun burst into rattling song, sending a stream of white flashes arcing across the sea. He kept at it, a mosquito harrying an elephant, until by the time they were into the third circuit the Japanese captain had got the message, and the ship began to slow.

"She's slowing down, Jay," called Winberg elatedly.

"Yowee," hooted Yaphank with delight.

"You take her, Mike," Schuman ordered Winberg. "Bring her up alongside . . . near the bridge. Just keep pace until she comes to a stop." Then he moved across and positioned himself by the loud hailer. Yaphank gave a savage grin, and nudged him in the ribs. "I told you we could do it, man," he crowed with exhilaration. "It's all ours, man—it's all ours."

Schuman ignored him. Luck was running with them, because he knew it would have been a hell of a job in a rough sea, and that luck would have to stay with them once they were aboard. The dark shapes along the railing had vanished, and he could see no sign of life. He hoped to Christ the captain understood English.

"Heave to, Awa Maru," he commanded. "We're coming aboard."

There was no answer, and he repeated the order at minute intervals. They throttled back, holding position, riding the ship's swell as she gradually came to a halt. Then two human figures appeared at the railing directly above the green cross, stared down at them for a moment, then vanished.

"Fuck 'em, back off and throw a few cannon shells at the bastards," growled Yaphank. "Show 'em we mean business."

Schuman made a dismissive motion of his hand. It might come to that, but the ship was almost stopped, so they were scarcely being ignored. "Let's give them some time," he cautioned.

Almost on his words the men reappeared above, and a ladder came snaking down over the green cross. The Awa Maru was dead in the water now, her engines muted, and faintly from above came the sound of Japanese voices.

He turned with a grunt of satisfaction from the hailer, and the small boarding party had already joined him in the cockpit, tightly bunched with apprehension, but in the glow of the Awa Maru's lights he could see their faces set with determination. They wouldn't let him down; the chance of riches beyond their wildest dreams was pumping adrenalin through their veins. Reflections flickered from the muzzles of the submachine guns, and he could even see the strange tattoo on Donlett's hand where he gripped the gun. He picked up the .45 and grinned at them, conscious of the upsurge in his pulse. His eyes moved from face to face, Ferras, Donlett, Halmstead, Martin, the pick of the crew; they'd seen blood, and they weren't squeamish about spilling more if it had to be done.

"Okay guys, we've been over it a hundred times, but has anyone got any questions?" He knew it was unnecessary to ask, but the inquiry was more prompted by nerves. They shook their heads in unison, and he jerked his thumb toward the ladder. "Watch yourselves on the ladder. It's not going to be easy, and I don't want to be fishing anyone out of the water. Once we're on board, play it hard, make like we're in complete control, and if anyone steps out of line they'll stop a bullet. Right? Any Jap tries to challenge you, that's exactly what they get."

He glanced irritably at Yaphank's grunts of approval. Even standing still, Carl was like uncorked champagne, ready to fizz out of the bottle. "You don't want me along?" he offered halfheartedly.

"No, it's better this way," said Schuman firmly. "These guys know what they're doing. You stay with Mike, he's going to need a hand with the loading operation if everything works out." He glanced at his watch, then turned to the ensign. "Give us twenty minutes, Mike. I'll send Ferras back by then, so you'll know what's going on. If you haven't heard from any of us by then, back off and put a fish into her up close to the bows just so she'll go down slowly. That way it'll give us a chance to get off."

"For Chrissake, get the gold off before you do a crazy thing like that," interjected Yaphank in alarm.

"That's only in case something goes wrong," said Schuman tersely. He nodded to Winberg. "Right, Mike?"

The chubby-boy-next-door face was made abruptly solemn by responsibility. "Right, yeah I've got it, Jay." Tension gave a slightly falsetto edge to his voice.

Schuman took a deep breath, stepped to the edge of the deck, balanced himself, then reached for the ladder.

"Okay then, guys, let's go make ourselves millionaires."

Vaguely Humbert became aware the front door bell was ringing again. His head oscillated slowly from side to side, eyes glazed as if emerging from a hypnotic trance. Perhaps the girl had come back, fearful of having to report failure to Roman. Maybe he should answer it after all; at least it would detach his mind from the past. He rose unsteadily to his feet, and stumbled toward the door.

Chapter 7

Detective Sergeant Harry Markby didn't particularly like Chief Inspector Scott Roman. But after all he was a big fish in the Sydney Police heirarchy, so he tried to maintain a respectful expression on his face. They were two constrasting styles of policeman. Roman was tall, his bulk scarcely thickened from his football days but his shock of hair now iron gray. He issued orders from a small tight mouth which hardly moved as he spoke. He'd begun as a uniformed cop on the beat, pushing himself up through the ranks, and the effort showed in an authoritative face lined beyond his fifty-five years. But it made him aggressively conscious of his position, and he dressed accordingly. A passion for the racetrack seemed his only human weakness, and unconfirmed rumor had him as a large bettor.

Even the way each man sat was a contrast in personality, Roman stiffly austere in his chair, Markby relaxed with hands interlocked over his portly belly, one leg crossed lazily over the other, all complimented by a rumpled gray suit and untidy necktie. Forty, married, overweight, freckled open face with an easy grin that had enticed many a confession, a few strands of sandy hair failing to conceal near-baldness. Over a beer or around the office, everyone called him Harry. It was a facade. He forgot nothing, missed nothing. He loved to probe, put it all together piece by piece, then show it to the suspect with a sympathetic smile and invite surrender. It was more satisfying than trying to solve it with a gun or a fist. If he'd been a studying man, he could have made inspector by now, but he preferred to spend his spare time drinking with friends. Or bowling with his wife, Helen.

Roman ran his eyes over the last pages of the report, then closed the cover with an air of finality.

"I'm sure there's more Lieutenant Zarich'll want to tell you, Harry, but that's the outline of why he's coming to Australia. I'm going to take you off all other duties so you can work closely with him while he's here. This report from the New York police was passed on to me by the assistant commissioner, who evidently considers you're the best man for the job." He smiled without warmth, and Markby had the feeling it was an opinion Roman didn't share.

"Sounds interesting—sir," he said casually. "I'll look forward to working with him."

Roman held out the report to him. "You'll need to go over this in detail, Harry. I want you to be fully briefed by the time you meet Zarich." The deep eyes appraised him coldly. "We want to put our best foot forward, show the New York people we do our homework."

Markby nodded, uncrossed his legs, and took the report. "This Donlett who was murdered in the New York hospital. I take it his wife's name and address is in here?"

"Yes. She lives in Bankstown, but her name's Shepherd now. We've been in touch, but it's up to you to arrange a meeting between her and Lieutenant Zarich."

"Yeah, I'll do that first thing." He caught the sour line of Roman's mouth. "Sir," he added. He had a disdain for rank that he knew rankled the chief inspector.

"The New York police have asked us to be close-mouthed about Zarich's visit. They don't want any publicity, anything at all that could warn the people who hired the gun man in New York. The assistant commissioner knows, I know, and now you know, Harry. That's the end of the line."

"Anything more on the money paid to this"—he paused, and examined the report a moment—"that's right, this Liavone?"

Roman shrugged. He appeared disinterested now he'd passed the assignment to Markby.

"Well, we're still trying through the Reserve Bank people, but I think it's a lost cause. We know the source was here in Australia, but there's no proof it was Sydney. I don't think that's going to help Zarich."

"It'd be a good start if we knew who paid this hit

bloke the money. Maybe even solve a few problems of our own."

"I don't believe it's going to happen like that," said Roman tersely. There was a short period of silence, then Roman glanced meaningfully at his watch. Markby took the hint, thrust the report under his arm, and shuffled his feet preparatory to rising.

"Well, I'll take this Zarich under my wing. Show him around and give him all the help I can." He grinned good-naturedly. "Good PR with the Yanks, and all that sort of thing. When's he get into Sydney?"

"Tomorrow around eleven I understand. Pan Am from Los Angeles. Maxie Church'll give you all the fine details. He's been booked into the Menzies Hotel. Of course I expect you to be there to meet him."

"Yeah, sure, I'll be there. Me and the wife went to Los Angeles a coupla years ago. Had a ball. You know, Disneyland and all that stuff. We'd like to go back one day."

"Yes, yes of course," murmured Roman. "I'd like that myself."

Markby had trouble imagining Roman enjoying himself at Disneyland. But the chief inspector wasn't really listening to Harry's words, his eyes on a distant target beyond the sergeant's shoulder.

"There is one other point, Harry," said Roman delicately.

"About Zarich?"

"Yes." He had a way of peering up from under his brows as if from ambush. "I'd like you to keep me completely informed about Zarich."

"Well, naturally I'll be putting in my report, sir."

"Of course. But you don't have to tell Zarich about that."

Markby looked puzzled. "I don't think I quite understand—sir?"

"We don't want these Americans coming here and trying to teach us our jobs, do we, Harry. Zarich's been promised cooperation, and of course he'll get it. But, ah, it's important I know what's going on. I mean he may think it's in his best interests to keep certain things from us, and I want to make sure that doesn't happen. After all, if the money came from here, it's our case also."

Markby's mouth wrinkled with distaste. He got the idea Roman expected him to act like some sort of pimp, and that wasn't his style.

"I couldn't imagine that happening, sir," he said in mild protest. "I'm sure they want to get the killers as much as we do."

Roman's lips compressed to a thin line of disapproval. He was quick to react to what he saw as the slightest challenge to his authority. "That may be so," he said sharply. "But keeping an eye on Zarich is part of the assignment, Harry. We don't know how these New York people work. There may be things we don't know, and we need to know." His mouth altered to a broad smile, as if to include Markby in a brotherly conspiracy.

"That shouldn't be too difficult for someone with your experience."

Markby nodded hesitantly, wondering if that was the assistant commissioner's instruction, or how Roman interpreted the brief.

"Then good luck, Harry," said Roman heavily. "I know you'll handle it the way I want."

Markby lumbered to his feet with the impression of an overloaded truck getting under way, his protruding belly more obvious.

"I'll be in touch then—sir," he said woodenly.

"I'll be waiting," murmured Roman.

He remained at the desk in the same rigid posture, staring at the door long after it had closed on Markby's bulk. The sergeant might have some dislike for playing watchdog on the American, but he was sure he was too good a policeman to disobey. Matter of fact that was the problem, he *was* too good a policeman. If the order to use Markby hadn't come down from the assistant commissioner, he would have felt safer with some easier controlled dullard he could have selected himself. Sade and Humbert weren't going to appreciate the involvement of someone as sharp as Markby. It was a worry, but if things got sticky he might be able to manufacture some excuse for pulling Markby off the case. He pondered for a time on

whether he should call Sade, then decided against it. It
would only draw pressure from Humbert, and he didn't
want that. He sighed absently, shuffled the papers about
on his desk, then placed his head despondently in his
hands. If he could just hang on until retirement, then
maybe Humbert would regard him as no longer useful,
and let him off the hook. Now he could scarcely remember back to when he was his own man. Did he ever
imagine he would finish his career as a high-paid puppet?
It had been easy at first, then all that extra money had got
to him like a drug habit impossible to kick, and he knew
Humbert would squeeze him until he was dry.

It was the longest flight in Zarich's experience. There
had been the occasional trips to the West Coast, an extra-
dition to Central America, the one or two vacations to
Europe with Rhonda, but they were like local stops compared to the haul to Australia. He flew American to L.A.,
then Pan Am direct, so at least there were no boring
stopovers. He could only wonder that tourists would vol-
untarily submit themselves to the long monotony. He
watched with envy those capable of drifting into time-
consuming sleep. He ate, dozed, browsed without concentration through magazines, walked the aisles, stared blankly
at the movies or the endless ocean below, listened to
accents he found difficult to understand, and thought of
the Old Tart, of Ella, Liavone, the strangled Donlett, the
drowned Musoveld. It all seemed a baffling maze, with no
exit in sight.

There was a hostess who seemed overattentive, with
eager smiles, but that was for another time. Besides,
Rhonda's bitter farewell was still festering in his mind.

He felt a sense of relief when the thrum of the jets
faded to an eerie hiss, and he saw the sprawl of Sydney
through an early morning haze, the same geometric tangle
as any other big city.

Someone was pulling strings because he was fast
through customs, then directed to a small side room.
There was a large man waiting for him, overweight, balding, about forty, bulbous stomach, and a suit that looked
like he'd slept in it. He warmed to anyone who could look

so less like a policeman. The man rose from the solitary chair, an engaging smile on his face, and extended his hand.

"Gooday. Lieutenant Zarich, I'm Sergeant Harry Markby of the Sydney Police." The voice was as large as the man, delivered in a broad nasal accent. Zarich put his hand into something resembling a bear trap.

"Glad to meet you, Sergeant," he said wearily.

"Call me Harry. Everyone else does."

"Okay, if you call me Ed." It was a good start.

"Beauty, okay Ed," replied Markby warmly.

Zarich wasn't sure if Markby was just a welcoming deputy or a working partner. Beuso had told him the Sydney police intended to assign a man to work with him.

"I'm the lucky bloke assigned to work with you while you're in Australia," replied the grinning Markby to the unasked query.

"That sounds great, Harry."

"How was the trip? Bloody drag I'll bet."

"You might say that."

"You cop any jet lag?"

"I didn't know what it was until now."

"Yeah, that's the bloody problem with us being so far away. I took my wife to Los Angeles for a holiday a few years ago, and I know we were zapped out for the first day. But then you had to come across from New York as well."

"That's right." He shrugged wearily. "I feel like I've been flying forever."

Markby gestured to the door. "You're going to need a few hours' sleep before we settle down to any serious talking. We can go out this way. I've got a car waiting."

"I'm booked somewhere?"

"Don't worry, Ed. Everything's taken care of."

Zarich let himself be led without questions, enticed by the thought of a soft hotel bed. It was difficult to make a judgment about Markby at first meeting, but there was a shrewdness about his eyes that belied the affable easygoing manner. He was sure Beuso would have pushed for a good man.

They went quickly to the car, and were soon out into

the main stream of traffic heading toward the city. It was April, springtime in New York, but the heat from the sun told him he'd been wise to pack lightly. He was forced to squint in the bright light, and he leaned back into the shade of the visor, nodding and offering short polite replies to Markby's chatter about Sydney. He took little interest in the surroundings for now.

"I'm not going to get into any details about your case right now, Ed," said Markby. "But from your New York report it seems you've got yourself a real mind-bender."

Zarich responded with a tilt of his head. "You read the report okay?"

"Yeah. Chief Inspector Roman, who assigned me to you took me through it, then I read up on the details. I guess there might be other things you can tell me, but I get the picture." He grinned wryly across the seat. "Or rather I get what you know, and what you don't know."

"The 'don't know' part heads the list, Harry, believe me." He shrugged, fighting drowsiness. "I just want to be sure no one else gets killed before I know more about the Old Tart."

Markby drove silently for a moment, the sound of his tongue reflectively clicking over.

"That's a bloody strange one," he murmured finally. "Weird. Jes', forty years is a long time to hide something in the closet. Then for some creepy reason it all explodes, and you've got two murders on your hands, and no answers."

"Hopefully we're not completely in the dark. We know about the Old Tart. We know Donlett was on her in '45, and that she operated out of Darwin. Maybe we can build on that."

"Well, I've got Donlett's onetime wife all lined up to talk to you."

"That's great, Harry. Great. Half the reason I'm here. I hope to Christ she can tell us something." He shook his head doubtfully. "Trouble is it all happened such a long time ago." He grinned with fatigue. "I don't have to tell you how hard it is getting people to even remember what happened yesterday."

Markby's understanding smile was an expression of

membership in a worldwide brotherhood. "Yeah, how right you are, Ed. Well, let's see what she's got to say. We might get lucky." The streets narrowed, and their pace slowed as they threaded through a traffic bottleneck. "Listen, Ed, let's forget it for now anyhow. We've got you booked into the Menzies Hotel in the city. You get yourself a few hours' sleep, then when you're freshened up we'll talk about it some more. Okay?"

Zarich nodded gratefully. "That sounds like the best idea yet."

Zarich didn't wake until four-thirty in the afternoon. The red message light was showing on the phone, and he dialed the number.

"I have to call a Mr. Markby when you wake up, Mr. Zarich," said the girl. "If you can give me a time he'll meet you at the bar down in the lobby."

Zarich scratched at his hair, and ogled his watch. He should have requested a wake-up call, for he had no intention of sleeping so long. But at least he felt like a human being again.

"Tell him five o'clock," he muttered.

"Thank you, sir. I'll send up the suit you asked to be pressed."

He thanked her, and hung up. It was a nice room within the tasteful stereotype of most classy hotels. He couldn't recall what floor he was on, but he was high, for when he went to the window, he could see across the magnificent harbor, the bridge flooded with traffic, the famous opera house. But apart from that, looking down had the sameness of every modern city, the clogged traffic, scurrying people, the boxed glass buildings jutting into the sky. His suit arrived, then he showered, shaved, dressed, and took the Old Tart file from his suitcase. It sounded as if Markby had a good grasp of what it was all about, but if they were going to operate together, he figured it best if the Australian was filled in on every detail. Especially on the photograph of the Old Tart crew. He liked what he'd seen of Markby, no bullshit, straight down the line, and he had a hunch they'd work well together.

He checked his appearance in the mirror. The boys at headquarters would have laughed, Beuso would have been proud of him, yet maybe Rhonda was right—he did look a little like a stockbroker.

He went through the hushed bustle of people coming and going in the lobby, and the sound of forgettable canned music, to where Markby was waiting for him in the dusky yellow light of the bar, a half-empty glass of beer before him on the table. Even as he sat down, Markby's hand was in the air, signaling for the waiter.

"Jes', you look ten years younger, Ed," he said cheerfully.

Zarich grinned, and scrubbed ruefully at his chin. "Tell you what, Harry, I feel ten years younger. Hell, I didn't figure on sleeping so long."

"Forget it. I was going to let you go until four, then have 'em wake you."

The girl arrived with two beers. She was dark and pretty, with a short skirt that gave Zarich a chance to appreciate her long legs.

"There's plenty around if that's what you want," offered Markby helpfully. "Or at least so they tell me. I got a wife that leaves me no time for side interests."

Zarich shrugged, and tapped the file. "First things first, Harry."

"Suits me," grunted Markby. He picked up the half-empty glass, drained it without pausing for breath, then put it down with a satisfied sigh, and wiped at his mouth. "Fosters, Ed," he laughed. "Best bloody beer in the world." He was half into his next glass before Zarich began drinking. "You married, Ed?"

"I was—once. Being a cop doesn't make it easy."

"Yeah, I know what you mean. Although my wife's used to it by now." He winked. "Trained y'know. It took fifteen years, but we finally made it. Sometimes I come crawling in at some crazy early morning hour, and she'll say, 'Harry, you've got to be out of your mind,' and I think maybe she could be right. Then comes the next day, and some crim wants to match it with you, and you think, I've gotta win this one, I've just gotta." His face creased in an apologetic grimace. "It gets in your blood I guess. At least that's what I keep telling myself. I never wanted to be anything else but a cop, my old man was one, and I suppose I never thought about nothing else."

Zarich gave an understanding nod. Now he knew it was the intuitive feeling for a soul mate that had warmed him toward Markby. They were on the same wavelength. "I know the feeling, Harry, believe me I know. 'Specially if it's a big fish."

"Yeah, but they're the ones who get off the hook, Ed. Who can hire the high-priced lawyers, know the right people. Anyone can nail a mug bank robber or a twenty-cent shoplifter. But putting the arm on a million-dollar shark, that's the joy. Seeing them swallow the hook whole." He held his beer dolefully to the light. "Not that it happens often."

"Well, I'll drink to it anyhow, Harry," said Zarich, raising his own glass.

"Right," agreed Markby. His beer disappeared again, then he was signaling the waiter once more. "Come on Ed, I can see I've got to educate you about drinking Australian beer," he said encouragingly.

Zarich tried to match Harry's drinking capacity, but then two more beers arrived, and he knew it was a lost cause. He pushed the glass determinedly to one side, and opened the file.

"From the size of the fee paid to Liavone in New York, maybe we've got a big fish here, Harry."

"Someone was prepared to spend a lot of dough to see those guys dead."

"Have your people got anywhere in tracing the source of the cash?"

"Don't hold your breath, Ed," Markby warned. "But I think that's a dead duck. They're working on it, but—" He shrugged.

"Okay, let's see what we've got," murmured Zarich.

He took Harry slowly through the file, clarifying points, elaborating details, until he was sure the Australian knew as much about the Old Tart as he did. Then he showed him the 1944 photograph of the crew from Musoveld's album. Markby studied it in silent concentration, even his beer forgotten.

"It gives me a strange feeling, you know, Ed. All these laughing young blokes dead like that." He grimaced. "Or maybe not. From what you've been saying, I suppose it's possible some of 'em might still be alive. I don't know how, but it's possible."

"Sometimes I think yes, other times no," admitted Zarich. "But this is what I want to show to Donlett's wife. See if I get any reaction. When's it set for me to see her, Harry?"

"Well, actually I had it arranged for tonight, Ed," answered Markby uncertainly. "That's why I was getting concerned about waking you. Maybe I should have left it until later, but she's pretty nervous about meeting you, and I don't think it'd be a good idea to put her off." He put his hands about the glass, and swirled the beer. "I've got a feeling it wouldn't take much to change her mind."

"What's she nervous about? I mean she thought Donlett died forty years ago."

"Yeah I know. But it's been a hell of a shock to her. Just talking to her over the phone she's a little secretive about the marriage. She was only a kid of seventeen at the time, and it might be a long time ago but I gather she doesn't like talking about it in front of her present husband." He pouted with his mouth. "Just one of those things, I guess."

"You're telling me she doesn't want us to go to her home, Harry?"

"That's the way she wants it."

"Well then where?"

"She's got a part-time job, coupla nights a week, behind the counter in the cafeteria at the back of the opera house." He grinned. "You've heard of our white winged wonder building?"

"Sure. I've seen photographs of it, and I can see part of it from my hotel window."

"Well, that's where she'll be. This is her last night on until next week, so that's another reason I don't want to put her off. She'll be through about nine o'clock, and she wants us to meet her there."

Zarich was silently pensive. He preferred a home, or the official feel of a police office, but he had to go with what she wanted. He drummed his fingers on the table as Harry's next beer vanished into his gullet. The sergeant's hand went once more automatically into the air, while he glanced meaningfully at Zarich's untouched glass.

"I'm getting ahead of you, Ed," he grinned.

Zarich smiled away the challenge. He tried to match Harry in the Foster's department, and he'd be too drunk to interview anyone.

"I take it she didn't know she was being watched?" he asked.

Markby stared at him blankly. "Watched? I don't get you?"

Zarich shuffled about uneasily on the chair. "Didn't my superior in New York, Captain Beuso, make a request to your people that she be placed under protection?"

"First I've heard of it, Ed. Roman said nothing about it to me."

Zarich scowled down at his interlocked hands. Fuck Beuso. It was like the captain to ignore his recommendation as a way of showing his authority.

"Maybe Beuso didn't think it was necessary, Ed," said Markby.

"For Chrissake, two people were murdered in New York, Harry. Donlett I'm almost sure because of what he might remember. Musoveld because he could have identified Donlett. Who knows how these fuckers' minds work. Whatever it is they're trying to cover up about the Old Tart, they'll kill anyone, Harry. That could include Donlett's wife."

"Don't tie yourself in knots about it, Ed. No one in this country knows about her. Only myself, Roman, and the assistant commissioner even know you're in the country."

Zarich pawed irritably at his mouth. "I hope you're right, Harry. Someone makes a connection between her and my being here, and she's in big trouble." He paused for a moment, hands nervously fiddling with the file. "I'd like to go and see her now."

"She's a very skittish lady, Ed. She won't like it, not if the arrangement's for nine o'clock."

"I figure we should take that risk. I just don't want

anything to happen to her, Harry. I've come a long way to see her. Would she be there now?"

Markby frowned, and consulted his watch. It was obvious he thought Zarich was getting into an unnecessary panic. "Five-thirty. Yeah, I think she goes on at five. I can't see why she could be in any danger if everyone thinks you're still in New York."

"But I'm here now, Harry," declared Zarich pointedly.

Markby hesitated, then suddenly grinned, drained his final beer, thumped the empty glass down on the table, and slapped Zarich on the shoulder. "Then if it'll make you feel easier we'll go, mate," he said agreeably. "If she doesn't like it, then we might have to use a little bluff." He winked knowingly. "Tell her we might have to take her to headquarters for her own protection. That should make her cooperative."

They hit peak traffic, and it was like being back in New York, the same torturous crawl, the tooting, drivers with identical expressions of frustration, the carbon monoxide haze. They turned slowly into a street with a park alongside, which Markby informed him was the Botanic Gardens, and from there it was an easier run down to the harbor. Markby parked the car, and they walked toward the Opera House. Apart from anything else it was dramatically sited on a spit of land jutting out into the harbor, surrounding the building on three side by the sea. The inlet to the left was a hive of bustling ferries, some skittling over the surface on raised legs like huge beetles. Across was the giant single span grid of the bridge connecting the north and south shores. And behind the usual sterile blocks of steel and glass formed the city skyline. Markby offered a running commentary, interspersed with dry humor, but there was no hiding the fact he took pride in the beautiful city.

They strode rapidly down the length of the Opera House, along the walkway at the water's edge. The building was larger than the impression left by photographs he'd seen, but it was a spectacular piece of architecture, the graceful curves of the white interlocking roofs like billowing sails.

"Looks like a good puff of wind would send her sailing out into the harbor, doesn't it," Markby said.

"It's more spectacular than I imagined."

"We ran a lottery to pay for it," declared the sergeant laconically. "If you Yanks ran a lottery to pay for your bloody missiles you'd have defense on the cheap."

"I'll make a recommendation to the President," grinned Zarich.

The attempted humor did little to dampen his underlying anxiety. Maybe he was merely creating monsters in his mind, but Christ, Beuso should have acted on security for Donlett's wife. Why take unnecessary risks?

At the rear of the Opera House was a small cafeteria of plastic and fast food that seemed out of character to its parent building. They went rapidly through the door, Markby leading. There was just a sprinkling of patrons, drinking coffee, munching food, and taking in the view across the water through the window. It was six-fifteen. He was looking behind the counter for a middle-aged woman, but there was only two young girls. Markby draped his arms on the counter, and offered his most engaging smile.

"G'day girls. I'm looking for Emma Shepherd. She anywhere around?"

One of the girls scowled. "If she is we haven't seen her."

"She's not working tonight?"

"She's supposed to be." She glanced about with a sour grin. "It's easy right now, but there's something on at the Opera House tonight, and we could be rushed off our feet later."

"Well, thanks anyway. If she comes in, tell her Mr. Markby was asking for her."

"Okay."

He crossed back to Zarich standing midway to the door, thrust his hands into his pockets, and stared moodily out to the harbor. Zarich could see some of his own anxiety had rubbed off on the Australian.

"Well, I guess we wait," Markby grunted. He glanced to one of the vacant tables. "You feel like some coffee?"

"Waiting makes me nervous, Harry."

Markby scratched thoughtfully at his chin. "Jes', you've got me as edgy as you, Ed. Maybe she just missed her train. She has to come in from Bankstown, and that's out of the city." His gaze went to the public phone at the end of the counter. "Perhaps I should call her home number." He took a small notebook from his pocket, and flipped through the pages. "I've got her number." He peered uncertainly at Zarich. "Just to check up, eh Ed."

"I think it might be worthwhile," said Zarich.

He wandered out through the door while Harry made the call, and stood at the water's edge, trying to still the qualms in his stomach. It was hot, and he undid his tie and stuffed it in his pocket. The dazzling reflections of the sun off the water hurt his eyes, and he turned away. There was a couple standing off to the left where the walkway ran down the other side of the building, and there was something in the way they held themselves that caught his attention, the woman's hand to her mouth in an attitude of distress. A young boy came running from around the corner, calling out, "Hey Nicky, come and have a look at this," as he passed. Zarich wandered curiously over to the couple, and glanced down the walkway. At the far end he could see two uniformed policemen and another man crouched at the water's edge, all reaching down as if trying to grasp something. He could feel a quiver traveling up his spine he recalled when he'd found Musoveld in the bath. He walked slowly down the walkway until he could see the gray hair from the woman's head trailing like seaweed in the water. One of the policemen saw him, and got on his feet. "Would you please keep clear, sir," he asked politely. "This isn't exactly a pleasant sight."

Zarich knew it was Emma Shepherd. He knew. He knew. Fuck Beuso, the sonofabitch. Maybe he had to take the lumps for Liavone's killing, but this fuck-up he could lay right at Beuso's feet. But worst of all, Harry was wrong in his claim. There had been a leak from some sonofabitch, either here or in New York, because the body floating in the water was all the evidence he needed that the bastards knew he was in Australia, knew why he was here. But they'd also tipped their hand. If he had any doubts at all that the answers about the Old Tart lay somewhere in

Australia, then the body they were trying to drag out of the harbor removed them for all time. He backed away and propped himself against the wall. He heard the sound of hurrying feet, and turned at the sight of Harry coming toward him, concern on his face. He guessed Harry wouldn't exactly relish the thought of taking this news back to his chief inspector.

It took all of Roman's self-control to keep the anger out of his face until Markby had finished his report about Emma Shepherd's death, and as soon as he was gone, he called Sade.

"You bastard, Sade," he declared hoarsely. "I told you I didn't want to be involved in any killing."

Sade was unperturbed. The silkiness of his voice was an indication he believed he had the chief inspector under control. "Inspector, I don't think these sorts of phone calls are wise. We should keep them to a minimum."

"The idea was to keep her and Zarich under surveillance. There was never any suggestion of killing. By Christ, Sade, I don't want . . ."

"I'm not interested in what you want, Inspector," Sade cut across him. "All we expect of you is to do exactly what you're told. After all, you're well rewarded for your services."

Roman let the conversation hang there for a moment, breathing heavily. "It's just not very smart," he managed finally. "In fact it's taking crazy risks. For everyone."

"Nonsense," said Sade flatly. "It must be as obvious to you as everyone else that the woman committed suicide. I see by the newspapers you've already issued a statement saying there are no suspicious circumstances." He clucked his tongue approvingly. "That's good, Inspector . . . very good indeed. I don't see why you're so uptight."

"The coroner may not accept a suicide theory."

"Then it's up to you to see that he does."

"What's it all about anyway . . . this Old Tart business?"

"The less you know the better, Inspector."

"If I'm not kept clean I'm no use to anyone."

"We understand that . . . we really do." Sade paused. "There's another problem giving us some concern."

"What's that?"

"Sergeant Harry Markby."

Roman pressed his teeth tightly into his bottom lip. He knew what was coming. "What about him?" he grated.

"He's a very smart policeman. I know something of his record."

"What of it?"

Sade cleared his throat with a threatening rasp. "Not exactly the sort of man we had in mind to work with Zarich."

"The decision was made over my head," declared Roman sullenly. "I had no alternative but to go along. Don't worry, he'll do what he's told."

"Maybe," answered Sade, unconvinced. "Let's say I have strong reservations about the sergeant. You may have to make other arrangements."

"What's that supposed to mean?"

"Not over the phone. We'll discuss it tonight. Meanwhile I suggest you try finding reasons to take Markby off the case. Think about it."

He'd already been thinking about it. "I'll have to convince the assistant commissioner."

"Well, you have influence. Give it serious thought, for your own sake." The inference was given weight by a short period of menacing silence. "I'll see you tonight, Inspector," he murmured, then hung up.

Roman slowly replaced the receiver, and stared forlornly at the phone. How in Christ had he arrived at this point in his life? A man works hard, raises a family, gains respect, then one day gets a tip-off about a horse race at the Randwick track being a fix. Temptation wins, he doesn't do anything but play the fix himself, and wins a packet. Maybe the set-up was just for him, because it's Humbert's horse, and soon there's some not too subtle requests for small favors, or the assistant commissioner is going to know about his winning big on a fixed race. So he's sucked in, the small favors turn into an avalanche where he's covering for heroin organizations. The money keeps coming the same way because it can't be traced, but he's in so deep there's no way he can get out. It's kept him awake nights, but his wife has enjoyed the life-style, yet he knows it will destroy her if the roof ever falls in on him.

It was the following afternoon before Zarich and Markby were able to settle down and talk to Emma Shepherd's husband. Up until then he'd been mostly incoherent, so they tried to give him time to cope with the sudden shock.

John Shepherd appeared to have been made in the same mold as the dreary furnishings of his small Bankstown house. Gray, weatherbeaten, worn by overuse. Maybe seventy, he was lean and lined, and bending with the wind all his life had left him with a permanent stoop. The clothes were as faded as the man. There was an ancient pipe almost constantly in his mouth, maybe in solace for a life that had never happened. He had hands like Zarich's uncle on the Kansas farm, large with knobbly callouses and permanently stained by the earth. When he rubbed them together the hardened skin made a sound like sandpaper.

"I spoke to the other police," he muttered softly." I don't know what else I can tell you blokes except what I told them. Emma didn't commit no suicide. That's a lotta bullshit. I know Emma better than that." He peered at them from under scraggly white brows. "I don't care what they say, she had no reason." He shook his head. "No reason at all." He stared blankly at them, then took a handkerchief from his pocket and loudly blew his nose. "We didn't have much, but we were getting by. She didn't have to do that job at the Opera House." He took the pipe from his mouth, and absently tapped it on the arm of the chair. "I suppose it was an interest for her, but she didn't have to do it. But she didn't commit no suicide. Maybe she accidentally fell into the water and hit her head, or something like that, but like I told the other police, she was a fair swimmer. But suicide"—he shook his head firmly—"forget it."

He fell silent, and Zarich took the opening.

"Can you tell us anything about your wife's first husband, Mr. Shepherd?" he asked.

The white brows arched in surprise. "Glory be, Em-

ma's first husband? You're goin' back forty years, Mr. . . .
Mr. . . . ?"

"Zarich," the lieutenant prompted him.

"Yeah, sorry, forty years, Mr. Zarich. Or longer. You
mean the Yank sailor, of course. Jes', Emma was only a
kid then."

"Something's come up, and we'd like to find out
about him," said Markby.

Shepherd puffed thoughtfully at his pipe. "It's such a
long time ago, an' of course I didn't know Emma then. I
know he was killed in the war." He looked to Zarich and
Markby in turn. "You knew that?"

"Yes, we know that."

"Emma never liked to talk about it. Maybe in the
beginning she thought I'd be jealous." He shrugged. "Then
it just went on in the same way, and I guessed if that was
the way she wanted it, then it was okay by me. I never
pried. And of course she had a kid when we married."

"She and Donlett had a child?" asked Zarich in surprise.

"Yeah, a daughter. I raised her as my own of course."
The frizzling sound of burning tobacco came from the
pipe, and smoke seeped from his mouth. "We never had
any of our own. Pity, 'specially now." He stared dolefully
at his hands. "That's the way of it, I s'pose. But crikey, the
girl was a real spitfire. I couldn't handle her, and neither
could her mother. Soon as she was old enough she cleared
out. We never saw her again."

"Any idea where she is now?"

"Dead. In a car accident about five years ago. We
didn't even know about it for a long time." He suddenly
thumped one of his large hands down on the arm of the
chair. "Listen, I'm not thinkin' too well." He unwound
from the chair, and creaked to his feet. "I think I can help
you blokes. Just wait here a moment." He motioned to
them with his pipe, then shuffled across the room and
disappeared through the door.

"It doesn't look like we're going to get much here,
Ed," observed Markby pessimistically. He was still ran-
kling over Roman's scathing comments on the death of
Emma Shepherd. How the hell was he supposed to know
the woman might need protection? He wasn't clairvoyant.

Yet he was surprised Roman had so quickly accepted the suicide theory.

"It doesn't look too hopeful," admitted Zarich. "Let's wait and see what he comes back with."

They heard the sound of drawers opening and closing in the other room, then Shepherd reappeared with a cardboard box under his arm. He placed it down on the small table beside Zarich, dropped himself back in the chair, and gestured to the box.

"Emma kept her special things in that. Letters, stuff like that. I knew it was in the bottom drawer, but I never looked. She would've got upset, and she had a thing about being private." He motioned again with the pipe. "Go on, you can open it now. Maybe there's something about her and Donlett inside."

Zarich opened the box. It was stuffed with letters and photographs. There was what appeared to be a recent picture on the top of an attractive young girl with fair, almost white blond hair, and he picked it up and held it out to Shepherd, while Markby looked over the letters.

"Any idea who this is, Mr. Shepherd?"

"Now that she told me about her, because she was so terribly excited. It's her granddaughter."

"Her granddaughter?"

"That's right. She traced Emma and got in touch with her just a short time ago. Emma was rapt. She'd never even known her daughter had a baby. They'd been spending a lotta time together. I even saw Emma take that box with her at times. Maybe she was telling the girl about her Yank grandfather."

"You know the girl's name, and where she lives?"

"Well, her name's Cassie Rehfield. I can't tell you where she lives, but she works at some club up at the Cross." His brow crinkled into a myriad lines with the effort of concentration. "Let's see, the purple something or other."

"The Purple Pussycat," interjected Markby.

"Yeah, yeah, that's it. The Purple Pussycat."

Zarich looked questioningly at Markby. "The Cross?"

"Kings Cross. It's just across from the city." He grinned. "Our pleasure center. Whatever you want, the

Cross has got it." He looked back at Shepherd. "Have you been in touch to tell her about your wife's death?"

"No, but I mean I intend to," he said apologetically. "Before the funeral. I just haven't been thinking straight, and I don't know where she lives anyway. I guess I could go to this—club?"

"Leave it with us, Mr. Shepherd," said Zarich. "It might be better if we tell her."

"Well, if you like. I suppose I don't really know her," muttered Shepherd uncertainly.

Markby leaned forward and showed one of the letters to Zarich. "Here's an interesting one, Ed," he murmured quietly. "Postmarked Darwin, 1944. And there's more here. Probably letters Donlett wrote to her."

Zarich took the envelope, and stared at it curiously. "We'll have to take these away with us, Harry, and go over them. There could be real gold inside."

Markby frowned, and ruffled his fingers through the contents of the box. "Okay, but let's do it in your hotel room instead of headquarters. After Emma Shepherd I've got a real thing about security. I've got a suspicion someone's looking over our shoulder."

Zarich nodded quick agreement. "Okay, I'll go with that. There has to be a leak somewhere, so let's play it safe." He studied the photograph a moment longer before putting it back in the box. If the shot was accurate, she was a very beautiful girl.

"Pretty, ain't she," remarked Shepherd.

"Yes, she is."

"Don't be fooled. From the little I heard I'd guess she's a lot like her mother. A real wild one. I think Emma was workin' on tryin' to straighten her out."

"Well, I think we should talk to her," said Zarich. He tapped on the box. "Have you showed these to anyone else, Mr. Shepherd?"

"No, you're the first. I guess your questions about Donlett made me think of it."

"Do you mind if we borrow it?" He smiled reassuringly. "They'll be well looked after, and we'll see you get them back."

Shepherd gestured acquiescence with his pipe. "Sure,

help yourself. I guess they're not that important anymore now Emma's gone." He hesitated, and looked quizzically at Zarich. "You're a Yank, too, aren't you Mr. Zarich?"

"That's right."

"You aren't a relative of this Donlett, or anything like that?"

Zarich stood back with a smile. "No, nothing like that."

Markby was closing the box, then tucking it under his arm preparatory to leaving.

"Well, best of luck whatever you're lookin' for," concluded Shepherd. He stared hard at Zarich. "But Emma didn't commit no suicide, Mr. Zarich."

"I don't believe it either, Mr. Shepherd," Zarich consoled him.

They were halfway back to the city before Markby voiced both their thoughts. "You think these bastards know about the granddaughter, Ed?"

"They knew about me, and Emma Shepherd," glowered Zarich. "But it's hard to see how they'd know about this granddaughter. Not if Shepherd hasn't shown this box to anyone else."

"It wouldn't make any sense to kill her anyway. What could she possibly know?"

"These people obviously don't think like that, Harry. They don't seem to give a fuck who they kill, just whatever they figure it takes to keep the secret of the Old Tart. But don't ask me what the hell it is."

"Well, we can't get to her until the club opens tonight anyway," said Markby.

They lapsed into silence again, each not wanting to contemplate another killing.

"I guess it's always possible Emma Shepherd did just fall in the water," ventured the sergeant.

Zarich responded with a sour laugh. "You believe that, Harry? You really believe that? It's the New York pattern all over again. Anyone with the slightest connection to Bart Donlett or the Old Tart is like having a death wish."

"Yeah, yeah, I know you're right. It's the leak that

bothers me. Someone knew you wanted to talk to Emma Shepherd and got to her first."

"I hope to Christ it doesn't work that way with the girl," declared Zarich fervently.

He didn't want to think about it. He'd batted a losing score in New York, and he wasn't doing much better here.

Chapter 8

The paper was yellowed, the ink faded, but the slightly school boyish writing was still quite legible.

"My darling Emma," Zarich read out. "I shouldn't be telling you but the skipper of the Old Tart has this screwball idea, and all the crew have decided to go along with him. It's crazy, but that includes me, sugar. It has to do with the Japs, but they're our enemies after all. Babe if it works out we'll be rich for the rest of our lives. But for Chrissake keep your mouth shut. Don't even mention this letter to your parents. I can't tell you any more, but I just know it's going to work. You can start thinking about your first fur coat, babe. I miss you since you left Darwin and went back to your folks in Sydney. I know it was no joy for you living here while I was out on patrol. Maybe we can figure out something when I get back. Keep it warm for me. Your loving husband, Bart."

Zarich ran his eyes through it again, then leaned back in the chair and dropped it on the table. The top was a jumble of opened letters, beer cans, and the remains of several fried chickens. Markby had a penchant for cigars, and the result hung like a smog haze in the hotel room. They both had their coats off and ties loosened, while Markby had removed his shoes with the claim it helped him concentrate.

"It's dated the fifteenth of March, 1944," added Zarich. "By comparison with the others that makes it the last letter he wrote to her."

Markby picked it up and gave it a fast scrutiny. "Jes', and it's paydirt, Ed. The others are just love letters. My God, Emma did know something."

"Maybe," said Zarich. He stood to his feet, took one of the cans, and wandered slowly to the window. Dusk was settling, and the city was donning its nighttime glitter. "I agree it is paydirt Harry, a real breakthrough. Confirmation of every hunch I've had about the Old Tart. Something happened on that PT boat forty years ago, something so significant, maybe even horrendous, that three people have been murdered to keep it secret." He scowled, took a swig from the can, then retrieved the letter from Markby. "The skipper has a screwball idea . . . it has to do with the Japs . . . we'll be rich for the rest of our lives . . ." he read again. He shook his head. "We're like Emma, Harry. We know something, yet we know nothing. Okay, Emma kept silent for forty years, yet what did she really know. Her husband wrote some crazy letter that probably made no sense to her, then he's reported missing in action. So she forgets about it. Whatever way Donlett had it figured to be rich, there was no way she was ever going to know what it was. And maybe saying something might have got her into trouble, for all she knew." He gave an irritated shrug, and dropped the letter back on the table. "Okay, I know more now than at any time since I first saw Donlett's body, but it doesn't seem to put me any closer. I'm not sure where the hell we go from here."

"Maybe the Old Tart wasn't sunk, Ed. Perhaps the crew are living like millionaires somewhere in the world, and they got the word about Donlett maybe recovering his memory in the hospital." He rapped his knuckles down on the letter. "I mean you get the feeling whatever they were up to on the Old Tart wasn't exactly official."

Zarich gave a morose shrug. The scent was lying around for him everywhere, but he didn't know which direction to run. "Anything's bloody possible. Harry. Anything." He bent over the table, sifting through the letters and photographs. "Christ, if only I'd taken Liavone alive. It might have given me a connection to someone here in Australia." He peered at a fading photograph of an Ameri-

can sailor and a young girl. He recognized Donlett, and
the young girl must be Emma. "Was there anything else
here important, Harry?"

"No, only that last letter means something."

"She must have stayed in Darwin for a time, according to that letter anyway. Maybe I should go up there,
Harry."

Markby scratched dubiously at his chin. "It's a long
time ago, Ed."

"There could be something up there, maybe records
that have been filed away and forgotten about the movements of the Old Tart."

Doubt remained in Markby's face. "Well, I could put
you in touch with a good friend up there. He'd help any
way he could. But perhaps a phone call is all you need to
get inquiries started."

Zarich shook his head firmly. The idea appealed to
him. "No, I always find it's better to be on the spot
yourself. It might be worth it. What's to lose?"

There was a thoughtful silence. Zarich prowled the
room, sipping at the can. He knew the deeper he was
getting into this, the more obsessed he was becoming to
find answers. There was someone in Australia crossing off
people as if they didn't matter, and he was going to nail
the bastard. He thought back to the photograph of the Old
Tart crew, and recalled that Schuman had been the name
of the PT boat skipper. What the hell was his screwball
idea to make them all rich? He drained the can in frustration, and glanced at his watch.

"We'd better get going to this Purple Pussycat Club
anyway, Harry. I want to contact the granddaughter as
soon as possible, just to play it safe."

Markby didn't answer immediately. He was crouched
over the table, head down, peering intently at something
amidst the clutter.

"Come on, Harry," urged Zarich. "You said the Purple Pussycat should be open by now."

Markby looked up with an absent grin. "Yeah, okay
I'm coming now, Ed."

"What's so interesting?"

"The photograph of the crew of the Old Tart you brought with you."

"What about it? You've seen it before."

Markby held it up to the light, a puzzled frown on his face. "Yeah I know. I guess it's nothing, but this Schuman who was the captain of the PT boat." His face broke with a slightly embarrassed snigger. "There just seems to be something vaguely familiar about him." He shrugged. "Perhaps it's only my imagination."

"Maybe not," said Zarich quickly. "We need everything we can get, Harry. Keep it for a while. You've got a cop's trained mind for faces, and you know the scene around here more than I do. Something might click." He glanced over Harry's shoulder, running his eyes along the picture until he came to Schuman. He hadn't taken that much notice before. It was a strong face, and the way he held himself in the group denoted more authority then the ranking uniform. "Keep it with you overnight," he murmured. "It might spark something in your memory." He slapped him across the shoulder. "Now, what about the Purple Pussycat?"

"I've been thinking about that too," said Markby.

Zarich paused in the action of donning his coat. "What's the problem?"

"I think it might be a good idea if you went alone. I could drop you off in the car, and you could get a cab back to the hotel."

Zarich slipped the coat slowly into place, and made sure his .38 was inside. "How come?"

"They know me around the Cross. We walk into the Purple Pussycat together, and you're going to see the word 'cop' light up like a flashing sign in everyone's face. They don't know you, Ed, so it might be easier if you were alone. It could get you to the girl with less hassle."

Zarich thought about it while he glanced in the mirror and pushed his hair into place. He knew what Harry meant. He thought of places in New York, like the bar where he'd picked up the information about Liavone, and recalled the old wary expressions that said "beware, cop."

"Okay, maybe you're right, Harry," he agreed. "Shepherd said the girl was a bit of a wild one, and we don't want to scare her off." He looked across as Markby began to shuffle into his own coat. "What'll you do?"

"Well, I'll think about this," grunted the sergeant, indicating the photograph. "And I have to report back to Roman again." He grimaced. "Who knows, I might even make it home before my wife's fallen asleep." He straightened his tie, and picked up a remaining chicken wing. "First chance I get I'll have you over to my place for dinner, Ed. I'd like you to meet Helen. You'd like her, she's the best." He bit off a portion of meat, dropped the bone back in the box, then took a card from his pocket and scribbled on the back. Then he handed it to Zarich. "That's my address and phone number," he mumbled through chicken meat. "You should know where you can get in touch, just in case of trouble."

Zarich slipped the card into his pocket. "Thanks, and that's a date for dinner, Harry." He moved impatiently to the door, while Markby butted his cigar. The pregnant bulge of his belly made it difficult to button his coat, so he always let it hang open. "I'd like to meet a woman who's taken fifteen years of this," added Zarich. "And can still smile—even be a little loving. I never got that lucky."

Markby tapped his finger against his forehead in mock solemnity. "It's training, Ed. You've gotta let them know the way it is."

Zarich had a feeling he knew the way it was. A man much in love with his wife, and he felt a twinge of envy.

Markby pulled the car to the side of the busy intersection, and pointed through the windshield.

"Better if I don't come any further, Ed. You'll see the club just along there in Ward Avenue. You won't have any trouble getting a taxi, they're around here like flies." He hesitated. "You know what you're going to do about the girl? It could be risky just letting her run loose."

"I'll play it by ear," murmured Zarich. "See how she takes it."

"Okay. Don't forget, you want anything, just call me anytime."

"Thanks . . . and I will," said Zarich appreciatively.

He stepped out, and paused on the corner until the

car slipped into an opening in the traffic. It reminded Zarich of the night-time hustle of Forty-second Street, the same part sleazy throb. Honking cabs claiming the road as their own, stuttering neons competing in garish colors, the swarming sidewalk, the tourists, pimps, hookers, characters, outsiders, the rich, the poor, those with money to spend on excitement but shopping warily, all rubbing shoulders in a jostling human goulash. Restaurants with windows like fishbowls, diners looking out with disdainful superiority, passersby looking back with contrived indifference. Young shabby boys gathering in protective huddles, white-faced girls in tight dresses or skimpy shorts, lounging sullenly in doorways, or parading the sidewalk with inviting eyes.

"Girls, girls, girls," shouted the doorman at the entrance to the Purple Pussycat. "See it all on stage . . . live." There was a board with buxom girls coyly concealing pudena. A narrow staircase led down off the street, the walls decorated in gaudy shades of purple.

"You won't be disappointed, sir," he shouted as Zarich descended the stairs, then he turned back to the street. "Another satisfied customer," he bawled raucously. "Girls, girls, girls."

It took Zarich's eyes time to adjust to the darkness, and he stood indecisively inside the door for a moment. There was a small bar to the left, spotlit in muddy yellow, vaguely outlining the heads of the seated patrons. There was a sudden burst of recorded music, and a naked girl wearing a huge picture hat appeared in a spotlight at the other end of the room. He could see in the added light it was only a small area, tables, chairs, and people clustered tightly in the center. There was a faint splattering of applause, and the girl removed the hat, using it like a concealing fan to tantalize the audience as she swayed her body to the music. Zarich had seen it all before; she had the sexual appeal of a tired performing seal.

"Just sit anywhere you like, sir," said a low voice at his side.

She was Scandinavian fair, straight hair almost white to her bare shoulders. Wide face shaping to a pointed chin, her mouth blooming with tasteful makeup. She was a few inches shorter than he, with a thin frame, but the vivid purple dress showed ample evidence she was well-shaped. Even in the gloom she looked stunning, and he recognized her at once from the photograph as Cassie Rehfield.

"Perhaps I could buy you a drink to begin with," he murmured.

"I'm sorry, sir, I can't drink with the customers while the show's on." She glanced toward the dancer. "The girls don't like it. Maybe later."

She went to turn away, but he caught her gently by the arm. She used a nice perfume that must have cost her. "I'd really like to talk to you about your grandmother, Cassie," he said politely.

She looked down at his restraining hand, then directly into his face with an expression that said, I'm not for touching, and he let go.

"My grandmother?"

"Yes. Is there somewhere we could talk?"

"Is it important?"

"Very important."

"You sound like an American. Are you a cop?"

The music moved up in volume, and the small room began to throb with sound. The dancer hurled her hat into the audience, and began frontal gyrations as some of the audience began to whistle.

"I said, are you a cop"? she repeated.

"Let's talk somewhere," he stalled.

"You got any trouble, Cassie?" There was a broad, swarthy man abruptly at his side, dark suit, white shirt, red bow tie, and hands that looked as if they'd fit twice around his throat. The girl hesitated, then shook her head.

"Give me five minutes, Ross," she murmured.

Zarich wasn't too sure the man heard the words, but her expression sufficed. She nodded curtly to Zarich, then led the way to a small door on the other side of the bar. The walls seemed to vibrate to the musical cacophony. She opened the door, gestured him through ahead of her, then followed. They were in a small dressing room, wall mirror, tatty dressing table littered with makeup paraphernalia, several rickety chairs, and clothes draped over a sagging rod along the wall. A bare light globe hung from the ceiling. The cracked walls had been painted purple, but a long time ago. There was an odor of stale sweat and sadness. Neither of them sat down. She leaned warily against the door, her hands behind her back. He guessed she was about twenty-two, but she looked older than the photograph, aged more by experience than time. Her skin glowed golden brown as if she spent a lot of time in the sun, and even without the tawdry glamour of the murky lighting she was still a looker. Maybe not beautiful, but she would turn heads in any company. He was impressed more than he cared to show. She glanced meaningfully at her watch, as if placing him on a time schedule.

"What about my grandmother?" she asked bluntly. The low voice reserved for patrons was gone, and replaced by a hard directness.

He placed a hand on one of the chairs. "Would you like to sit down?"

"I prefer to stand." She tilted her head as if listening to the music.

"They won't like it if I'm not there when the show finishes."

"My name's Zarich . . . Ed Zarich."

"Well, what's your business about my grandmother, Mr. Zarich?"

He shrugged. She wasn't the sort of woman to respect evasive tact.

"I'm afraid I have some bad news about her."

"What do you mean, bad news?"

"She died last night."

He knew it hit her, but it seemed part of her tough exterior to feel the need to hide it. She stared at him wordlessly for a time, then directed her eyes to the floor. "Now would you like to sit down?" he asked quietly.

She pushed herself reluctantly from the door, and crossed to the chair. Even with her slim build it creaked ominously as she sat down. She crossed her hands on her lap, and stared mournfully at her reflection in the mirror.

"What happened?" she asked huskily.

"She was drowned near where she worked. In the harbor by the Opera House."

She swung around in the chair, wide-eyed. They were an incredible shade of blue, and the expression of concern gave her a surprisingly elfin look. "My God . . . drowned? How could that happen?"

"We're trying to find out."

"Drowned," she muttered again. "It doesn't seem possible. Was it an accident?" She stared at him suspiciously. "Are you a cop?"

He thought about how to answer her for a brief moment, then when he finally decided to show her his ID she registered surprise.

"New York. You're a New York cop? I don't get it. What's a New York cop got to do with my grandmother drowning?"

"It's a long story. Maybe we'll catch up on it later."

She stared at him in bewilderment, then shook her head and turned back to the dressing table. "If you'd told me she had a heart attack I may have understood. But my God, drowned. She couldn't just fall in the water?"

"Like I said, we're trying to find out."

"I wouldn't expect her old creep of a husband to bring me the news," she said derisively. "He's not my real grandfather you know."

"He's had a lot on his mind," said Zarich shortly. "He would have got around to it." He reversed the other chair and squatted down facing her, his arms folded over the back. The music hammered against the door like someone urgently demanding entrance. She slumped in the chair not looking at him, one arm resting on the dressing table. She had a physical allure about her he hadn't experienced since the early days with Rhonda, a heat some women generated that he found hard to resist.

"I'd only just found her after a long time," she muttered.

"So I understand from her husband."

"We got real close. She never got on with her daughter . . . my mother, but that didn't surprise me." She laughed bitterly. "My mother threw me out when I was fifteen. She was a real bastard." Her eyes narrowed with hostility at the memory. "It's one way to learn, a great survival course if you go the distance." Her eyes flicked to the door. "Even if you finish up in a dump like this, at least you're eating regularly. It was one of the things I talked about with my grandmother, getting out of this place." Her hand stroked mournfully at her hair. "It's no joy, guys pawing at you and figuring you're an easy lay, then having to be nice to the creeps or you get fired. But somehow I could never make the break. But we talked about it, and she said she'd help . . . I mean not with money, but just by being there." She shrugged. "Maybe it wouldn't have worked anyway." A wistful smile passed over her face, and it was like a brief glimpse of lost innocence. She was really very lovely. Her grandmother had been right; she didn't belong in this shit place.

"Maybe you owe it to her to make the break on your own," murmured Zarich.

"Yeah, it sounds easy when you say it. I don't fancy myself in a factory, and . . ." She tilted her head to the wall. "Out there on the street the competition's fierce, and all you get for your trouble is a heroin fix."

"The street's no answer. I don't see why someone with your looks should have any problem."

"Yeah, like I said, it sounds easy."

There was a silent pause. The begrudging reluctance about talking to him was gone, and now she seemed in no hurry for him to leave.

"I still can't imagine how she'd drown," she said faintly.

"When you were having these talks with your grandmother, did she ever say anything about your real grandfather?"

She thoughtfully shuffled some of the makeup items about on the dressing table. "You mean the American sailor she married during the war?"

"That's the one."

"You know about him?"

"A little. What did she tell you?"

"Not much. She showed me some letters he wrote to her once. She was only a kid at the time, but she must have been crazy about him. I think life stopped for her after he was killed."

"Did she ever mention the Old Tart?"

Her bewildered expression was supplemented by words. "Is that some sort of joke?"

"No, I want you to think about it a moment. It could have been mentioned in one of the letters."

She half turned back to the mirror, listlessly pushing at her hair, and it shimmered in the weak light. The outside music seemed to reach a crescendo with a machine gun rattle of drums, a clash of symbols, then the applause of the audience.

"I think you're right," she answered slowly. "I do remember the Old Tart." She placed her head questioningly to one side. "Yes, I do remember. Wasn't it the nickname of my grandfather's boat during the war?" Full recollection came into her eyes. "That's right, it was in the letters. We talked about it one day, and she was laughing about some idea he had for getting rich. I don't think it made any sense to her, and it certainly didn't to me."

He nodded without comment. She was part of the clan now; she knew something yet she knew nothing, and it was probably the most dangerous knowledge she could possibly have. He thought of Donlett, Musoveld, her grandmother floating like discarded garbage. He wasn't going to let them turn this beautiful face into a death mask.

"Say, what's this all about?" she demanded in sudden exasperation. "Why all the questions about my grandfather? What's a New York cop doing here telling me about my grandmother's death anyway?"

"I've a feeling—well more than a feeling, that your grandmother was murdered."

That really seemed to get to her, even more than the news about her death. The sky blue eyes expanded to dominate her face. "Murdered? You've got to be kidding, Mr. Zarich."

"No, I'm very serious."

"You mean she was mugged, or something like that?"

"No I don't think it was anything like that."

"My God, who would want to murder a harmless lady like her?"

It was like an echo from New York. Harmless Donlett. Harmless Musoveld. "Like I said, it's a long story," he stalled.

"Then I think I should hear about it." She looked at him wonderingly. "Don't tell me you're all the way from New York because of my grandmother?" She shook her head in disbelief. "No, that sounds crazy. She was an ordinary woman, living a dull life in Bankstown. I just don't understand any of the questions you're asking me. And as for her being murdered. . . ?" The expression of incredulity widened on her face. "That sounds like fantasy."

"Listen, Cassie, what time do you finish here?" he asked.

She was instantly wary. "What's that got to do with it?"

"I think . . . I'm sure it might be a good idea if you had protection."

"Protection from what?"

"I think your grandmother shared some information with you that could be dangerous."

"Dangerous for me?"

He could sense her backing cautiously away. "Yes. Where do you live?"

She hesitated. "Just out of the city in Paddington."

"I'd prefer you didn't go there tonight."

"And you've got a better idea, like with you," she jeered.

"Something like that."

"Christ, do I really look that easy?"

He rested his chin on his arms, and solemnly studied her. It would be so delicious with her; he hadn't felt so turned on by a woman in a long, long time. But her world required an armor-plated shield and that wasn't why he was there anyway.

"I'm trying to save your life," he declared sharply.

That shook her defenses for a moment. He waited while fear and distrust alternated in her face, then he took Markby's card from his pocket and held it close to her.

"That's Detective Sergeant Harry Markby's card, from the Sydney Police. You can call him for confirmation if you like. But I warn you, what he'll probably want to do is put you under protective arrest."

She stared at the card, but didn't take it. Fear made

her look once more like the young girl in Emma Shepherd's box of memories.

"He can't do that, I haven't done anything," she whined.

"He'll think of something. He wants to keep you alive too."

She obviously wasn't going to take up the challenge, so he placed the card back in his pocket.

"Your kind are always hassling me, you know that," she said huskily. "It's the story of my life."

"I'm not trying to hassle you. I've seen three people murdered, your grandmother one of them, and I don't want you to be the fourth."

"It's as bad as that?"

It could be. I just don't want to take the risk."

She silently studied her red nails. He hadn't wanted to frighten her, but maybe it was the only way to save her.

"What do you want me to do?" she asked sullenly.

"Come back to my hotel with me."

"I see. You get a freeby, and I get protection."

"It won't be like that."

"Then you tell me what it'll be like."

"I'll book you into a room next to mine."

"And as soon as I squeal, you'll come running?"

He tired of the game, stood to his feet, and shoved the chair aside. There was more applause from outside, so maybe the girl onstage was doing a special without music.

"This case is really bugging me, know that," he said coldly. "It's brought me halfway around the world. I'm going to level with you, Cassie. I'm not too sure keeping you alive is going to get me any closer to a solution, so it's up to you. You want to finish up floating in the harbor like your grandmother, I guess it's your decision."

The sudden change in tactics took the edge off her brittle distrust. She was suddenly vulnerable, like prey caught in the open. The door opened and the man she'd called Ross poked his head through. He threw an aggressive scowl at Zarich, then concentrated on Cassie.

"You okay, Cassie. You've got some thirsty customers out there, and Pat wants to use the room."

She nodded, and eased herself out of the chair. "Okay Ross, I'll be right there."

He hesitated, and gave Zarich another challenging stare. "You got any trouble?"

"No, no trouble, Ross," she assured him. "I'm coming now."

"I hope so." He closed the door heavily to indicate his displeasure. Zarich didn't move, watching as she went slowly to the door without looking at him, then she half turned with her fingers on the handle. It didn't matter if she told him to go to hell, he wasn't going to let her finish up like her grandmother.

"All right," she murmured. "I don't understand any of this, but I'll come. Wait by the bar. I'll speak to Ross and see if I can get away early."

He felt relieved. "You're very wise," he said simply. "And I'll try and tell you as much as I can later."

He remained in the room after she'd gone. He wasn't too sure how much he could tell her; he'd have to feel his way and just feed her sufficient to keep her insecure enough to want protection. But he'd be lying to himself if he didn't relish the thought of having her close.

The door burst open, and the still naked girl from the stage bustled through. It took him by surprise, and in spite of himself he gawked at all the bare flesh.

"Okay, goggle eyes," she shot at him harshly. "This is my den. You can piss off outside with all the other fucking perverts."

They didn't have a vacant room adjoining his, so Zarich changed to another floor. They'd stopped off at Cassie's Paddington apartment so she could change and pick up a few overnight things. She looked just as terrific in the red blouse and white jeans, and her mood of sceptical cynicism was gone. Now she was subdued, saying little, just going along, letting him lead and make the decisions. He carefully checked her room, then pointed to the wall.

"I'm right next door," he said. "I don't believe this is going to be any problem, but if you need me and don't want to come out into the passage, just thump on the wall."

"It would be a lot easier if I knew just what the hell I'm supposed to be afraid of," she whispered. "You haven't told me much, Zarich."

"Ed," he insisted.

"Okay, Ed. What is it my grandmother's supposed to have told me that's so dangerous? Is it something to do with those questions you asked me about my grandfather, and the Old Tart?"

He rubbed doubtfully at his chin. Maybe he should talk with Harry about how much they should take her into their confidence. It was a leak from somewhere that had cost Emma Shepherd's life, and he didn't want to risk anything like that happening again.

"When I say you're in danger, just trust me . . . please," he said. "Let's get through tonight, then we'll talk about it in the morning."

"But it is to do with my grandfather?" she persisted.

"Something like that," he admitted guardedly.

She surprised him by conceding abrupt defeat. "All right then, in the morning," she smiled. "I guess being here and not knowing is better than being in a cell and still not knowing." She looked hesitantly at her watch, then at the telephone. "I guess I should ring John Shepherd and find out about the funeral and a few things like that, but it's after twelve." She grimaced. "Not that I particularly want to talk to him."

"Why not leave it until the morning," advised Zurich. Maybe Emma had bad-mouthed her husband, because it was obvious Cassie had some antipathy toward him.

"All right then," she agreed quickly.

He smiled and went to turn away, but she caught at his arm.

"Listen, Ed," she said softly. "If, if this is on the level, and I guess it is or you wouldn't be going to all this trouble . . . well, thanks for trying to help, for coming and telling me about my grandmother. I'm sorry about back there at the club, but I'm so used to creeps trying to con me." She smiled apologetically. "Some of them can be pretty persistent."

"That's okay, Cassie. We'll talk about it some more in the morning."

"You really think I might be in danger? If it's to do with my grandfather it all seems such a long time ago."

"Don't worry about it," he reassured her. "I'm playing safe, so this is only a precaution." She had a marvelous mouth. In another time, another place he could fall off the deep end with a girl like this. Prying information out of her in bed would be more pleasure than duty.

"Well, thanks anyway."

"Would you like a drink before you turn in?" he felt compelled to ask.

It was a mistake; he could see the defenses come up in her eyes like sprung traps.

"Thanks anyway, but it's been a long day, and after the news and everything I'm pretty washed out."

He made a swift retreat. "That's okay. Get a good night's sleep. Like I said, we'll talk in the morning."

She closed the door on him with a soft smile impossible to read. With another woman he could have inferred a subtle suggestion they use only his room, but you couldn't tell with her. He'd met plenty like her who'd been around, who were survivors, but there was something about her that intrigued him.

He put the .38 within reach on the table before he got into bed. Maybe he was running scared, but after Emma Shepherd anything was possible.

Sleep eluded him. Perhaps he missed the night-time sounds of Manhattan, but there was no point in fooling himself that the girl in the next room wasn't on his mind. For a time she even competed with his obsessive brooding over the Old Tart. He must have dozed off, and he wasn't too sure what had woken him. He picked up his watch, and peered blearily at the time. It was three-thirty. Then he became aware of a faint bumping noise beating in the room with a regular pattern. He sat up in the bed and listened for a moment, trying to locate the direction of the sound. He slipped quickly out of bed, crossed to the wall separating him from Cassie, and placed his ear to the surface. It was clearer there, not a regular beat like he first imagined, but intermittent.

He swiftly pulled on his trousers, thrust the .38 into his pocket, opened the door, and glanced out into the corridor. It was deserted, nothing but the feel of a hotel asleep, and the sound no longer audible.

He paused uncertainly, then stepped out and padded barefoot to Cassie's room. He put his ear to the door and heard it again, just faint, like the beating of a muffled drum. He lifted his hand to knock, and the door opened at his touch. He felt an instant tightness in his throat.

"Christ," he moaned. "Christ not again, not again."

He moved fast into the room, the .38 in his hand, and closed the door softly behind him. The bedside lamp was on but the bed empty, the covers thrown back as if in haste. The sound was more distinct now, and he traced it across to the closed bathroom door. He stopped, ear to the door, and it was coming from inside the room as if someone was beating feebly against the wall. He tried the handle, but it was locked.

"Cassie," he called urgently. "It's Ed Zarich. Are you in there? Are you all right?"

The sound abruptly stopped, and he rattled the handle furiously. "Cassie, for Chrissake open the door."

For a second there was only silence, then he heard her strained whisper from the other side of the door. "Ed? Ed, is it really you? There's no one else with you?"

She sounded terrified. "Open the door," he demanded. "Of course it's only me." But he still held the .38 ready, for even if she opened the door he wasn't too sure what he'd find.

Finally there was the rattle of the door chain, and the click of the latch as the door swung open. She was kneeling on the floor just inside, dressed in a white nightie, hair disheveled, mouth slack, eyes wide with glazed fear. He pushed the .38 into his pocket as he moved quickly into the room, and crouched down beside her, hands on her shoulders.

She leaned her head thankfully to his chest. "Ed, thank God," she gasped.

"For Chrissake, what happened?" he asked. He hooked his hands under her armpits, and began to lever her to her feet. "Can you stand? Are you hurt?"

He pulled her upright, and she leaned heavily to him, her breath coming in long sobbing moans. "No . . . no, I'm not hurt." He caught at her chin with his fingers and turned her face to him. "Ed, I was terrified. My, my legs just wouldn't hold me anymore. I fell down after I locked the door, and . . . and I couldn't get up again." The blond hair swirled about her face as she shook her head. "I . . . just . . . couldn't . . . get up."

She would have fallen again, but he braced himself against the shower recess, holding her tight. "I couldn't do anything," she moaned. "Anything at all. I didn't even have enough strength to beat the wall properly. I, I just kept hitting it with my hand, but I didn't seem able to do it hard enough to make you hear me. Jesus," she muttered exhaustedly. Her hair brushed his face, and he could feel her body trembling. "Jesus," she moaned again.

He swept her up off her feet, carried her to the bed, lowered her as gently as possible, and pulled the covers over her. She just lay there with her eyes closed, while he sat down on the bed and patiently waited. She was breathing rapidly and looked so vulnerable, yet strangely it made her seem more beautiful than when he'd first seen her.

She didn't open her eyes, but took one arm from beneath the covers and gestured listlessly to the front door.

"I don't know what woke me," she whispered. "But the bedside lamp was on. I must have forgotten to switch it off before I went to sleep. I thought I heard a noise from the front door, but at first I wondered if it might be you, maybe coming to check I was all right." She paused, her throat pulsing as she swallowed. "So I went and listened." Her eyes finally opened, and she stared at the ceiling. "There was a scraping sound, like someone was trying keys in the lock. I didn't know what to do. I hadn't put the locking chain on, and when I tried to do it I could see the door starting to open. I was sure then it wasn't you, I mean you hadn't said anything about having a key to my room." She turned her eyes in the direction of the bathroom. "I don't know why I didn't put the chain on. I guess I was so tired, and I just forgot, but I ran across to the bathroom, and just closed the door enough to see out.

Well . . ." She paused again, tongue flickering nervously over her lips. "Well, the door opened, and this man came in." She shook her head. "Don't ask me to describe him, because I can't, I just can't. I was so scared I could hardly see. I closed the bathroom door, locked it, and just slid to the floor. God, it was awful, I just couldn't stand up. I guess he must have known I was in the bathroom because he came over and tried to force the door, then he began trying to break it down. But I still couldn't move, I just lay on the floor praying to God the lock would hold." Her breath was coming rapidly again at the memory. "Even when he stopped I still couldn't get up. But there was no way I was going to unlock the door anyway, he could have been just waiting for me to do that. So I stayed where I was, beating over and over at the wall in the hope you'd hear me." She rolled her head from side to side on the pillow. "God, I'm not exactly lily-white, but I never thought anyone would actually want to kill me." For the first time she looked directly at Zarich. "It's these people you say killed my grandmother isn't it, Ed? I want to know what it's all about, I've got a right to know why someone's trying to kill me. I've got a right."

He took her hand and tried to calm her, thinking of what would have happened if he hadn't persuaded her to come to the hotel.

"You should have put on the chain," he remonstrated quietly.

"I know, I know. It was crazy. I guess way down I didn't really believe all the things you were telling me about being in danger."

"You're going to be all right now, you can believe that. They won't try again tonight. I want you to try and get back to sleep."

She seized his hand in a fierce grip. "You can't be serious," she cried. "There's no way I could get back to sleep if I was here alone. My God, don't you leave me here alone, Ed. Please don't leave me."

"Okay, okay, I'll stay with you if that's what you want."

He went to shift his position on the bed, but her grip

on his hand was like a vise. "Just don't leave me . . . please," she whimpered.

He didn't move. After a time her eyes closed, her breathing became more regular, and even though she stirred restlessly about the bed, she seemed to fall into an uneasy sleep. He pried his hand loose, put the .38 on the bedside cupboard, then eased himself carefully down beside her. He didn't believe they'd make another try tonight, but the bastards seemed desperate enough for anything. But for Chrissake, where was the leak? Someone knew every move he was making. They knew about Emma Shepherd. They had to know he was going to see this girl, maybe had followed them to the hotel. He was going to have to resolve it some way with Harry in the morning, or he wasn't going to do anything except get more people killed. He scowled, pushed his head into the pillow, and closed his eyes.

He didn't know what time it was when he woke, but it was still dark. It seemed as if he was locked into an erotic dream, with Rhonda playing the lead, only not cold and bitter like he'd last seen her, but with all the warmth and passion of the old days. He didn't open his eyes lest the dream vanish, but the mouth clamped fiercely on his was full of promise and heat. Then there were probing fingers at his trousers, opening him, pushing inside, finding his erection, teasing, tantalizing, gently squeezing. "Rhonda," he whispered.

"Rhonda if you like, baby," said the low voice throatily at his ear. "Anyone you want it to be."

He didn't want it to be Rhonda; he wanted it to be Cassie; it was Cassie. He tried to reach for her, but she was already over him, positioning her legs astride, lowering herself slowly until he slid deep into her. He grasped at her thighs, matching her driving rhythm, and when he came, for a moment even the Old Tart didn't seem to matter. She lay over him for a time, her movements gradually subsiding, holding him close, his nostrils full of the perfume he'd first noticed at the club.

"You're a doll, Ed," she whispered. "A real doll. That's for my life, that's for everything."

Then she eased off him, and fell back alongside. He

waited until his heart ceased hammering, then put out an arm to draw her close, and she nestled to him like she belonged. He didn't know if it was only gratitude, but he hoped it was more. There was something stirring in him he thought had died a long time ago.

It was daylight when he next woke, and they went at it again with exploring caressing hands, moans intermingling, throwing sparks off each other like striking flint, and he knew then it was more than gratitude. They came in mutual paroxysm, and even when she snugged close again afterward he felt guilty about immediately calling Markby. Harry would be anxious to know how he'd got on, but he wasn't going to tell him about this part of it.

"I'm not easy, Ed," she murmured suddenly. "I'm not easy at all. I pick and choose, and maybe I didn't show it at the club, but I liked you as soon as I saw you. I didn't know it was going to work out this way, but I knew it'd work out some way. It's more than you saving my life, Ed." She lifted her head until their faces were close, her blue eyes so wide they filled his vision. "And I can tell you feel the same. I can. I know when a guy's got somehing going for me. And about all these things that are happening, whatever they mean, I'll go along with you to the end if that's what you want."

He stroked at her hair, and pressed her close. "That's what I want," he whispered. Then he told her everything he knew about the Old Tart, because he figured if they had her on their kill list then she had a right to know. It was another hour before he called Harry.

It was eleven o'clock by the time Markby arrived, and by then at his insistence they'd canceled Cassie's room, and she'd moved in with him. Zarich wasn't too sure how to protect her, whether to keep her at the hotel, or go back with her to the Paddington apartment. But he wasn't going to leave her alone.

It didn't take the sergeant long to sniff what was going on; there was an almost touchable aura between Zarich and Cassie they made no effort to hide. He offered only a lift of his eyebrow, and a sly smile that could have been envy, then listened silently while Zarich told him about the meeting at the club and the attempt on Cassie. She took no part in the conversation, but sat over by the window staring moodily at the skyline.

"We've got a real problem, Ed," said Markby soberly. "They know every move we're making. Someone must have followed you back here to the hotel." He glanced cautiously in Cassie's direction. "And I was thinking about you last night. They're ruthless assholes and I was wondering if they might make a try at you."

Zarich looked across at Cassie, and she turned her head with a faint smile of intimacy. It had crossed his mind, but it was a two-edged thing. Maybe they figured he was just as far away from an answer as when he was in New York, but if he ever got close he could start looking over his shoulder.

"How about I make some coffee?" asked Cassie suddenly.

"That sounds like a good idea." Zarich smiled.

He was sure she thought they might talk easier with her out of earshot, so he waited until he heard the clink of cups and the gush of water.

"I can take care of myself, Harry," he said. "But what about this fucking leak? Who the hell else knows what's going on apart from your Chief Inspector Roman, and the assistant commissioner? There has to be someone."

Markby's face took on a slightly harassed expression. "Crikey, then I'm damned if I know who, Ed." He hesitated. "Of course I've been making detailed reports to Roman."

"What do you mean, 'detailed reports'?"

Markby shuffled uncomfortably in the chair. "Well, the usual thing, Ed. He's my superior, and he wants to know what's going on." He stared at his hands for a moment. "I'll level with you, Ed, I don't think Roman likes you being here that much," he confessed candidly. "I guess I'm playing a sort of watchdog . . . you know, apart from anything else." His face mirrored embarrassment. "It's not the sort of role I like playing, but I've got to take orders the same as you. But you seem a real decent sort of bloke, so . . ." His voice trailed away uncertainly.

"That's okay, I understand, and thanks for filling me

in, Harry. Then that makes you and me and Roman who know about day-to-day details."

"He's a longtime cop, Ed. From all I hear a bloody lucky punter, but a good cop. I don't see how the leak could come from there."

"These reports you've been making have only been verbal?"

"Yeah, for the time being until I can get something down on paper."

"Is it possible someone's bugging his office?"

Markby's lower lip protruded doubtfully. "Well, I suppose anything's possible, but Christ I'd be surprised. Still, there's some pretty strange people get bugged in this city."

Zarich pushed back in his chair, and thoughtfully considered the ceiling. Cassie brought the coffee, placing a cup carefully beside each man.

"You've had a rough time, are you feeling okay now?" asked Markby solicitously.

She passed a fleeting smile full of meaning to Zarich. "I'll survive, thanks to Ed," she murmured. She took her own cup back to the position by the window. "Maybe I should go for a walk while you guys talk," she offered.

Zarich shook his head firmly. "I want you to stay put here until we figure out what we're going to do."

She shrugged and settled down in the chair again, while the men sipped at their coffee.

"You've got a nice thing going there, Ed," said Markby softly.

Zarich only grinned in answer. Nice thing? Was that what it was, having her on his mind almost as much as the Old Tart?

"She couldn't identify this bloke who made a try for her?"

"No. I think she was so terrified she couldn't have identified her own mother. Anyway she only got a brief glimpse of him through the bathroom door." He paused, and blew reflectively on his hot coffee. "I want you to do a favor for me, Harry," he requested carefully.

"Name it."

"When we make our next move, whatever the hell it is, leave Roman out of it?"

Markby silently considered the request for a time. "That's making it tough, Ed," he said finally.

"I'm not asking you to lie to him. Tell him I've gone off on my own if you like. I don't want him to know anything more, especially about Cassie."

The sergeant frowned. "It's stretching things to suspect him of passing anything on, Ed." He shrugged. "Then again, we've had bad apples surface in the force in the past. What police force hasn't? But Roman?"

"I'm not saying he's passing anything on, Harry. But there's only you and me, and Roman. I'm bloody sure it's not me." He gave Markby a crooked grin. "And I figure I'm a good enough judge to know it's not you, Harry."

"Well thanks for that," said Markby gruffly.

Zarich didn't put it into words, but it had crossed his mind. But he'd made an assessment about the Australian, and he was going to back his judgment.

"Will you do it, just until we see where we're going?" he asked.

Markby nodded hesitantly. "Okay, I'll give it a try. But he's a shrewd bastard. He won't be easy to fool."

"Just try it," urged Zarich. "If someone is bugging his office we'll soon know."

Markby balanced his cup on his portly belly, and studied Zarich through half-closed eyes. "I did a little survey after I left you last night. You know, a word here and there with a few informers."

Zarich gave a grin of understanding. "Yeah, I know, I've got my own New York rounds."

"No one knows a thing. They'd drop something if they knew, but it's a closed book. Whoever or whatever it is we're up against, it's nothing to do with the usual crims. Not a thing."

Zarich nodded without surprise. He'd had the feeling all along that this was much bigger than some hoodlum organization. Cassie was sitting profile to them, eyes still pensively to the window. If she was listening, she gave little evidence of interest. He had the impression that after last night she was quite confident to leave her life in his hands.

"Did you think any more about Darwin?" asked Markby.

"I still want to go. Maybe I'm just scratching around for anything, but it's where the Old Tart operated."

"Forty years ago."

"Forty years or not, there might just be some record that'll give me a way to go."

Markby nodded, and grinned knowingly. "I reckoned you sounded pretty determined last night, so I made a few calls to Darwin this morning and set it up for you. I've got a pal up there who knows how to keep his mouth shut. He's a retired cop called Dennis Charlton. A real character. He'll meet you at the airport. And he can open doors for you. He's lived in Darwin all his life, and that includes right through the war. If anyone can help you, he can."

Zarich laughed, and slapped his hand down on the arm of the chair. "I might've guessed. Thanks, Harry. I only figure on a short stay, but it could be worthwhile." He paused, eyebrows raised. "But nothing to Roman. Okay?"

"Okay," muttered Markby. He was thoughtful a moment, then nodded cautiously toward Cassie. "What about her? I'm going to have to put her under twenty-four-hour protection, and that'll be hard to keep from Roman."

She turned to them, and put her coffee cup down on the floor. "I'll have something to say about that," she declared tersely. "Ed was right here in the room next to me last night, and that didn't stop them trying."

"Well, I suppose we could lock you up, but you wouldn't like that either," said Markby laconically.

"How would you like to come to Darwin with me?" asked Zarich.

She stared at him thoughtfully. He could see her mind turning over like his. There was more than protection, it was them together nights, and he knew she was as hungry as he thinking about it.

"I guess that's the only way I'm going to feel really safe," she murmured slowly. "At least I'll be out of Sydney."

"What do you think, Harry?" asked Zarich.

"Sounds like a good idea," Markby shrugged. "It's better if she's out of Sydney."

"Okay, that's the way we'll play it. There's no problems for you at the club, Cassie? I don't want you to tell them you're going away."

"I'll get one of the girls to phone in sick for me. It's happened before."

"Great." He turned back to Markby. "You can arrange it, Harry?"

"Sure. I'll book you both on the first flight out tomorrow morning." He glanced to them in turn. "If that's okay with both of you?"

They both nodded quick agreement as he picked up his case from the floor, opened it, took out the photograph of the Old Tart crew, and passed it over to Zarich. "I guess you'll be wanting to take that with you, Ed."

Zarich studied it for a moment, then placed it down on the small table to the side. Every time he looked at the photograph it was almost as if he was willing one of those smiling faces to speak to him, to tell him what had happened on the Old Tart. "Thanks, Harry, I will." He tapped his finger down on the head of Schuman. "Did your memory turn up any answers?"

The sergeant spread his hands in a perplexed gesture. "To be honest, Ed, no. But I'm sure there's something niggling around in the back of my head, and I just can't dig it out." He motioned to the picture. "I had a copy made this morning and I'm going to keep it by me, just looking at it and hoping whatever it is that's bugging me comes out." He grinned. "Maybe I'm just gettin' old, and the brain cells don't stir so fast anymore."

"If there's something there, it'll come to you, Harry. Christ, we need some sort of break. Listen, if it'll help why don't you keep the original, and I'll take the copy. What's the quality like?"

Harry took the copy from his case and showed it to Zarich.

"That looks fine," said Zarich. "Why don't I go with this one. I might not even need it in Darwin. The sharper print might help your memory."

Markby shrugged agreement, and they exchanged

prints. Zarich drained his coffee, and pushed the cup aside. "There's something else you could do while I'm away."

"What's that?"

"It's to do with the last letter Emma got from Donlett. Are there old newspaper files around here you can check?"

"Sure, no sweat."

"That letter was dated . . . ah, just a moment." He went across to the dresser, brought the file back to the table, and extracted the letter. "Yeah, here it is, the fifteenth of March, 1945." He motioned with it to Harry. "It might help if we knew just what was happening in the Pacific war at that time. There could have been something going on that might tie in with the disappearance of the Old Tart." He raised his eyebrows hopefully. "Anyway, it's worth a try."

"Sure, sure, good idea, Ed," agreed Markby affably. He stirred on the chair. "Well, I've got a few things to do, so I'd better get moving." He offered a faint smile to Cassie. "You'd better keep yourself out of sight as much as possible."

"I'll have to go to my apartment to get some things for the trip."

"I guess Ed'll go with you, but leave it as late as you can," he advised. He stood on his feet, and picked up the case. "Listen, I should have your tickets this afternoon. What about I pick you both up later, and take you out to my place for dinner?" He glanced from one to the other, obviously pleased with the thought. "I know Helen would like to meet you . . . and the kids."

Zarich glanced toward Cassie, and she indicated agreement with a smile. "All right, Harry," he said. "That sounds like a nice idea."

They walked to the door together, and Zarich had the sudden impression all their talking had achieved very little.

"I feel like I'm going nowhere, Harry," he confessed. "I should call Beuso in New York, but I keep stalling. I tell him Donlett's wife's been killed and he's just as likely to tell me to forget the whole deal, and come back home instead of spending the department's money on a lost cause." He screwed his mouth into a rueful line. "But I'm absolutely sure the answer's here somewhere. It has to be. I'm not leaving until I find it, and the hell with Beuso if he objects."

"Well, you know a bloody sight more than when you were in New York, Ed," Markby commiserated. "Emma Shepherd's letter told us that. We know the crew of the Old Tart were up to something. We're not completely in the dark."

Zarich patted him on the shoulder. "No, just feeling our way like we're half blind."

"Well, I gotta go report to Roman before anything else."

"Don't forget our agreement. I especially don't want him knowing about Darwin."

Markby grimaced doubtfully. "I'm no great actor, but I'll give it a try." He moved through the door, then stopped and peered back at Cassie. "I'll pick you up about five. I guess you can manage to fill in the day."

"She's something else," murmured Zarich.

"Half your luck," came the sergeant's parting envious remark.

Zarich stood by the open door, watching until Markby's rounded form disappeared down the corridor. The warm feeling he had for the Australian was growing, and if he was going to crack this thing he couldn't wish for a better partner.

"I would like to have gone to the funeral," said Cassie solemnly.

He crossed, and softly kissed her. "I know. I just think it might be dangerous if you did."

She stood close, with her hair brushing his face. "I know, but I feel bad about it."

"I want you with me in Darwin, for many reasons."

"And I want to be with you," she whispered.

He gently consoled her, then they went to bed again. He was breaking all his ground rules, such as never getting distracted emotionally when the scent is running, but he was captivated by her in a way he'd never experienced before. Even in the beginning with Rhonda he'd always been conscious of a wary holding back, a fear she might

try to own him, and maybe that had soured the marriage
as much as anything else. But everything about this girl
entranced him, her feel, heat, sexual initiative, fervent
response. Yet he knew nothing about her—she could have
been a part-time hooker, but it didn't seem to matter.
Some time during the day he heard himself say "I love
you" as if the words were coming from another person,
and it surprised him almost as much as her.

She raised herself on an elbow, and soberly appraised
him. "Really?" she challenged. It wasn't so much cynical
disbelief as wonderment, and brought a return of natural
caution.

"Well . . . almost," he retreated with a grin.

She sank back on the pillow, and softly caressed his
face. "Almost is good enough for both of us," she whispered. "For now."

Chapter 9

Sade had never risked his own skin for Humbert as
he had with Emma Shepherd, and it angered him. He was
an organizer, not a hatchet man; there was any amount of
garbage around like Liavone who would do anything for a
price. But the pressure Humbert had exerted over the
urgency of the Shepherd woman had forced him into the
role of executioner. He hadn't been that since Vietnam,
and he found it just as distasteful as he had then. But
Christ, the risk he'd taken of being seen dropping the
unconscious woman's body in the water. It chilled him to
think of it in retrospect.

All his life had been plagued by shits like Humbert.
The old man had been a Humbert, and he'd lost that
confrontation to finish up on the streets. There had been
another Humbert at reform school, and he'd lost that one
too. Christ knows how many Humberts he might have
found in jail, but he fled to the Army to avoid that. Yet he

wasn't too stupid to learn. By the time Vietnam came he'd learned the safety of fake toadyism as a mask for his true feelings. Give a creep a feeling of superiority and it made him careless, then when he least expected it you had him. He got himself an education in the Army, and there were Humberts there, too, but he knew how to handle them by then. When he found out how easy it was to get killed in Vietnam, that contrived subservience kept him alive. Fuck them all, he had more brains and cunning than the college-educated brass. Yes sir, no sir, let me kiss your ass, sir, ferrying them around in a helicopter while mentally giving them the up-yours sign, because he could see through their glory games like they were glass.

But it had got him an introduction to Humbert, and give the devious bastard his due, he was perceptive enough to recognize a soul mate. It took him a while to realize Humbert was a man who made up his own rules, then he willingly let himself get sucked in, each job a little more outside the law than the last, and it made him rich. But he had never really worked Humbert out, and he figured Humbert had the same trouble with him. He never let the mask drop; he didn't give a damn if Humbert despised his fawning. He also learned the fear of the wealthy, that it might all be taken away from him one day, and he craved foolproof insurance. Maybe this Old Tart business was a way of skinning off Humbert's outer layer, finding out what really made him tick, where all the ghosts lay, then he would have him. No more yes sir, no sir, but equal partners.

Humbert told the new girl to come back the next night. It could have just been she was different, or Asian, but she had an originality that made him realize how much the other girl had paled. And she spoke very little, which was good, for he hated gabby women. But she provided much needed distraction when he was passing through such a nerve-racking time waiting to hear from Sade. Already he'd canceled a dinner with Hayes, the attorney general, wary that his state of mind might betray him.

He lay on his back, eyes closed, taking pleasure in

the skillful manipulation of the girl's fingers. If an erection was possible, he had no doubts this girl could do it. If his wife had some of this girl's expertise, maybe they would still be married.

But it was stupid to imagine anything could drive the Old Tart from his mind, or his sense of anxiety over the American detective. He wished he knew more about this Zarich, his strengths, his weaknesses, something he could exploit. Maybe it was possible for Sade to make discreet inquiries in New York. But if the man got even marginally close to the truth about the Old Tart, then he would have to go. All this killing did nothing for his sleep at night, but for God's sake, what alternative did he have?

The phone on the bedside table jangled against his ear, and he opened his eyes. The girl's fingers suddenly stilled, and she looked down at him questioningly.

"You want me to take it off the hook, Mr. Humbert?" she murmured throatily.

He licked at his lips, and raised himself on his elbows. His skin glistened in the light from the oil she was using. It might be Sade, so he couldn't possibly refuse the call.

"No, I'll have to take it," he muttered.

He slid away from her, picked up the receiver, and instantly recognized Sade's flat voice.

"I thought I should let you know about the problem we discussed, Mr. Humbert," Sade began.

"I've been waiting to hear from you," he grunted.

"It wasn't easy. Because of the urgency some unfortunate risks were necessary. There was no time for careful planning."

He wasn't interested; it merely sounded as if Sade was doing a promotion job for a high fee. One day something would have to be done about Sade also. The girl's fingers traced caressing lines over his back, and he shrugged her irritably aside.

"Never mind that," he said bluntly. "That's part of your executive responsibility. Has the problem been resolved or not?"

"Yes it has. There'll be no one for the American tourist to interview."

"Not ever?"

"No. Not ever."

This time his sense of relief was tempered with caution, because there were still so many dangerous intangibles. It wouldn't stop Zarich from digging, and while it didn't seem possible he could turn up anything now, there was always the chance.

"Well, at least you've made amends, Sade," he muttered surlily. "Is there anything else?"

There was a brief pause. "No, everything's under control."

He was suspicious of the hesitation. He hated to be in a position of being so reliant on Sade, and he knew if there were any other bungles the man would be reluctant to tell him.

"You're keeping an eye on the American tourist?" he asked sharply.

"Yes. That's in Roman's court. We'll even know when he blows his nose."

"Good." He thought for a moment. "You might consider some discreet inquiries in New York. It could help us to know a little more about his background."

"I'll see what can be done," replied Sade politely.

"Keep me informed."

"Of course."

He hung up and lay back on the bed, but his mind was far away from the girl now. She looked down at him with a practiced smile.

"Okay, Mr. Humbert?"

"Yes . . . yes, sure," he murmured vaguely.

He scarcely gave the Shepherd woman a thought; there was no guilt, no remorse. Right from the days of the Old Tart he'd always considered such emotions a dangerous luxury when he was fighting for survival. But the call had spoiled his concentration with the girl, and orgasm took him almost by surprise, quickly over.

"Now wasn't it nice having your rocket go off like that," murmured the girl.

He didn't answer, but closed his eyes again. Rockets, torpedoes, machine guns, they'd all gone off on that long-ago night. He made a weary dismissive gesture with his hand.

"You can go now," he said.

"Go"? she asked in surprise.

"Yes, it's over for now."

"You want me to come again?"

"You'll be contacted."

He didn't open his eyes, and there was a period of silence, then the rustling sound of her dressing followed by the door softly closing. He half smiled to himself. Rockets. He could still hear the explosions, feel the blast of hot air, see night turning starkly to day.

Taiwan Straits, April 1945

At first glance the deck of the *Awa Maru* appeared deserted to Schuman, apart from the two sailors at the ladder. But the way to the bridge was crowded with huddled groups of people, watching silently, white apprehensive faces flowering from the darkness. Gushing steam from the brightly lit funnel filled the night air. No one challenged them, they saw no weapons, and they strode as if in command, machine guns held with menacing authority.

The captain was built like a squat barrel, heavily mustached, and expressed indignation with a good command of English. Two of his junior officers watched impassively from the far side of the bridge.

"I do not understand," he protested. "You explain, please? This is hospital ship. *Awa Maru*. You have no right . . ."

Schuman prodded him with the .45. "Shut up," he snapped harshly. "Have you sent out any radio messages?"

The captain stared uncomprehendingly. "Radio message? I do not understand. Is part of our agreement with American forces that we keep radio silence. I do not . . ." He fell back several paces as Schuman prodded him again.

Schuman gestured with the pistol to one of the other officers. "Tell him to take one of my men to your radio room."

For a moment he thought the captain was going to

refuse the order, and he pressed the muzzle tightly against his throat. "Radio room," he repeated.

The captain awkwardly turned his head and spoke in rapid Japanese to one of the officers, then the man nodded, stared at Schuman, and shuffled hesitantly to the door.

"Go with him, Ferras," ordered Schuman crisply. "Make it fast. You know what to do."

Ferras nodded, wagged the machine gun threateningly at the officer, then followed him from the bridge. Schuman could see the Old Tart below, floating like a match box toy. On the deck the dark blobs of huddled onlookers stirred like wary prey. If things went wrong and Winberg had to put a fish into her, it was a long jump down to the water.

"Explain please," the captain tried timidly again. "We have done something wrong?" He gestured to the table at the back of the bridge. "Can show you agreement from American Armed Forces that *Awa Maru* can proceed to Japan with safe passage. Is guaranteed from your own command. Please, we are hospital ship. Perhaps you do not hear of agreement?"

"You're cheating, Captain," grated Schuman. "This is more than a hospital ship."

The captain looked bewildered. "Please . . ." he began.

"You have a cargo of gold bullion aboard . . . appropriated from the occupied countries by your forces, and you're taking it back to Japan. You're risking the life of everyone on board your ship, Captain."

"No, no, is not true," the captain protested. "This only hospital ship."

Schuman put the muzzle of the .45 back at his throat. "Suit yourself, Captain. I can blow your head off, and deal with one of the other officers if you don't want to cooperate."

For a short time no one spoke. The other Japanese officer stepped forward, and Donlett swiftly covered him. Schuman hoped to Christ the captain was only bluffing. Yaphank would sell his own grandmother, but he wouldn't lie about a thing like this.

"Put a bullet into the sonofabitch," said Martin hoarsely. "We'll deal with this other monkey."

"Think of your ship, Captain," scowled Schuman. "We get the gold, or you all go to the bottom." He jerked his head in the direction of the Old Tart. "I've got men down there just waiting for the order to put a torpedo into your ship."

The Japanese captain tried to fend off the muzzle with his hand, but Schuman only pushed harder.

"Can then proceed to . . . to Japan?" the captain gasped.

Schuman eased off the pressure. "Yes, once we've got the gold loaded on my ship. You broke the agreement, Captain."

"Please, I have to obey orders too."

Schuman nodded, and slowly lowered the gun back to his side. The captain staggered back against the glass of the bridge, and teetered for a second as if about to fall, then he grasped at the railing and held himself upright.

The other Japanese officer stepped back on the bridge, trailed by Ferras.

"Everything go okay?" asked Schuman.

"Yeah, I gave it a real working over," Ferras reported. "They won't be able to use that radio again."

Schuman gave a grunt of satisfaction, and returned his attention to the captain. "Detail a party from your crew, Captain. Two of my men go along to supervise. Put a boat over the side, and ferry the gold across to my ship, and keep going for as long as it takes." He waved the .45 aggressively in the captain's face. "Anything goes wrong, any tricks, and your ship goes to the bottom of the Taiwan Straits," he threatened. "Understood?"

The captain tentatively nodded his head, paused to recover his breath, then began to issue a stream of orders to the other officers.

"I hope he's telling 'em the right things," muttered Donlett uneasily. "I don't trust any of these monkeys."

"They won't try anything," said Schuman confidently. "This is an old bucket. We put a couple of fish into her and she'll go down like a cardboard box. He knows that."

"Then he won't be surprised," growled Donlett.

"You and Halmstead go with the officers," directed Schuman. "Don't take your eyes off 'em." He tapped the submachine gun nestled in Donlett's arms. "Anyone tries anything, don't be afraid to use that. They think we're operating an official mission, so let 'em keep thinking that. They're not going to risk being sunk."

"Gotcha," said Donlett. He leaned back and rapped Halmstead on the arm. "Come on, Ham, let's go and watch these monkeys making us into millionaires."

It took three hours, but during that time no one on the bridge spoke. Schuman and Ferras were silently watchful, while the Japanese captain kept his face averted, staring out to the bow of the ship, perhaps with thoughts of hara-kari on his mind.

Schuman impatiently stalked the bridge, occasionally pausing at the railing to glance down at the small boat plying backward and forward between the freighter and the Old Tart, but his mind was already surging into the future with the possibilities of what life could mean to him with all that wealth. It was another world after his family's two-bit existence, the constant haggling, the insecure quarrels, the frustration, the old man's fury when his mother paid too much for a cut of beef. Fuck all of them, no way was he going back to that. But he'd break away from Yaphank. "More" was the only word Yaphank understood, more of everything, and you could never be sure Carl wasn't cooking up some scheme to cheat you out of your share. But he had Yaphank by the balls this time, because he was the one who had the gold.

The captain edged away as he paced restlessly to the front of the bridge. Even the watchers scattered around the deck were no longer visible, but had merged with the shadows. He had no idea of the number on board, but doubtless there were many packed below, wondering what the hell was going on. Then the small boat disappeared, and from somewhere along the hull came the rasping sound of a winch. Below he could see the Old Tart maneuvering back close to the freighter, and even from up on the bridge he could see she was low in the water. He swore softly. Maybe he hadn't calculated on the weight of the gold, but if they ran into any bad weather on the return trip it could be a problem.

Donlett's head appeared through the door, a grin almost splitting his face in two.

"Okay, it's all aboard, skipper."

"Any problems?"

"Smooth as silk. Jesus Christ, I've never seen anything like it. All that gold. We're millionaires, fucking millionaires."

Schuman nodded briskly to Ferras. "Okay, let's get the hell out of here." He tapped the captain on the shoulder with the gun, but the man ignored him. "It's all yours, captain," he said mockingly.

The Japanese stood stiffly to attention as if turned to stone, eyes fixedly out to sea, hands tightly gripping the railing. Schuman didn't wait for an answer, but turned away with a shrug. He knew the captain was covering for his own high command, but that was his risk, even if it wouldn't bother him much longer.

But he was disturbed when they were all finally back on board their own boat, maybe Yaphank and the rest were almost delirious with joy, yet the Old Tart was even lower in the water than he had first realized, wallowing in a growing swell like an old duck. It was useless trying to draw it to anyone's attention for now—Yaphank was laughing with a sound close to hysteria, and Winberg was dancing around the cockpit as if he couldn't control his limbs.

"Jay, it's unbelievable," he chortled. "Christ, unbelievable, fucking unbelievable. You've gotta come and look below. We've got it stacked everywhere around the engine room. For Chrissake, the Old Tart's a bloody floating Fort Knox." He seized Schuman's arm. "Just take a look, Jay, for Chrissake, just take a look."

He angrily broke the ensign's grip, and pushed him fiercely to the other side of the cockpit. He liked the idea of being rich the same as all of them, but the job wasn't finished yet. The *Awa Maru* made it back to Japan, and the only thing they'd be looking forward to was a court martial. He stabbed a finger toward the horizon, where a faint whisp of gray was beginning to separate sea and sky. Even as they backed off from the Japanese ship the muffled thump of her engines gathering power again came clearly across the water.

"You stupid fuckers," he roared. "Get back to your posts. It'll be light soon. You want the *Awa Maru* back in Japan? The only money you'll be spending then will be your jail allowance." He sprang to the front of the cockpit. "You crazy sonofabitches. Berger . . . Berger," he bawled. "Where's the torpedo guys? Get their eyes off that gold and back at their posts."

Winberg looked momentarily startled, then quickly grasped Schuman's urgency. "Jesus I'm sorry, Jay, I'm sorry," he apologized. He tried to raise his voice to equal Schuman. "Torpedo men, torpedo men, on deck on the double."

The gap between the ships began to widen as the Awa Maru got under way.

"Give her all four fish," Schuman shouted. "One at the bow, two amidships, and one at the stern. I want her to go down fast."

The torpedo men were scrambling along the deck, stumbling in their haste. He could see Donlett groping forward to the machine gun as if drunk. He gunned her to half-power, and she lifted like a sluggish snail as he swept around in a wide circle away from the freighter. "Stand by torpedoes," he bellowed. He glanced furiously about the cockpit. Where the hell was Berger? For Chrissake, they all knew what had to be done, they'd talked about it often enough. "Berger," he screamed.

The bulk of the quartermaster emerged from the chart house, instantly formal. Yaphank crouched to the side, a bewildered expression on his face.

"Here sir," came Berger's Midwestern drawl.

"Get down there and make sure those guys know what they're doing. They're all goddamn gold drunk. Tell 'em they'll be jail birds if they foul this up."

The quartermaster lumbered out of the cockpit as the Old Tart came around at the apex of the turning circle. Already the *Awa Maru* was increasing speed, trailing white foam, but still well within range. Schuman lined up on the bow of the freighter.

"By Christ I'll throw those sonofabitches overboard if

they haven't armed the torpedoes," he said, gritting his teeth.

"It's been done, Jay," Winberg hastily assured him.

"Fire one," he shouted.

"Fire one," Winberg repeated.

He heard the splash of the torpedo hitting the water, and altered his alignment.

"Fire two."

"Fire two."

He realigned. "Fire three."

"Fire three."

He realigned for the last fish. "Fire four."

"Fire four."

Maybe he was caught by the gold fever himself, marring his judgment, because he ran in too close, and even as he swung hard away he saw Winberg's hand raised in alarm. He was almost deafened by the explosions, the four of them rolling together like succeeding claps of thunder, then the night sky turned to day with brilliant flashes of white and yellow and red, all overhung with a billowing cloud of smoke expanding upward at incredible speed. Then he felt heat as if from a blast furnace rush over his face. He couldn't even see the freighter now, but he was feverishly pushing the Old Tart up to top speed to correct his mistake, and widen the gap from the doomed ship. Debris came down like rain, and they all ducked instinctively, conscious of the ping of hot metal ricochetting off the deck. Then they were finally clear, and when they raised their heads from cover she was gone, disintegrated, and in the gloom there was only a large oil slick dotted with pieces of bobbing flotsam, like a thick soup.

"Jesus," muttered Yaphank shakily.

"Goddamn," whispered the ensign.

They couldn't quite believe what they'd done.

"Now you're not only rich . . . you're safely rich," added Schuman. He cut the speed to dead slow while he ran through the slick, but he knew from the force of the explosions there'd be no survivors to finish off. It would have been impossible for anyone to get away when she went down so fast. Even the crew's attack of gold fever was subdued by the sudden impact of all they'd killed. He shrugged. It'd pass. In the years to come when they were wallowing in luxury, no one would give a thought for the Japs at the bottom of the Taiwan Straits. They were, as Yaphank said, the enemy.

The strip of gray to the east was widening to warn of approaching dawn, and he wanted to be far away before the sun rose.

"Come on Mike, let's get the hell out of here," he muttered. "We've got a long way to go."

It wasn't until daylight that they realized Bart Donlett was gone. There was blood on the deck near the forward machine gun, and his dog tag, as if in some way whatever had hit him had wrenched it from his neck. They ran back a few miles, but there was no sign of him, and it was too dangerous to stay around. No one said anything, but it showed in their faces that they figured there was one less to split with now.

Humbert opened his eyes and stared blankly at the ceiling for a short time, until he realized he must have fallen asleep. He propped himself awkwardly on his elbows and glanced blearily about the room, trying to remember if he'd told the girl to go, or if she was in another part of the house. Then he recalled the rocket going off, shivered in his nakedness, and wearily pulled the bed covers up over his body. At times like this he felt old, tired, even resigned, but he was sure, come the morning, he would be full of fight again. These fresh, vivid memories of the Old Tart would renew his spirit. He hadn't come this far, achieved so much, to let it run through his fingers like sand. He knew now that it was inevitable he would have to do something about Zarich. But then he'd killed so many that night on the Taiwan Straits, did another few matter?

It was a pleasant dinner at Harry's home in the seaside suburb of Cronulla, even if Zarich's hunger for Cassie had such an insatiable edge any interlude made him horny again. It was like being in love for the first time, back to the teenage crush with the young girl on the neighboring farm across from his aunt. And unbelievably almost as difficult to control as if the intervening years had taught him nothing.

It was stupid, disconcerting, and he knew he was going to have to put it back in perspective. Sometime. The Old Tart was why he was in Australia, nothing was more important than satisfying the old hound dog urge, and yet, and yet. As he'd confessed to Harry, she was something else again. He knew his eyes rarely left her—Harry and his wife Helen would have to be blind not to notice—but they made no comment.

Helen was charming, with dark Greek looks, and overweight like her husband. "My favorite wog," Harry called her affectionately, but there was no mistaking the bond. They had a set pattern of banter between them, for she talked incessantly, avid for any information about America. He'd never been to Disneyland, and that stunned her. An American who had never been to Disneyland seemed inconceivable, but no crook had ever left a scent to follow in that direction, and such an explanation baffled her even more. There were two boys, ten and eight, who formally shook hands, then listened fascinated to his American tales before being dispatched protesting to bed. He chatted, he answered questions, but at times the conversation seemed an indecipherable buzz, then he smiled at Cassie and she smiled back with knowing intimacy.

Later he had time alone over a beer with Harry, while Helen and Cassie talked clothes in the bedroom.

"You seem kinda thunderstruck," commented Harry drily.

"Does it show?"

"Shit, are you kiddin', mate. Do you know anything about her?"

"Only what I know from sleeping with her. Sometimes that can be the best dossier you'll ever get."

"Is gathering information what you're doing?"

Zarich shrugged. He would have had no trouble answering yes to that question only a few days ago, but now he felt slightly foolish. "Maybe. No—for Chrissake, I don't know. I'm looking after her, Harry. Okay, maybe I'm falling in love with her. She needs someone badly."

"That's okay, it's your business, Ed. But there's still the Old Tart."

"Don't worry, that comes first, Harry," replied Zarich vehemently. The vehemence seemed more for himself than Markby. "But she is part of the pattern, Harry. She only knows what her grandmother passed on from the letter, but I figure the bastards are trying to kill her just to play it safe. That's the way they operate." He paused. "How did you go with Roman?"

"Well, he seemed convinced." He shook his head. "Jes', I'm backing you, Ed, but he'll be mad as hell if he finds out."

"You told him about Cassie?"

"That I had to tell him. It'd be too easy for him to check the Purple Pussycat."

"How far did you take it?"

"I said she'd gone into smoke. That we're not too sure what she knows, but her grandmother had obviously confided in her. That's what we're supposed to be doin' now, trying to find her again."

"Good man," said Zarich appreciatively.

"I just hope you're right about the leak coming from his office."

"It's worth trying, Harry. What about Darwin?"

"You're on a TAA morning flight, under the name of Wilson." He grinned. "Mr. and Mrs. Wilson."

"That's terrific, Harry." He hesitated with a sense of guilt he might have put Harry's head on the chopping block with Roman. "Listen, when I get back from Darwin why don't we both go to Roman. Lay it out for him, why we had to play it this way. If someone is bugging his office, then he has to know for Chrissake."

"Yeah, well let's see if you turn up anything in Darwin first," said Markby doubtfully. "I'll pick you up around eight in the morning and take you to the airport. I don't think we should risk any taxis."

"Did you have a chance to check those old newspaper files?"

"Yeah." Harry put his beer aside, opened the case, and took out several photostats of newspaper pages. "I had copies made, Ed. I had a look through, but I'm fucked if they told me anything."

Zarich spent a few minutes examining the copies. The headlines were mostly to do with the war in Europe. In the Pacific there was fighting on Bouganville. A tank battle in Mandalay. Marines mopping up on Iwo Jima. Heavy Japanese casualties in raids on Tokyo. But nothing that offered any connection to the Old Tart. Maybe they needed more detailed scrutiny, but it was disappointing.

"It was just an idea," he murmured pensively. "But you're right, nothing really connects."

"Well, anything's worth trying," said Markby. He put them back in his case. "We'll have another look at them when you get back." He reflected a moment. "I hope you've got some light clothes, it'll be pretty warm in Darwin."

"Then I'll have to buy some gear," said Zarich. He could almost hear Beuso screaming about his expense account. Through the door came the sound of the two women returning from the bedroom.

"This Dennis Charlton you'll be seeing in Darwin, Ed. I know him from way back. If there's a way to dig out anything on the Old Tart, then he'll find it for you. He's a good bloke, you can trust him with your life."

"I've already met one Australian like that," he said warmly.

Markby shuffled his feet about in embarrassment. "Yeah . . . well there's more than one of us, Ed," he muttered.

It was a long flight to Darwin, but it could have continued on to the moon the way Cassie sat close to him, fingers interlocked, head down on his shoulder. He was already figuring out a way for her to return to the States with him when it came time to leave. Maybe when he should have been concentrating solely on the Old Tart it was a bad tactic to take her to Darwin with him, but what the hell could he do? There was only death for her if she stayed alone in Sydney.

He was intrigued by the vast empty stretches of Australia passing below, so much in contrast to flying across most of the States, which was sprinkled liberally with cities and small towns. He had the same feeling as flying out to Australia over vast tracts of unmarked ocean. The 727 banked and the wing pointed up to a dazzling blue sky. Cassie stirred beside him, then looked out the window, blinking in the vivid light. She looked marvelous in the red slacks and white lace blouse, and Zarich's beige tropical clothes looked innocuous in comparison.

"I don't know anything about you," he murmured. "You come into my life and hit me like a tornado, but I don't know anything about you."

"As much as I know about you," she countered.

"I'm a New York cop, far from home."

"What does a New York cop mean?"

"It means long hours, low pay, sometimes being shot at, sometimes abused by the public, sometimes praised, most times like you're lost in a jungle full of wild animals."

"Sounds like a fun time. Why do it?"

He couldn't answer that question. Rhonda asked him often enough. *I crave the hunt. I enjoy the kill at the end.*

"Like you said, it's a fun time," he replied instead. "Is the Purple Pussycat a fun time?"

"You have to ask?" she said with a grimace.

"Are you going to get out like your grandmother wanted?"

"She's not around to help now. I needed her."

"I'm here now."

"Then I'll get out. You want it, then I'm out," she declared stoutly.

"There's a man?" he asked tentatively.

She laughed with a bitter inflexion. "There's always a man, darling. There was a creep my mother was living with who tried so hard to screw me when I was twelve I was too scared to go home. There was another jerk who offered to feed me heroin if I'd go on the street for him—if I really loved him." She paused, and uttered the same laugh. "I'm about surviving, Ed. Staying afloat." He thought of Ella. "I have a nasty habit of attaching myself to bloodsuckers."

"I'm different."

"I'll say you are, lover. You're more real than anything I've ever met. A man. Someone to love like I haven't loved before."

"I'm glad," he said simply.

"Don't tell me a guy like you hasn't got a woman somewhere?"

"Not anymore. Some women don't like being tied in with a cop. At least not the ones I meet. The last one divorced me."

She leaned across and nuzzled him with her face. "Then I'm going to change all that, lover," she whispered.

His memory had to go back again to the time with the girl on the farm to recall such a glow in his belly. He talked to her as if he hadn't opened up in a long time, of things he'd half forgotten himself. His dead parents, the dutiful aunt barren of affection, the loneliness, the wanting to belong. If he painted a biased portrait with only a suggestion of the hunter, it was because he didn't want anything to disturb what was going between them. But she offered little more background about herself, and he didn't question her. When the seatbelt lights blinked on, and Darwin appeared below ringed by brilliant blue water, he still didn't know a great deal about her. Not that it mattered.

It was noon by the time they got their luggage. Dennis Charlton was standing by the airport exit, and as soon as he saw Zarich and Cassie he stepped forward, hand outstretched. A large man, maybe up to six foot four or so, he was dressed in a casual blue shirt and white shorts. His body had the shape of a giant pear, small head on top and matchstick legs defying the improbability of supporting the weight. He was a two-color combination of sun-tanned skin and snow white hair, eyebrows, and bushy mustache. Pouched brown eyes, large nose, and drooping facial lines mournful in repose, but when he smiled there was a magical conversion to sparkling amicability. He looked about seventy.

"From everything Harry Markby told me you have to be Ed Wilson," he declared in a gritty voice. He glanced quickly about the airport. "Although I guess Ed Zarich's okay here."

The large hand was freckled, and grassed with white

hair. Zarich accepted the handshake with a grin. "Sure, I guess Zarich's okay here. You're Dennis Charlton."

"That's right, Chooka Charlton. Everyone calls me Chooka, so you may as well." His eyes switched appreciatively to Cassie. "Harry told me to watch for a beautiful young blond girl, so I knew it was you."

"Well thank you," Cassie simpered.

"This is Cassie Rehfield, Chooka," introduced Zarich.

Chooka grasped enthusiastically at her hand. "Pleased to meetcha, Cassie," he said with a broad grin. He quickly picked up her suitcase, and nodded to the exit door. "C'mon, let's get out of this. I gotta car waiting outside."

Outside the sun threw a pleasant dry heat from a cloudless sky, and Zarich quickly shed his jacket.

"You're lucky it's not the wet season," smirked Chooka. "That's when it turns into a steam bath up here, and you'd really sweat, m'boy." He put their luggage into the back of a battered, aged utility truck, then they all crammed into the cabin, Cassie in the middle, but she bore the squeeze with stoic calm. For the moment she seemed to have left all her fear back in Sydney.

The engine vibrated as if threatening to tear itself loose from its mountings, but Chooka drove carefully, as if handling a frail, elderly parent.

"Harry didn't tell me too much," he declared above the racket of the truck. "Don't even know how long you're supposed to be stayin'."

"We're not too sure about that ourselves," said Zarich.

"I was goin' to book you into a motel and there's plenty of good ones around, but then Harry made it clear you didn't exactly want a lot of publicity about visitin' here." He paused to check the road, then turned cautiously out of the airport. "I guess it's up to you, Ed, but I reckoned it might be best if I put you up at my place . . . at least for tonight." He slowed for an intersection, and a huge multiwheeled stock transport rumbled past, blasting its horn. Chooka ignored it, and jerked his thumb to the left. "I can take you that way back inta the city, or out the other way to my house. It's quiet out there, and no one'll know you're around."

Zarich glanced at Cassie, and she shrugged the decision to him.

"If it's okay, then your place sounds the best idea to me," said Zarich. "As long as it's no trouble."

"Trouble," Chooka snorted. "No bloody trouble at all. Not if it's for friends of young Harry."

He turned right at the intersection, and drove hugging to the side of the road, heedless of the constant whoosh of passing traffic. But he refused to be deterred from conversation by the clatter of the truck.

"How is young Harry?" asked Chooka. "Still a smart city cop?"

"Well, he looks that way to me."

"Always said Harry'd do well. Me and his old man were mates all our lives until he died a few years ago. I didn't marry myself." He grinned at Cassie. "Although blimey, if someone like you had been around, it would have been hard to resist, Cassie. Anyhow, I took an interest in Harry. I reckon I was the one who talked him into joining the force although at the time I was hopin' it'd be up here in Darwin." He shrugged. "You can breathe up here, not like in Sydney."

Zarich nodded absently, glancing around at the green countryside. Water lay everywhere, and it reminded him of summertime in New Orleans.

"We had some rain here a few days ago. Last of the wet season I'd say." He had the knack of pitching his voice so it could be heard above the engine. "You're a Yank, aren't you, Ed. Harry tells me from New York."

"That's right, Chooka."

"Never been there. Been most places, but not New York. We get Yank tourists comin' through here all the time now, and I got to know some Yanks when they were stationed here during the war."

"Maybe you knew the one I'm trying to trace."

Chooka shook his head doubtfully. "You're talkin' forty years ago, Ed, and there was a lot of you blokes around then. I've forgotten most of 'em."

"Well, I'll show you a few things later, and see if they mean anything to you."

"Sure, sure, only too willing to help. Harry told me

you were trying to track down the movements of some PT boat operating outa Darwin durin' the war."

"Something like that."

"That's a toughie. It might be on the port records. I spoke to a woman friend of mine in the Port of Darwin office called Judy Werrin. She's willing to let you glance over the old records if it's any use."

Zarich's throat was growing tired from competing with the engine. He'd much rather have left this until they were at the house, but it was obvious the old policeman could scarcely restrain his enthusiasm from being involved in a case again.

"That's great, and thanks, Chooka."

"And I might be able to help in another way."

"How do you mean?"

"Well I've been around here all my life, and right through the war when lots of people were hightailing south after Darwin was bombed. I stayed on duty, and I kept my own records."

Zarich looked at him curiously, but the old cop didn't elaborate. They rapidly left suburban Darwin behind, and the ocean appeared again over to the left. "My place is up near Lee Point," said Chooka. "It's not far outa town."

The road and sea gradually converged, then Chooka slowed, turned right, cautiously negotiated a flooded drain, then pulled into the side of a neat white bungalow set amidst the trees.

"Home sweet home," he grinned. "It ain't the Royal Palace, but it's comfortable, and I like it."

He took the cases from the truck, ignoring Zarich's attempt to help, and led them toward the house. The sound of clucking chickens came from the bottom of the yard, where a section of ground had been wired off to form a pen. Chooka gestured to the pen with one of the cases, and laughed. "That's where I got me nickname, Ed. It's a long time hobby of mine. We call chickens chooks over here. Reckon I kept the Darwin police force in eggs for twenty years."

They followed him into the house, and he put the suitcases down on the living room floor. It was a pleasant room, cane furniture, bare boards with colorful rugs scat-

tered about, and a large window looking out to sea. A
ceiling fan did little but stir the warm air. Cassie wandered across to the window, and Chooka's voice dropped
to a confidential whisper as he pointed Zarich to one of the
doors leading off the room.

"I guess you and Cassie are in together, Ed?" he
asked quietly. "I mean, it makes no difference to me, if
you're goin' to sleep together you may as well be comfortable, and I know that's the way it is with you young'uns
these days."

"Yeah, sure, Chooka," murmured Zarich. Funny, he
was only thirty-two yet he rarely thought of himself as still
young. Maybe what he had with Cassie had softened some
of the cynical lines.

They both showered while Chooka made some king-
sized sandwiches, then all three sat down at the small
table by the window with the inevitable beer. The sea
sparkled white in the bright sunlight, and the far-off trees
shimmered in a misty haze.

"I dunno how you're runnin' for time, Ed," muttered
Chooka between mouthfuls of beer and sandwich. "But if
you wanted you could go and look at those records this
evening."

Zarich looked questioningly at Cassie. "Sounds like a
good idea. How do you feel, Cassie?"

"Do you want me to come with you?"

"It might be better if you look on your own, Ed,"
interrupted Chooka. "Attract less attention." His eyebrows
contracted in an expression of comic lechery. "Don't worry
about Cassie. I'll drop you off at the Port of Darwin office,
then take her on a tour of the town. I tell you, by the time
I'm through, you'll be bloody lucky if she wants anything
more to do with you, Ed."

Cassie laughed, and patted Chooka's hand. "Don't
tempt me, Chooka."

"We'll see, we'll see," smirked Chooka. He turned to
Zarich. "After you've finished at the office, then you can
take a look at my records. Dunno if it'll be any help, but
you might find it interesting."

"You mentioned that before, Chooka. What sort of
records?"

Chooka grinned mysteriously, and made a dismissive gesture of his hand.

"No, I'm not sayin' for now. Let's wait until after."

"Well, are there any other old timers I could talk to?" asked Zarich. "Guys like yourself who were here during the war?"

"Could be," mused Chooka. "We've gotta sort of club. There's a few old Navy blokes there who were stationed in Darwin during the war. I'll see what I can arrange for you." He shook his head. "But don't expect any miracles, Ed. Some of the blokes are gettin' on a bit." His eyes sparkled. "Not in the prime of life like me."

Zarich had learned his lesson with Harry, and made no attempt to match Chooka's beer consumption. He waited patiently until the old man had finished prattling of Darwin, Chinese cooking, tracking aborigines in the old days, the bombing of Darwin, of cops and women and travels through Southeast Asia. Then he brought out the photograph of the Old Tart crew, and gave him a brief summary of what it was all about.

Chooka slipped on a pair of worn glasses, and spent a long time poring over the photograph. The overhead fan did little to alleviate the rising heat of the day. Zarich could feel sweat forming on his skin, and Cassie lounged on the cane settee, using a newspaper as a fan.

"Nope," murmured Chooka finally. "Don't recognize anybody. I'm sorry, Ed, maybe it's too long ago, but they're just faces to me. Dead faces, from what you tell me."

Zarich shrugged. He was resigned to disappointment by now. "Well, perhaps I'll get a lead from the Port files."

"Here's hoping." He tapped Zarich's beer can with his own. "Finish your beer, and we'll get going."

Chooka dropped him outside the Port Authority on Harry Chan Avenue, promised to be back in an hour, then with Cassie at his side drove off toward the port area. Zarich felt quite relaxed about leaving her with the bluff ex-cop. Despite the old man's banter, he sensed Harry was right—you could trust him with your life.

Judy Werrin was an uncut flower left too long in the garden, the bloom long gone from her gaunt, primly dressed frame, and there must have been a foul-up in the retirement files, for she looked about the same age as Chooka. But her faded eyes behind the frameless spectacles softened at the mention of Chooka's name, and Zarich wondered if cooperation was part of a campaign to undermine the ex-policeman's bachelorhood.

She put him in an isolated small room where he could pore over the old files undisturbed. The records on the PT 524 were surprisingly easy to locate, departure dates, arrival dates. He noted them all down on the chance some pattern might emerge. But it was all so inconclusive. Perhaps Harry had put his finger on it; the Old Tart was never sunk. Whatever Schuman's screwball idea had been about getting rich, it had come off, and the crew were living the lives of millionaires somewhere in the world. Or maybe in Australia, and had formed some sort of assassination club to protect the secret of the Old Tart. The last letter Donlett wrote to his wife had been on the fifteenth of March. The final departure date of the Old Tart was noted down as the twenty-fifth of March. The date had to mean something. Yet if the caper with the Old Tart had come off, how did Donlett miss out of his cut, and finish up in a New York hospital forty years later? He thought about it until his head ached, then pocketed his notes, thanked Judy Werrin for her help, and assured her he'd tell dear Chooka how much assistance she'd been. He knew he couldn't stall off calling Beuso much longer.

He stepped out on to the street to the gargled sound of a horn as Chooka's truck pulled up to the curb. The old man's grin was as bright as the sunlight, but Cassie was slumped in the seat as if about to evaporate. He climbed aboard, and Chooka accelerated down the road with his usual snail-like caution. Cassie offered a wan smile of greeting, and when he squeezed her hand, wet suction fused their skin.

"I've been tryin' to persuade Cassie to clear out to Sydney with me," chuckled Chooka. "But she wasn't havin' any. You must have somethin' I ain't got, Ed." He took in Zarich's weary expression of fatigue. "Looks like you didn't have much luck?"

"Oh, the records are there all right, Chooka, but I

don't know if they tell me anything. I'll think about them for a while, and see if the last departure date of the Old Tart helps me or not."

Chooka leaned across and slapped him on the knee. "What you need is a coupla beers, Ed. You and Cassie. That'll make you feel like human beings again."

For once Zarich was in full agreement. A couple of beers, and maybe twenty hours' sleep.

"Then you get to look at my records," said Chooka. "They ain't got a thing in common with what you've just seen, but well"—he shrugged—"let's see."

Zarich nodded. He was curious after Chooka's mysterious buildup. "Incidentally, Judy Werrin sends her love. She said to tell you she'd be out at your place same time tomorrow night," he murmured innocently.

The white eyebrows arched into a multifurrowed brow, and the truck almost careered to the wrong side of the road before Chooka brought it under control. "What?" he roared.

"She was talking about you asking her to move in."

"Shit . . . in the pig's bloody ear," he exclaimed.

Cassie placed an anxious hand on the steering wheel as his head slewed about the cabin until he saw Zarich's teasing grin.

"Jes', don't give me a scare like that, Ed." Then he laughed, and the sound reverberated in the cabin. "Judy's a good sort, but jes', she ain't moving in with me. Not bloomin' likely."

"I thought you'd make a nice couple," said Zarich mockingly.

Chooka contented himself with a snort of derision. But Zarich must have hit a tender spot, for he scarcely broke the silence until they were back at the house.

It was actually a small museum Chooka had created in a large room at the rear of the house. He stood aside at the door, and proudly ushered them inside. The collection was set up on shelves along each wall, leaving a narrow viewing corridor.

"Not that many people know about it," he confessed. "Some of the blokes at the club reckon I'm crazy, that I could make myself a nice packet if I opened it up to the

tourists. I let a few through, but not many." He motioned
them impatiently ahead. "I suppose they're right, but I
don't like the thought of all those gawkers clumping through
my house, takin' photographs, askin' fool questions. It's a
hobby for me, same as the chooks outside. Not that I add
much to it these days, 'cause it's all to do with the war."
He moved to one of the shelves, and picked up a rusty
army pistol. "I bought this a coupla months ago from a
buffalo shooter who found it out near Koolpinyah. Haven't
had a chance to clean it up yet." He pointed to the wheel
of a plane. "A bloke brought this to me about a year ago
from Finke Bay. Some of the planes just disappeared like
your PT boat, and now and then bits and pieces wash up
outa the sea." He gestured expansively around the collection. "But there it is, Ed. My record of wartime Darwin."

It was an incredible array of military paraphernalia,
rifles, bayonets, bombs, bomb fragments, assorted small
weapons, remnants of uniforms, American, Australian,
Dutch, Indonesian, English. Pinned to boards were rows
of various Army, Navy, and Air Force insignias. Place of
honor was given to a wing section from a Japanese bomber,
hung from the ceiling by a cobweb of wires. Items of
Japanese flying gear, instruments from downed planes,
and a gallery of faded photographs of Darwin during wartime, bomb-damaged buildings, fighter planes taking off,
smiling faces of Air Force crews, anti-aircraft guns in
action at East Point, crashed aircraft, dead bodies.

"About two hundred people died in that first air raid
in '42," he informed them. "The Japs came over about sixty
more times after that." He gently urged them along the
corridor. "There's some photographs of PT boats like the
Old Tart, Ed." He shook his head. "With a nickname like
that it's a wonder I don't remember her."

Zarich moved slowly, peering at the photographs,
handling the pieces. Cassie was ahead of him, turning
over a collection of servicemen's hats, again of all branches
and countries.

"Maybe there's nothin' here," cautioned Chooka. "But
I was kinda hoping something might start the ball rolling
for you. You know, give you an idea."

"How does that look?" asked Cassie.

She had a faded Australian Air Force cap perched cockily on her head.

"Anything would look good on you, Cassie," commented Chooka.

Zarich picked up a dirt-stained American Naval officer's cap, and held it out to her. "Maybe this is more your style," he suggested.

She turned quickly, knocking it from his hand to the floor.

"That's somethin' I only got recently," said Chooka. "I reckon it'd be about a year since I bought it. I checked it out, and it is an American Navy ensign's cap from the war. Not in bad condition either."

The cap had dropped bottom up, and as Zarich bent to retrieve it he seemed to freeze in a crouched position. Chooka and Cassie stared at him wonderingly.

"What's the matter, Ed?" asked Cassie.

He didn't answer, but picked up the cap, strode rapidly to the window at the end of the room, and held it up to the bright sunlight. He couldn't quite believe what he was seeing.

"Have you ever looked just above the lining inside this cap, Chooka?" he asked tersely.

Chooka pushed past Cassie toward him. "In the lining?"

Zarich tilted it for Chooka, as he fumbled for his spectacles.

"Yes, take a look."

"Well, I just had it checked out for rank. I didn't pay much attention to the inside." He took the cap from Zarich's hands, and put it closer to the window. "Where . . . what am I lookin' for, Ed?"

Zarich reached over and pointed inside the cap. He could see his fingers visibly trembling with expectation. "There, just to the side. It's in some sort of marking ink."

Chooka peered silently at the cap for a time. "Jes'," he whispered suddenly.

"Read it out, Chooka."

"Old Tart. For crying out loud, the words are 'Old Tart.' It's bloody faint, but still readable, and the letters following it are PT five two four." He lowered it, and stared at Zarich. "Crikey, this cap must have belonged to one of the crew of the Old Tart."

Zarich swiftly retrieved the cap, and grinned triumphantly at Cassie. "For Chrissake, Harry won't believe this." He had a feeling close to exultation. Christ, what a break. "Where the hell did you get this from, Chooka?"

The startled expression remained on his face. "Like . . . like I said, about a year ago," he stuttered. "A black fella brought it in, and I bought it from him."

"Did he tell you where he found it?"

"Not exactly. I wasn't particularly interested, but I think he said it was somewhere up along the South Alligator River."

Zarich turned the cap carefully in his hand. Cassie was staring at him wide-eyed, and he could feel the upsurge of his pulse. Jesus, was he holding the key to the Old Tart right in his hand?

"It can't have been out in the open, Chooka, not to be in this condition after forty years?"

"I honestly don't know, Ed. I reckon I didn't ask too many questions. I thought he may have been lying at the time, 'cause I couldn't for the life of me see how an American Naval cap could be up there. The place is alive with crocs. You'd be lucky to get in there during the wet season."

"You remember the man? Could we get in touch with him?"

"Sure, if he's still at the same place. It was an aborigine called Tom Kalangi. He comes from a place called Jabiru, out near Arnhem Land, and he was working at the Ranger uranium mine at the time. He doesn't come into Darwin very much, matter of fact I ain't seen him since I bought the cap." He scratched absently at his white hair. "Starve the lizards, that's bloody incredible. Old Tart. I guess with my eyes and all I just never noticed." He shrugged. "Anyhow, it wouldn't have meant anything to me then."

"How quickly could we see this Kalangi, Chooka?"

Chooka propped his wide buttocks against the plane wheel, and considered for a moment.

"Well, I don't see why not tomorrow morning. I

mean, I can't guarantee he's still at Jabiru, but a phone call could answer that. Then Jabiru's about, oh . . . two hundred and fifty kilometers from Darwin."

Cassie took the cap from Zarich, and held it to the light to see for herself.

"Could we fly out there?" asked Zarich.

"Sure, if that's what you want, Ed. It's easy enough to hire a plane, but it'll cost you."

"Don't worry about that," he said quickly. Beuso would scream his head off, but he was too far away to hear.

"I s'pose it could have got there before the Old Tart disappeared." mused Chooka. "They could have been patrolling around there, and it got blown overboard." He shrugged apologetically. "I'm just thinking out loud, Ed."

Zarich didn't want to consider it a possibility. The scent was running again, filling his nostrils like sweet perfume. "I think we should go," he declared positively. "That doesn't explain the good condition of the hat, Chooka. Could you make the flight arrangements for me?"

"Nothin' to it. You want me along?"

"Of course. You know this Kalangi."

"And Cassie?"

"I've got a stake in this too, darling," she cut in quickly. "I want to find out what happened as much as you do. I'd love to come."

"It might be pretty rough out there," warned Chooka.

"I still want to come. I do, Ed. I feel safer when I'm around you."

Zarich smiled agreement, and turned his attention to the cap again. He suddenly recalled there was an ensign in the Old Tart photograph. He gestured with the cap to Chooka. "Mind if I keep this for a while?"

"Sure. You'll need to take it to Jabiru anyway."

He nodded, then brushed past Chooka, and returned swiftly to the living room. In his excitement he was scarcely aware of his brusque manners. He was sure the cap was the first direct tangible link to the Old Tart, he had no idea what it meant, but it had to lead him somewhere. He took out the photograph, placed it down on the table beside the cap, then moved his eyes rapidly along the line of smiling faces, checking off the names. Ferras, Berger, Donlett, Schuman the captain, and alongside him the chubby-faced Ensign Winberg. Surely it had to be his cap. He lifted the picture, and stared intently at the smiling youthful face. "Jesus, tell me, tell me," he whispered. "Tell me all you know about the Old Tart?"

He heard the others entering the room behind him, but ignored them.

"I'll make that call to Jabiru to see if Kalangi's still there, Ed," Chooka volunteered. "Then if he is there I know a coupla charter blokes who'll take us out."

"Fine, Chooka, fine," he muttered, without turning. He wondered if he should call Harry about this, then decided it would be better if he waited until he spoke to the aborigine. Cassie came up beside him, and stood close, one hand draped intimately on his shoulder.

"I'm glad for you, darling," she whispered. "So glad for you. It's the sort of break you wanted."

He nodded, and gripped her hand. Yes, it was running for him again, he could feel it, like blood in his veins.

"I love you, I love you," whispered Zarich. It came easy for him now as it never had before, not with Rhonda, not with any woman. He had a cynical distrust of instant love, but this was different. Cassie was different. She bucked and moaned under him until all his love gushed into her, then when her shuddering finally ceased he eased gently off, and lay beside her. Maybe this would make it impossible for him with women like Ella now, perhaps make him a less effective cop, but he didn't want to think about that. She lay on her back, eyes closed, and the moonlight through the window made a white mask of her face. He raised himself on his elbow, and kissed her with lingering tenderness.

"I love you," he said into her mouth.

"I know," she murmured.

He moved back and rested his head on his hand, watching her. Her eyes remained closed, her expression passive with the contented aftermath of orgasm.

"That was terrific," he said.

"Me too," she whispered, her mouth scarcely moving.

He wanted an expression of answering love, but for once the woman was more cautious in making such a quick commitment. He rarely made any at all, so it was a unique situation for him. "Are you all right?" he asked.

"Yes . . . yes, I feel great. Sleepy, that's all." She rolled her head into the shadows. "I think I love you, if that's what you want to hear, but it's all going too fast, darling. You love me too fast, Ed, when you know nothing about me."

"I know all I want to. All I need to."

Her face shifted into white profile again. "It's only for now, Ed. When you know about the Old Tart, you'll go back to New York. End of fairy tale. They never work out anyway."

"It needn't end like that. You can come back to New York with me."

She stared at the ceiling. "You really want that?"

"I really want that." He caressed her shoulder, but she shrugged his hand aside, and turned away. He watched her for a time, then lay back on his pillow, hands cupped behind his head. Her mood puzzled him, for he thought telling her he wanted her to come back with him to the States would please her. He decided on sleep, with the vision of the ensign's cap floating in his mind like a succulent meal.

When he woke during the night she was gone, and there seemed to be a shadow passing intermittently across the moonlit window. He lay quietly waiting for his eyes to adjust to the light, catching the sound of muffled footsteps from across the room. Then he realized the silhouette edged in moonlight pacing back and forth past the window was Cassie, arms crossed, her head bent down. He watched for a moment, unsure what to do. She was obviously disturbed, but Christ, he should have been aware of how much pressure she'd been under. The death of her grandmother, the attempt on her own life, and he was adding to it with talk of love and coming back to the States with him. He was on the point of slipping out and going to her to offer comfort, when she suddenly came softly back to bed, so he closed his eyes and pretended sleep. But she didn't touch him, and he made no attempt to touch her. But he wouldn't push her about New York anymore, at least not until he was no longer plagued by the Old Tart. If the time ever came.

Chapter 10

Chooka had a security friend at the Ranger mine who confirmed that Tom Kalangi was still working there, so they flew out by Cessna at nine-thirty in the morning. It was a clear bright day, which made a sparkling landscape of the great swathe of green below, the rivers coiling inland like giant snakes from the ocean to the north. Chooka sat beside the pilot, Cassie and Zarich in the rear seat. His hand softly caressed hers, and while she didn't draw away she seemed listlessly disinterested. The strange mood of the night persisted, and he couldn't put a finger on the reason. Perhaps he was right in his suspicion that he'd come on too strong after all the pressure she'd been under. For now he pushed it determinedly out of his mind.

But when the plane began to descend as the small town of Jabiru came into sight, her mood seemed to brighten. Maybe, like him, she was trying to postpone everything until the Old Tart was resolved.

The town was a cluster of buildings at the edge of a lake, dwarfed by a flat landscape stretching to infinity. Across to the right was the mine layout, a tight-knit collection of buildings, mining machinery, storage tanks, and vehicles dotted everywhere. Beyond that was a series of obviously man-made lakes, the shapes cut with precision, the sun glinting on the blue water in strong contrast to the dour red earth. To the side of one of the lakes was the open cut itself, like a huge gouge in the ground, the earth-moving machinery and trucks reduced to the magnitude of toys by their environs.

Chooka's security friend, whom he introduced merely as Ginger, was waiting at the airstrip with a Land Rover. Like Chooka, he was dressed in the inevitable shorts and short-sleeved shirt, and Cassie's white slacks with bright yellow blouse and his own city-bought tropical clothes made them seem like interlopers. Ginger was maybe ten years younger than Chooka, the red hair from which he evidently derived his nickname flecked with gray, his features and skin with the same gnarled weathering as the harsh countryside. They shook hands, exchanged a few pleasantries, and like most men, Ginger cast an appreciative eye at Cassie. But he was doubtless an important contact to have, because he drove them without questions directly to the mine, deposited them by one of the outbuildings, then left with the assurance Kalangi would join them shortly.

They moved into the shade, and stood looking out over the mine. From the open cut came the constant growl of earth-moving machinery, and the rumble of giant ore-carrying trucks emerging like moles from their burrow. It was perhaps ten minutes before Tom Kalangi stepped tentatively around the corner of the building. He looked to be in his midfifties, with all the characteristics of his race, heavy eyebrows, squat nose, thick lips, his heavy dark beard and hair already streaked with white. He wore earth-stained jeans, a red-checked shirt, and heavy boots, all finely coated with dust. He was about Zarich's height, with the lean hardness of his homeland. He came to a halt a few feet from Chooka, but his eyes were never still, moving warily from one to the other. Even when he shook hands he held his body in a cautious attitude, as if prepared to bolt at the slightest sign of danger.

"I haven't seen you for about a year, Tom," began Chooka affably. "You never come into Darwin these days."

Kalangi smiled guardedly. "No reason, Mr. Charlton. Don't like Darwin . . . all that city life."

"Nothing more to sell me, Tom?"

"No. I ain't found nothing else, Mr. Charlton."

Chooka motioned to Zarich and Cassie. "These two are friends of mine. Cassie Rehfield from Sydney, and Ed Zarich all the way from New York."

Kalangi nodded acknowledgment, but didn't offer his hand. "America. We got Americans here sometimes too." His eyes moved back to Chooka. "You come all the way from Darwin just to see me, Mr. Charlton?"

"Well, we've got a bit of a problem, and we're hopin' you might be able to help us."

"Problem, Mr. Charlton?"

Chooka nodded, opened his small carrying bag, and took out the ensign's cap. "Remember selling this to me, Tom?" he asked, holding it out to the aborigine.

Kalangi stared suspiciously at the cap. "Is there something wrong with it? You want your money back or something?"

"No, no, the cap's fine, Tom. Looks just great in my collection." He gestured to Zarich. "Mr. Zarich's interested in the cap, and we'd like to know exactly where you found it."

"Just like I told you, up along the South Alligator River, I didn't do anything wrong."

"Nothing's wrong, Tom," Chooka hastily reassured him. "No troubles at all. It's just important to us to know the exact place."

Kalangi was silent for a time, staring warily at the cap. One of the huge carrying trucks growled past, and they momentarily turned away from the dust thrown by the wheels. Kalangi waved his hand vaguely in the air.

"Up north, near the coast, Mr. Charlton."

"Crikey, that's one hell of a lot of country up there, Tom. A lot of wild country. Don't you remember the exact spot?"

A hazy expression came into the aborigine's eyes. "Maybe."

"Were you doin' some croc shooting up there?"

"Maybe."

"Listen Tom, Jes', I don't give a damn if you were doin' some illegal shooting. Y'hear, not a damn. All we want to know about is the cap."

"It's important?"

"Bloody important."

There was another brief period of silence, while Kalangi shuffled his feet about in the red earth.

"I'll pay you well if you'll take us there, Tom," Zarich intervened.

Kalangi stared at him without expression. "In a cave," he finally admitted. "Up from Munmarly, and not far from the river. I was skinnin' some crocs up there, an' looking for a place to leave the skins to dry out, and I found this cave."

"The hat was in the cave?"

"Yeah. I . . . I reckoned it might be worth something to Mr. Charlton."

"Was there anything else?"

Kalangi dropped into another period of wary silence. "I don't want any trouble, Mr. Charlton," he muttered.

"There isn't goin' to be any trouble for you, Tom," said Chooka persuasively.

"If I tell you, it don't go no further? No runnin' to your cop mates?"

Chooka held up his hand as if taking an oath. "You've got my promise, Tom."

The black eyes made a cautious assessment. "You my friend, Mr. Charlton?"

"Of course I am. And don't forget. Mr. Zarich'll pay you well."

The aborigine hesitated, breathing deeply, then nodded. "Well, there was what was left of a man."

Zarich sucked in his breath, and glanced quickly at Chooka. "What do you mean what was left, Tom?"

"A skeleton, an' bits and pieces of some sort of uniform."

"You should have told someone about it," said Chooka reprovingly. "Even me."

Kalangi shrugged, and stared pensively at the ground. The sun gave a sheen to his skin like black velvet. "I didn't want no trouble," he said. "I reckoned selling you the cap was safe, because you don't ask questions."

"Did you move the skeleton?" asked Zarich.

"No, I didn't touch it. Just took the cap, because it was laying away to the other side of the cave."

"Will you take us there?"

Kalangi crossed his arms, and plucked thoughtfully at his beard. "It's pretty rough up there, Mr. Zarich." He glanced sideways at Cassie. "Pretty rough. It ain't easy to get in, and it ain't easy to get out."

"We could go up the river by boat," said Chooka.

"You got to be bloody careful," warned Kalangi. "I tell you there's a lotta crocs up there. Some big buggers too."

Zarich seized Chooka by the arm, and drew him aside. "For Chrissake, we've got to get to that cave, Chooka. The skeleton has to be Winberg. It has to be. This makes it another ball game. Don't ask me how the hell the bones of an American ensign supposedly lost at sea forty years ago turn up in a cave in the north of Australia, because I don't know. But that skeleton might give us some of the answers we're looking for."

"If it is Winberg, you'll soon know, Ed."

"What do you mean?"

"All those boys had dog tags . . . you know, metal identification disks around their necks. I'll bet it's still there."

Zarich turned back to Kalangi. "How far is this place, Tom?"

The aborigine scratched uncertainly at his hair. "Let's see, you go down the Arnhem Highway about, oh, twelve or fifteen miles, then turn off to Munmarly, which is another twenty miles or so. I can take you up the river from Munmarly in my boat. It's about a two- to three-hour trip from there."

Cassie frowned, and prodded Zarich in the ribs. "Don't get any ideas about leaving me behind, Ed," she stated firmly.

"Rough country up there, miss," grunted Kalangi.

"Would Ginger be able to fix us up with a vehicle?" Zarich asked Chooka, ignoring Cassie.

"Maybe. I could ask him."

"Try and impress on him how urgent it is. Tell him I've come all the way from New York to find something like this. Can Tom get away for a time from his job here?"

"Don't worry, Ginger can fix that."

"You hear me," Cassie interjected again. "Don't you two get any bright ideas about leaving me behind."

The men seemed to hear her for the first time.

"Rough country," repeated Kalangi.

"You ain't exactly dressed for that sort of country," ventured Chooka.

She scowled, and glanced at Zarich's lightweight clothes and city shoes. "Neither's Ed for that matter," she observed sharply.

"I've got to go, baby," said Zarich gently. "There's no other way, I just have to go. This is so important."

"I don't want too many in the boat," added Kalangi. "It's only small. Coupla people got tipped outa their boat by a croc a few months ago. Bloody lucky they didn't get grabbed, I can tell you."

"You could stay with Ginger's wife in Jabiru," said Chooka. "She's a nice woman. We'd be back before dark." He glanced toward Kalangi, and received a nod of confirmation.

Zarich took Cassie by the arm and drew her away to the shade of the building, while Chooka and Kalangi made plans. "Darling, this time I really want you to stay," he murmured. "It'll be faster for us, and you're safe enough in a place like this."

Her mouth drooped sullenly. "I can match it with any of you," she declared.

"I know that, baby . . . I really do. But I want you to stay, for me. Please." he squeezed her hand. "Sure as hell it's not going to be a picnic, and I'll tell you everything when we get back." He smiled persuasively. "Okay?"

He kissed her as she conceded grudging agreement. He couldn't quite figure what the fuss was all about, if they were going to be dodging crocodiles and tramping through rough country, but he suspected it was a carryover from her mood last night.

They didn't need to trouble Ginger about a vehicle, because Tom insisted on using his own old tray truck, which made Chooka's vehicle seem like the epitome of luxury. The battered aluminum dingy with the ancient outboard was strapped to the back of the truck, and seemed even smaller than Tom had described. It made Zarich relieved he'd left Cassie behind.

They went back along the Arnhem Highway toward

Darwin, then north to Munmarly on a loose gravel road,
throwing dust like a covering screen. Every spring and
shock absorber on the truck seemed worn to the point of
exhaustion, and the bone-shaking rattle made conversation
impossible. The country was mostly flat, with sorghum
grass and eucalyptus trees thick over the red earth. Black
cockatoos soared overhead, and the trees disgorged flocks
of brilliantly colored rosellas, twittering protest. A wallaby
darted across the road in front of them, and small groups
of horned buffalo scattered as they passed. Kalangi drove
with silent concentration, his old army 303 rifle propped
between him and Zarich.

Munmarly was only a clearing with a few scattered
huts, and no sign of habitation. From there the road
deteriorated into a narrow winding track, where the birds
became more prolific both in number and variety. The
surrounding vegetation took on a richer shade of green,
and the undergrowth spotted with cycad palms, until
through the trees Zarich saw the wide blue-green expanse
of the South Alligator River. Kalangi pulled into the trees,
and cut the motor. The silence was overwhelming after
the clanking roar of the engine, just the lap of the water, a
soft breeze moaning through the branches, and the call of
the birds. They untied the boat and carried it to the water
where Zarich noted with relief at least it seemed to float
with no sign of a leak. Kalangi positioned the rifle carefully
beneath the seat, then jerked his thumb toward the river.
"We're going up to a big deep hole off the river near the
Culaly Plain, so you watch out for crocs up there, Mr.
Zarich. You, too, Mr. Charlton. Like I said, there's some
big buggers up there." He patted the rifle, and grinned.
"Don't worry, this old gun can still put a bloody big hole
in 'em if they give trouble. I know."

It took Kalangi a little time to persuade the outboard
into life, to the accompaniment of threatening curses, then
he set a course north, hugging as close to the shoreline as
the shallow mud banks would permit. It was a wide stretch
of calm water, with low scrubby vegetation along the
banks. The sun was high now, with only scattered clouds,
turning the surface of the river into a shimmering heat
reflector, and Zarich was soon wiping at the sweat oozing

down his face. The pop-pop of the outboard echoed in the still air. An occasional crocodile basking in the mud slid rapidly into the water as they approached. Elegant white egrets, long necks stretched in alarm, launched from surrounding trees at the sound of the outboard. There was little conversation, Kalangi staring mutely ahead to the river.

He spoke only once. "There's a Hessian bag under the front seat, Mr. Zarich," he muttered. "Just in case you want to bring the skeleton back with you." Then he lapsed into watchful silence.

They ran on into the growing heat of the day, occasionally passing around the water bag to relieve parched throats. Zarich anxiously consulted his watch. The boat was very slow, and the trip was obviously going to take longer than he'd been told.

"Maybe we should have tried to charter a helicopter," he said.

Chooka shrugged. "Maybe." He grimaced. "Maybe we rushed it a bit." He mopped at his face and glanced into the sky. "Bloody hot, too, ain't it."

Zarich didn't reply. He guessed he'd pushed it hard, but the thought it could be Winberg's skeleton in this cave filled him with an irresistible urgency. If Winberg was dead, what about the rest of the crew? Did that make nonsense of the theory the crew were still alive, and were their remains scattered about this remote part of northern Australia? He leaned to the side, scooped up a handful of water, and sluiced it over his face. He had that terrible frustrating feeling again that perhaps he would never know. He refused to contemplate such a stalemate, and thought instead of Cassie pacing the floor last night. Now he regretted pretending sleep; he should have taken her in his arms, comforted her, tried to draw her out. He'd make it up to her, but the longer he was with her, the more determined he became to persuade her to go back to New York with him.

The river widened until the open sea came in sight, an island standing like a sentinel to the west of the mouth.

"Barren island," called Kalangi. "Not far now."

"You're doin' great, Tom," encouraged Chooka. "Crikey, I won't forget this, mate. Neither of us will."

The aborigine shrugged it aside, then swung the boat right into a narrower waterway branching off the South Alligator. "More crocs up here," he warned. "The buggers are hard to spot sometimes, until you bump into 'em. They can tip the boat if you're not careful."

He cut the speed and chugged cautiously along for another thirty minutes as the course narrowed, with trees overhanging from the banks, and crocodiles more visible, some perched on gnarled trunks running down into the river. Then abruptly the river widened into a large area of still water, speckled with bird life and water lilies.

"Very deep here, very deep," said Kalangi. "Even stays that way when the tide's running out." He turned off the outboard, and ran the boat into the bank. Birds rose like winged rain at the intrusion. To the right a large crocodile slithered swiftly into the water, and sank quickly from sight. Kalangi stepped out onto the bank, glanced hesitantly about with his rifle held ready, then gestured for them to follow. "We walk from here," he grunted.

It was only ten minutes away, on a rising slope of red earth, the small entrance so covered with foliage it would have been easy to miss the cave completely without Kalangi. The aborigine pushed back the covering branches, then stood aside and motioned them in ahead of him. Zarich could feel a sense of expectation similar to when he'd first seen Old Tart inscribed on the ensign's cap.

He hesitated. "Where's the skeleton, Tom?"

"Just inside the cave, Mr. Zarich." He pulled on the branches until they broke away to allow more light into the opening. "You'll see it all right." Zarich dropped to his hands and knees and crawled through, with the others following. Inside, the cave widened to about ten feet, with ocher-colored walls, but not sufficiently high to allow them to fully stand. It was cool after the outside heat, with the smell of newly turned earth. It was difficult to know how deep it went, for the light only penetrated a short distance.

"Over here, Ed," called Chooka. "Against this side." Even though he spoke in a low tone, the sound echoed about the walls.

The skeleton was about twelve feet from the entrance, on its back, one bony arm extended, the other draped across the chest. Even in the soft light the skull had an eerie whiteness. Scraps of clothing clung in patches to the bones, but sufficient for them to see it was the remnants of an armed forces uniform.

"This 'uns been here a long, long time, Ed," murmured Chooka.

"Like over forty years."

"You reckon it's that Ensign Winberg in the photograph?"

"It's got to be, Chooka. See if you can see any sign of his dog tag. Don't ask me how in Christ he got here, but it has to be him." He turned to Kalangi. "Where did you find the cap, Tom?"

Kalangi was squatted back near the entrance, and made no attempt to approach the skeleton. He pointed to the other side of the cave. "Just over there against the wall, like I said."

"And you didn't touch the skeleton?"

Kalangi nodded firmly. "Not a finger." He threw the Hessian bag across to Zarich. "Here's the bag if you want it, Mr. Zarich."

Chooka rapped Zarich's arm as he picked up the bag. "There's the tag, Ed," he said, indicating the neck.

Zarich crouched forward, pushed a fragment of uniform to one side, then detached the chain, moving delicately as if he was in some strange way infringing the privacy of the long dead man. Then he shuffled closer to the entrance, and held the disk to the light. "Michael Winberg, USN," he read out triumphantly. There was a serial number, but it was irrelevant. He switched around, and thumped Chooka across the shoulders. "I was right, Chooka." He shook his head wonderingly, and stared down at the skeleton. "For Chrissake, how did the poor sonofabitch get here? If the Navy Department were surprised about Donlett turning up in New York, wait 'til they hear about this." He propped on his knees, pawing thoughtfully at his chin. "What the hell connects it all, Chooka? I've got so much now, the Old Tart, the link to Australia,

Emma Shepherd's letter, and now this, yet the answer seems as far away as ever."

"There's something else here, Ed," said Chooka.

"What's that?"

Chooka pointed to where Zarich had pushed the uniform fragment aside. Even in the pale light the shape was metallic in contrast to the white bones. "See, underneath the skeleton."

"Yeah, I see." He slipped the tag into his pocket. "I'll have to move the skeleton to get to it."

"Then let's do it."

They shifted the bones carefully to the center of the cave with gentle propriety, then Zarich picked up the object, brushed away the film of dust, and held it to the light.

"Jesus," he whispered. "It's a gold ingot, Chooka."

Chooka sat back on his haunches and ran his fingers aimlessly through his hair, a bewildered expression on his face. "I don't get it," he muttered. "I don't bloody well get any of it, Ed. It's like trying to work out some crossword puzzle."

Zarich glumly agreed. He ran his fingers over the ingot, and his fingers felt a series of indentations. He held it again to the light, trying to see the indentations. "There are some sort of markings on it." He scrambled forward on his knees toward the cave entrance, ignoring the damage to his light trousers, then peered at it again. "It's some sort of Oriental writing, Chooka. Chinese . . . Japanese, something ljke that."

"I can read some of that lingo, Ed. Let me take a look?" said Chooka. He shuffled up behind Zarich, fumbling for his spectacles, and took the ingot from Zarich's hand. He perched his spectacles on the tip of his nose, then examined it for a time, turning it backward and forward to the light. "It's Japanese," he declared. "Awa . . . ah, then Ma something. Wait, a minute, it's in two words. Awa . . . Maru. That's right, Awa Maru." He put the ingot down in his lap, and stared blankly at Zarich. "Starve the lizards, what's that supposed to mean?"

"Awa Maru? Sounds like some sort of place, or name.

Perhaps a person, a company, maybe a bank . . . even a ship."

"Could be any of them," shrugged Chooka.

They were silent for a time. Kalangi had moved back outside the cave, and they could see his shadow, black against the red ground.

"The skipper has a screwball idea," Zarich pondered out loud. "It has to do with the Japanese . . . we'll be rich for the rest of our lives."

"What's that supposed to mean?" asked Chooka.

"The letter I told you about, the last one Donlett wrote to his wife before the Old Tart vanished. That's what he told her in the letter, not that she had the faintest idea what he was talking about." He tapped his hand against the ingot. "But sure as hell it had something to do with this. Maybe there was hundreds more like this, Chooka. That's what was going to make them rich for the rest of their lives." He held up his hand to still Chooka's questioning look. "I know, Chooka, I know, but I don't have the least idea how it got here, or Winberg, or if there is more gold, what happened to it." He paused, and solemnly contemplated the white bones. "But that's one of the crew who never got rich, that's for sure." He took the ingot back from Chooka, and balanced it in his hands. "But someone in Japan has to know what this means. Where it came from."

"In Japan?"

"Sure. It either came from Japan, or was going to Japan. There's no other way to account for the Japanese markings. It has to be on record somewhere in Japan." He switched about on his haunches, and looked toward the back of the cave. "Maybe there's more gold back there. We'd better make a thorough search before we leave." He shrugged. "Perhaps even another skeleton."

"Yeah, you're right, mate," agreed Chooka. He gestured toward the bones. "I guess next thing is to find out what killed him. He might have crawled in here to die, or maybe he was killed outside and someone put the body in here."

Zarich shrugged himself to his feet, and began to move at an awkward stoop toward the back of the cave.

"Your guess is as good as mine, Chooka. I'll send the skeleton back to New York. They can do tests there that should show how he died."

There was no more gold or skeletons in the cave, and they searched the surrounding area, but found nothing. But it didn't require a pathology examination to tell them how Ensign Winberg met his death. In the dirt under where the bones had originally lain they found three bullets, and Zarich knew from experience where to look for the signs. Two ribs in the rear rib cage had been severed, not breaks from deterioration, but smashed by the impact of bullets. Someone had shot him in the back, and he must have just made it to the cave to die. If the killer had known he was there, surely he wouldn't have left the ingot. What did it mean? Yet a hazy picture was gradually forming. Somehow the crew of the Old Tart set out on that long ago March day to pull off some caper over Japanese gold. What went wrong? Did gold greed get them, and there was a falling out over dividing the loot? If Donlett was picked up by a Chinese gunboat, what happened to him? Did they throw him overboard to cut him out of a share? Perhaps he should forget about the possibility of all the crew being alive, although there could be a few survivors, perhaps only one, with the rest of the bodies scattered God knows where, like Winberg. Luck had led him to Winberg, but he had virtually no chance of finding any others. Even if they were somewhere in the area. But the ingot could give him the one final link. He sighed. He was so obsessed to know what it all meant, in some way the killing of Donlett, Musoveld, and Emma Shepherd was becoming irrelevant. Not knowing would niggle him, and keep him awake nights forever. He slipped the bullets into his pocket along with the dog tag. He'd be able to find out what sort of weapon fired them, although he doubted it would mean anything. They packed the skeleton carefully into the bag, and took it back down to the boat.

"It's a bloody puzzle all right, Ed," said Chooka sympathetically.

"The best," grinned Zarich ruefully. The sun was already low in the sky, and Kalangi waited crouched impatiently by the outboard. It would be dark by the time they got back to Jabiru. "I don't want the authorities in Australia knowing anything about this now, Chooka. I'll ship it straight to New York. Then as soon as we get back to Darwin I'll call Harry."

It was dark by the time they took off for the return flight to Darwin, but from the plane a few crimson strips still hung along the western horizon. Zarich had already decided what he was going to do. Cassie listened silently while he gave her a concise outline of the find in the cave.

"You still don't know who killed my grandmother though, Ed," she said forlornly. "Or the people in New York. Or would like to see me dead."

"I'm getting there," he grinned tightly. Was he? She was right; he knew so much, but he still couldn't point a finger at anyone. "I'll check with New York and see if they've turned up anything there," he added. "What I want to do is make a quick trip to Japan." He tried not to think of Beuso and his accountant's mind.

She studied him with wide eyes. "You want me to come there with you too?" The light from the cockpit outlined her face, and she looked incredibly beautiful. But he shook his head. Beuso would scream about one fare, let alone two. "No, I want you to stay with Chooka. You'll be safe up here with him. Believe me, you can trust Chooka with your life," he murmured softly.

She tilted her head, and even in the dim light he saw some of the old fear. "Yes . . . yes, I know you're right, darling," she said hesitantly.

"Then when I get back we can talk about us," he added.

She knew he was talking about going back to New York with him, but she offered no protest, merely nodded her head. He felt a warm buzz from her reaction, for at least it indicated she was thinking about the idea.

As soon as they were back in Chooka's house he called Harry, and told him what had happened.

"That sounds like a terrific break to me, Ed," commented Harry enthusiastically. "You're right, there is a picture coming together about what they were up to on the Old Tart. If you can identify the gold ingot it might just be the link we're looking for." He chuckled delightedly. "I told you, Chooka was good value, Ed. A great old bloke. I'll bet he's just lapping up being involved in a case again."

"You might say that," said Zarich drily. "Listen, I'm going to get Winberg's remains down to you in Sydney together with a letter and address in New York. It might be better if you send them off for me."

"No worries, mate. How long before you come back yourself?"

"I'll only be gone a few days." He clucked his tongue. "Beuso'll squirm when he gets the tab."

"That's a problem?"

"No, no I didn't think so. It certainly won't stop me going."

"How's Cassie?"

"She's fine. It's better she's away from Sydney. I'm going to leave her with Chooka while I'm in Japan."

"Good thinking. He'll watch her like a hawk."

"How's everything with Roman?"

The way he cleared his throat was an indication of unease. "Well, he keeps asking what you're up to, but he's not pushin' me. Reckon I can stall him off for a coupla more days. I've got a feelin' he thinks you're only chasing your tail anyway."

"Good, let him think that. You haven't got anything more on Emma Shepherd's death?"

"Not so far, Ed. Roman hasn't budged from the suicide theory, which surprises me. I went to her funeral, but I didn't learn anything. But I'm still working on it. Whoever killed her at the Opera House took an awful risk, but no one saw a thing."

"How's it with the Old Tart photograph? I keep hoping something's going to slip out of your memory, Harry."

"So do I, Ed. So do I. But I've got an idea goin' that might just open up whatever's niggling me."

"What's that?"

"I'm not goin' to try and explain it over the phone," said Markby mysteriously. "Maybe nothing'll come of it. I'll give it a try, and tell you about it when you get back to

Sydney. Jes', who knows, you might have the whole thing cracked wide open by then."

"I should get so lucky."

He hung up, and called the Australian airline Qantas. There was a flight the following day, not direct to Japan, but to Singapore, where he could pick up a flight to Tokyo. He confirmed a booking, then called Beuso in New York. The middle of the night wasn't the greatest time to fire the captain with enthusiasm, and he knew he was in for a hard time as soon as the sleep-raddled voice crackled over the line.

"For Chrissake, Ed, what the hell do you mean getting me out of bed at this time of the night?"

"Captain, this thing with the Old Tart is all coming together. I'm sorry calling you at this hour, but I'm taking a flight to Tokyo in the morning, and I wanted to bring you up to date."

He opted for a bold approach, and for a moment silence was the only reaction.

"Tokyo?" questioned Beuso thickly. "Tokyo . . . Japan?"

"It's a hell of a lead. It'll only take a few days."

"Jesus Christ, Tokyo? Are you figuring on running a tourist service for the New York Police Department?"

"Captain, believe me, if it wasn't necessary I wouldn't go."

"Where the hell are you now?"

"Darwin. You know, the port where the Old Tart operated from during the war."

There were muffled, indecipherable sounds from the other end of the line, as if Beuso might have fallen out of bed. "You're jumping around like a cat on hot coals," he growled finally.

"I found the remains here of another crew member of the Old Tart . . . just a skeleton. I'm going to send it to you along with a report of everything that's happened since I arrived in Australia."

"What the hell do you want me to do with the skeleton?"

"I'm positive it was Winberg, who was an ensign on the Old Tart. Get it to a pathologist. I want it confirmed how he died. I'm sure he was shot in the back, so I'm sending the bullets along as well."

Beuso's sleep-clouded brain began to clear. "You mean murdered, like the others here in New York?" he asked sharply.

"Yeah, only forty years ago."

"You think that ties in with the sonofabitch who put out the contract on Donlett and Musoveld."

"Probably. I hope I'll know when I get back from Japan."

"What about Donlett's wife? Did she know anything?"

"She's dead."

There was a series of barely recognizable expletives. "What?"

"They got to her before I did, Captain. That's why I know they're here in Australia . . . for sure now."

"Christ," grunted Beuso in disgust. "They're running ahead of you, Ed."

It quivered on Zarich's tongue to stick it to Beuso over the foul-up on Emma Shepherd's security, but he let it pass for another time. That was one he owed the captain.

"Listen, everything's in the report. For now I want you to open a few doors for me in Tokyo. Before I get there."

"Well, I guess I can make a few calls. Who do you want to see?"

"I guess there's a Department of War Archives where I could start. Something like that. If they don't have answers, then they'll know who does. I just want to make sure I get cooperation."

"Just a second," muttered Beuso. There was the scratching sound of pen on paper. "I'll see what I can do. What airline are you flying?"

"Qantas, the Australian airline."

"Okay, I'll get it lined up for you at the Tokyo airport so there'll be someone there to take you to the right people."

"That's terrific, Captain."

There was another pause, filled by the harsh clearing of phlegm. "Jesus, Ed, I'm not too clear what this is all

about, but it better pay off. Dawkins has run into a dead
end with the investigation here."

"Believe me, it will, Captain. You'll understand when
you read the report."

"Okay. Get in touch again when you get back from
Japan. You hear Ed, I want to know it all."

"Sure, sure," said Zarich hastily, then hung up. He
grinned with satisfaction as he replaced the receiver. Catching Beuso in the middle of the night was a piece of
uncalculated luck, because come the clear light of day he
might have second thoughts.

He said good-bye to Cassie that night with all the
passion that seemed to be growing every hour he was with
her. It was as if storing memories to carry with him like
luggage. He rode her hard, and long, and she seemed to
respond with equal zeal, and yet he was aware of a subtle
holding back he found impossible to define, except he
knew it was there. Ego wouldn't allow him to accept there
might be something almost contrived in her fervor, that it
was only a performance because she didn't know how to
tell him she was already tiring of the affair. Not when he'd
saved her life. It might be only a continuation of the mood
from the previous night, but he hesitated to question her,
and was careful to make no more references to New York.
That could wait until he got back from Japan, but somewhere along the way he had to know what was bugging
her. It was more than fear, for he was sure she felt safe
enough to be left here with Chooka.

Maybe it was something with him, which Rhonda had
felt, even some of the others, and he winced at the remembrance of Ella's scornful words.

"You don't touch people," said his aunt. He was only
a kid then, and he hadn't the least idea what she was
talking about. He missed the city kids he was used to
running with, and there was nothing to touch on the bleak
Kansas landscape.

"It's like I'm holding my hands in front of a dead
fire," she had declared. "Just no warmth coming out."

The hell with her, he had more warmth for this girl than she'd ever had. He closed his eyes, but held off sleep, relishing the feel of her, the soft sound of her breathing.

Chapter 11

Ricky Bossley was home working when Harry Markby called at his small Balmain house. Bossley was a young man of small build, thin frame, and quick nervous mannerisms, who had made a determined effort to expunge his features under a luxuriant growth of hair on both head and face. Markby described him once as two bright eyes set in a black mattress. He wore a black shirt, old sneakers, and jeans that had probably never seen a washing machine.

He led Harry into the small studio, casually indicated a chair, squatted himself down at the drawing board, offered the detective a cigarette, shrugged at the refusal, then lit up with a cloud of smoke. An overfull ashtray testified to the fact that few cigarettes were smoked to their full length.

"What is it this time, Harry?" he inquired. "You got a rapist you want drawn?" He spoke rapidly, running the words together. He was an artist who often did identikit portraits of suspects wanted by the police.

"No, not this time, Ricky, but something that might be a little harder."

"Then you've come to the right place, Sarge. I'm only interested in the tough ones."

Markby opened his case, and laid the photograph of the Old Tart crew down on the drawing board. Bossley crossed his arms, and peered intently at the picture.

"Not bad, not bad, Harry. Nice photograph. Vietnam? Korea?"

"No, Second World War."

Bossley grinned, and picked up the photograph. "Shit, I love looking at stuff like this. All those young guys . . . old guys now. Makes you think, eh mate. It all runs out bloody fast, too bloody fast for my liking."

Markby didn't elaborate. He put his finger down on the head of Schuman the captain. "How would you go about making a portrait of this one if he was forty years older?"

Bossley twisted in the chair, and scrutinized him through a haze of smoke. The cigarette bobbed in his mouth as he spoke. "This a gag, Sarge?"

"No, I'm quite serious. You're the best, Ricky. I know you can do it."

Bossley switched back to the board, and picked up the photograph again. "I guess it's a bloody waste of time asking why?"

"You said it."

Bossley mused awhile. "Well, it's a fantastically good print for its age. Some photographer knew what he was doing. What I'd do is get maybe half a dozen large blowups of this guy's head, then work over each photograph with alternatives. You know, the guy could have gone bald, that'd be one. Or maybe he kept his hair and went gray, or even white . . . that'd be another. Then others with spectacles, lines, get what I mean?"

"That sounds great."

Bossley took two quick drags on his cigarette, then added to the pile in the ashtray. "You want it yesterday of course, Harry?" he asked, with a trace of sarcasm.

"Even the day before if possible, Ricky."

"Jes', you bastards are impatient."

"All in the course of justice, mate."

"Yeah, sure, I'd hate to have someone like you on my tail, Harry."

Markby patted him on the shoulder. "It wouldn't be the first time you worked all night for me, Ricky."

"And not the last."

Markby lumbered to his feet, and headed for the door. "I'll leave it with you. Call me as soon as you've got something."

"It'll cost you," Bossley called after him.

"We'll charge it to the taxpayers," Markby answered as he closed the door.

There was an urgent message for him to see Roman as soon as he got back to headquarters, and one look at the chief inspector's face told him he was in trouble. He sat down nervously, perched on the edge of the chair. Roman was never a man to mince words.

"Zarich's in Darwin," he challenged in a clipped voice. "I received word from one of our local people up there." He hunched his shoulders, and scowled at the sergeant. "I thought you might like to give me an explanation, Harry?"

Markby felt as if someone had kicked him in the groin. He couldn't believe Chooka would have taken Zarich anywhere near the local police. He shuffled uneasily on his buttocks, fishing desperately for an answer.

"He mentioned he might want to make some inquiries out of Sydney," he muttered evasively.

"You disobeyed my orders, Harry," rasped the chief inspector. "You ignored my request for a report on every move Zarich made in Australia." He picked up a piece of paper from his desk, shook it furiously in the air, then angrily discarded it again. "Now I get this information about Zarich in Darwin from another source."

Markby was bewildered. How the hell could the Darwin police have tipped off Roman? Could it have been Chooka? The old guy liked to talk big at times, but he couldn't make himself believe that. He kept his cool, and tried for an orderly retreat.

"I've obeyed orders, sir," he complained in an aggrieved tone. "I've told you everything that's been happening. About Emma Shepherd, and the granddaughter. Zarich being in Darwin would have been in the report I was going to make to you this morning," he lied.

He didn't mention Ricky Bossley. Maybe there *was* a bug in the office, and he didn't want to put the young artist's life at risk as well. But he could tell by the expression on Roman's face he didn't believe a word of his excuse.

Roman cleared his throat abrasively, and glared across the desk. Markby had never seen such a high color in his superior's face. What the hell was he so uptight about?

"You're usually much more prompt with your reports than that, Harry," he said with acid sarcasm.

"I've got other assignments goin' as well," Markby tried defensively.

Roman scowled, and shuffled the papers about on his desk. Markby had the feeling a decision had been made long before he stepped into the office.

"Then it might be a good idea if you just concentrated on those other things, Sergeant," he said coldly.

Markby felt like a chastised schoolboy, and he was forced to swallow hard before answering.

"Where does that leave me with Zarich?"

"I'll find someone else for Zarich."

"You mean you're taking me off the case?"

"We're obviously overtaxing you, Harry. If you've got too many investigations going at once, it just means none of them get proper attention."

Markby glowered at the paper on Roman's desk. His complaint of overwork had backfired on him. It stank. He could smell it like a rat had died in a corner of the office. "I can still handle the thing with Zarich," he declared hotly.

"Obviously not, if I have to wait on a report from our Darwin people to find out something it was your duty to report quickly to me."

"I can't leave Zarich high and dry. He needs someone in Australia batting for him . . . and I know the case now."

"No," said Roman firmly. "I'm sure we can find someone not under so much pressure as you, Harry. It won't take them long to acquaint themselves with the case." He leaned forward with a pretense of examining the papers on his desk, but it was a blunt indication the meeting was over.

"Just let's say I'm disappointed, Harry. Very disappointed. This Zarich must have really got to you, if he could undermine your loyalty to your own department."

"It wasn't like that," protested Markby weakly.

"Well, I'm not going to argue about it. Your assignment to Zarich is finished. I'll assign someone else when Zarich gets back to Sydney." He concluded with a curt nod. "That'll be all, Sergeant."

He refused to look at the sergeant until he heard the door close, then he pushed the papers aside with a forlorn sigh. Well, at least Sade would be satisfied now; he'd been under unceasing pressure to get rid of the sergeant, yet now that it was done, it left him with an uneasy feeling. He knew Markby too well. Even if he was officially removed from Zarich, there was no guarantee it would shut off the sergeant's inquiring mind. He'd obviously formed a friendship with the American, and he wouldn't let go easy. He'd have to keep careful watch to see that didn't happen, and if he saw any sign of it he'd come down hard, even squash Markby into a demotion situation. He clasped his hands, and placed them pensively at his mouth. He'd held off mentioning he also knew Zarich was on his way to Japan, because that could have created suspicion. But God, he was flying blind. He knew so little of what this was all about, how it connected back as some enormous risk to Kepler Humbert. No wonder his wife was so concerned over his inability to sleep nights. If only he could try to be fatalistic, then if it all fell in on him one day at least he'd be prepared for it. But he had his special race meeting coming up on Saturday, and at least he knew that would be rewarding.

Markby seethed over his dismissal from the case for a day, then gradually the situation began to crystallize in his mind. It had to be more than his failure to report Ed being in Darwin. Roman wanted him out, but why? He was confident enough in his own professional ability to know that wasn't the reason, yet in a way it had been so clumsily done he was sure Roman was being pressured by someone else. For Chrissake, why again? It took him back to Zarich's suspicions about the leak. If Roman was being pressured, then perhaps Ed's theory about a bug was wrong, and it was Roman himself. Markby had been a cop for a long time, took some pride in being a good one, but he also knew Sydney's reputation for corruption, and a rotten apple as highly placed as Roman was always possible, even with his squeaky clean image. He couldn't put it out of his mind. The hell with Roman; he'd play it careful, but he owed it to Ed not to let go. He was glad now he'd said nothing about young Ricky Bossley.

He let it all simmer until Friday morning, turning over alternatives in his mind, then he received a call from Bossley to come over to his studio. When he got there Bossley had them lined up along the studio wall in presentation form, all the prints about twelve inches high. The usual cigarette dangled from his mouth, and his wiry frame bobbed about the room as if manipulated by a puppeteer's strings. Markby stood back and carefully examined each of the six portraits in turn.

"I did six blowups like I told you, then I worked straight down on the prints," Bossley cackled delightedly. "Jes, I reckon I done you proud, Sarge. Take your pick." His hand darted out, flicking from one picture to the next. "See, this one's bald, this one's gray-headed, this one's had a tough life and he's pretty lined, this one's put on weight with all those extra chins, this one's got lousy eyesight now, and wears glasses. I guess for that matter after forty years you could put spectacles on all of 'em."

"You've done a fantastic job, Ricky . . . really great," said Markby. "You must have worked all bloody night."

"Tell you what, I enjoyed myself, Harry. Bloody lot of fun."

Markby's eyes came to an abrupt halt at the fifth portrait. He stared for a long time, then he stepped forward for a closer examination, paused, then moved back again. Bossley had created a distinguished portrait of late middle age. Gray hair, lined face, but a man who had looked after himself, enjoyed the good things of life. Whether it was luck or good judgment, he'd caught an eerie likeness that jogged Markby's memory.

"Jesus," he murmured in astonishment.

"That one rings a bell, Harry?"

"It mean anything to you, Ricky?"

"Nope, not a thing. But then I'm not up in the social register, and the way that one came out the guy looks very social register to me."

Markby nodded, but said nothing. He'd done some work for the Company Squad a few years back over a bogus share deal, and this man had been discussed, al-

though not in any criminal context. Kepler Humbert. It
had to be him; it had to be. Yet a sense of frustration
mingled with the revelation. If he was right, there probably wasn't a thing he could do about it, at least not without
cast-iron proof, and even then the man was virtually un-
touchable. Few ordinary citizens knew the man with his
immense wealth, but he was the confidante of some of the
most powerful men in the country. Christ, it would cause
a political storm, but he didn't have the slightest doubt
now that he was also Schuman, the captain of the Old
Tart. This was the man who had the screwball idea to
make Donlett rich, and all the rest of the crew. Was he
also the man who had ordered three people killed? It
sounded incredible, but then everything about the Old
Tart challenged the imagination. Was the gold Ed had
found in the cave part of what had been the source of
Humbert's wealth? And where was the rest of the crew?
And more depressing, what could a detective sergeant do
against someone with Humbert's enormous clout, except
maybe finish up dead himself if he opened his mouth?

"You're not saying much, Sarge," commented Bossley.

Markby gave a resigned shrug. "Some things it's best
not to know, 'specially for you, Ricky."

"It's like that, eh?"

"You've done a great job for me, Ricky. I wouldn't
have believed it would work so well."

"We aim to please," Bossley smirked. "What d'you
want to do with 'em?"

"I'd like to take them all with me . . . wrapped."

"Sure thing," grinned Bossley. He collected the portraits, took them to a small side table, and carefully wrapped
them in brown paper. He handed them to Markby with a
shrewd smile.

"I've got a feeling I might've opened a can of worms,
Sarge."

Markby dropped them in his case, showing nothing of
the cauldron bubbling in his mind.

"You just might have Ricky, you never know," he
replied grave-faced. He didn't want to put the fear of
Christ into the young artist, but unwittingly he knew he'd
pushed him into the firing line. "I don't want a word about

this outside your studio, Ricky," he warned. "Not a bloody word. I'm dealing with some blokes who are pretty rough customers. Understand?"

Some of the good humor washed from Bossley's face. "You'll protect me, Sarge," he said confidently. "I know I'm safe with you."

Markby preferred not to disillusion him. "Sure, but keep your mouth shut anyway, mate. Just remember I can't be in two places at the same time."

He didn't know what to do with it. Going to Roman was out of the question. He scarcely ate dinner, his wife's voice a far-off burr of words, until she gave up in disgust and sullenly turned her attention to the television set. In a way life had been a smooth run for him, caring parents, capable schooling, a good marriage, a job that never ceased to interest him. Suddenly it was as if he were walking around trying to balance a can of nitroglycerin on his nose. One misstep, and he was gone.

Finally he called Chooka in Darwin, but the old man didn't know when Zarich would be back. A subtle inquiry that Chooka might have shown Ed around to some of the Darwin police was easily seen through, and brought a volcanic denial. All he could do was back off with muttered apologies before he hung up, but the call got him nowhere. Yet it did serve to strengthen his doubts about Roman. Christ, a chief inspector, on the take from a man like Kepler Humbert. What the fuck was the force coming to? There was a sinking feeling in his stomach that one of Roman's spies must have followed Zarich from the Sydney hotel. He hoped to Christ they hadn't put a bug on Chooka's phone, because then they could also know about Ed's Japanese trip. It was a depressing outlook.

"I'm going to bed," said Helen, around eleven-thirty.

He looked at her blankly, as if she were speaking another language.

"Bed, you know . . . that place where you sleep," she added caustically. "Are you coming, Harry?"

He nodded absently. "Sure, you go along. I'll be there in a minute."

"Famous last words." She leaned to the door, and concern replaced resentment. She was no stranger to the day-to-day pressure, had lived with it for fifteen years, but she'd never seen him like this. "I never interfere, Harry, but if you want to talk about it, then I want to listen."

He smiled while he thought about it, but he was so wary of taking anyone into his confidence when these people killed so easily. Especially someone like Helen.

"I . . . I might later," he said evasively. "Thanks, honey, but I want to try and work it out in my own mind first."

"Something to do with Ed Zarich?"

"He's part of it," he admitted. "But the good part."

She waited a moment, but he didn't add anything else, and she knew better than to push him. She moved to his side, ruffled his few remaining strands of hair, then kissed him gently on the forehead.

But he sat there until almost four o'clock in the morning, because he knew the revelation Ricky Bossley had provided about Kepler Humbert was the most dangerous piece of information he'd ever possessed. Dangerous for him, for Zarich, for Cassie, God, even for Helen. But he couldn't back away and hope for the best; that was a sure way to go down the gurgler. From now on he'd wear Roman like a shadow. Saturday was race day for the chief inspector, and that's where he'd start, for he knew the ideal man for the job.

A polite young man in a dark suit and white shirt met Zarich at Narita Airport. He held a card aloft in the arrival lobby which read, WELCOME TO TOKYO MISTER ED ZARICH. So much for security, but he was sure no one in Australia knew he was there. He offered a friendly smile as he shook hands with the young man, who introduced himself as Shinzo Kuroki.

"Ah, we have arranged for you to talk to someone at the Defense Agency, Mr. Zarich," he said. "We hope that may satisfy your inquiries."

"I hope so too," answered Zarich, with matching politeness.

"We have booked you in Asaka Tokyo Hotel. Very good hotel, Mr. Zarich, you will be most comfortable." He gave a short bow. "I am to be your guide while you're in Tokyo. The Defense Agency is in Rappongi, not far from your hotel. Everything has been seen to, your worries are my worries." He gestured to the exit door. "I have a car waiting outside."

Zarich was impressed. For all Beuso's sour response to his phone call, he'd obviously been busy opening doors for him.

It was his first time in Japan, but he'd never been in a large modern city that didn't share all the problems of New York. The roads were a jungle of jostling traffic, the smog even heavier, the bustle, the noise, the claustrophobic crush of people, hemmed in by the same walls of steel, glass, and concrete. But as a counterpoint the parks were oases of green and multiple shades of springtime blossoms, gleaming in the late afternoon sun. Glimpses of shrines, the great gate of the Meiji Shrine, the strangely European fence of the Askasaka Palace, all unobtrusively pointed out by Kuroki on the way to the hotel.

The guide made sure he was booked into the hotel, then wished him a pleasant evening, and left with the information he would return to pick him up at nine o'clock in the morning. Zarich didn't object to being left to himself for the remainder of the day. He'd flown more hours since first hearing the words "Old Tart" than ever in his life before, and he was still trying to catch up on sleep. But not before he checked out on the ingot in his suitcase. Nightmares of misplaced luggage had plagued him during the entire flight, and he decided there and then he wouldn't put himself through that again. Wherever he went from now on, that ingot would stay close by him in hand luggage. He turned it over in his hand, once again studying the Japanese markings. Surely there had to be a chance that this was finally the key to the Old Tart. The picture of what had happened in 1945 was still like peering through a fog, and he hoped to Christ this trip would provide clarity.

He thought of calling Cassie, but decided against it. He had no doubts about his own feelings for her, but maybe a few days' clear break would give her a chance to sort out her moods, whatever the reason. Yet he wasn't going to let go; there had never been such intense feeling about any woman in his life before. But already he'd grown used to the feel of her beside him in bed, and it was a long time before he found sleep.

At nine o'clock Kuroki drove him to the Defense Agency, where in a small office a grave, middle-aged man who identified himself only as Mr. Anami listened patiently to his reason for coming to Tokyo. Zarich told him no more than the finding of Winberg's skeleton together with the ingot in the cave, then he produced the gold from his carryon bag, and placed it carefully on the desk as a climax to the story.

"So if we can identify the source of the ingot, Mr. Anami, it might hopefully give me a lead as to how the body came to be in the cave," he concluded.

Anami said nothing for a time, a slight smile on his face, his fingers caressing the imprint on the ingot.

"Awa Maru," he murmured finally.

"I have no idea what it means," said Zarich. "I'd guess maybe a bank, or a company, perhaps even a ship."

"A most interesting story, Mr. Zarich."

Zarich thought of Emma Shepherd's body floating in the water. Of Donlett and Musoveld. Winberg's rib cage smashed by the impact of bullets. "Yes, interesting," he agreed drily.

Anami slipped the steel-framed spectacles from his face, and stroked thoughtfully at his completely bald dome. "Please, can you leave ingot with me for a time, Mr. Zarich?"

He saw hesitation come into Zarich's face, and offered a quick smile of reassurance. "I give you promise not to steal, Mr. Zarich. It will be perfectly safe with me, but I must speak of this to various people." He offered an apologetic gesture with the spectacles. "After all, is forty years ago, and is better if you get correct answers." He tilted his head questioningly to one side. "Yes? Is a long way to come, and not get real truth, yes Mr. Zarich?"

Zarich was reluctant to let the ingot out of his possession, but he knew he had no choice but to agree. It was a long way to come, and Beuso would have his ass if he went back to Australia with nothing to show for the trip. He returned a smile which he hoped projected confidence.

"Sure, you're right, Mr. Anami. It is a long way to come, and I really want the truth about that ingot."

"Then with hope can give it to you, Mr. Zarich." He picked up a pen, and glanced inquiringly at Zarich. "You are staying at Asaka Tokyo Hotel. I can contact you there?"

"Yes."

"Good. As soon as I have news, will call you, Mr. Zarich."

Zarich restrained a sense of disappointment. But then it was foolish to believe it was just a matter of walking into an office, and all the mists surrounding the Old Tart would magically lift. Anami was right about the same thing that had bugged him from the start—it was forty years ago, so he'd just have to endure hanging around for a time.

He mooned about the hotel room for the remainder of the day, waiting for a phone call from Anami that never came. Around evening he went for a stroll, and dropped in at the Neboke Restaurant for a quick dinner of Shikokee seafood. There was a depressing sense of being alone he'd never felt before. The streets were swarming with nighttime crowds, but he could see only Cassie's face. His mind was always so concentrated on a hunt like this, and it was a weird experience having a woman competing for space. It gave him for once an uneasy sense of vulnerability. It would give Mal Dawkins back in New York a horse laugh, the old hound dog himself with his foot in the trap, yet his tongue hanging out drooling to stay there.

When he got back to the hotel there was a message from Anami telling him Kuroki would pick him up tomorrow afternoon at three to take him to the Defense Agency again to see a Mr. Koiso. It meant more time he had to kill, and he hoped to Christ he wasn't getting the runaround, as he already had misgivings about letting the ingot out of his hands. If it vanished into some bureaucratic bottomless pit, then he could be back to first base. And there was another uneasy thought pushing into his mind. Revealing the ingot to Anami had staked him out like bait if the killers had any contacts in Japan, which he guessed was possible. He took the .38 out of his suitcase, and placed it on the bedside table. From now on it would travel everywhere with him like an old friend.

Koiso was a younger man than Anami, although much broader, with matching black mustache and immaculate business suit. The size of the office and the furnishings indicated a higher rank in the hierarchy. He had a slightly depreciating air, as if he considered policemen to be one of the lower orders. The ingot sat in the exact center of an almost bare desk, like a prize exhibit.

"Your, or should I say, our gold ingot, has created quite a stir, Mr. Zarich," he began. He spoke very precise English, in a light youthful tone.

Zarich ignored the inference over ownership of the ingot. "Then I take it you know something about it, Mr. Koiso?"

"Oh yes indeed, Mr. Zarich. It has created quite a stir. This ingot shouldn't even exist, it should be at the bottom of the Taiwan Straits, if it was anywhere."

Zarich stared at him blankly. "The Taiwan Straits?"

"Yes. One of your guesses was correct. The *Awa Maru* was the name of a ship, or more accurately a hospital ship, which vanished in the Taiwan Straits towards the end of the war."

"The ingot came from the ship?"

Koiso shrugged. "That is the story."

"You mean it was part of the cargo? It was being carried on a hospital ship?"

Koiso didn't answer immediately, but stared silently at the ingot, then he cleared his throat and patted delicately at his mouth. Finally he picked up a sheaf of papers from the desk, and began to read. "The hospital ship *Awa Maru* left Singapore on March 28 in 1945. It was brightly lit, and marked with large crosses to show it was a hospital ship. It carried over two thousand passengers, some ten times more than its registered capacity. It was returning to Japan, and the U.S. Forces Command had guaranteed it safe passage from any attack." He glanced up briefly. "You understand?"

Zarich nodded impatiently.

"However," Koiso continued, "according to Singapore prisoner-of-war dockworkers who loaded the ship, it was also carrying strategic war materials, rubber, tin, things like that. And also gold bullion supposedly appropriated

from Southeast Asia by Japanese commanders, and worth
millions of dollars. I understand this information was somehow conveyed to American Intelligence." He paused,
pinched at his nose, and dropped the papers down over
the ingot. "From there the events become rather hazy.
There was a brief message from the *Awa Maru* that she
had stopped in the Taiwan Straits, but it was presumed to
be engine trouble. But then . . ." He shrugged. "Only
silence. There were no survivors." Koiso's mouth puckered hesitantly as if carefully choosing his next words. "Of
course there was an official denial by the Japanese government that such gold ever existed, Mr. Zarich. There were
bitter accusations from both sides of treachery. The Americans were accused of breaking their safe guarantee, and
sinking the *Awa Maru*. The Japanese were accused of
deceit for carrying war booty in a hospital ship."

"But the name of the ship has been stamped on the
ingot," interrupted Zarich.

Koiso twitched his broad shoulders, and the corners
of his mouth lifted in a frosty smile. "Then you have to
draw your own conclusions, Mr. Zarich. I find it difficult
myself to believe the dockworkers would contrive such a
story. However in 1975 the Chinese government signed a
peace and friendship treaty with my country, and as a
good will gesture they located the wreck of the *Awa Maru*.
Divers managed to salvage some of the bones of those
drowned in the sinking, and they were presented to their
families." He gave a solemn tilt of his head. "Such things
are important in this country, Mr. Zarich." He paused for
emphasis. "But the Chinese divers found no sign of any
gold in the wreck. No gold at all."

He fell silent, and interlocked his fingers carefully on
the desk. "As I said, you must draw your own conclusions,
Mr. Zarich. But how this ingot, together with the remains
of an American Naval officer, came to be in a cave in the
north of Australia is a mystery no one here can answer for
you." He paused again, eyes shrewdly assessing Zarich.
"There are perhaps . . . ah, elements of the mystery we
don't know about, Mr. Zarich. Perhaps there are things
you know of which we are ignorant. I'm sure if you are

ever able to fit all the pieces together, then the Japanese government would be interested in knowing the result."

Zarich figured Koiso was probing, but he had no intention of going right back to Donlett's murder in New York, at least not at this stage. "Yes, yes of course," he murmured. He stood to his feet, and they shook hands. "I don't know who's the rightful owner of this, Mr. Koiso," he said, motioning to the ingot. "But it's important I keep it at least until my investigations are complete. I hope you understand?"

"Of course," said Koiso affably. "You have something to carry it in?"

Zarich picked up the carryon bag from the floor, deposited the ingot inside, and they shook hands again.

"Thank you again, Mr. Koiso. You've been a great help."

"A pleasure," murmured Koiso. "I hope you won't forget, Mr. Zarich, that my government would really like to know the end result of your investigation."

Zarich nodded agreement. Perhaps Koiso figured if there was a billion dollars worth of bullion floating around, the Japanese government could forget their stance of innocence forty years ago, and lay claim to the gold. But Zarich had little doubt the gold was long gone by now.

He was like a blind man while Kuroki drove him back to the hotel, seeing nothing, his mind on fire. There was the same sense of frustration that every new insight still didn't give the complete answer to the Old Tart, yet he was excited by what Koiso had told him. He had a complete story now; it all connected. Donlett's letter to his wife. *The captain has this crazy idea to make us rich.* The ingot in the cave. Those crazy bastards forty years ago must have been tipped off about the bullion on the *Awa Maru*, they'd hijacked the gold, then sunk her. That had to be the way it happened. The ingot in the cave also had to mean they'd taken the gold to the water hole off the South Alligator River, and probably hidden it there with the intention of coming back for it after the war. What happened there? Who killed Winberg? No doubt the same one who'd taken out Donlett and Musoveld, and Emma Shepherd. The sonofabitch must have felt bloody safe for

forty years, until Donlett turned up in the New York
hospital. He still didn't have a positive theory about the
rest of the crew. Maybe they'd been killed along with
Winberg, and the crocodiles had taken care of any evidence. Yet the Old Tart itself had vanished. He sat stiff in
the seat of the car, his eyes half closed. For Chrissake,
with three bullets in his back Winberg wouldn't have been
able to go far. Maybe the Old Tart was at the bottom of
that bloody water hole. Kalangi had said it was very deep.
If there had been a massacre of the crew there was no way
a lone survivor could risk taking the PT boat back to
Darwin on his own. What-the-hell story could he give
without raising suspicion? Zarich shook his head as theory
piled on theory in his mind. He still couldn't point to
anyone, but the only thing of which he could be absolutely
sure was that some sonofabitch had survived the hijacking,
was now sitting somewhere in Australia rich as hell, ready
to kill anyone to protect the secret of the Old Tart, and
living in fear of being found out after forty years.

    He couldn't wait to get back to Australia, and fill
Harry in on the *Awa Maru*. With luck something may
have jogged Harry's memory about Schuman by now. And
there was Cassie waiting for him in Darwin. When he
stared into space the image of her face was so vivid he felt
he could reach out and touch her.

Chapter 12

    Humbert felt an uncomfortable flutter in his chest
when his secretary announced Sade had arrived at the
office to see him. He preferred meetings with Sade to be
restricted as much as possible to his home, and on the last
few occasions the man's visits to the office had coincided
with bad news. He forced himself to relax behind the desk
as Sade entered the office, and as usual his face was totally
unreadable. It could be good news, bad news, anything,

but a meeting without warning was a bad omen. One day all that bottled-up darkness in Sade would explode, and he hoped he was there to see it.

"Roman has passed through information about Zarich's movements I thought you should know about," murmured Sade.

Humbert nodded, almost fearful of asking what new disaster had loomed, and he still had the lurking suspicion there was some foul-up Sade was keeping from him.

"The Shepherd woman is still being written off as suicide?"

"Of course. Roman has that under control. No, Zarich has gone to Darwin."

He stared at Sade, the flutter still there. "Darwin? What the hell is he doing in Darwin?"

"Roman's informant still hasn't provided him with complete details," continued Sade, unperturbed. "But he evidently was given some information that took him to a location near the mouth of the South Alligator River."

"The South Alligator River," said Humbert hoarsely.

"That's right. It seems he found the remains of a man in a cave there."

Humbert turned momentarily away to conceal the nerves he felt twitching in his face. He paused before asking further questions, disciplining any tremor from his voice.

"A man? What sort of man?"

"A man who evidently died a long time ago. He's been identified as an American Naval ensign called Winberg. Michael Winberg." He paused, head poised to one side. "The name means something to you, Mr. Humbert? There's a suspicion he was a member of the crew of the Old Tart."

Humbert closed his eyes. Sade was a fucking snide bastard, sitting there blank-faced, when he must know it was earth-shattering news. God, he never did find Winberg's body, had spent hours searching, then concluded a crocodile must have taken it.

"It may," he admitted thickly. "Go on."

"There was also a gold ingot found in the cave, lying under the skeleton. There was some sort of Japanese marking on the ingot. Roman's information is that the marking is the words 'Awa Maru.' " He hesitated for another questioning stare, but Humbert said nothing. He felt temporarily beyond words; there was a sensation as if his entire stomach were draining out through his bowels. Poor stupid Winberg. How in God's name had he got hold of one of the ingots?

"What's happening to the gold ingot?" he managed to ask.

"Zarich has gone with it to Japan. I understand he has a feeling if it can be identified it might tell him a good deal about the Old Tart, and about the crew. There was a letter Donlett wrote to his wife." He coughed discreetly. "I mean the late Emma Shepherd of course. Zarich has the letter, in which Donlett mentioned that the captain of the Old Tart had an idea which was going to make the entire crew rich." He shrugged. "I doubt poor Emma had the slightest idea what her husband was talking about. Nor Zarich perhaps . . . until now." His mouth crooked into a cunning smirk. "Nor I," he added.

Humbert nodded slowly, his eyes still to the window. The view across the harbor was marred by a veil of rain. Donlett had always been a fool, never able to keep his mouth shut. God almighty, imagine what would have happened if he'd recovered with his restored memory. Disaster. But then he was already facing disaster anyway.

"Let . . . let me think on it for a while," he muttered.

Sade's head bobbed deferentially. "Of course. Whatever you decide we have all the details of Zarich's movements in Tokyo. I . . . ah, was quick to inform our contacts there to watch for him."

Humbert put his head back on the chair, breathing deeply to try and keep his mind under control. This sonofabitch Zarich had got closer than he could ever have imagined possible, in spite of every maneuver he'd taken, those he'd killed. In the beginning the killings hadn't seemed that important. Donlett, well, he should have died forty years ago, and Musoveld was a nobody. Emma Shepherd perhaps an unfortunate necessity. But the danger of Zarich had no need for rationalization.

The reports through from New York were obviously accurate—he was a persistent bulldog of a man who would never let go, could never be bought, and would gnaw and gnaw until he brought him down like a multimillion-dollar pack of cards. Well, he could be just as persistent, just as ruthless; there was no turning back now. Zarich was the linchpin of the investigation, and it was quite plain the only way to stop that was to stop him. Maybe this entire trauma could have been avoided if he'd realized that from the moment he heard Zarich was coming to Australia. Well, it still wasn't too late.

"You say you're already in touch with your contacts in Japan?" he inquired huskily.

He looked back at Sade as his head mechanically dipped in his usual servile manner.

"Yes. I thought it wise to act quickly."

He gave a grunt of satisfaction. Give Sade his due; he could be very efficient. "I want Zarich's investigation to come to an end in Japan." He stared meaningfully at Sade. "Do I make myself perfectly clear. The man has become too dangerous, and we should have seen that from the very beginning. But it ends in Japan. I don't want him back in this country. Ever."

"I understand perfectly, Mr. Humbert."

"Your contacts are reliable?"

"They have been in the past, and I don't see why it should change. The right money always guarantees reliability."

Humbert shook his head mournfully. "Perhaps if we'd known earlier the type of man Zarich is we would have acted sooner. He's always been the real danger point."

"An oversight, Mr. Humbert," consoled Sade smoothly. "It can easily be corrected. What about Markby, the Sydney detective? I don't know how much he knows, but you'll be pleased to learn Roman has managed to shift him off the case."

Humbert reflected a moment. "No, we'll leave that with Roman. Once the Zarich problem's resolved I'm sure that'll make Markby ineffectual. If there's any problem I'm sure Roman can figure some way to have Markby disgraced, even pushed right out of the force. Better that way than Markby disappearing. I don't want to cause any problems for Roman."

"Roman's payment is due also."

Humbert gave an irritated gesture of his hand. "I don't want to hear about those trifles. That's what I pay you for, Sade. You know how to handle it."

"He's an expensive item."

"Well, this whole exercise proves he's worth it. I always said a high-placed policeman on the payroll was essential." His mouth twisted in an unpleasant grin. "Don't worry, Sade, he's still a long way short of what you're paid."

The barb made no effect on Sade's flat expression. They both lapsed into silence, then finally Sade stirred in his chair, and stood to his feet.

"If there's nothing else, then I have some urgent telephone calls to make now, Mr. Humbert," he murmured.

Humbert merely gave a languid gesture of dismissal in reply. He turned back to the window as the door softly opened and closed. Sade wouldn't fail him. After the foul-up with Musoveld, he'd done well with the Shepherd woman, and he'd make doubly sure nothing went wrong over Zarich. And there were other considerations after Zarich was gone. Sade's inference that he was also learning more about the Old Tart was cause for concern. He'd have to think about that.

The rain was becoming heavier, splattering against the window, completely obscuring the view. He'd seen that countless times over the years, but now every remote image took him back to the Old Tart. The sea coming over the cockpit, drenching him, every huge wave threatening to drag her down, all of them clinging on as if riding a roller coaster in pitch darkness. Yaphank crouched down in the chart room eating his liver, and he could hear again Winberg slobbering at his side. "I'm not going to be rich, I'm going to be dead. . . . Jes', I'm going to be dead."

North of Australia 1945

The cyclone came from nowhere. Perhaps the constant mood of jubilation on board the Old Tart made them too careless to notice the ominous signs. It had gone easy up until then, hiding along islands during the day, run-

ning at night until they made the Banda Sea off Timor. By
then of course they were long overdue, and Schuman
knew they would have been reported missing. Then it
came so fast, a puff of wind that turned in minutes to a
raging fury, waves that built rapidly from an uncomfortable chop to foaming monsters intent on drowning them
all. The problem was an overweight boat responding like a
tired slug to every crushing wave sweeping over her,
leaving the cockpit like an isolated island until the hull
fought its way back to the surface. And each time the
effort seemed to take her longer. Some of the gold had to
go. It was Schuman's decision; he figured no one was
going to be rich as fish food at the bottom of the Banda
Sea. Even with half of it gone there was still more than
enough for all of them. Maybe the crew were aghast at the
order in the beginning, but as the cyclone increased in
fury, greed was quickly supplanted by desperate self-
preservation. With the exception of Yaphank, surprisingly
overcoming his terror, stampeding out of the chart house
like a raging bull as the ingots began to disappear overboard, screaming obscenities that were snatched away by
the roar of the wind. For a moment there was a ludicrous
struggle in the cockpit, where it was almost impossible to
stand on the bucking deck, let alone fight. Winberg grimly
riveted in one corner, while Schuman and Yaphank grap-
pled like two half-drowned bears. Then the boat rolled
crazily into a deep trough, and Yaphank went over backward, striking his head, and that was the end of the
opposition, at least until he recovered consciousness. But
the Old Tart began to ride easier, lifting to the waves with
restored buoyancy, and they made it through the night
until a gray dawn revealed a smoother sea. Maybe they
weren't as rich, but at least they were alive.

   He was almost out on his feet, but he took some
coffee down to Yaphank in the chart room.

   "You stupid bastard, you panicked, Jay," declared
Yaphank sullenly.

   "What was the last PT boat you skippered?" said
Schuman angrily. "Jesus Christ, don't tell me how to run
the Old Tart. She would have gone down if I hadn't

lightened her." He jerked his thumb savagely to the floor. "You crazy sonofabitch, there's no rich men down there."

It was as if Yaphank couldn't hear him. "All that fucking gold over the side. You gotta be out of your mind, Jay."

Schuman cut him off with a derisive snort of contempt. "Have a look below when you feel up to it. There's still plenty there to make rich men of all of us. I'm dead on my feet right now, so I'm going to get some shut-eye. Maybe you'll come to your senses by the time I wake up."

But Yaphank couldn't get it out of his mind; it was as if he felt the crew had deliberately cheated him, and every time he got Schuman alone in the chart house it was like a sore that refused to heal. His eyes were sunken, there was a yellowish tinge to his skin, and the fact that he hadn't shaved in days gave him even more the look of a wild wolf. Schuman knew from the old days at Columbia he could be an ugly bastard if things didn't go his way, and it merely confirmed his feelings that once the gold was split he'd cut off from Yaphank, run his own race.

"You don't seem to realize we're not going to get the true value of the gold," Yaphank hammered at him again, when they were making the final run toward the Australian coast.

"For Chrissake, Carl," exclaimed Schuman in exasperation. "You've seen what's left. I tell you there's still plenty for everyone."

"And I keep telling you it won't work like that."

"What do you mean?"

"The South American connections I've got lined up to take the stuff. Those sonofabitches aren't going to give us anywhere near the full value of the gold. They'll screw us for everything they can get."

"You said you could do a good deal with them."

"So I could with the amount of gold we had originally."

"There's still plenty," insisted Schuman stubbornly.

"They'll screw us. The split won't work."

"Now you're the one who's panicking. Anyway, we can't do anything until the war's over."

"That won't change anything."

Schuman was sick of the argument. He knew Carl;

something was building in his mind, and he could tell it was on the point of spilling out.

"Well, I say there's enough, and I'm fucking sick of you whining about it."

"You bloody hope," sneered Yaphank. He jerked his thumb contemptuously to the door. "What about the rest of these jerks?"

"What about them?"

"That's a lot of guys to keep their mouths shut for the rest of their lives."

"Christ, you really think they're going to go around talking themselves into a court martial? Are you nuts? Forget it, they know the score."

"Do they? Do they?" He wriggled his ass across the seat until his mouth was only a few inches from Schuman's face. "You and I, man . . . we know the score," he whispered fiercely. "I know you, man, you're like me, you want to be rich in a way these jerks can't imagine. And are you going to spend the rest of your days wondering if one of these creeps gets pissed at a party one night, and shoots his mouth off about the great *Awa Maru* heist? Then there's a knock at your door, and they cart you off to spend the rest of your life in the can. Is that what you want? And I keep telling you there's not enough to go around now, not for you, or me. Christ, you want to go through all this, and finish up with peanuts."

He fought it, but for the first time he could sense Yaphank was getting through to him. And he had to admit the thought of so many guys sharing the secret bugged him. But what the hell could he do about it?

"You're crazy, we can trust these guys. I know 'em," he protested feebly.

"My ass we can. You're finally seeing I'm making sense, Jay."

"I don't know what you're talking about," he protested.

"My ass you don't. We ditch 'em, Jay."

"What do you mean?"

"Like I said, just you and me. It's the only way we can ever be really rich . . . really safe."

He glanced warily about the chart room with a nagging sense of guilt. "You mean kill 'em?" he whispered. "You're out of your mind. I know these guys."

"I know you, man, from way back. Don't give me that conscience crap. How many do you figure you killed back there on the Jap ship. A thousand? Two thousand?"

"That was different."

"My ass it was. We're talking about surviving, you and I."

Schuman didn't want to hear. Those demons had already come to him in the night, and he'd shut them out of his mind. "You're crazy," he repeated.

"You stupid jerk, you know I'm not crazy, you know it."

He had to get away from Yaphank, think about it. "I . . . I've got to think about it," he muttered.

"You'll think yourself out of doing anything, and right into a lifetime in the can."

"Where . . . how?" God, he was weakening, yet how could he do it?

"Easy, leave it to me. After we've stashed the gold and got rid of the other jerks we sink the Old Tart, then head for Darwin in the life raft, the only bloody heroic survivors. It's sweet, man." Up close Yaphank's sweat stank like the hogs on the Kansas farm. "I just know a split won't work. And so do you."

He stared with repulsion at Yaphank. The hell with him, even if he hadn't been forced to dump the gold he suspected the sonofabitch had this in his mind right from the beginning. He pushed himself violently away, and went to the chart table. Yaphank had read him like a open newspaper and he was amazed to see his hands trembling. It was all right for a bloody-minded bastard like Yaphank, but how could he possibly cut these guys down? He tried not to think about it, and tapped his fingers down on the chart.

"What about this place you picked out where we can put the gold ashore?" he growled. "How well do you know it?"

Yaphank dropped the subject of the crew, moved alongside Schuman, and stared moodily at the chart. The slap of the waves beat with mechanical rhythm against the hull.

"I've only been there once," he grunted.

"You need daylight?"

"Well, I need some sort of light."

Schuman scratched doubtfully at his chin. "Daylight's too risky. We're running down into the Arafura Sea now. I figure to pull into one of these islands in the Tanimbar Archipelago for today, then make a nighttime dash for Australia. We can time it to arrive off the mouth of the South Alligator River by about dawn, so we can sneak in at half-light." He glanced at the morose Yaphank. "That suit you?"

"Sure, as long as it's high tide. I'm aiming for a deep water hole off the east bank of the river, but if we don't make the right tide we're risking being stranded on the mud."

"It's not going to be easy."

"Getting rich never is."

"We've got to find a place to hide the gold, sink the boat, make it back out to sea in the life rafts, then convince them back in Darwin we hit a mine."

"We haven't decided who goes in the rafts yet," muttered Yaphank.

Schuman didn't want to think about that, not yet. "Let's get there first," he said tersely. "You do your part, Carl, and I'll do mine."

Yaphank draped himself on the chart table, and grinned at Schuman. It was an ugly expression, his mouth tight and jagged at the corners. "I've done my part, making you rich, but I didn't figure on you being lily-livered, Jay. You think about what I said, man. Maybe you don't mind running the risk of spending the rest of your life in the can, but I'm not buying that."

"I'm still running this boat," he came back harshly. "And what I say still goes. Just don't try pulling anything without my okay."

Yaphank was instantly into retreat, his hands raised in an expression of innocence. "Okay, okay, it was only a thought. But you think about it, man. It's the only thing that makes any sense for both of us."

Schuman signaled the end of the subject with a curt scowl. He wasn't the least convinced by Yaphank's back-down; he knew him too well. Maybe none of this would have been possible without him, but from now on he'd watch the sonofabitch like a hawk.

It went exactly as planned. They slipped past the small island at the mouth of the river just as a pale smudge was lightening the horizon. The sea was a flat gray plain, but he took the Old Tart slowly, feeling his way into the opening, Yaphank at his side instructing directions. The black mass of the coastline gradually evolved into shapes and trees, separating it from sea and sky, as they probed cautiously into the broad river.

"There," pointed Yaphank suddenly. "Over to the left. See the opening."

It was a smaller stream running east off the South Alligator, and he cut down to dead slow as he turned into the new heading. It was the eerie quiet of dawn, just the soft hush of the parting water, and the muffled throb of the engines. Startled birds winged out of the surrounding trees with shrill cries, and occasionally there was the grating sound of the Old Tart scraping bottom. He scowled at Yaphank, carefully holding her dead center. "We've had it if we run aground," he muttered.

"It'll take it," Yaphank assured him confidently.

Schuman could sense the tension on board, as if everyone were breathing in concert with the Old Tart. The crew had never recaptured the jubilant mood of before the cyclone, but unlike Yaphank, no one had voiced objections to dumping part of the gold. The brush with death had subdued them. They would have been even more subdued to see into Yaphank's mind, and maybe even his.

It was almost full light by the time the stream broadened out into a large lake, dotted with water lilies, and teeming with bird life. Along the bank crocodiles either lay like inert logs, or slithered rapidly into the water.

"It's deep," said Yaphank. "We can sink her here, and she wouldn't be found for a hundred years."

"It's perfect," chortled Winberg. "Jesus, it's perfect."

"Here," declared Yaphank curtly. "Right here, Jay."

Schuman brought the engines to a dead stop, and they dropped anchor to Berger's bawled orders. In the

silence his strident voice ricocheted across the water, and
he gave Schuman a startled grin. It was as if they were the
only people on earth, the war nothing but an uncomfirmed
rumor.

"Bloody perfect," said Winberg again.

Schuman nodded. He was right. Maybe they could
be spotted from the air, but if they found a place for the
gold and worked fast, then scuttled the Old Tart, there
was only the chance threat of a passing aircraft.

"Just no one fall overboard," warned Schuman. "Not
with all those crocodiles about." He rubbed his hands
vigorously together in the crisp early morning air, and
glanced about with satisfaction. "Okay you guys, let's move
fast." His eyes searched the sky. "We probably won't get
any aircraft this way, but don't let's chance our luck."

He detailed Berger to supervise bringing the gold
ashore in the life raft, while together with Yaphank and
Winberg, he searched for a suitable hiding place. They
spread out as the land rose to a ridge three or four hundred yards from the river, until a call from Yaphank brought
them together. He was standing at the base of a rocky
outcrop, thumping his heel into the red soil.

"I figure this is a good place," he grunted. He gestured back down to the lake. "They tell me this is sometimes a flood plain in the wet season, but it'll be safe on
this high ground."

Schuman offered no objection, but it was difficult not
to have a sneaking regard for the way Yaphank had figured
out all the angles. He must have spent a lot of time asking
questions and working out details before he even approached him about the *Awa Maru* in Darwin. He glanced
down to where the crew were already ferrying the gold to
the bank, then back to the site Yaphank had chosen. The
ocher-colored rock loomed above the ridge like a craggy
totem pole, and it would be a good location marker.
Overhead the whisps of dawn cloud had dispersed, and
already the sun was giving promise of heat.

"Okay, get the guys up here with the shovels, Mike,"
he ordered. "It's going to be tough digging, but let's get it
done before the sun gets too hot."

"Well, at least there isn't so much gold to carry now," Yaphank sneered.

Schuman let it pass. Maybe Yaphank had a point about the crew, but he wasn't going to go along with any killing; he'd been with these guys too long. There had to be another way.

It took longer than Schuman estimated, what with the digging into the flint-hard ground, the slow process of bringing the gold ashore on the life raft, then each man carrying the ingots to the burial site. By midmorning they were all bare-waisted with sweat running freely, so they took a break on the bank, while Ferras and Halmstead went across to the Old Tart for rations.

Schuman sat down, propped his back against a tree, and lit a cigarette. There were ten of them with Yaphank— although that bastard wasn't exactly breaking his back, if he pushed them hard it could be finished in another hour. He guessed he should stop worrying about aircraft; the Old Tart was only about fifty feet off the bank, and she'd be hard to spot with her camouflage colors. Spotty-faced young Corum stood by with the carbine in case of any inquisitive crocodiles. It was a good time for dreaming speculation about what he would do with the money after the war. But Yaphank's fears kept turning every vision sour. Was it really crazy risking all these guys keeping their mouths shut for the rest of their lives? And in spite of his confident reassurances to Carl, now they were actually burying the gold he was stunned by how much they must have thrown overboard. If Yaphank's concern about the South American sale was true, maybe he wouldn't be as rich as he imagined. Could he really push himself to Yaphank's solution after all?

"I'm going up to stand guard by the gold," said Winberg abruptly.

Schuman rolled lazily on his side. "What's the problem, Mike? For Chrissake, there's not another soul for hundreds of miles."

Winberg moved determinedly toward the ridge. "I've been told back in Darwin there's plenty of blacks around here," he called back. "I thought I saw signs when we were working up there earlier."

"You didn't say anything."

"I wasn't sure. I'm just going to take a look. Sure as hell it'd be crazy if they've been watching what we're doing."

Schuman shrugged. Winberg was always jumping at shadows, but if he wanted to satisfy himself, let him. For now he wasn't budging. Damn Yaphank, he'd been under so much pressure from the time they'd left Darwin, what with the attack on the *Awa Maru*, then the cyclone and the run back to Australia, and now Carl had turned his mind into a can of worms. But he couldn't make a decision. He stretched out by the tree, and tried to force himself to relax. He'd just play along for now, and see what chances offered, for he figured there was still danger in the life raft trip back to Darwin and anything could happen.

Ensign Winberg didn't like Carl Yaphank; every instinct warned him to distrust the man. He'd always hit it off reasonably well with Schuman, but he couldn't help feeling that Yaphank and Schuman together could be a dangerous combination. Maybe he could trust Schuman because of the way the captain had it figured to dispose of the gold, but Yaphank was something else again, especially with the way he kept moaning about the gold thrown overboard. He'd sold insurance before the war, and he needed some insurance now. Maybe he'd been a little crazy getting himself into the goddamn hijacking, but he wasn't going to get cheated out of his share. He could still remember his old man's words when he took his first job. "You're goin' out into a world full of sharks, kid, so just make goddamn sure you don't get eaten." Well, Yaphank was a shark if he'd ever seen one.

He halted at the lip of the hole, the gold at the bottom shimmering yellow in the sun. He glanced back to the crew on the bank, lolling about, talking, smoking. They were partly screened by the trees, and from his high vantage point he could see them, but he figured unless they stood up and looked toward the digging site, they couldn't see him.

He'd stumbled on a small cave when they were doing

the preliminary search, but he hadn't said anything to Schuman or Yaphank, because there had already been the kernel of an insurance idea forming in his mind.

He dropped to his knees and reached down swiftly into the hole, seized one of the ingots, then concealing it in his shirt he went quickly to the cave, and threw it inside. No one was doing a count, and perhaps if he could stash four or five ingots in the cave he'd have his own nest egg, just in case Yaphank or Schuman tried any cute double cross. He was almost back to the hole when he saw Berger halfway up the rise toward him.

"See anything?" shouted the quartermaster. He gave a negative wave of his hand, silently mouthing obscenities. Berger's rubbery face creased into a smile.

"I thought I'd better help you," said Berger. "Just in case you did see any blacks."

Winberg nodded sullen thanks. Maybe Berger meant it, or perhaps they were all getting to a stage of not trusting each other. But he never got another chance to add to his nest egg in the cave.

They were finished in another hour, and they stood around as if observing a funeral service, while the gold gradually disappeared under each shovelful of red earth.

"Best bloody funeral I've ever been to," cracked Halmstead.

They all laughed uneasily. Maybe the thought of when they'd get their share was on every man's mind, if trust would last, if they could rely on each other to keep their mouths shut.

Ferras voiced some of their unease. "Just let's hope we can convince 'em back in Darwin that we hit a mine, that's all," he muttered. His eyes took in his fellow crewmates one by one. "Just make fucking sure everyone tells the same story."

There was a murmur of assent from the group.

"They probably think we're all fish food by now," said Schuman.

"You'll convince them, Jay," said Winberg confidently.

"Yeah, you'll tell 'em, skipper," joined in Berger.

They were halfway down the slope before Schuman

suddenly realized Carl wasn't amongst them. "Where's Yaphank?" he asked Winberg.

The ensign glanced around, then shrugged. "Search me, Jay. I saw him when we started filling the hole. I guess he went on ahead down to the bank."

It irritated Schuman. There was a sense of aggravation that Yaphank had got to him, and whatever happened he anticipated a wrangling hassle when it came to converting the gold into cash.

When they arrived at the bank the life raft was moored over against the side of the Old Tart. They could see Yaphank's skinny frame moving toward the bow, and Schuman stood hands on hips, glaring across the water.

"What the hell do you think you're doing, Carl?" he shouted.

Yaphank waved back reassuringly. "I'm coming, I'm coming. Just hold on a minute."

"Come on, you sonofabitch, get that life raft back here."

Yaphank halted by the machine gun. "Don't you guys move," he called urgently. "I spotted two giant crocs off to the side of you, about twenty foot long. I'll get the bastards with this."

"Fuck the crocodiles," declared Schuman furiously. "Get that raft back here, you crazy bastard. You don't know how to use that thing."

"Yes I do. Berger showed me." He cocked the gun, and pointed it along the bank.

"Lay off, you jerk," roared Schuman.

The words caught suddenly in his throat, and he stepped back from the water. Maybe it was instinct, an awareness of how dangerous Yaphank could be, and even as the muzzle was swinging rapidly toward the crew he was throwing himself back behind a fallen tree trunk. He squirmed into the mud as the machine gun yammered death, the sound mingling with the screams of the crew as Yaphank cut them down. Splinters ricocheted about him; he could hear the sickening thud of bullets impacting against flesh, and the soft squelch of bodies dropping in the mud. The bastard, the fucking double-crossing sonofabitch, Yaphank not only figured on crossing the crew out of their cut, he was going to cross him out too. The fear he should have felt was overwhelmed by fury.

It was all over in a few minutes, even the bird life stunned into silence. He didn't move, gradually opening his eyes. There were bodies sprawled everywhere, mud blended with blood, and he saw Winberg laying on his stomach near the undergrowth, still alive, his eyes wide in shocked disbelief.

He silently berated himself. He'd told himself over and over to watch Yaphank, yet he'd been taken completely off guard. He should have known from the old days that a creep like Carl was never going to settle for just a share, certainly not when the take had been cut in half. He didn't know how he was going to do it, but he'd kill the bastard. Doubtless Yaphank would come across to confirm the slaughter, and all he could do was hope the murdering shit believed he'd got him along with the rest of the crew.

The tree completely cut off any view of the Old Tart, but he still kept perfectly still. Berger lay just a few feet away, on his back, the carbine within easy reach.

After a while he heard splashing sounds which he guessed came from the life raft, and he knew it had to be Yaphank coming ashore. If he wanted to live, he had to move now. He cautiously reached out and grasped the carbine by the muzzle, pulled it gingerly toward him, then began a crablike shuffle backward until he was behind an upward curve in the trunk that provided a view of the bank. Yaphank was already out of the life raft, picking his way carefully through the massacre, the .45 from the chart room in his hand. Then he passed out of view, and he must have found someone still alive, maybe Winberg, because the sound of a shot suddenly reverberated around the trees. He knew it wouldn't take the shit long to realize he wasn't among the bodies. He cocked the carbine, raised himself stealthily on his knees, braced his elbows on the tree trunk, and positioned the gun at his shoulder. Yaphank's back was to him, the .45 held loosely at his side, stepping carefully around each body. To Schuman's surprise he saw Winberg had disappeared.

"You shit Yaphank . . . this is for you," he muttered hoarsely.

Yaphank turned suddenly to stone, then ever so gradually he moved around, and stared at Schuman. For a time neither man spoke. If Yaphank felt any fear, he was expert at keeping it out of his face.

"Jay, I was just coming over to take you back to the Old Tart," he said finally.

God, he was smooth; he made it sound like an invitation to a party.

"You could see I was aiming to miss you," he added.

"The fuck you were."

"No, it's the truth. We talked about it, you know we're in this together, man. We need each other." He made a small gesture with the gun. "You know these guys are nothing. Christ, you can't keep a secret like this with ten guys, we agreed about that. I don't want to finish up in the can, and neither do you." He laughed, and for the first time he was betrayed by the bubbling sound of fear in his throat. "You know I'm right, there's just not enough gold to go around now. This makes us safe . . . safe and rich. Just the two of us." He nodded toward the slaughtered crew. "You wanted this just as much as I did. I could see it in your face when we were talking about it, but I knew you'd never have the guts. So I did it for both of us."

Schuman listened, but he didn't let the carbine deviate a fraction from Yaphank's chest. Maybe what he was saying was true; perhaps he had secretly wished for this, might have even done something about it himself in time, but he knew it was bullshit Yaphank had aimed to miss him. Trusting Yaphank was a good way to finish up dead.

"Come on, Jay, put down the carbine," Yaphank implored. "We can make it together. We dump the bodies in the Old Tart, sink her like we planned anyway, and take off in the life raft. We got it made, Jay."

"No," said Schuman slowly. "*I've* got it made, Carl." He squeezed the trigger and hit him twice before he went down, once in the chest, then his head disintegrated into a crimson explosion. After a while he stood to his feet, and stared at the bodies for a long time. He'd known these guys, shared good and bad times with them, yet all he could think of was that the gold was his now. Yaphank had done the killing, but it had always been in his own mind. He could leave the bodies there for the crocodiles, but that was risky. There just might be blacks around, and it would blow everything if they found them. No, it would be safer to lock them below in the Old Tart before he sent her to the bottom.

But he couldn't find Winberg's body. Maybe he would only have finished him off anyway, but the ensign must have crawled away somewhere to die. In the end he had to assume a crocodile had done the job for him.

It was late, but Humbert felt no pressing urgency to go home. Water coursed down the office window like an incoming tide, and the lights of Sydney quivered as if a mirage. So Winberg had crawled into some cave, and left his bones to threaten him forty years later. But it was still a mystery how one of the ingots was found with him. God, he could recall so vividly the sense of power that had come to him that day standing on the riverbank, surrounded by bodies. A feeling anything was possible for him, and it ran just as strongly in his veins now. The memory served to strengthen the feeling he'd made the right decision about Zarich.

Chapter 13

Markby waited in his car outside the Randwick racetrack until after the last race, watching the select few departing with contented smiles of success, and the defeated majority slinking homeward to lick their wounds. Hating to lose made him a bad punter, so he seldom went to the races. Helen had an occasional flutter, but it was strictly a one-dollar affair. He was parked a little away from the track, slumped low in the driver's seat. It had to

be a million-dollar chance against Roman's seeing him, but
he didn't want to take the slightest risk.

The opposite door opened, and Ferret slid in beside
him with his usual grin. The little man was nattily dressed,
sharp suit, pale tie against a dark shirt, and a small hat
perched cockily on the side of his head. Fate had nomi-
nated Ferret Westy a loser the day he was born. When
the other babies were screaming to make themselves heard,
he was screaming for breath. He was around fifty, an
ex-jockey, five feet tall, nuggety build, and ugly. Big
beetle nose, thick lips, lank hair, almost no jaw, an unjust
facade for a man who only wanted to be loved. He had
failed as a jockey, a husband, and a burglar, and was
heading for the gutter when Markby picked him up. The
sergeant had a feeling for losers, and he made a project of
the Ferret. He fed him, got him a job, gave him back his
self-respect, and in the process discovered the one real
talent Ferret possessed. He was a brilliant tail, and could
follow a man around undetected as if he'd taken up residence in his pocket. For his part Ferret would have thrown
himself under a train if Markby had asked.

"You can relax now, Sarge," he chuckled. "Everyone's gone home with empty wallets, except the chief
inspector." He shook his head. "Jes', you learn somethin'
every day."

"Tell me what you learned, Ferret?"

"I learned how to make a packet at the races without
bettin' on a bloody horse, that's what I learned."

"Tell me who you learned that from."

"The bloke you asked me to tail, your old mate Chief
Inspector Roman. From the collect I saw him make I'd say
he picked up a cool hundred thousand on Flyin' Fox in the
fourth, but he didn't back it."

Markby lit up a cigar, and fouled the air with acrid
smoke. The Ferret coughed several times, and the detective apologetically diffused the smoke with his hands. "I
don't get you, Ferret."

"Okay, this is the way it goes, Sarge. Roman sits in
the stand before the fourth race. A well-dressed geezer
comes and sits alongside, and puts a rolled-up form guide
on the seat between them. They don't talk, act like total

strangers. After a while the well-dressed geezer gets up an' walks off, but leaves the form guide, all nice'n'casual, y'know. Roman picks up the form guide, see, and when I'm followin' him I see him dump the form guide in the garbage bin, and guess what, there's a nice little envelope inside the form guide."

"An envelope?"

"Yeah . . . with a bettin' ticket inside. When Flyin' Fox's number comes up he takes his ticket to the window, and they've practically got to give him a wheelbarrow to cart the dough away." He laughed, and the great nose bobbed like a pointer dog in action. "Jes', talk about smooth. What a fuckin' payoff operation."

"Whoever was doing the paying would have to be very sure Flying Fox was going to win."

Ferret gave a derisive snort. "You know better than that, Sarge. It can be done. You shoulda told me your big-time mate was on the take."

Markby nodded slowly, eyes moodily on his cigar. He felt no satisfaction. Fuck Roman, the greedy bastard, there were so many decent guys on the force playing it square, and the chief inspector dragged them all down in the shit with him. He might suspect Kepler Humbert was the one paying off Roman, but he couldn't prove it. Would Roman really play ball with a creep who had already contracted for three murders, with Cassie a possible fourth if she hadn't got lucky? That was a deep, deep hole. He knew he was right now; the leak that had been bugging Zarich had come directly from Roman.

"This well-dressed geezer, the one providing the winning ticket for Roman. Have you ever seen him before?"

"Nope. Creepy-lookin' bloke, bald, thin-faced, tall, and I'd reckon about my age. Maybe younger. Looked like he'd make a good funeral director."

"Did you see him around the track again?"

"Sure. You told me to play it by ear, so I did, Sarge. Soon as I saw Roman collect his wad, I switched to the well-dressed geezer. He was still around, just checkin' to see Roman collected his payout, then he took off."

"You tailed him?"

"Only to the car park." He reached into his pocket,

and produced a scrap of paper. "I've got the registration number of his car all written down, Sarge."

Markby grinned delightedly, and affectionately pushed Ferret's hat down over his eyes. "Ferret, you're a bloody genius. Check it out for me, and call me at headquarters soon as you can on Monday morning."

"Sure thing." He hesitated, eyes concerned. "You gonna try and nail Roman, Sarge? That's big stuff, you watch yourself, mate."

"Don't worry, I can take care of myself. I'll play it so cool you'll think I'm Cary Grant."

They both laughed, but there was a note of unease in Ferret's voice.

Markby dropped Ferret off in the city, then drove thoughtfully home. What he had now was growing so big, it scared the shit out of him. A chief inspector on the take. Probably the wealthiest and most powerful business man in Australia a murderer. Yet he knew he couldn't prove any of it. Did it all connect up with the gold ingot Zarich had found in the cave up north? Roman must have put a bug on Chooka's phone for him to know about Zarich in Darwin. Did that mean he also knew about him flying to Japan? He decided the only thing he could do was sit on it all for now until Zarich got back from Japan, then maybe they could compare notes, and see if they had a case.

As soon as he walked in the door and saw the expression on Helen's face, he knew something was terribly wrong.

"There's no need to look like that, I didn't even have a bet," he tried jocularly.

It didn't work. She came to him with her eyes brimming, put her arms around, and dropped her head down on his shoulder. Someone had to have died to warrant that sort of behavior. An aunt, an uncle? A brother?

"What's going on, honey?" he inquired gently.

She lifted her head, and dabbed at her eyes. "I just got a call from Japanese Airlines."

An icy finger probed at his spine. "Japanese Airlines?"

"Ed Zarich left our number with them as a forwarding contact. There's been a crash, Harry."

He stared at her. "A crash?"

"A Japanese jumbo jet . . . somewhere over the South China Sea they said . . . it just, just blew up. There were no survivors."

He felt as if he had to unglue his tongue to speak. "Ed . . . Ed was on the plane?"

She nodded dumbly. He released her, somehow found a chair, then sat back and stared blankly into space. "Jesus Christ," he muttered.

Helen stood there as if unsure what to do. "I, I didn't know him that well, but he seemed such a nice man . . . and that poor girl . . . Cassie. They seemed so much in love."

"Yeah, yeah," he mumbled tonelessly. He scuffed absently at his strands of hair. He felt stunned. "I'll call Chooka. They'll both have to know as soon as possible."

"I'll . . . I'll go and make a cup of tea," murmured Helen.

It was her timeless remedy for any crisis, but he didn't stop her. In just a short time he'd formed a close affinity with Zarich, and he felt a real sense of loss. The plane just blew up. My God, would they really go that far; was Ed so close to the truth with what he had found out about the ingot in Japan? He'd been on a 747, and he tried to imagine all those people dying because some creep thought Ed was too dangerous to stay alive. Whatever it was Humbert was trying to hide about the Old Tart, if he'd go this far he was nothing but a lunatic psychopath. He'd get the bastard, he'd get 'em all, including Roman. He owed it to Ed. He silently drank the tea, and Helen left him alone. She knew how troubled he'd been over the last few days, and maybe he should take her into his confidence. Christ, he had to talk to someone. He thought of going over Roman's head to the assistant commissioner if possible, but with what? Some photographs, artist's drawings, and suspicions that a smart ass lawyer would blow out of court. If it ever got to court with the clout Humbert had. Besides, how high up did Humbert's corruption go? He opened his mouth, and it might be an invitation to a bullet in the back. Well, the bastards got Ed, but they wouldn't get him. He'd dig like he was trying to find his way to the center of the earth, even if it meant going to Japan himself, and trying to backtrack on Ed. But he didn't have the evidence of the gold now, with the ingot at the bottom of the South China Sea. He waited until he reckoned he had himself together, then he called Chooka.

"Bloody hell, Harry," said the old man in dismay. "That's terrible . . . absolutely terrible. Jes', he was so excited when he found that ingot, reckoned he was really on to something." His tongue clucked mournfully over the phone. "I suppose we'll never know now."

"I've got a strong feeling there are some people in Sydney who'll be bloody glad we'll never know, Chooka," said Harry savagely.

"Are you sayin' what I think you're sayin', Harry?"

"What do you think?"

"I heard about the crash. They reckon the plane just blew up in midair. Christ, Harry, all those people. Would they go that far because of Ed . . . I mean that's bloody terrible. They'd have to be insane."

"I'm not saying anything for now, Chooka, and don't you either. If they're not going to stop at a planeload of innocent people, then you and I don't count for much, mate."

Chooka was at once subdued. "Right . . . yeah, you're bloody right, Harry." He paused. "Listen, you want to tell Cassie, or will I? It's going to be rough on her whichever way."

Markby thought about that for a moment. He wasn't trying to chicken out, but it could sound so unfeeling over the phone, and Chooka was good at that sort of thing.

"No, I'd prefer you to tell her, Chooka. You've got good broad shoulders for her to cry on. Don't say anything about what I suspect, just that the plane crashed."

"It won't be easy."

"You can do it."

"Okay, leave it with me. Should I send her back to Sydney? I mean she can stay here as long as she likes, but she was only waiting for Ed to come back. You reckon she'd be safe in Sydney now?"

"I . . . I don't know," answered Markby warily. "Maybe. With Ed dead they might reckon she isn't a threat anymore. Not that she ever was anyway. See if you can talk her into staying on a week or so until I see how things are going."

"Okay, I'll be in touch. But it's bloody terrible about Ed."

"Yeah. It won't stop me, Chooka."

"You watch yourself, young fella," warned Chooka. "Seems to me like these bastards'll stop at nothing."

"I can handle myself."

"So could Ed."

He let it pass, and hung up. He called New York, and spoke to the police captain Beuso that Zarich had told him about. It was difficult to cover the shocked silence with expressions of regret. Not that he gathered Beuso had meant any great deal in Ed's life, but he had to be told. But Markby said nothing of his suspicions of sabotage. Maybe that would come later, because the way the plane went down people were bound to start asking questions eventually. He promised to send over everything Ed had on the case before he hung up.

Then he called Roman, and even that worthy seemed slightly stunned by the news. Maybe he was more taken aback by the ruthless way Zarich had been dealt with, for there was a choking timbre to his voice. Yet he got some satisfaction in hearing the chief inspector squirm.

"That's tough luck," said Roman gruffly. "I'm sorry to hear it."

Lying bastard, thought Markby bitterly, but he managed to keep the rancor out of his voice. "I called his chief in New York to let him know."

There was a moment's silence. "That was the department's responsibility," snapped Roman. "You should have left that to me, Markby."

"Well, I guess you can make a follow-up call."

"I intend to."

"He didn't say if he was sending a replacement."

"That's something I'll discuss with him. The investigation obviously wasn't getting anywhere." He paused, and grittily cleared his throat. "Besides, it's nothing to do with you now, Harry," he concluded offensively.

It was apparent that Roman's initial shock had quickly

passed. Well, let the chief inspector believe the fantasy he
was no longer interested in the case, but he'd stick it to
him for Ed if it took forever.

"I was just letting you know," he grunted sullenly,
then put the phone down. There wasn't the slightest doubt
in his mind that Roman would quietly sidetrack the case
into obscurity now.

He spent the remainder of the weekend cut off from
his surroundings in a detached state of mind, his feelings
alternating between fear and fury. He kicked a football
with the boys, but with such obvious disinterest they
abandoned him in disgust. Helen crept about the house as
if fearful of waking the dead, providing cups of tea, and
inviting confidence with sympathetic smiles.

"I'm here if you want to talk, Harry," she offered
again several times, and he silently declined for the same
reasons. He guessed he was giving her a hard time, and
toward Sunday evening he made a determined effort to
snap out of it. But there was no way he could leave it
alone, it was a challenge to everything he believed himself
to be. It would be so easy to creep away into a safe hole,
keep his mouth shut, his eyes closed, and no one would
ever be the wiser. Humbert would go on being the most
powerful man in Australia; Roman would go on into comfortable superannuated retirement, with all his take from
Humbert carefully invested. But how could he live with
that when so many people had died? Yet he was a rela-
tively unimportant detective sergeant in the Sydney Police Force, and he knew if he tried to nail the powerful
bastards he risked being crushed like an ant. And maybe
Helen, and his sons. By Sunday night it was still unre-
solved, and he was beginning to think it would just remain
in a state of flux, until it all drifted away into nothing.

Chooka called him back.

"She's gone, Harry."

"You mean Cassie?"

"That's right. I told her about Ed as gentle as I could,
and she took it as if the earth fell on her. Then she just
said she was going back to Sydney, that she couldn't stay
any longer."

"Shit. Did you tell her I thought it mightn't be safe yet?"

"Yeah, I tried to tell her, but she said she didn't care, and with Ed gone why the hell should they bother with her. Maybe she's right."

"Maybe. I'll try and keep an eye on her." Could he do that? If one of Roman's watchdogs saw him with Emma Shepherd's granddaughter they'd know he was still poking his nose into the case. He'd have to handle it carefully. "Did she say if she was going back to her place in Paddington?"

"Didn't say anything, Harry. Just took off."

"Well, thanks for letting me know, Chooka. I'll try and watch for her."

"My pleasure. And don't forget what I said, mate. Just keep looking over your shoulder."

After the call he brooded awhile in the chair overlooking the small back garden. The dog had knocked down one of Helen's plants, and he could hear the boys trying to defend the culprit. They would have to come first, but if he went on with this thing he'd have to pull out every trick he'd learned in fifteen years on the force. And maybe invent some new ones.

He got through most of Monday, but the mental fog still refused to lift. He kept himself strictly out of Roman's way. He'd always considered Roman a good cop, but never liked him, and now he was wary of the contempt showing in his face.

Around three o'clock he received a call from Ferret.

"The man's name is Irwin Sade, Sarge. Lives in a swank house at Palm Beach. I drove out there and took a look. Lotsa dough I'd say."

The information stirred his interest again. Maybe he needed something like this to get himself started.

"Nice work, Ferret. Give me the address?" He scrawled it down quickly on his pad. "Do you know anything else about him?"

"Not right now. You want me to follow it up?"

He sharpened his voice to conceal his sense of depression. "No, not right now, but thanks, mate. I want anything else from you I'll be in touch."

"You've only got to say the word, Sarge."

He put the phone down, rested his head on his hands, and stared blankly at the name and address. He could check through the files, but he doubted he'd find anyone there with the slightest connection to Kepler Humbert. In the end he did the simplest thing possible, but one which had served him well over the years. He looked up the Humbert Corporation number, dialed, and asked to speak to Humbert's secretary. Trying to talk to corporation big shots was like trying to get through to the moon, but their secretaries were invariably courteous projections of their company's image.

"I'd like to speak to Mr. Sade, please," he asked crisply, in his best executive-style voice.

"I'm sorry, but Mr. Sade is out of the office most of the time. Can I take a message?"

Bull's-eye. As simple as that. All he'd wanted was a connection between Roman and Humbert, and he had it right in his lap.

"No. We have a new insurance policy we've evolved for company executives, and I believe Mr. Sade would find it interesting," he said smoothly.

"Well I'm sorry, sir, but I've no idea when Mr. Sade will be in the office again. You understand we can't give out private addresses."

"Of course. Thank you, I'll try again next week."

He cut the connection with a grin of satisfaction. Well, he had a line from Sade to Roman to Humbert, but he wasn't too sure where that led him with Ed Zarich. No wonder Roman was so intent on knowing Ed's movements, when he was passing it straight to Humbert via Sade. It only strengthened his conviction that Ed's plane had been sabotaged. But he still didn't know how he was going to handle all this stuff without getting himself killed.

He was kept late that night trying to run down a lead on a heroin pusher who got stuck with a knife, but it proved to be a dead end. He considered dropping off at the Purple Pussycat to see if Cassie was already back at the club. He owed her some expression of sympathy, but he hadn't figured out how to handle her yet, whether she was still in danger or not. He picked up a newspaper on the way home, and already the questions were coming thick and fast about the way the Japanese airliner just blew out of the sky. Trouble was how would they ever know with the pieces at the bottom of the South China Sea.

He pulled into the driveway of his house, cut the motor, then sat for five minutes trying to figure out what was wrong. Helen never turned the lights off at the front of the house like that, except maybe when he was very late, and it was only nine o'clock. He finally stepped out, stood by the car for a few moments, then padded quietly around to the side of the house. At the bottom of the side path he could see a solitary light burning from the laundry window. He was sure Helen would have called him, or at least left a message if she was going out. He moved swiftly to the back of the house, poised listening for a time, then gently tried the rear door. It was unlocked. Alarm bells were ringing loud and clear in his head now, and he slipped the .32 into his hand before he stepped into the house. The fear creeping up from his belly into his throat wasn't for himself, but for Helen and the boys. He was instantly plagued by doubts that he hadn't been careful enough, he should have sent them away somewhere until he knew what he was going to do, but by God if anything had been done to them he'd go to Roman and put a bullet in the bastard's head.

Apart from the laundry there was only darkness, but his familiarity with the house required no light. He felt his way cautiously through the small dining room, around the kitchen island bench, and halted at the entrance to the living room. There was nothing but the vague outline of furniture, except for the pale fuzz of the outside street light through the window curtains at the far end. He raised the pistol, and flattened himself against the wall.

"Helen," he called in a hoarse whisper.

There was only silence. A car purred along the street outside, the headlights flicked briefly about the room, then there was hushed darkness again. "Helen," he tried once more.

There was a click from the standing lamp at the far

end of the room, and for an instant his eyes refused to adjust to the sudden flush of light.

"Take it easy, Harry," murmured the man standing by the wall, one hand still at the lamp switch.

He gaped. Ridiculously he lost control of his fingers, and the gun clumped to the floor. His mouth opened, but shock strangled the words in his throat.

"Ed," he croaked finally. "Jesus . . . Ed . . . is it really you . . . It can't, my God, Ed . . . Ed Zarich."

A wild thought rushed through his mind that he was seeing a vision—all the strain he'd been under was creating mirages in his mind—and as he stumbled into the room with outstretched arms Zarich moved swiftly to grasp him.

"Easy, Harry, easy," soothed Zarich. "Easy . . . yes, it's me, really me. You didn't think the bastards would get Ed Zarich as easily as that, did you?"

Then Markby was accepting flesh and blood reality, laughing crazily, thumping Zarich repetitively across the shoulders, and crying out, "For Chrissake, it is you . . . my God, my God, it is you . . . you're right, Ed, you old son of a gun. I shoulda known . . . you fooled 'em, mate, you beat the bastards."

It took quite a time for the usually phlegmatic Markby to calm down, and even then he kept looking at Zarich as if he couldn't believe his eyes. Then as sanity gradually returned, he glanced quickly about the room. "Wait a minute, hell, where's Helen and the boys?"

"I only got here about an hour ago, Harry. I had to wait until dark. I hated to give Helen such a fright, but she damn near fainted when she saw me. But being around me is a dangerous business now . . . mate. I persuaded her to go to her sister's with the boys for the night at least, while you and I sort out what we're going to do."

"You crazy bastard sitting in the dark, I might've shot you."

"I wasn't sure it was you, Harry. After what those psychopaths did with the Japanese airliner I'm trying to walk around as if I've got eyes in the back of my head."

Markby shook his head. "You figured the same as I did about the airliner?"

Zarich eased himself into the chair by the lamp, his mouth set in grim lines. "I can't be sure, Harry. No one can. It's hard to imagine they'd go that far, but . . ." He shrugged. "Yeah, I haven't the slightest doubt it was meant for me. They had to know I was in Japan, why I was there, like they've known every move I've made since I arrived in Australia."

Markby shook his head glumly. "They're crazy, Ed. They've got to be. Jes', all those people."

"They'll do anything, Harry."

Markby made a quick gesture toward the kitchen. "Listen, I know you've got a lot to tell me, and Christ I want to know how the hell you weren't on that plane. I'm going to get a coupla beers, and we're going to sit here and talk this through." He grinned ruefully. "You've got me in a state of shock, Ed, and I need something."

Zarich nodded, folded wearily back into the chair, and closed his eyes, while Markby scuttled from the room. He was back quickly with two cans, and even as he handed one to Zarich there was still glazed disbelief in his eyes. "I'm still not sure this isn't some bloody dream," he muttered with a forced grin.

Zarich's tongue flicked nervously over his mouth, and he solemnly contemplated the can for a second. "Let's say more like a nightmare, Ed," he whispered. Then he shook himself as if trying to break free from the horror, and raised his can with a grave smile. "Here's to survival, Harry. Survival, and luck, because that's why I'm sitting here with you now."

He held the can long to his mouth, and the cold beer sluicing into his throat was like the feel of survival, of being alive, of wanting to see Cassie again, hold her and tell her he was safe.

Markby motioned to him with his can. "You first, Ed. I've got some pretty startling news to tell you myself, but you first."

Zarich shrugged. "It was simple really. I flew up with the ingot packed in my suitcase, and it bugged the hell out of me. I know luggage doesn't usually go astray, but I kept thinking of the consequences if it did. After all, it was the only real piece of evidence I had. So I figured no way was

I going to let it out of my sight for the return trip, I'd just put it in my carryon bag as hand luggage. Well, it got picked up as I was going through the security check at Narita Airport. Christ, in about two seconds I found myself under arrest. There was no way the security authorities were going to let me take the ingot aboard, and there was no way I was going to leave it behind. There was a hell of a lot of telephoning trying to locate the people I'd seen in Tokyo, but it was a weekend, they weren't in the offices, and I didn't know their home numbers. They had me locked in a private room as if they figured I was involved in some sort of gold smuggling racket." He gave an embarrassed grin. "I mean if I'd been thinking straight I would have got it cleared first, but I was trying to keep the trip so low-key." He swirled the can in his hand, then emptied it with another long swallow. "By the time I was cleared the plane had gone. My name must have stayed on the passenger list, but that hassle over the ingot saved my ass, Harry." He fell silent. "Saved my ass," he repeated softly, as if like Markby he could scarcely believe it. "Anyway, I decided to stay dead," he continued. "I figured if they wanted me dead that much then it gave me an advantage to let them think they'd pulled it off, they might just relax enough to let me nail 'em. So I got on a Qantas flight, flew into Sydney today, and came straight here . . . with the ingot." He grinned uncertainly. "A real Lazarus job, Harry, only I came out of a plane instead of a cave. But I figure I haven't got much time, for I'm sure it won't last. My name'll go on the computor somewhere as a Qantas arrival, then someone's going to start checking back on the Japanese passenger list, and they'll know I survived." He paused, thoughtfully turning the empty can over in his hands. "With luck I should have a few days to play with." He ducked his head apologetically toward Markby. "Sorry about Helen and the boys, but I couldn't think of anywhere else to go, Harry. I mean not if I was going to keep out of sight. I guess it puts you on the spot, but . . ."

Markby cut across him with a quick gesture of his hand. "Forget it, Ed. Christ, forget it. You had to come here, there was nowhere else. I just think it's fantastic you're alive." He leaned across with sudden enthusiasm, and slapped Zarich affectionately across the shoulders. "Bloody fantastic."

"What about Cassie?" asked Zarich. There were many other things, but he had to know about her.

"She's back in Sydney," said Markby uneasily.

Zarich's eyebrows tilted in surprise. "She knew about the crash?"

"Yeah. I called Chooka, and he told her." He offered a rueful expression of concern. "She evidently took it pretty badly, Ed. I wanted her to stay with him awhile, I reckoned it might still be dangerous for her in Sydney, but Chooka called back to say he couldn't hold her." He twitched his shoulders. "I don't know if she's back at the Purple Pussycat or not, but I haven't had a chance to get to see her. I've been sorta walking around half-stunned since I heard about you."

"I want to see her as soon as I can so she knows I'm alive."

"You might have another near fainting fit on your hands."

"I guess so, but she has to know as soon as possible."

"Well, you can't go to the club, Ed, too much risk of being spotted. Maybe we can go around to her Paddington apartment later tonight and see if she's there."

Zarich nodded agreement. "Okay. Anyhow, I've got a lot to tell you, Harry. I've got a total picture of what I believe the Old Tart crew were up to in 1945."

"I'm bustin' to hear, mate. First I'm goin' to get another coupla cans, then when you've finished I've got something that'll knock your bloody eyes out. Perhaps if we put both our stories together we'll have something to take these psychotic bastards apart."

They compared notes. Zarich went through what he'd learned of the disappearance of the *Awa Maru* in 1945, and his belief that the Old Tart had hi-jacked the gold, and sunk the Japanese ship. Then his theory that they'd hidden the gold off the South Alligator River, with the possibility the PT boat could still be there. He was still uncertain about the fate of the crew, but Winberg's remains certainly indicated some killing had taken place.

Then Markby took Zarich through everything he'd uncovered in Sydney, his dismissal from the case, which had originated his suspicions about Roman, the corruption of the chief inspector, his connection through Sade to Kepler Humbert, and finally Humbert himself with Ricky Bossley's drawings.

Then they reviewed what they had, with the realization it was a dovetailing of an incredible story that had lain dormant for forty years, until Donlett's operation had acted as a catalyst to waken a crazed psychopath from hibernation. Yet there was still the frustrating feeling expressed by each man that they couldn't prove a thing. Not in court. Not against a man like Humbert.

"Harry, what you've done is marvelous," congratulated Zarich earnestly. "Fucking marvelous." He gestured to Bossley's drawing. "Just great. What you've got here is just as important as what I found out in Japan. Maybe more so." He hesitated, staring intently at the portrait. "This man's really big, eh?"

"Ed, this bloke calls the Prime Minister on the phone. No one's been able to even calculate his wealth yet."

The corners of Zarich's mouth dipped mournfully. "You've got no doubts it's him?"

"Absolutely not. Besides everything connects, Ed. Roman to Sade to Humbert. No, Schuman of the Old Tart and Humbert are the same man. If he was the one who finished up with the *Awa Maru* gold, then maybe he reckoned he was safe starting up in Australia instead of going back to America. Take another name, make himself look like an enterprising businessman. Maybe he killed the rest of the crew. If his psycho strain went underground for forty years he certainly didn't lose his touch. I wonder how he got on to Donlett in New York."

"I guess we'll have to ask him," commented Zarich sourly. He scrubbed wearily at his face. He couldn't come this far, know so much, yet not be able to do a thing about it. How could he tell that to Beuso? To himself? All those people on the Japanese airliner?

"I think you're right, Harry," he muttered. "This Humbert, Schuman, whatever you like to call him, is the only survivor of the Old Tart. He's calling the shots.

Maybe that was the finale of the Old Tart off the South Alligator River. He killed the rest of the crew, kept the gold, and used it to create this business empire." He clasped his hands together in agitation. "What if we went to your police commissioner with all this, Harry?"

"I don't know, Ed. I just don't know. I've a suspicion he'd back off so fast you wouldn't see him for dust. Say it was all inconclusive, and throw it to the politicians like it was burning a hole in his hands. And the politicians would throw it back. It's so hot no one would want to get stuck with it."

"For Chrissake, there's got to be a way into this, Harry," declared Zarich fervently. "We've got a complete picture here. Why Donlett was killed. Musoveld. Emma Shepherd." He glowered at Markby. "And how the fuck did Roman know I was in Japan? What I was doing there?"

"He must have put a tail on you, Ed. It figures he wouldn't trust me. Remember you called me from Darwin and told me everything about Winberg, finding the ingot, going to Japan. They only had to have an electronic listening device on Chooka's phone, and they would have got the lot." He thumped a fist into the palm of his hand. "I'm bloody sure it didn't come from Chooka."

Zarich stared pensively into space. "No, I'm sure it wasn't Chooka," he muttered. He shook his head. "But my big mouth cost an awful lot of people their lives."

"Don't blame yourself for that, Ed," said Markby quickly. "I should have been on to Roman. I didn't even think of Chooka's phone being bugged."

The words of comfort did little to erase self-recrimination from Zarich's expression. He dropped his empty beer can down on the floor, and studied Markby through half-closed eyes. "Tell you what I think we should do, Harry," he said slowly. "All this stuff is running around in our heads now, and shooting off in all directions. Why don't I put it all down on paper tomorrow, here if it's okay with you. A logical step-by-step progressive report, right from New York to the point we're at now. Then we'll both look at it, see exactly what we've got, and decide where we go from here. Maybe it'll be possible to show it to someone else, get another opinion."

"Like who, Ed?"

"Well, I'm not sure, but someone right at the top. If you're not sure of the commissioner, then maybe a political big shot. Your attorney general, or someone like that."

Markby sunk down into his chair, doubt on his face. "Maybe. But like I said, even the politicians are wary of Humbert. I'd bet my last buck he's been ladling out plenty of gravy to the political parties. It's the sort of insurance he'd want. Still, I think it's a good idea to write it all down. I'll go along with that, then we'll make a decision."

They both lapsed into morose silence, then Zarich glanced at his watch.

"I'd still like to get to Cassie's place, Harry," he urged. "If they bugged Chooka's phone, then they'd know all about her being in Darwin. Perhaps they don't consider her a threat anymore if they think I'm dead, but I'd feel easier in my mind to see her."

"She might still be at the Purple Pussycat," warned Markby.

"Perhaps. But I've got a feeling she wouldn't have gone back there yet. She was trying to break away from that place."

Markby dropped his beer down on the table, and stretched to his feet. "Only one way to find out. Christ, I'd like to see her face when she claps eyes on you. I know how I felt. You'd better be ready for a slight case of hysteria." He paused. "Not that it's any of my business, but what happens with her? Once they know you're alive, she'll be in the firing line again, Ed."

"We might get her out of town somewhere. But I'm taking her back to the States with me eventually, Harry. If she'll come. Marry her if I can."

"It's like that?"

"Yeah, it's like that, Harry."

"Well maybe Helen and I can get over for the wedding."

"I'd expect my best man to be there," grinned Zarich.

Markby parked in the narrow street across from the small apartment block in Paddington, and left Zarich inside the car while he went across to check if Cassie was at home. He was back in a few moments.

"No one answering the door, Ed," he muttered. "I checked down the side of the building, and there's no lights showing in the windows of her apartment."

"Maybe I'm wrong, she has gone back to the club."

"Could be."

There was a hesitant silence, then Zarich gestured down the street to a public telephone. "What if I call the club, just to check if she's there?" He grinned uncertainly at Markby. "I know I'm a pain in the ass, Harry, but I've just got a bad feeling."

Markby patted him good-naturedly on the shoulder. "Forget it, Lazarus, I was in love myself once, but don't tell Helen. You stay put, and I'll make the call. It's too dangerous for you to be wandering around the streets."

"I guess I wish the hell she'd stayed with Chooka."

"Stop worrying, she'll be okay," Markby reassured him. Then he was gone, his large bulk moving swiftly down the dimly lit street. Maybe he had the build of a workhorse, but he compensated with the agility of a ballet dancer. Zarich sighed, and hunched down in the seat. It was crazy, but she was still as much on his mind as the Old Tart, and he prickled with the anticipation of seeing her again, feeling her, holding her, but she should have stayed with Chooka. There was still so much danger, and for Harry too. If Roman found out Harry was still investigating into the Old Tart, they'd just as likely blow him away as if they were swatting a fly. He waited impatiently until the rap of Harry's footsteps came again, then the sergeant reappeared at the door of the car.

"Well, she's not at the club," he grunted.

The news added to Zarich's unease. "Then I wonder where the hell she is?"

"Could be she didn't come back to Sydney after leaving Chooka. Maybe she figured out for herself the heat would still be on. She could have gone into smoke to Melbourne, Adelaide, anywhere. Let's face it, Ed, I haven't seen her, and she made no attempt to get in touch with me."

"Perhaps she was too scared?"

"Of what? And if she was, why leave Darwin?" He opened the car door, and squeezed himself back in alongside Zarich. The snap of the closing door was like a pistol shot on the deserted street.

Markby's fingers thoughtfully caressed the steering wheel. "Perhaps she wasn't thinking straight when she left Darwin. She'd be in a state of shock over you, maybe frightened. I don't know where she'd go, Ed."

Zarich could sense Harry becoming infected by the same misgivings. "Let's just wait here for a while," he suggested. "She could just be out for dinner."

"Okay, if that's what you want to do."

"You don't mind?"

Markby uttered a soft laugh. "What's to go home for. It's a shit place without Helen and the boys."

It was on Zarich's tongue to apologize again for their absence, but he let it go. He knew Harry wanted it like this, and it was crazy to expose them to the possibility of danger.

They waited, mainly in silence, exchanging occasional desultory ideas about the Old Tart. But it had all been said for now. Once it was all laid out before them on paper they could theorize, make plans, decisions. Little traffic passed along the street. There was a streetlight directly outside the apartment block, and the walls gleamed white in the glow. It was an old area, small houses huddled together in comforting dotage, the modern apartment building like a flashy interloper. A sharp breeze played with discarded newspapers in the gutter, and the quiver of the overhead lights made shadows dance eerily about the road. From somewhere to the right came the constant drum of heavy traffic.

"I'm concerned for her, and I'm concerned for you, Harry," murmured Zarich. "Roman's just as fucking dangerous as Humbert . . . especially for you."

"I'll watch him. He doesn't know I'm on to him. That's an advantage."

"He gets even a sniff you are, and they'll take you out as easy as drawing breath."

"I'm not that easy. He won't find out."

It was a confident assertion, but Zarich didn't have

the slightest doubt the thought hadn't occurred to Harry. Markby gave him an appreciative smile that was like an affirmation of the strong bond that had formed between them. "But thanks for worrying, Ed," he said.

Zarich punched him lightly on the shoulder. "You worry for me . . . mate."

Then their attention was caught by a large dark car pulling up to the curb outside the apartment complex. They eased lower in the seat as the throaty purr of the engine came sharply on the night air. The streetlight caught the driver as he leaned forward on the steering wheel, then there was the sharp slap of a door closing, followed by a woman's voice calling, "If I hear anything else I'll let you know."

There was a muffled indistinguishable reply, the beat of the engine rose to a powerful throb, and the car accelerated rapidly away down the street, leaving a woman standing on the sidewalk staring after the car. She wore slacks, and her hands were thrust into the pockets of a fur jacket, but it was a face Zarich was never supposed to see again, white in the streetlight, yet even from the car he could see her features were drawn and exquisitely sad.

He reached quickly for the door handle. "It's her, Harry," he whispered.

Then Markby's fingers were like pincers into his arm. "Hold it, Ed," he whispered urgently. "For Chrissake, hold it . . . don't move . . . don't call out."

His head swiveled around to Markby in astonishment. "What the hell's wrong with you," he muttered savagely.

"Wait, please, just wait," pleaded Markby softly.

Zarich failed to comprehend, but there was no misunderstanding the intensity in Markby's voice, so he waited, hand still resting on the door handle, and his mouth drooped open in bewilderment. Harry's fingers were still fiercely into his arms, like hooks that refused to let go.

Cassie turned slowly away, walking as if she dragged a heavy weight at her heels, until she disappeared into the apartment building, then Zarich reached around and pried Markby's fingers loose.

"What the fuck are you on about, Harry?" he demanded angrily. "For Chrissake, she's what we've been waiting here for."

"The man driving that car."

"What about him?"

"It was Roman, Ed. Chief Inspector Roman."

He wanted to kill her. Strangely he'd never really wanted to kill anyone before. There were hoods he'd blown away in tight situations, where the only choice was staying alive, but dispassionately done, the professional cop playing an avenging god. But the rage like an inferno in his belly was something new, almost frightening, and as much directed at himself as her. The smart ass New York cop, conned like a rookie, and deep down inside where it hurt, where he kept all his secrets.

His first reaction was to go storming immediately into her apartment, but Markby sensed his mood, and insisted on driving back to the house.

"Just cool it for a while, Ed," he pleaded. "Just cool it. She's not going anywhere, she'll be there tomorrow. We can decide what to do when you've got yourself together." He didn't take his eyes from the road, but there was nothing patronizing about the sympathy in his voice. "I'm . . . I'm sorry, mate, I really am," he murmured. "It's a lousy break, and I know that doesn't make it any better, but I am sorry."

He appreciated the words, but he couldn't answer. He knew Harry was right; he went into her apartment the way he felt now, and anything could happen. For a time neither man spoke; there was only the drone of the motor, and the whisk of passing cars. In the pale green illumination of the lighted dashboard Zarich's face was set like an emerald mask.

"I . . . I just never thought of Cassie," said Markby finally. "I thought of you being tailed, and telephone taps, but I just never thought of Cassie." He shook his head. "Jesus, no wonder they knew what we were doing."

"I feel such a fucking asshole," said Zarich bitterly.

"I'm as much to blame."

"The hell you are. She sucked me in like a kid out of school."

"No, I should have checked her out, Ed. I'm just as much an asshole. I accepted her right from the start without question. I'd take a guess she isn't even Donlett's granddaughter, but was just set up by Roman as a watch-dog on poor Emma Shepherd." He bobbed his head for-lornly. "I just took her word for what she was. Don't ask me why I didn't check her out. Maybe it was the beautiful big blue eyes. But I shoulda checked . . . I'm sorry, Ed."

Markby still kept his eyes to the road, and Zarich was grateful for even that small measure of privacy. He was experiencing a sensation close to grief, of immeasurable loss that took him back to his time as a kid when he'd been told of his parents' death, and he groped to handle it.

"You didn't check her out because of that night in the hotel room," he gritted dully. "That whole attempt on her must have been nothing but a phoney act."

"You never did see anyone that night, did you?"

"Not a soul. Christ, the bitch was so convincing," he muttered. "A real academy award performance." He licked at his lips, and stared morosely through the windshield. "Oh she has talent, real fucking talent. Those beautiful blue eyes got to me more than you, Harry. What a joke. She scarcely left my side in Darwin, and I told her every-thing, Jesus, everything. She must have called Roman as soon as I left for Japan." He uttered a short, curdled laugh. "I wouldn't have believed any woman would get to me like that."

No woman ever had, not Rhonda, not any of them. Maybe he was being paid off in spades for the fact he'd never let any woman get inside him like she had. "I love you," a voice whispered in his head, echoing from a dark-ened bed where her skin glistened with the moonlit sheen, and he winced as if stuck with a knife.

"She damn near had you killed," said Markby quietly.

He didn't reply. He knew that, and thinking about it only made the ache worse, to love her so much, and realize she'd taken him for a ride, was even an accessory to murder.

"I think we should let this hang overnight, then talk about the best way to handle it in the morning, eh Ed," murmured the sergeant. "It's bloody tough, I know, mate, but don't waste your time on her, not if she's runnin' with those psychopaths."

He nodded agreement, but for Chrissake if only it were as easy as that, just push a switch and wipe her out.

"Yeah sure, we'll talk about it, Harry," he managed gruffly. Then he lapsed back into silence, because he wasn't sure how much longer he could control his voice.

He stepped from the car outside Harry's house, and stood for a moment looking down to the luminous water of Cronulla Beach at the end of the street. It was one o'clock. He heard the front door open, then Harry called. "Come on Ed, let's try and get some sleep."

Good old Harry. He figured the sergeant was afraid he was going to head back to the Paddington apartment and blast Cassie. No, he wasn't going to do anything like that, but he knew sleep was beyond him. He hesitated, then waved his hand vaguely in the direction of the ocean. "You go on in, Harry. I might just walk awhile."

"You sure you're okay?" Markby questioned with concern.

"Yeah, I'm fine. I won't be long, but I'll see if I can walk this out of my system." He should be so lucky.

Harry didn't answer immediately. Perhaps the sergeant figured it was risky for him walking around the streets, but no one was going to see him on a deserted beach at one o'clock in the morning.

"Okay, but watch yourself," called Harry reluctantly.

But he was already on his way, hands thrust into his pockets, head down, mind still in a turmoil. He'd never walked along an ocean beach in the middle of the night, but it helped. The breeze pushed scattered clouds swiftly across the moon, so that the light on the sea alternated between glittering silver and lifeless gray. The air was warm, so he took off his coat, loosened his tie, and walked slowly, scuffing his feet in the sand. He was conscious of a numbed feeling, like the aftereffect of the impact of a bullet. He walked close to the water's edge, and the surf was a comforting roar, foam swirling up as if to suck him away, then just as quickly gone. He kept going until the lights of Cronulla twinkled behind him like a remote galaxy, then he sat down, arms crossed over drawn-up knees, and stared at the sea advancing and retreating, advancing and retreating. He was doing neither, jammed in a static world where he'd never been before. "You don't touch people," said his aunt, and that was the second time those long ago words had sprung into his mind within a few days. Well, he tried with Cassie, he really tried, but he may as well have pissed it into the Pacific Ocean as use it on someone playing him for a fool. God, she must have thought he was some sort of softheaded meatball, listening to his moonstruck declarations of love as if from an adolescent jerk. He felt an urge to fling himself into the surf, as if the swirling water could wash it all away and let him start clean again. Perhaps it was the drumming roar of the surf, or the isolation, but after a while the ache became more bearable. He knew it would take a long time to go away, maybe never, but at least his mind began to function like a cop again. They had so much on the Old Tart now, and surely he could figure some twist to bring it all into focus, nail a psychopath like Schuman. Or Humbert as he called himself now. He owed it to Donlett, and Musoveld, and Emma Shepherd, and all the sacrificed passengers on the Japanese jet. He owed it to himself not to sit around like some moonstruck kid disappointed in love. He was a cop, and if some bitch had deflated his ego like a pricked balloon, then he just had to puff himself back on his feet, and run again. He would use her, the way she'd used him, because an idea was already forming in his mind. Yet he knew no matter what happened he'd still love her, but he was just going to have to learn to live with that.

Harry was asleep when he got back to the house. He thought of waking him to fill him in on the idea, but he was close to exhaustion, so he lay down on the couch in the living room and drifted into a doze around four in the morning.

He woke around nine-thirty, ambled blearily into the dining room, and found Harry seated at the table surrounded by papers.

"Gooday, mate," said Harry cheerfully. "I didn't want to wake you, so I thought I'd let you get as much sleep as possible. How do you feel?"

He draped himself into a chair, scuffed wearily at his hair, and stared owlishly at the papers. "Well, I've felt better," he grunted. "What are you doing, Harry?"

"What we suggested, Ed," shrugged Markby. "Putting all the Old Tart thing down on paper. I didn't know whether you'd feel up to it, so I reckoned I'd make a start. I called in sick this morning, so I've got time." He shuffled the papers about, and looked cautiously at Zarich. "I guess after last night with Cassie we've got another step now."

Zarich nodded morosely. "Good man . . . yeah, you're right, Harry."

"I called Helen too. I want her to stay with her sister for another coupla days or so . . . at least until we've got this lot sorted out." He paused, his eyes carefully appraising Zarich. "Are you okay, Ed? I mean after last night?" He clucked his tongue sympathetically. "Why do the bitches of the world so often get the breaks in the looks department?"

It was ludicrous, but he felt almost a stir of resentment at Harry's remark. Yet he guessed it was an accurate observation about Cassie; he just had to get used to thinking about her in those terms.

"Well, I gave her a lot of thought last night, Harry," he said thickly. "And I've an idea how we can use her to wrap up Schuman."

"That'd be great, Ed." His mouth curved in a sly grin. "And maybe even the score with her at the same time, eh?"

He dismissed the comment with a scowl. Perhaps that was part of it, but he wanted to believe it was more than that.

"Just let's say my theory about the Old Tart is right, that she is at the bottom of the water hole where we found Winberg and the gold ingot."

"Well, I guess we could find out," said Markby. "It would take time, and I'd have to go careful so Roman didn't know what was going on, but we could get some divers up there . . . if they're prepared to risk the crocs."

Zarich frowned and hunched himself forward over the table. He wanted a shower, he craved coffee, his brain felt as if thickened with glue, but this had been on his mind since the beach last night, and he wanted it out.

"No, even if I'm right, Harry, finding it isn't going to prove a connection to Humbert. But what if we leak it to the sonofabitch that we know it's there, that we're going up there to organize a salvage operation. He'd get there so fast to try and stop us he'd burn up the countryside."

"You think he'd react like that?"

"He has to. It'd be in character. The man's prepared to do anything, and after the plane sabotage I mean anything, to stop his connection to the Old Tart being uncovered. He's a frightened man, Harry. Okay, a bloody-minded frightened man, but if he believes we know the Old Tart is at the bottom of the water hole he might just panic. There's a chance it would push him out into the open. And we'd be up there waiting for him."

Markby silently considered the idea, rubbing reflectively at his scalp. "Okay, let's say you're right, Ed. He did sink the PT boat there, but it's forty years ago." He shrugged. "Maybe since then Humbert had it . . . I don't know, removed, even destroyed by now."

"Why should he? He attempted anything like that, and he'd take a crazy risk of exposing his connection to the boat. Surely he'd feel safe enough with it in such a remote place. Sure he would have had to go back for the gold, but he wasn't a powerful public figure then. My guess is he wouldn't dare go near the place again. Unless we force him."

Markby nodded slowly, absorbing the idea. "It might work, but it's a long shot, Ed."

"What have we got to lose, Harry." His hand swept out over the papers. "We've got everything else. Humbert turns up at the water hole, and that'll be all the proof we need the Old Tart is actually there. That Humbert is Schuman. It might even tell us what happened to the crew."

"If the Old Tart's there," said Markby pointedly.

"Okay . . . sure, if the fucking thing's there," he scowled in exasperation.

"He'll know you're still alive, Ed."

"The hell with it, that'll be the extra bait that forces

him to go. Maybe even pushes him to the edge of panic. He must know the ingot would lead me to the *Awa Maru* story."

"He takes the bait, what then? Do we arrest him at the water hole?" He gave a warning shake of his head. "If he does come, sure as hell he won't be alone. He'll be going there to stop us . . . kill us, and that means he'll have some gunsters with him. There'll only be you and I, Ed. I mean a stake out in force would be terrific, but I can't trust anyone else with this . . . not after Roman."

Zarich knew it could be dangerous for both of them, and he silently considered options for a time.

"We'd have to play it as it comes, Harry," he muttered. "Maybe if he just comes to the water hole it'd be all the proof we need. But it'd be stronger in court if we could take him right where it all happened."

"If he comes."

Markby was being negative, but he brushed it aside. "Yeah, if he comes. We get there first, and I figure we can hide out in the cave. We've got to work it so they believe they're there before us, which means they'll wait around. Then at night we can move in and take 'em." He felt a sudden flush of enthusiasm that it was all possible. "We'd have the murdering sonofabitch on ice, Harry," he exclaimed eagerly. "If I know politicians they'd break speed records disowning him once we salvage the Old Tart." He knew the more he talked about it, the more he was convincing himself the PT boat was there, he was almost craving for it to be there. And why not? Winberg had been there. The ingot had been there.

"I guess there's always the chance he mightn't go himself, but just send some gunsters," Harry said.

"You mean like this Sade?"

"Yes, someone like that."

Zarich shook his head firmly. "I don't believe that. If I'm right about the Old Tart, it's too important to him. To how many people would a man in his position entrust a secret like that? My guess would be no one. And he would be the only one who knows the exact location." He clasped his hands, and rapped forcefully on the table. "No, this one he'd have to take on himself, Harry, he wouldn't have any option."

Markby sighed with resignation, and absently sifted the papers about on the table. "Well, like I said, it's a long shot, mate, but I'm game. You're right, what've we got to lose"—he grinned—"except our bloody necks."

"Thanks, Harry. Don't worry, I'm sure I'm right about the Old Tart."

"Well, how do we tip off Humbert? I guess it has to be through Roman, but it would backfire if I tried to do it. He'd know I was still involved in the case, and . . ." He grimaced, and meaningfully drew a finger across his throat.

"Cassie takes care of that for us," said Zarich curtly.

Markby stared at him. "Cassie?"

"Sure. I come back from the dead and she falls into my arms with a passionate welcome. After she gets over the shock, of course. Then I give her the complete story about us knowing the Old Tart's sunk in the water hole, that in a few days we're heading north to look it over ourselves before we arrange salvage. She'll be on the phone to Roman as soon as I'm out of the apartment. Simple as that. Then we get the hell out of here, so Humbert doesn't get any ideas about trying to get to us while we're still in Sydney."

There was a taste in his mouth like the sidewalk of Times Square. He knew facing her wasn't going to be as simple as that, and the ache inside flared up again. He forced his mouth into a confident smile that he knew didn't fool Harry for a moment. "It's a nice touch of irony," he managed to conclude.

I love you, said the voice. He didn't want to listen, but the words kept bouncing around in his head.

"Well, if you reckon you can handle it, Ed. I mean . . ." Markby hesitated, embarrassed.

"I can handle it," replied Zarich incisively.

Markby solemnly studied him for a second, then folded his arms with a smile. "Then it's beautiful, Ed," he crowed. "Just beautiful."

Zarich shrugged, and clambered wearily to his feet. "Yeah . . . just beautiful," he murmured. "Think about the details while I take a shower, Harry, then I'll fill myself up with coffee until I feel like a human being again."

"Chooka can set it up for us. He'll get everything we need."

"We might have to stay out at the water hole for a few days."

"That's okay. He'll get the supplies for us."

Zarich paused at the door. "Then see if he can also arrange some heavy firepower for us. I don't feel like being out there with just a .38 considering the sort of playmates Humbert has working for him."

"With Chooka's contacts, he can get anything," asserted Markby. He leaned back in the chair, and frowned. "But Ed we'll have to know for sure Cassie calls Roman before we go charging north."

"Don't worry, she'll call him," said Zarich heavily. "Oh yes, she'll call him all right."

"I guess you're right, but I think it's important to be sure. Give me a few hours and I can set it up so there's absolutely no doubt."

Zarich leaned to the door frame, and scratched at his unshaven chin. "I guess it makes sense," he conceded. "What've you got in mind?"

"I don't think we'll have any trouble putting a bug on her phone. You'll be in the apartment, and I know where I can lay my hands on the equipment with no questions asked."

"Sounds like a good idea. I'll leave it with you." He hesitated, his expression abruptly solemn. "You know this puts you right in the shooting gallery along with me, Harry. Humbert figures you know as much as I do, and it makes you a prime target too."

Markby nodded soberly. "Yeah, I know that."

"All I'm saying is if you wanted to back out I'd understand. There's Helen and the boys. You've got more to lose than me."

"No, I'm with you, mate," said Markby promptly. "I reckon I've got a break on the ones like Emma Shepherd. They didn't know they were sitting ducks." His face broke into a broad smile. "No, hell, let's do it, Ed. But it might be a good idea to keep Helen and the boys away from the house until it's over."

Zarich returned the smile with warmth. He'd take on an army with this guy at his side.

It took longer than Harry allowed for, and it was midafternoon before he had the equipment set up in a hired van. Zarich called Chooka while Markby was preoccupied, and it took some time to convince the bewildered old man he was still alive. He didn't tell him about Cassie, but just gave him a list of what they'd need for the trip to the water hole. Chooka was stunned enough at finding him alive without adding the shocking news of Cassie. That could come later.

Then Markby drove him back to the Paddington apartment in the van. They both wore dark glasses, but the remote chance of being spotted was a risk they had to take.

"How are you goin' to handle it, Ed?" queried Markby. "Just knock on the door, and say guess who? She'll pass out."

"She might. But I figure the shock'll work for me, Harry. Throw her off guard."

"Maybe. But . . ." The sergeant stirred uncomfortably behind the wheel, struggling for words. "Just . . . just watch her, mate. I mean I don't think she's the type to put a bullet in your back, but just watch her that's all," he warned. "Jes', she's some performer. I didn't exactly come down in the last shower, and I've been around, but she fooled me."

Zarich silently dipped his head in acknowledgment. He could have been irritated by Harry's inferred doubts, but he understood. Unspoken in Harry's words was a warning that his feelings for Cassie could be more dangerous than any chance bullet. It wouldn't happen. He was a cop again, the old hound dog from New York running once more with the scent, and he already had steel shutters in place so she wouldn't get to him.

Markby pulled the van up to the curb at the bottom of the street, and gestured toward the apartment.

"I'll set up down at this end, Ed. It's well within

range, and I should be able to pick it up easy. It'd be better if you walked from here." He glanced uneasily around the street. "Should be okay. There's no one much around."

"Nothing's going to happen until I leave her."

"Yeah, but I want to be ready, mate." He scowled in the direction of the apartments. "It's goin' to be a fuckin' anticlimax if she's not home."

"We can always wait. I'll come back to the van if she's not there."

Zarich glanced warily up the road as he opened the door. The street dozed in the bright sun, and the old houses seemed more aged in the daylight, leaning into each other as much for comfort as support, the apartment complex still like an intruder from another time. Two women strolled languidly at the other end of the street, arms draped with shopping bags, and across the road a dog pissed nonchalantly against a fence. It was clear as it would ever be.

"I'll tip you off when I'm leaving by calling a cab on the phone," Zarich muttered. "I'll take it back to the house, and wait for you."

"Watch yourself," grunted Markby.

But even as he walked to the apartment he knew he was only fooling himself if he thought it was going to be in any way easy. There was a dampness in the palms of his hands, and his heart ticked over with an uncomfortable beat.

He rang the bell, then took off the dark glasses, and just stood there in the corridor with a half-smile on his face as she opened the door. He thought he was ready, but he should have known better; the steel shutters fluttered like tissue paper at the sight of her face. But it was a face suddenly devoid of the color he remembered, now chalk white, the blue eyes widened to unbelievable orbs, mouth half-open and surrendered to uncontrollable trembling.

"I guess I'm not that easy to kill, darling," he said huskily.

She wore a beautiful quilted blue housecoat he'd never seen before, and he wondered if Roman had paid for it. She couldn't move, couldn't speak, and he could see her hands white with the tension of gripping the door, as if she would fall if she let go. He stepped quickly inside, put an arm around her waist to take her weight, then pushed the door shut with his foot. Her eyes closed, and he thought she'd passed out until her mouth quivered again.

"Ed," she whispered faintly. "Ed . . . my God, it can't be . . . Jesus, it can't be you, it can't be."

He carried her to the divan, laid her down, then sat quietly alongside, holding her hands. It wasn't the way he'd thought it would be at all, not fighting to control himself from hitting her, from hurting back, but only aware of the smell of her, the closeness. Harry's misgivings were right. She was a bitch, a murdering two-timing bitch like the rest of them, yet he still loved her.

Several times her eyes half opened as if trying to convince herself it wasn't a dream, or more likely nightmare, and she would whisper his name again so faintly as to be almost inaudible, then her eyes would close once more. The color began to come back into her face, but after a time he figured she was using it as a ploy, laying there inert with her mind turning over at a thousand miles an hour trying to unscramble what had gone wrong. So he kissed her, despising himself for loving the feel of her lips again, then her arms went tightly about his neck, and he could feel the heat from her mouth saying over and over, "Ed, you're alive . . . darling, you're alive, I can't believe it, you're alive, you're alive."

He thought of all the other times, the kisses, the passionate words, the rutting, then she nearly had him goddamn slaughtered, and the steel shutters regained some of their strength. It matched the hardness coming in his groin as if demanding retribution. Right then it was the only thing that seemed to matter, so he picked her up and carried her into the bedroom, all the time her mouth still moaning against his neck, "you're alive, you're alive," and he would have given half his life for her passionate welcome to be real.

Her housecoat was quickly discarded, and he didn't even bother to undress, straddling over her until he was in deep, yet his cock wasn't a love piece but a dagger, not thrusting in response to her heaving thighs, but stabbing as if trying to wound her until it all spilled from him in a frenzy of love and hate.

He lay exhausted for a time, trying to put himself together again while she waited patiently in his arms for an explanation.

In a low voice he told her everything, right from the time he left Darwin to the revelations about the *Awa Maru* in Japan, and how he survived the plane crash. But he didn't tell her he knew Roman was a shit of a cop on the take, or that Kepler Humbert was also Jay Schuman, onetime captain of the Old Tart, and a murdering sonofa-bitch he would burn if it took a lifetime. Or betray by the slightest hint he knew she'd set him up. "The best thing of all," he concluded, "is that Harry and I have found the Old Tart. We have information that the crew sunk it in a deep water hole off the South Alligator River in 1945. The same place Chooka took me to when I found Winberg's bones and the ingot. It's all we need. We raise that boat, and I'm positive it'll tell us everything we want to know. What happened to the crew, who it is from the Old Tart who's living in Australia and ordering all these killings to prevent the secret of the PT boat ever coming out. Harry and I are going up there in a couple of days to have a look, then we'll arrange salvage."

She placed her hand on his chest, and her hair whis-pered softly against his face. "It all sounds incredible," she whispered. "I'm just so grateful you're alive. It's more important than anything about the Old Tart. I can't be-lieve anything this wonderful could happen to me."

Liar. Oh, she was good. Fucking brilliant in a way.

"It's hard to believe people like that exist. To put a bomb on a plane just to kill one man. Especially when I love that man," she added.

Liar, liar, liar. "I love you too," he murmured.

She nuzzled into him. "When are you and Harry going up there?" she questioned softly. "I guess now I've got you back I don't want to lose you again too soon."

He felt the taste of vomit in his mouth, and it took time to find words. "Well, I'd say in a few days. It'll take time to organize a salvage operation. I figure we'll fly up there around the end of the week, and have a look around the water hole. I'm hoping Chooka might be able to help in some way."

It was as if he could hear the tape running, with everything he was saying being recorded in her mind.

"Will it be dangerous? Can I come with you? Maybe I could stay with Chooka again?" She raised herself on one elbow, and stared at him wide-eyed. With all that serious innocence she'd never looked more beautiful, eyes soft, blond hair strewn about her face. She really had got under his skin, but he laughed inwardly at her suggestion. It would be the same direct line to Roman for everything that was happening.

"No, you should never have left Chooka," he reprimanded her. "But now you're here I think you should stay put. It could be more dangerous for you up there."

"I didn't care what happened after I heard about the crash," she pouted. "Nothing seemed to matter anymore. I . . . I didn't mean to do that to Chooka, he'd been so kind. But I just had to get back to Sydney. I thought I could handle it better here." She paused, her eyes slowly traversing his face. "And I still can't quite believe you're alive. I'm frightened I'll wake up and find it's all been a dream."

Bitch. Bitch. Maybe if he hadn't loved her he would have felt grudging admiration for the way she was handling the situation.

"I had to let you know," he murmured. "But I can't stay. I have to make arrangements with Harry. Once this is over we can spend all the time together we want. I don't think it's dangerous for you while they think I'm dead," he added glibly. "But I've got to stay out of sight until we get out of Sydney."

Her arms tightened about him. "I don't want you to go . . . not yet." He lay there a moment, with love and hate coming like alternating waves of fever, until he couldn't stand it any longer, then he shrugged her aside and clambered off the bed.

"I'm sorry, but I have to go, Cassie," he muttered. "There's a lot of planning to do, and Harry's waiting." He

tried to ignore her nakedness, the way she propped invit-
ingly on her elbows. "I didn't intend to stay this long, but
it was important to let you know I was alive."

"And thank Christ for that," she whispered.

For the first time he felt an almost uncontrollable
urge to reach across and smash her off the bed, so he
smiled instead.

"Will I see you again before you leave?" she asked.

"I don't think so. It's dangerous for me even being
here now. I'll let you know."

She slid languidly off the bed, and back into her
housecoat. "Then all I can do is hope. Have you time for
just a quick drink, darling?"

He hesitated, then gestured to the phone by the bed.

"Maybe a quick one. I'll call a cab while you're pour-
ing. Do you have a number?"

She pointed to the teledex. "Look under A . . . the
Ajax Taxi Company."

Before he had a chance to look, she pushed her body
tight to him, put her arms around his neck, and gave him
a lingering kiss.

"I still can't quite believe you're alive," she purred.

She baffled him. He couldn't figure how she could be
so utterly convincing, what motivated her. Did she love
Roman? Did the chief inspector have something on her
that could exert so much pressure she'd do anything to
stay afloat?

"Well, I just showed you how alive I am," he
murmured.

"Then I want you to show me over and over again."

"I will, but it'll have to be another time." He pulled
her arms from around his neck. "And I won't even have
time for that drink unless you're careful."

She stepped away, and blew him a kiss. "I love you,"
she said, then walked swiftly from the room.

She must have felt the need to be even more convincing, because she'd never said that to him before; those
words had always come dribbling out of his own idiot
mouth.

He quickly picked up the phone, disconnected the
cap, and put the bug in position, then screwed it back into

place. From outside he could hear the snip of cupboards opening, followed by the clink of glass. He called the number and asked for a taxi in fifteen minutes, with the knowledge Harry would be picking up his voice now. Then he put on his coat, and moved gingerly from the bedroom. He hoped he'd been as successful a liar as Cassie, yet she still baffled him, perhaps always would, but no matter what he wouldn't make love to her again. Harry had understood his state of mind more than he had himself; he was on a razor's edge, and it would be so easy to let her sucker him again. Somehow he was going to have to find a way to stop loving her.

He waited four hours at the house, restlessly prowling the rooms, emptying Harry's refrigerator of beer, convinced that something had gone wrong. He'd already put the arrangements in hand to disappear from the house as soon as Cassie had the information by booking a room at a hotel near the airport, and he was dressed, packed, and ready to go. But what the hell was taking Harry so long? Surely she would have made the phone call as soon as he was out of the apartment. Doubts began to eat at him, that they might have been too hasty, jumped at the obvious without asking questions. Perhaps Roman had just been interrogating Cassie last night, but Christ would he drive her home as if they were old friends? Maybe he was longing for his doubts to be true so he could go on loving her, then the sound of the van pulling into the driveway broke into his thoughts.

Markby came in the door as if he'd just completed a marathon, and sprawled wearily into a chair. Zarich opened the last can of beer, put it in the sergeant's hand, then squatted anxiously in the opposite chair.

Harry lifted the can in a disdainful toast, and squinted at Zarich. "Jes', that was a bloody long haul, I can tell you, mate. Cooped up like a chicken in that shitty little van."

"Harry, we've been packed and ready to pull out for the last four hours. For Chrissake, what took so long? Did she make the call to Roman?"

"Yeah," said Markby in exasperation. "She made the call to him all right, but she took her bloody time."

Zarich eased his weight slowly back into the chair as all niggling doubts evaporated. Well, that was it. He winced again from the renewed sting of his gullibility.

"She told him everything?" he asked dully.

"The works, Ed. The whole bit about the Old Tart being at the bottom of the water hole. And about the salvage attempt."

"What the hell took her so long?"

"Search me. Perhaps she was thinking it over, trying to make up her mind."

"How did Roman react?"

"He didn't say much, just took it all in. They didn't exactly sound like the best of friends. Matter of fact he treated her like shit."

"Then he must have something pretty strong on her."

"I guess so."

"You came straight back here after she made the call?"

"Yeah. I'd say the wires are probably runnin' hot to Humbert by now." He held up the beer can, studying it as if it contained some profound message. "She didn't exactly tell him everything," he muttered awkwardly.

"What do you mean, Harry?"

The sergeant lowered the can, a strange expression on his face. "She didn't mention you, Ed. That you were still alive . . . anything."

Zarich stared at him in astonishment. "You can't be serious?"

"Bloody hell I am. Your name wasn't mentioned. She put it all on me, mate. I'm the one who knows where the Old Tart is. I'm the one who's going up there for a look around before I organize a salvage operation. I'm the one who visited her, and told her all about it." He gave a wicked grin. "You're out, mate. As far as Roman's concerned he thinks you're still at the bottom of the South China Sea."

Zarich was stunned into silence. It was crazy, but did she feel something for him after all; was she so convincing because it wasn't all pretense? Yet she set him up to die in the Japanese airliner.

"I guess she's got something going for you after all,

Ed," Markby voiced his thoughts. "I mean it's pretty crazy and mixed up, but I reckon she does anyway." He raised the can in a cynical gesture. "Poor little bitch, this time it's only me she's tryin' to get killed."

"She set me up for the plane crash, Harry."

"Well, she tipped them off you were goin' to Japan. Maybe she didn't know they were going to try and knock you off."

He wanted to try, but he couldn't excuse her. "She must have known about Emma Shepherd . . . that they were killers. You're right, there's no way she was really Emma Shepherd's granddaughter."

Markby shrugged, and drained the can. "Don't ask me to read her mind, mate. It's beyond me. I only know she's working for Roman, and that's enough for me. Roman's got something big on her, I'd say. Anyhow right now she doesn't matter. What do we do now?"

"We go, Harry, fast as we can. Out of this house. The hotel room's booked, and the flight in the morning. We'll just have to stay out of sight as much as possible until takeoff."

"Humbert might just say it's all shit. The Old Tart's not in the water hole. I mean I'm not saying you're wrong, Ed, but it's possible."

Zarich's mouth set in a resolute line. "We've been through that, Harry. We've come this far we'd be crazy not to go for it." He raised his hand in warning. "He's not going to ignore you now anyway, not after what Cassie passed on to Roman. The sonofabitch could already be arranging a contract. He'll move fast, try for you here in Sydney first, then maybe even fly up to Darwin by private plane." He grimaced. "I'm sorry you ended up as bait, Harry, but it wasn't intended that way."

"Forget it. We'd better call Chooka first and let him know we're on our way."

Zarich was gripped by a sense of urgency. Humbert was going to scour Sydney for Harry, and they should get out of the house fast.

"Call him from the hotel. You'd better dump the van somewhere, and we'll pick up a cab."

His theory about the Old Tart had grown to certainty in his mind. He didn't want to think about Cassie, but he wondered how he was going to feel when she was in the net along with all the other sharks.

Chapter 14

Humbert's meeting with Sade began in a coldly brusque manner, for he was still rankled over their last contact. All the strain he'd been under the last few months had erupted in a furious denunciation of Sade over the sabotage of the Japanese plane. It was ludicrous, idiotic, a heavy-handed way of killing an ant with a cannon, and unforgivably drawing international attention. It meant questions, inquiries, God-knows-what repercussions, and it was irrelevant for Sade to protest his Japanese agents had gone outside his instructions for a quiet elimination in Tokyo. It was the final touch to his growing loss of confidence in Sade—he had to go. Besides, with Zarich dead he had no need for such a hatchet man now, and with the information Sade was gathering piece by piece about the Old Tart, there was always the possibility of blackmail.

But those thoughts vanished when Sade told him of Markby's discovery of the Old Tart in the water hole off the South Alligator River. The same dull ache returned to his chest with the feeling he would never be free, never be safe, new threats would constantly emerge until it finally destroyed him. On and on, and now he had to kill another one. He wouldn't have believed Markby would be so smart, so persistent. How in God's name could he have found out the whereabouts of the Old Tart? No doubt it had something to do with the discovery of Winberg's bones, and the ingot. Once again he couldn't allow it to happen. If the Old Tart was salvaged they would find the bones of the crew inside and it could trigger a chain of inquiries that led directly to him. And why did the information come through the girl? If Markby hadn't told Roman, did that mean he no longer trusted the chief inspector, but suspected his involvement? He sighed despondently. At least there was some consolation in realizing that this would force the sergeant to keep it to himself.

"It's taken all morning to get this absolutely vital information to me. Where the hell have you been, Sade?"

Sade tilted his head with the usual blank-faced deference. Even the tirade over the Japanese plane hadn't penetrated that expression.

"I've been trying to locate Markby. That seemed the first priority. If we could get him here in Sydney it would save the hassle of a trip north. End all our worries."

He didn't believe that anymore. It was an endlessly repeating nightmare. He got rid of Markby, then something else would emerge. But he had to forget his thoughts about Sade because he needed him now.

"You couldn't find him?" he rasped.

"Not yet. His house is deserted."

"Roman has no idea where he is?"

"No. He called in sick yesterday. Roman tried to contact him after he got the call from the girl, but without success. Markby told the girl he'd be around Sydney for a few more days, but he could have changed his mind and headed north."

The ache in his chest was almost like the onset of angina, and Humbert wrapped his arms around his torso in an effort to suppress the pain.

"You want me to go after him?" asked Sade. "I could take a few men with me. Markby didn't speak to Roman about the Old Tart, so I doubt he'll confide in anyone until he confirms it himself. We could get him at this water hole."

"If he's talking salvage he might have someone else with him."

"Then we'll get them too. I'd guess he'd have to spend a few days in Darwin making arrangements, so if we move fast we can get to the water hole before him."

"You'd have to find the place."

"You can tell me where it is."

Humbert considered a moment. The pain in his chest

was making it difficult to think fast, and he knew he was being forced into a reliance on Sade which could prove as dangerous in the end as Markby. Was that the next unknown monster? No, he couldn't afford to let him run any longer without a leash.

"I think it's important I go too," he muttered.

Even Sade's impassive face registered mild surprise. "Is that wise?"

"It's too important, and now Markby's vanished, too urgent. It'll save valuable time if I take you straight to the place. There's no chance of anyone seeing me in that remote area."

Sade shrugged obvious disagreement. "Well, if you feel you must, but it could be a tough trip."

"I can handle it," he snapped. Sade's disapproval only reinforced his decision to go. He needed the sonofabitch badly, but the time had come to watch him just as carefully as everyone else. "Call the airport and get the plane readied," he ordered sullenly. "We'll fly straight to Darwin, then take a helicopter to the location." He glowered at Sade. "You haven't forgotten from your Vietnam days how to fly a helicopter, Sade?"

Sade's eyebrows minutely lifted. "I can handle it."

"You'll need to take someone with you."

"I can think of two I can get right now. They'll do what they're told, and no questions asked, if the money's right."

"All right, do it." He made a quick, nervous gesture to the door. "Make all your arrangements on the phone in the side office. I'll need to make a few calls myself first."

Sade hesitated, moved slowly to the door, and halted again. "This . . . this could be a very expensive operation, Mr. Humbert," he warned softly.

"Forget the money," flared Humbert. "Just do it."

"In the long term," persisted Sade, "when I'm handling such important operations for you it might be better if I was, ah say, a member of the board." He gave a predatory smile. "It could make things easier for both of us."

Humbert smiled in return, but he was like a fighter who takes a heavy punch, and uses the expression to disguise pain. God, it was laughable to imagine a hoodlum like Sade on the board, but the threatening suggestion confirmed all his suspicions. Yes, Sade was the next monster.

"It sounds like a good idea, Sade," he answered smoothly. "We'll talk about it when we get back."

"I have some documents prepared. It might be a good idea if we looked them over during the flight. Of course I wouldn't have to attend board meetings. Just so long as I was a member."

Humbert kept his smile in place, but he knew he was being stood over. He felt a sense of inevitability, but Christ he'd see him dead first. The ache in his chest was suddenly gone. "You've shown a great deal of initiative, Sade," he murmured. "Yes, we can have a look at them."

Sade's head dipped in mocking deference. "I was sure you'd see it that way, Mr. Humbert." Then he passed quietly from the room.

Humbert remained at the desk, his hands clenched so tightly the nails bit into his flesh. He disposed of Sade, and maybe Roman would be next. He was trapped on an endless merry-go-round. Perhaps in retrospect he'd handled it wrongly from the very beginning, been panicked by Donlett's shock reappearance in New York. After all, Donlett would have known nothing about the events after the hijacking, and it might have been better to risk leaving him alive. He stared despondently out the window. It was useless anguishing over a past he couldn't change, and he had no intention of letting go. The fierce desire to survive had always been part of him, had kept him alive forty years ago. Dragging the bodies back to the Old Tart, sinking her in the water hole with a depth charge, then standing on the bank by the life raft as she went down, until there was only the silence, the birds, the crocodiles, and the knowledge he was richer than he could ever have possibly dreamed.

But he still had to make it back to Darwin, and convince them he was the only survivor when the Old Tart hit a chance mine. But he never made Darwin. At the mouth of the South Alligator River the tide caught the life raft and pushed him out into the Timor Sea, where he drifted for days, until he was picked up half-dead by an

Australian destroyer. But he still had enough presence of mind to discard his dog tag so he couldn't be identified. Chance altered his plans, and he went along with it, pretending total loss of memory. He spent months in a Brisbane hospital, where patient doctors tried to establish his identity, but he played the game too well for them. In the end they shipped him back to the States, and in the euphoria of the war's end he quietly disappeared.

It took him nearly four years to realize on the gold, taking it a little at a time, cautiously working through dealers in South America. Yaphank had been right—the bastards cheated him, offering only a fraction of its worth, but he had no option but to take the price. By the time he was through he was still a rich man, but not the multimillionaire of which he'd dreamed. Yaphank had been right about that too; a split with the crew would have left them all with peanuts. But he'd been astute. There was too much risk for him to stay in America, but Australia was a safe haven where he made the money work for him to create an empire. Position, prestige, wealth, and power, even if he indulged in some profitable deals the law would have considered dubious.

Then a doctor chasing fame performs a brain operation on an unknown man, and a smart ass New York detective with a talent for digging like a badger arrives in Australia. Perhaps it would never be the same again. It was traumatic to be forced into a position where people had to die, but what alternative did he have?

He wearily detached himself from the chair, and shuffled to the window. It had crossed his mind on numerous occasions to attempt to do something about the Old Tart in the water hole, but he always pulled back from what seemed the unnecessary risk involved. After all it was an isolated area, and the chance of someone stumbling on it close to impossible. Besides, the crocodiles made excellent guards. Or so he'd thought, which only made it more inexplicable how Markby knew it was there. And now there was Sade.

He leaned unsteadily against the window, and the glass felt refreshingly cool against his forehead. He refused

to be sidetracked by that problem for now, but he had
little doubt the sonofabitch could prove as dangerous as
Markby.

Once Chooka had them safely inside his house he
welcomed Zarich with the special fervor reserved for those
returned from the dead, vigorously pumping his hand,
and slapping him heartily over the shoulders, while chor-
tling, 'You beat 'em, mate . . . you beat the bastards."

They waited for his enthusiasm to cool, then told him
quietly about Cassie, and it quickly defused his ebullient
welcome for Zarich. He gave an awkward shake of his
head, and grimaced at both men in turn. "Jes', it's hard to
believe. I'm sorry, Harry, and it's tough on you, Ed. You
can never tell about a woman, least I never could. That's
why I left the buggers alone."

"Forget it, Chooka," muttered Zarich. "We all got
sucked in. I just want to concentrate on trying to make
this setup work."

"Sure, sure," agreed Chooka hastily. "Come and have
a look at what I've got for you blokes."

Chooka had done a great job of organization in Darwin for the short time they'd given him. Three days'
provisions, sleeping bags, two SLR 7.62-millimeter army
rifles with ammunition, a set of powerful army binoculars,
and even a change of clothes, tough green-colored denim
jeans and boots. Neither Zarich nor Markby asked questions about the weapons. The old man had a talent for
scrounging, and it was better not to know. Besides, the
excitement of his involvement seemed to have taken ten
years off his age.

"The helicopter's all set to go," he exclaimed eagerly.
"I've just got to pick up the phone and call the pilot. He's
the son of an old pal of mine. See nothin', hear nothin',
speak nothin'," he said with a grin, miming the ancient
fable.

"Sounds great," declared Markby.

"Listen, from what you've told me it sounds pretty
sticky. Just watch yu'selves. Anything else I can do, just
ask." He looked searchingly from one to the other. "Okay
fellas?"

"You've been a terrific help already," said Zarich warmly.

"You want the helicopter to drop you as close as possible to the cave?"

"Right," said Zarich. "We'll stash ourselves inside and wait for them."

"When do you want him to come back for you?"

Zarich hesitated, and glanced questioningly at Markby. "What do you think, Harry?"

Markby shrugged. "I'd reckon if the creeps haven't turned up in a coupla days, then they're not coming at all."

"Okay, I'll buy that," agreed Zarich. "Say he comes back for us on the morning of the third day. We'll ask him to make a run along the water hole before he lands. If he doesn't see us standing on the bank he'll know something's wrong, and get the hell out of there."

"Shit, something better not go wrong," said Chooka vehemently. "Those buggers play for keeps."

"It's just a precaution," Zarich assured him. "Don't worry, nothing's going to go wrong. If we're hidden in the cave they'll assume they're there before us. They won't leave, but settle down to wait." He patted the rifles, and grinned confidently. "Come nighttime and we'll move in. They won't know what hit 'em." It sounded so simple he convinced himself more than Chooka.

The old man doubtfully shook his head. "Well, it sounds bloody dicey to me. Maybe I should come, too."

"Jes', Chooka, we want to give them a sporting chance," grinned Markby.

Chooka cackled appreciatively, and reached out to grip each man's shoulders. "Okay, but I offered. You'll get 'em, boys, you'll get 'em." The words were a cover for the anxiety clouding his eyes. "Now let me go and call the pilot."

They spent some time disguising the entrance to the cave as much as possible with shrubs and rocks, but still leaving sufficient opening to enable them to observe the bank below. Then they set up in the cave with their gear, each taking a watch, sprawled on their stomachs at the entrance with the binoculars. It wasn't a totally clear view, with sections of the bank blocked by clumps of trees, but it sufficed for now. The important thing was to remain under cover in the daylight hours, because if Humbert took the bait, he was almost certain to arrive by helicopter. Zarich knew Harry still had unspoken doubts Humbert would come, but he had the old hound dog gut feeling that told him he was right.

He made a sweep of the area below through the binoculars, but there was nothing. It was a scene of tranquil peace, brilliant blue sky, ocher-colored earth, green trees, all reflected in the still surface of the water hole. The late afternoon sun drew a misty haze from the earth, and occasionally flocks of magpie geese rose from the water hole, circling as if equally watchful. He felt a sense of unreality to be here in this remote place so far from the bustle of New York.

"I wonder just what happened down there forty years ago, Harry," he mused thoughtfully. "Who killed Winberg? Did Humbert? Did he kill the rest of the crew?"

Markby was spread out on one of the sleeping bags, munching an apple. "I guess only Humbert can tell us that, mate," he answered laconically. "I mean, we've got a complete framework now, the *Awa Maru*, the gold, the hijacking, Humbert as Schuman, and I guess as the one who's been ordering all the killing." He cleared his mouth, and motioned with the apple to the cave entrance. "Even if the Old Tart's down there full of bones, I don't figure Humbert for the confessin' kind. And if we get him to trial, he'll have the best legal brains in the country. And lots of political favors he can call in."

Zarich turned his head with a wry grin. "You figure we should just pack up and go home, Harry? Let the fucker get away with it?"

"Hell no. I want to get the bastard same as you, Ed." He shrugged. "There's no goin' back for either of us now, mate. I mean Cassie's put my head on the chopping block as much as yours. We get Humbert, or he gets us, it's as simple as that."

It was a sobering reminder, and it jogged Zarich's mind with Cassie. The fact she hadn't told Roman he was alive still occupied his thoughts. But even if she really did have something for him, how could he ever come to terms with her treachery? For Chrissake, maybe loving her had changed him, but could he ever live with that?

They talked in low tones of life and loves and experiences while expectations for that day slowly withered. Sunset turned the sky blood red along the eastern horizon, tinting the countryside with a crimson glow, then it was quickly dark, and overhead more stars than Zarich had ever seen. They took three-hour shifts, even though it was improbable Humbert would arrive at night.

Zarich took the first shift, but there was nothing but the rustle of night creatures, and down in the water hole an occasional splash and squawk of alarm as predator and prey played the perpetual life-and-death game. Overhead the moon painted the landscape in stark black and glittering white in contrast to the rich colors of the day. Then it was his turn to sleep, but he only dozed fitfully, plagued by the sound of her voice, the memory of her feel. Perhaps his first reaction outside the apartment had been right, and only by killing her could he ever free himself.

Then he became aware Harry was vigorously shaking him awake, and he sat up, startled, at first unsure of his surroundings. It was pale first light, but there was no mistaking the excitement in Harry's face.

"What . . . what is it, Harry?" he asked thickly.

Harry glanced up to the roof of the cave. "Listen, Ed," he said urgently.

At first the sound seemed little more than the drone of bees, then it swelled fast to the unmistakable chutter of a helicopter, and they both scrambled for the cave entrance.

It came in fast and low from behind them, barely at tree top height, then as it swept past they could see the menacing muzzle of a machine gun poking from the side of the cabin. It banked in a tight circle over the water hole, sending swarms of startled birds fluttering into the air, and Markby hastily tried to get a fix with the binoculars.

"It's them," whispered Zarich. "Christ, it has to be them."

"I can't make out anybody in the cabin," exclaimed Markby. He followed the helicopter around until it disappeared behind the trees. "Just as well we're under cover," he grunted. "I guess they reckoned if anyone was here they'd catch 'em asleep at first light." He grimaced. "We'd been down there on the bank, the bastards would have cut us to pieces."

They waited, but the eerie dawn light seemed to create muffled echoes, making it difficult to pinpoint the direction of the chopper. Then it came again, up over the trees and straight for the cave, and they shrank down as it swooped away on another tack, repetitiously criss-crossing the water hole, the machine gun pointing like a threatening finger.

Zarich experienced more elation than fear. "For Chrissake, I was right, Harry," he crowed. "I was right. The Old Tart is down there in the water hole." He thumped Markby enthusiastically over the shoulders. "We pulled it off . . . mate. We pulled it off."

"Yeah, just so long as we can stay alive long enough to tell someone about it," muttered Harry cautiously.

Zarich peered across the water hole, where the helicopter was at the arc of another sweep.

"We'll do it. We've got surprise on our side, Harry. We stay put until they stop tarting about. Soon as they figure no one's around they'll put down somewhere close by. Then we sweat it out until nighttime, and move in on the bastards."

Markby nodded uncertainly, chin resting on his crossed arms, eyes following the helicopter. "Yeah, sounds like a piece of cake," he said with a trace of sarcasm. "I just hope Humbert's aboard to make it a complete party."

Zarich shivered in the coolness of the early morning, or perhaps it was part exhilaration. He sensed Harry's reservations, but he was sure it wasn't lack of courage. Maybe Harry was thinking of his family. It would be nice to have someone like Helen and the boys on his mind than the bitch in Paddington. But Harry's caution tempered his spontaneous reaction. Now they were actually facing it, even with surprise they were taking a hell of a risk. Beuso would never have approved. To be honest, there was a possibility the thing with Cassie had turned this into a personal vendetta for him, something he had to prove to himself as much as her.

The helicopter finally settled to the ground behind a low slope to the right, and it was only about five to ten minutes before the passengers appeared at the bank of the water hole. There were four of them, three dressed in jeans and open shirts, the fourth ludicrously out of place in an immaculate business suit. He was the only one not armed with a submachine gun. Markby silently studied them through the binoculars.

"Well?" whispered Zarich impatiently. "Is it him?"

"Yeah, the one in the suit is Humbert all right." He passed the glasses to Zarich. "Take a gander at the murdering shit."

Zarich shuffled into position, and quickly focused the binoculars to his eyes. Murder with a distinguished face and beautifully cut clothes filled the frame. They were grouped on the bank facing the water, Humbert's hands gesticulating as he spoke to the others. Zarich shifted from Humbert's face, and slowly scanned the other three.

"You know any of the others?" he muttered.

"The big dark guy fits the description of Sade that Ferret gave me. Nasty-lookin' customer."

"What about the other two?"

"I'd say hired guns, but I don't know them." He scowled. "They've got some pretty heavy armory with 'em. Let's hope they're sound sleepers."

Zarich merely grunted agreement. He didn't want to add to Harry's misgivings, but in a straight-out fight they wouldn't stand much chance against that firepower. But he'd make sure that never happened.

The group began to spread out, Humbert staying by the bank, the other three heading in opposite directions with weapons held in readiness.

"Looks like Humbert wasn't satisfied with his air search," murmured Zarich. He lowered the binoculars, anxiously adjusted the foliage over the entrance, then gestured to Harry as he edged back into the cave. "The cover's okay from a distance," he warned. "But if any of them come too close we might have trouble. Let's get back a way."

Markby silently complied. He crawled back alongside Zarich, picked up a rifle, cocked it, and laid it across his legs with his eyes fixed at the cave entrance. They both sat immobile, faces strained, listening, but no one came. There was a brushing sound from somewhere outside, but it could have been the wind tugging at the trees. Half an hour passed without a word between them, then Zarich motioned silently to Markby, and wriggled back to the entrance. He lay on his stomach with the rifle at his side, and squinted through the binoculars at the water hole.

They were all gathered together on the bank again, Humbert had removed his coat and was standing staring at the water, hands clasped behind his back, while the others lolled around, smoking and drinking beer.

"We're right, Harry," he called quietly, with a relieved laugh. "Search is over."

Markby moved swiftly to join him. "Okay, but let's keep an eye on the buggers," he growled. "I'm goin' to get ulcers unless I know where they are every minute of the bloody day."

They stood watches again. It was cool in the cave, but as time passed, heat waves began to shimmer off the surrounding countryside. They kept the group under constant surveillance with the binoculars, but no one strayed from the bank. As the sun climbed higher, it penetrated the cave entrance, reflecting flashing darts of light from the lens of the binoculars.

It was thirty-five years since Humbert had last stood there, yet it was totally unchanged. There were memories of the hazardous trips in the cockleshell boat to recover the gold, yet when he looked out across the water hole, it was the image of the Old Tart that dominated his mind. He couldn't even remember the exact place where the Old Tart had gone down, but maybe when this was all over he could find some discreet way to have it destroyed. If it would ever be over. But the calls of the birds could have been the screams of the crew as crazy Yaphank cut them down. If he closed his eyes, visions of bodies sprawled at his feet seemed so real; he almost expected the crew to be there when he opened them again. It was becoming increasingly hot, and he mopped his brow as he paced restlessly about the bank. After that long ago massacre it was scarcely conceivable that so much killing would be necessary forty years later. And there was still the problem of Sade. He wasn't even sure now that he should have come; it was the first time he'd ever personally involved himself, and it was a dangerous precedent, but he was committed now, and all he could do was sweat it out until Markby arrived.

He turned as Sade came up beside him.

"Bloody hot, isn't it," muttered Sade.

It wasn't his imagination, but the man's subservient attitude was already changing. It was even more apparent now than on the plane.

"Yes, it is," he murmured.

"How long do you think we should stay?"

"As long as it takes until Markby arrives," he answered sharply. "There's no time problem. I left word at the office I was taking a short vacation."

"I'd say we only had supplies for two, maybe three days if we're careful. It was all such a hell of a rush."

"Then if it's necessary for you to fly back to Darwin for more supplies, that's what we'll do." He scowled at Sade. "We don't leave here until Markby shows, Sade."

Sade shrugged. He kicked idly at a loose rock, the machine gun held slackly in his hand. On the opposite bank a crocodile slid swiftly into the water, and sank from sight.

"Those things give me the creeps," Sade muttered. He gestured with the weapon. "One comes anywhere near me, and I'll empty this into them."

"No shooting," exclaimed Humbert irritably. "There'll be enough of that when Markby shows."

Sade gave another sullen shrug. "Tell me, Mr. Humbert, is there really a PT boat sunk out there?" he sneered.

One of the hired guns saved Humbert the trouble of answering. Sade had introduced him only as Mick.

"Listen, Sade, there's something funny back up there on the hill," he said. He was a small red-headed man, but wiry, and he handled the machine gun as if it were a natural extension of his body.

"What do you mean . . . funny?" asked Sade.

Mick pointed a multitattooed arm up toward the slope. "Watch," he grunted.

For a time there was nothing, then came an intermittent flashing like a polished surface reflecting the sun.

"Maybe a piece of metal," said Sade. "Something dropped by a croc shooter. Or when you were up that way, Mick, did you drop anything?"

"No, not a thing."

"If it was just laying in the sun the reflection would be constant," interjected Humbert. "It looks as if it's moving."

They watched a while longer, then it vanished.

"Probably nothing," declared Sade.

"I think someone should go up there and check it out," ordered Humbert curtly.

Sade shrugged, and jerked his thumb in the direction of the slope. "Okay, take a look, Mick. It'll give you something to do."

Mick gave an ugly grin, and cocked the machine gun. "Well, if there's any black bastards up there spying on us they'll get a bullet."

"Anything happening?" asked Zarich from the back of the cave.

Markby didn't answer immediately. "You'd better come and have a look at this, Ed," he said sharply.

Zarich edged up alongside, and took over the binoculars. He could see one of the hired guns moving laboriously up the slope toward them, submachine held ready in his hands. He directed the binoculars quickly down to the bank, and saw the others standing watching.

"What the fuck's goin' on?" muttered Markby apprehensively.

"I don't know."

"He's headed straight towards us, Ed."

Zarich lowered the binoculars, and pushed himself tighter to the ground.

"They can't have seen us. It's not possible from down there."

"Well the bastard's comin' up as if he has."

"Let's move back in the cave again," murmured Zarich.

They cowed away from the entrance, both clutching cocked rifles, listening tensely to the approaching sound of footsteps clumping over the rough ground. They could see him through the gaps in the foliage as he came to a halt perhaps a dozen yards away, the submachine gun swinging loosely in his hand. Both men scarcely breathed. Someone called from below, but they couldn't distinguish the words.

"Well, I don't see anything flashin' up here now," the man bellowed in answer.

There was a muffled reply from the bank. Zarich stared at Harry in silent bewilderment. Flashing? What the hell did he mean by flashing? His eyes went to the binoculars at Harry's feet, and he felt a sudden sickening jolt in the chest. Christ, could they have been that stupid, not noticed the sun reflecting in the lens? He motioned to Harry, and they wriggled further toward the back of the cave, then flattened themselves to the ground. The footsteps started up again, coming closer until they could see only the man's legs, then the muzzle of his submachine gun poked inquiringly through the foliage. Zarich put the rifle carefully to his shoulder, aimed at the entrance, and rested his finger gently on the trigger. The creep came any further, and he had no alternative but to blow him apart. He could hear Harry's breath like whispered sighs beside him. He killed the man and they'd have to run for it, or they'd be sitting ducks in the cave. But after a few moments the man backed away to his original position. Zarich lowered the rifle, breathing deeply.

"There's some sort of cave up here," the man called.

Another blur of words floated up from the water hole.

"Yeah, okay . . . good idea," shouted the man. "Then we'll know for sure."

Zarich didn't know what was meant by good idea, but he didn't like the sound of it. He scuttled forward on all fours to the entrance again to get a better view. The man had placed the machine gun in the crook of his arm while he fumbled at his pocket, then when his hand emerged, Zarich could see the oval black pineapple shape gripped in his fingers.

"Fucking hell, he's got a grenade," he whispered in sudden panic.

The man's arm was already raised to throw the grenade toward the cave as Zarich slammed the rifle back to his shoulder, and opened fire. The detonation rebounded off the cave walls like cannon fire. He saw blood spout from the man's chest as he collapsed from sight, and the grenade curved back through the air and down the slope. Then there was a shuddering crump as it exploded, and the mouth of the cave was clouded with dust, and gravel, and shredded vegetation.

Zarich grasped urgently at Markby's arm. Jesus, he'd known the risks, but it had all gone wrong, and now there was a chance it could mean their lives.

"Let's get the hell out of here, Harry," he barked. "This is a fucking death trap now."

They scrambled frantically through the opening, blinking in the bright sunlight. The body was sprawled twenty yards down the slope, the machine gun between his legs. The smoke from the grenade drifted through the trees, and coiled lazily into the air like a smudge against the blue sky.

"I've got to get that machine gun," shouted Zarich.

The machine guns below were already yammering for their blood, and he could hear the zip-zip of bullets scything the grass.

"The hell with the bloody machine gun . . . run for it," screamed Markby, already scampering in a stumbling crouch across the crest of the slope.

Zarich realized Harry was right; he tried for the weapon, and he was a dead man. He switched around and followed in Harry's wake, half running, half falling, conscious of hissing strands of lead probing for his life. When he reached the crest Harry was already out of sight, and he threw himself over stretched out full length as if making a tackle, clinging grimly to his rifle as he tumbled down the other side.

Harry was propped behind a fallen tree, rifle defen-

sively poised, mouth open and panting like a distressed
dog.

"Jes'," he wheezed. "Jesus Christ. Get behind here
with me, Ed."

Zarich hastily straddled the tree and fell down beside
Markby, gulping air, his chest heaving. There was an ugly
red graze on his left hand he must have got from the fall.

"They have to come for us over the slope," gasped
Harry. "We don't stand a chance against the machine guns
out in the open, but we might be able to pick them off
from here."

Zarich scrambled up on his knees beside Harry, and
rested his rifle across the tree trunk. "Christ, what a
fuck-up," he panted.

Markby gave him a lopsided grin. His face also showed
the consequences of the tumble, blood seeping from a
gash across his forehead. "They haven't got us yet, mate."
He tapped his finger sardonically against his head. "They've
got the firepower, but we've got the brains."

Zarich felt a sense of guilt. Maybe the entire idea was
never any more than a lunatic way of getting themselves
killed, driven as he suspected by an urge to pay off Cassie.

They waited, trying to steady their breathing, but
there was no sign of an assault over the crest. Yet with the
water hole at their backs there was no other way for
Humbert's men to come.

"What the hell are the bastards doin'?" muttered
Harry suspiciously.

After the rattle of the machine guns the silence was
unnerving. Behind them the water lapped soothingly in
the breeze, and a bird called shrilly from a nearby branch.
But that was all.

"You watch behind, Harry," warned Zarich. "I'll cover
the slope."

Markby was shuttling around on his buttocks when he
was halted by the sound of the helicopter, and they both
turned startled eyes to the sky. "What the fuck?" croaked
Harry. He swallowed hard, and swiveled the rifle about in
the air. "Jesus, maybe the buggers are leaving," he muttered hopefully.

"Not Humbert. We know the sonofabitch better than

that. He can't afford to leave now he knows we're here. He wants blood, and he won't leave until he gets it, Harry."

The sound expanded, coming fast, but they couldn't see from where, and Zarich half rose to his feet, searching desperately around for better cover. Then it came over the crest like an avenging angel, blades glittering in the sunlight, churning the ground to a swirling cauldron of blinding dust. He wasn't such a hot pilot because he came over too fast, and when the machine gun began chattering the bullets only pruned the tree tops, then he was forced to bank abruptly away over the water hole.

Zarich threw several quick shots after the machine, but it was only a token gesture for he was momentarily blinded by the dust. Then it began to clear, and he saw the helicopter circling low over the water to come back for a second try, and he knew there was no chance they'd be so lucky next time. He seized Harry by the shoulder, and shoved him violently in the opposite direction.

"Split, Harry," he screamed. "We've got a better chance that way." He waved his rifle frantically in the air. "Run for it . . . I'll try and draw their fire."

Markby nodded and took off, sprinting like a crazy man toward a clump of trees farther along the bank. Zarich scrambled over the tree trunk, and down to the water's edge. He could see the helicopter maneuvering around to line up on him, and he got off another wild running shot before the machine gun began spitting again. He threw himself down behind a mound of rocks as the air became charged with flying chips, and the spang, spang, spang of ricocheting bullets. He'd never seen himself as a sacrificing jerk, but he owed it to Harry. Harry had Helen and the boys, and he had fucking nothing. He leaped to his feet again, running as he'd never run in his life before, dodging around trees and rocks, then he saw the shadow of the chopper flit past like the touch of death as it zoomed over the trees. He didn't look back but he knew they were lining up on him; he was blanketed by the chuttering roar, hair flailing in the down draft, deafened to everything save the pounding of his heart. Jesus, he was going to die. A fallen tree loomed in his path, and as he took a desperate leap to try and clear it, his foot caught in a protruding branch, then he slammed violently to the ground. He lay there half-stunned, barely aware of the bullets thunking into the tree, and peppering the ground in front of him like a hailstorm. He didn't move, spread-eagled in an attitude of death, and he knew they thought he was finished because the roar of the machine faded as it veered out in a wide circle across the water hole. They were going to try for Harry now, and he wasn't going to let that happen. He turned his head just sufficiently to see the chopper edging cautiously along the middle of the water hole, maybe only twenty feet about the surface. He reached carefully for the rifle, then waited until it was almost level with him, and partly obscured by foliage. He balanced himself painfully against the trunk, and drew a bead on the cabin. They were all hunched forward searching for Harry, and he could see Humbert at the back pointing directions. He felt incredibly calm. He had to save Harry, but if he could bring them down maybe he'd still get Humbert in court. He emptied the magazine, firing rapidly, and he could see the hits registering as one of the figures slumped forward. The nose of the helicopter suddenly rose to point skyward at a crazy angle, then it slipped slowly backward, shuddering like a wounded bird. One of the blades struck the surface and it sheered off, spinning wildly in the air. Then the fuselage crunched heavily into the water, somersaulting until it was upside down, and immediately began to sink in a gurgling mass of bubbles.

He drooped wearily to the tree, aching in every muscle, and the rifle slipped from his hand. He glanced back along the bank, but there was no sign of Harry. The chopper went down fast until there was only the tail end showing, then the water hole seemed to take one last swallow, and it disappeared. Two heads bobbed to the surface, the men floundered indecisively, then began swimming feebly for the shore. It was Humbert in the lead, with one of the hired guns following, so it must have been Sade he hit. Maybe he'd have his day in court after all.

He moved down to the water's edge, and waited. The hired gun suddenly threw up his arms, a look of terror on his face, and his mouth opened wide to scream, but he went under so fast there was no time to utter a sound. Zarich anxiously waded a few feet into the water. It was probably a crocodile, and he didn't want to risk losing Humbert. Christ not now, not when there was still so much he didn't know. There was an expression of exhaustion on Humbert's ashen face, the coiffured gray hair now lank about his head. He came close enough for Zarich to reach down and grasp him beneath the armpits, then as he began to drag him toward the bank he saw the swirl of water at the man's feet and the vague outline of the huge prehistoric body. The long snout broke the surface with the jaws open wide to expose the fearsome rows of teeth, then it clamped shut on Humbert's leg. Humbert tried to scream, but only a strangled whine escaped from his throat. Zarich desperately tried to brace his feet in the mud in an effort to pull Humbert loose, but the man's body gyrated uncontrollably in his hands as the crocodile jerked the leg savagely from side to side, the long tail threshing at the water. It was an uneven contest; he didn't have the strength to win a tug-of-war with a twenty-foot monster, and horror finally found Humbert's voice with a high-pitched inhuman scream. Zarich could feel his feet sliding through the mud, his fingers gradually losing their grip on Humbert's armpits, and the man's face distorted with fear. Zarich glanced despairingly over his shoulder at the sight of Markby coming at a shambling trot along the bank.

"Harry," he screamed. "Harry . . . quick, for Chrissake . . . I can't hold him much longer."

Even as Harry broke into a stumbling run, he knew he was beaten, his fingers slipping through the soaked material of Humbert's suit, and he made one last frantic effort to switch his grip to the shirt. He fell back as it tore away in his hand, and Humbert was dragged swiftly back into the water, eyes bugged with terror, mouth no longer capable of sound, arms waving wildly as if in macabre farewell, then he vanished beneath the surface, leaving only a few bubbles to mark his death.

Zarich staggered back to the bank, and dropped exhausted to the ground. He lay there gasping for breath, watching Markby's horrified expression as he stepped hesitantly to the water's edge.

"Jesus," muttered Harry in awe. "Jes', what a way . . ." He broke off, shook his head, then turned around and knelt beside Zarich. "Are you all right, Ed?"

"Yeah, I'm okay," panted Zarich. He nodded toward the water. "I . . . I tried to save him, Harry. I wanted to see him in court. Let the whole world see what a murdering sonofabitch he was." He stared morosely at the place where Humbert had disappeared. "The bastard took it all with him. Christ, now there are some things we'll never know, Harry. You know that? The crew. The gold. Winberg." He snorted in disgust. "Shit, to come this far, and just have it slip away at the last minute."

"I know, I know," Markby consoled him. He dropped his rifle to the ground, and squatted down beside Zarich. "We know the Old Tart's somewhere out there," he murmured, gesturing to the water hole. "That should tell us some more. But perhaps it's better this way, mate. Jes', all the lawyers, all the politicians, they would have made it bloody hard for us. Maybe impossible."

"I lost him, but I'll make shit of his reputation," gritted Zarich.

Markby didn't answer. The transition of the water hole back to peaceful calm seemed strangely eerie in comparison to Humbert's ferocious death.

"I owe you, Ed," said Markby. "I really owe you, mate. I thought we were both gonnas then."

Zarich raised himself on an elbow, and wearily slapped Harry over the shoulder. "No, I owed you, Harry. You stuck by me right from the beginning. None of this would have been possible without you." He shrugged into a sitting position, trying to ignore the ache in his body. "For Chrissake, I owe you more than you'll ever know . . . mate."

They both fell silent, staring mournfully out across the water hole.

"So what do we do now?" asked Markby.

Zarich shrugged. "We've got a day's wait before the helicopter comes back for us, so we've got plenty of time to think about it."

Chapter 15

Once they were back in Sydney they spent three days putting it all together. Helen and the boys returned, but they all insisted Zarich stay on with them.

Markby still had a paranoid distrust of how far Humbert's fingers would have extended into the police force, so after Zarich made a number of phone calls, Mark Hopkins, the Attorney General, agreed to see them.

The aura of the office proclaimed ministerial responsibility, as did the immaculately groomed, spectacled youngish man behind the impressive desk.

"You realize how unusual this is, Sergeant Markby," he began affably. "Normally I'd refuse a meeting like this and deal through your superiors." He smiled at Zarich. "But you were very persuasive, Lieutenant Zarich. As a policeman from another country I considered I owed you the courtesy of at least letting you explain what this was all about."

"Thank you, sir," murmured Zarich appreciatively. He smiled encouragingly at Markby as he placed the portfolio on the desk. "I think if I begin at the New York end, then you take it from there, Harry. Maybe I should talk about Japan as well."

"Sounds fine," agreed Markby.

They went through it methodically, step by step, and even to listen to it again themselves it was an incredible story. Hopkins said little, asked few questions, and it was difficult to tell what impact they were making. Even after they'd concluded he stared silently into space for a time, hands clenched and pressed to his chin.

"Unbelievable," he finally murmured. "Absolutely unbelievable. And Kepler Humbert is dead?"

"Yes, but I wouldn't bother searching for a body,"

said Zarich drily. "I don't figure there'd be much left after the crocodile got through."

"No, no of course," Hopkins agreed hastily. There was a contemplative pause. "And you believe this American PT boat . . . the Old Tart, is at the bottom of the water hole."

"I know it is," stated Zarich confidently. "It has to be. Humbert would never have come otherwise. What we need now with your help is a fast salvage operation."

"Yes, you're right, of course," said Hopkins smoothly. "But first things first. You must understand this is much too big for just the Attorney General. There will have to be inquiries made, and of course it will need to be discussed in Cabinet. But I want to congratulate you both on a fantastic job. Absolutely fantastic. You put your lives at risk, and believe me, I'm grateful." He leaned forward and proprietarily placed his hands on the portfolio. "I'll have to insist on complete security on all this for now." He glanced searchingly from one to the other, and they nodded solemn agreement. "I knew I could rely on you." He smiled. "Now if you'll just leave it all with me, I'll get back to you as soon as I can."

He shook their hands with practiced political warmth before they left.

"I don't like it," said Zarich in the car on the way home. "I've got a good nose for bullshit, and I smelled plenty of it in that office."

"Let's give him a chance," countered Markby. "There's nothin' else we can do for now, Ed. Hopkins does have a reputation as a straight shooter."

"He's a politician," observed Zarich cynically.

Zarich called Beuso in New York, and asked for another week to try and tie up all the loose ends. The captain was still too much in a state of shock from learning Zarich was alive to do anything but agree.

Another two days passed before he succumbed to the temptation to go and see Cassie. He didn't quite understand it himself, but in the report to the Attorney General he'd toned down her involvement, yet if Hopkins started digging he guessed there was a good chance she'd finish up in a cell. Perhaps he had a sadistic kink for self-inflicted punishment, but he was sure he had his emotions under control now, and he'd never sleep easy until he knew why.

That certainty of control dissolved the moment she opened the door, robed again in the blue housecoat, still beautiful, still able to make him ache, and he felt like a pathetic jerk for still loving her.

But she offered no loving smile or passionate welcoming embrace, and he knew from the sullen expression on her face she'd been tipped off the bubble had burst.

"Am I under arrest?" she asked churlishly.

"Let's talk about that inside," he muttered, and brushed past her into the apartment. He halted by the window, hands clasped at his back, watching her light a cigarette. He hated her for being so cool; he wanted her to fall at his feet whining for mercy, plead she was forced into it.

"Well, am I?" she challenged curtly.

"You've been talking to Roman."

She shook her hair behind her shoulders, and blew a nervous puff of smoke into the air. "Everyone's been talking to Roman, including the Attorney General."

He felt good about that; at least Hopkins was moving. He was silent for a moment, wishing to Christ she'd break, wanting to hold her, hit her, fuck her, kill her.

"Why?" he asked bitterly. "Just tell me why?"

She sat down on a chair, crossed her legs, and made a pretence of examining her cigarette. "Why?" She twitched her shoulders. "We've all got our problems."

"Do you have any idea how many people died in the Japanese airliner?" he asked furiously.

She didn't answer, but kept her eyes fixedly at the floor.

"You really scored, you know that," he grated. "No woman ever sucked me in like you did."

It was a tactical error, an admission of weakness he shouldn't have made, but it was an indication of how she could throw him.

"That's what really gets to you, isn't it, Zarich," she jeered. "Not how many people died, but the smart ass New York cop who got taken. Your bruised ego is what

hurts, not the killing. You shit, you really think you can
make it big for your career between my legs, or any other
woman?" She jabbed the cigarette contemptuously in the
air. "You were easy, baby. You know that? Easy. You
never loved anyone all your life except yourself, and you
were riding for a fall, just waiting for someone to plaster
egg all over your face."

He felt as if she'd stripped him naked. He couldn't
think about it now, for her scornful words had burst the
dam walls. He strode the few feet to her chair, brushed
the cigarette from her fingers, and dragged her by the
housecoat to her feet. His action dissolved all her composure, but God she smelled marvelous.

"Don't hurt me," she whimpered.

He'd never been so close to loss of control. "You
fucking bitch," he screamed at her. "You lying tramp.
Laying all over me like some Judas whore. You fingered
Emma Shepherd, got her drowned. You're no more her
granddaughter than I am. Everytime you tipped off Roman someone died. Hundreds in the Japanese plane, but
not me, baby, not me. Even that wasn't enough, you put
Harry Markby in. Well, we suckered you this time, because they were the ones who died, not us." Her face was
so close, lips parted, eyes wide enough to drown him, and
he clamped his mouth fiercely down on hers, burrowing
in, arms clenched about her, loving and hating her equally
fervent response. She wasn't just angling for a way out; it
was all the confirmation he needed she did have something for him. He broke angrily away, pushed her back in
the chair, and wiped furiously at his mouth. "Bitch," he
panted.

She didn't look at him, breathing fast, crouched apprehensively in the chair. He crossed to the other side of
the room to put as much distance between them as possible, then crossed his arms and leaned to the wall.

"It wasn't like that," she muttered dully. "I . . . I was
just Roman's watchdog with Emma Shepherd. I didn't
even know why. He told me she committed suicide." She
hesitated, her mouth trembling. "I guess I just wanted to
believe, even after what you told me." It was like she was
a different person to the one who'd just spewed hot words

over him. She nervously twisted strands of hair in her fingers. "I'd never have told him about you going to Japan if I'd known the terrible thing they were going to do. I reckoned you could look after yourself anyway."

"That didn't stop you putting Harry Markby in," he commented vehemently.

"But not you, I didn't tell him about you. I thought that would give you an edge." She glanced up, and for the first time there was a hint of pleading in her eyes. "And I was right, wasn't it?"

"Why leave me out?"

He knew why, but he wanted to hear her say it. She remained silent for a long time, her mouth quivering as if she couldn't find the words. "You know why," she whispered finally. "You've got it for me too, you just showed me. I felt it coming strong when we were in Darwin, and I couldn't sleep for not knowing how to handle it."

It took him back to her inexplicable moods, the way she paced the floor at night, and he wanted to believe her. But it excused nothing.

"Then why?" he questioned urgently. "Why Roman?"

She struggled again to form words, and when they came the tone was so low he strained to hear.

"I . . . I took a holiday . . . about a year ago. A paid holiday to Bangkok." She shrugged. "A couple of friends paid. I didn't ask question, I didn't want to know, I just wanted the holiday." She stared into space, not seeing him. "When I got back customs found the lining of my suitcase full of heroin. Christ, I was scared to death, I could have gone to jail for maybe fifteen years. I still could." Her eyes went back to him, and now there was no mistaking the pleading for understanding. "That'd be a death sentence for me. I couldn't stay alive locked up for all that time. I couldn't. I don't know how he worked it, but Roman held the case over with some crap about me leading them to the other couriers. But it was only to get me on his hook. He said I could be useful to him. It wasn't a sex thing, he wasn't like that. I did a few jobs, then he told me to play granddaughter to Emma Shepherd, pass on anything she might say about Donlett. Then when you came on the scene he told me to answer your questions straight so you wouldn't get suspicious. That phony attempt on my life at the hotel was his idea, once again so you wouldn't get suspicious of me." She gestured helplessly. "I mean I didn't even know what it was all about until you told me." She sighed mournfully. "Roman was always holding the heroin thing over me, and I guess there's nothing like fear to turn you into the greatest actress in the world." She fell pensively silent, then her mouth twisted into a forlorn smile. "I was acting at first, then I fell in love with you," she whispered.

He stayed by the wall, not trusting himself to go near her. How could he be sure this wasn't another skilled performance?

"I love you," he muttered.

"I know," she breathed. "But they'll put me away forever."

He tried to shrug. "Perhaps, I don't know. This isn't my country."

"The attorney general must know I was working with Roman."

"It depends. I didn't say so in the report."

Her eyes widened with surprise. "Why?"

"You have to ask?"

"Harry went along with you?"

"Yes, he did it for me. He had it all figured about us when you didn't tell Roman I was still alive."

She studied her hands locked together on her lap. "They're sure to find out eventually."

"Maybe."

If he touched her, even went close, he knew he was gone. Too much innocent blood had been spilled for him to ever trust her; he would spend his life wondering how much was love, and how much was performance. Perhaps they'd lock her up forever, if that was the way it had to be, but he wouldn't turn the key, and he'd never stop loving her. He walked slowly across the room, and carefully past her to the door. She turned in the chair and watched him, until there was just her melancholy face over the back of the chair. He didn't say good-bye, but just went out and closed the door softly behind him.

*   *   *

He told it all to Harry when he returned to the house, then the sergeant showed him a newspaper. There was a banner headline about the death of Humbert in a tragic hunting accident. He threw the newspaper disgustedly on the table.

"What the hell's all that shit about?" he asked hotly.

"Search me," exclaimed Harry. "I didn't get asked. It's all on the television and radio as well."

"What about Hopkins? Christ, it's a whitewash job, Harry."

"Maybe. Hopkins called while you were out. He wants to see us in his office first thing in the morning."

Zarich scowled at the newspaper. "I'll be interested to hear what smooth-talking bullshit he tries to feed us."

The beautifully garbed Hopkins welcomed them with the same affability, but there was no sign of the portfolio on his desk.

"I expect you've seen the news," he said.

"It's hard to miss," said Zarich sarcastically.

Hopkins offered an apologetic gesture. "Time was going by, we had to say something about the absence of an important man like Humbert."

"Then why an accident?"

Hopkins paused for a discreet cough before answering. "As you can understand, Lieutenant, this is a difficult situation, most difficult. The ramifications are enormous, both here and overseas. Ah, some investigations have been made. Divers have been up to the water hole and located the helicopter . . . and the PT boat." He smiled. "You were right, there were numerous bones inside the boat, so there's no denying the crew were murdered." He shrugged. "Although whether by Humbert we'll probably never know for sure."

They were both taken aback by the speed with which Hopkins had acted. Someone wanted it resolved, and quickly out of the way.

"Then you've got a salvage operation going?" asked Markby.

The preliminary cough came again. "Not yet . . . but we will in time."

"What do you mean by 'in time'?" queried Zarich suspiciously.

"Well, from this point I think we need to move fairly cautiously. There are . . . considerations. When we have all our facts straight there'll probably be some sort of, ah . . . judicial enquiry."

Zarich and Markby exchanged sour glances. Zarich was sure his first impression of a whitewash was right; the politicians were scrambling for cover, intent on burying it all in a legal maze. "It's a cover-up," he declared with blunt hostility. "You're letting Humbert off the hook. He was a murdering sonofabitch, and I want the world to know it."

"I consider that unfair criticism," said Hopkins firmly. "I think you have to leave it to the government to do what's best in the interests of the Australian people."

Zarich gave a scornful laugh. "That won't satisfy my people in New York," he warned harshly.

"Yes, ah, well we regard this as a security matter, Lieutenant. You may not be aware but there are severe penalties in this country for breaking security." He turned cold eyes to Markby. "I'm sure you realize that, Sergeant."

Markby merely replied with an offhand twitch of his shoulders.

"Our ambassador has been in touch with your government, Mr. Zarich," continued Hopkins. "And they see our point of view. They've agreed to hold down on everything until our, ah, enquiries are completed."

Zarich knew it was bullshit; they'd blocked him off, but he had a feeling there wasn't a thing he could do about it. For the first time he felt a sense of relief he'd lost the tug-of-war with the crocodile. They would never have nailed Humbert; the entire story of the Old Tart would have been smothered under a blanket of secrecy.

"What about Roman? Does he get a medal?" he sneered.

Hopkins ignored the sardonic remark. "Well, we've been questioning him, but of course you wouldn't have heard about the chief inspector."

"Heard what?"

"He shot himself early this morning."

There was a short period of stunned silence.

"Jesus," croaked Markby.

Hopkins spread his hands in a motion of regret. "Unfortunate, but in the light of everything that's happened perhaps it's just as well he couldn't face the disgrace." He grimaced. "He could have done nothing but harm the reputation of the force."

Even then Zarich's mind went immediately to Cassie. That would probably put her in the clear, because doubtless the evidence of her involvement had died with Roman. And maybe the heroin charge too. Did he care?

"Of course there are so many things none of us can ever know," Hopkins continued. "There is still so much that is only conjecture. The hijacking of the *Awa Maru*. Who killed the crew of the Old Tart." He carefully scrutinized the faces of the two policemen. "I know you agree with me."

The words were softly spoken, but he left no doubt that the case of the Old Tart stayed right there in his hands, with his discretion to do whatever he thought fit.

Zarich didn't bother to answer. How considerate of Roman to blow his brains out. He had the feeling if he stayed listening to this crap much longer he'd puke all over the expensive carpet. He just wanted to be out of the office, back to the sights and sounds and smells of New York—there was only frustration here. Yet Hopkins was right, there were so many things they would never know. He was suddenly sick of the sound of Humbert's name, of the Old Tart. It had changed him, Cassie had changed him, and he wasn't too sure how he was going to cope with the new Zarich. He nodded curtly to Markby. "Come on, let's get the hell out, Harry. It's only shit in here."

There was no further communication from Hopkins, and after three days Zarich decided he couldn't play the waiting game any longer. The politicians were probably too concerned with burrowing madly to conceal any connection to Humbert. Maybe it would all come out eventually, but safely bundled in legal jargon. He wanted only to go home. He said a fond farewell to Helen and the boys.

"It'll heal, Ed," she advised softly. "It always does."

He smiled and wished there was another Helen.

Harry drove him to the airport, and they stood close together amidst the bustle and chatter of the departure lounge, savoring a bond that had taken on special meaning for both of them. They would exchange letters, perhaps the occasional telephone call, but this marvelous sense of brotherhood would fade into wistful memory.

"Watch out for her, will you, Harry," he muttered.

Markby gave an understanding smile. "Sure. I'll see what I can do."

When the boarding light began to flicker he took Harry's hand in a tight grip, and held it as long as he could. "I wish I could find the words," he muttered huskily.

"It's all been said . . . mate," replied Markby gruffly. He slapped him across the shoulder. "Take care of yourself, and stay in touch."

Zarich turned abruptly away, and was headed for the embarkation doors when he saw Cassie standing to one side by the check-in counter. Merely watching, face serious, very erect, very still, but she made no attempt to approach him, just her mouth curving in the faint suggestion of a smile. Maybe Harry had told her he was leaving, or more likely Helen. She looked superb in a pink outfit. He came to a sudden halt, but he knew nothing had changed; he loved her, and she loved him, but there was no way he could handle it. Not now. If he stayed with her, after a while every time he looked at her he would have a vision of a pathetic body floating in the water, or imagine the screams of passengers as a jet plunged out of the sky.

He nodded slowly, returned the smile in kind, then went slowly through the embarkation door. He held it ajar for a short time, looking at her, remembering the way it had been, then he let it go and shut her from sight.

Introducing Ben Perkins, a hard-boiled, motor city PI who doesn't exactly look for trouble, it has a way of finding him.

THE BACK-DOOR MAN

by Rob Kantner

Coming in July, from Bantam Books

"Sure, I'm sorry the bastard's dead. He got killed before I could get back the money he stole from me."

When it comes to cash, the milk of human kindness is nowhere to be found in Joann Sturtevant. That isn't how she got to be filthy rich, but it's one of the reasons she's stayed that way.

I leaned back in the comfortable, upholstered patio chair and lighted a short cork-tipped cigar. The sunroom of Mrs. Sturtevant's Bloomfield Hills mansion was ablaze with mid-day light, and glowed with exquisite taste in furniture, paintings and other appointments. There's prettier places in the world. There's prettier places in Michigan. There may even be prettier places around Detroit. Or so I've heard.

Through my fresh, fragrant (at least to me) cigar smoke, I watched her stew. Mrs. Sturtevant is the classic specimen of Bloomfield Hills widowed wealth: well-fed yet thin, well-dressed yet understated, well-coiffed yet simple. Angular, taut, blonde, smooth. Who is very picky about spelling Joann with no "e" at the end. A very damn good looking 60ish. A tough old broad who pays well.

When she didn't enlighten me further, I prompted, "Papers said it was some kind of commodities flim-flam?"

"That's right, Ben." She pulled her elbows against her sleek flanks and gazed out a broad expanse of sunlit glass toward the golf course. This wasn't hers, she informed me once. Though it had been offered to her, and she certainly could afford it, but, after all, she'd added innocently, she already owned a country club in Palm Springs, Florida, and one golf course was enough for the average person.

Right.

As her gaze faded into the past, I saw the coarse uncaring sunlight revealing all her little facial lines, but she was rich enough and tough enough not to care. "Arthur Barton was a top rep for Trans-Ocean Commodities out of Cincinnati. Really knew his stuff. I invested heavily with him, made a lot of money. Then about seven years ago he simply vanished. Along with about $150,000 of my money. Plus, so I learned, huge sums that belonged to other people."

"Didn't Trans-Ocean make good?" I asked.

Her voice went hard, gaze clicking back to the present. "Didn't have to. Turned out Barton was in business for himself, on the side. He'd set up my investments, and a lot of others, through a paper company that he controlled. When he disappeared, the company's money disappeared with it. Trans-Ocean, 'regretfully,' " she added sarcastically, "had no obligation to us since our business wasn't placed through them."

"Seems to me a good lawyer could—"

"A good lawyer tried, Mr. Perkins!" she flared. "I sued his estate, I sued Trans-Ocean, everybody else we could get our hands on. We turned them upside down trying to shake money out, and came up empty."

Poor old Joann. 'Course I didn't say this, I only thought it. Insulting clients can be bad for business. "So then he turned up again."

"Yes." Her voice had the quiet of impending disappointment. Of course I knew part of the story, at least what had been in the papers, but you let Mrs. Sturtevant tell things her own way. "Couple weeks ago. Turned himself in to the FBI in Cincinnati. Apparently he'd undergone some kind of religious awakening. Came from nowhere to do penance for his crimes. And, so I'm told, turn a lot of the money back over to the people he stole from."

She went silent as the maid came in and gave her a large chunk of cylindrical crystal filled to the brim with sparkling something and ice and shavings of lime peel. Of course the maid brought me nothing. I was as much a hired hand as she was. And, the way things were shaping up, this time Mrs. Sturtevant would be hiring me for more than driver and bodyguard and stuff. Good. I could use the excitement and the money, not necessarily in that order.

Mrs. Sturtevant sipped her drink, ice clinking, and, uncharacteristically, didn't continue with the story. Not that she really needed to. According to the papers, Barton refused to tell the FBI where he'd hidden the seven years he'd been away. But he did tell them he'd hidden a lot of the money around the Detroit area, and offered to lead them to it.

So the FBI chartered a plane, and Barton boarded it in Cincinnati along with four special agents. Just east of Detroit City Airport, the plane went down, killing all aboard. An accident, they called it.

"What struck me as ironic," I mused, "was that Barton's wife in Cincinnati had just had him declared legally dead when he turned up out of nowhere."

"So she was put to some inconvenience," Mrs. Sturtevant said acidly. "Too God-damned bad." She set her drink down on the glass table between us, fixed me with a piercing gray stare, and said with great precision: "Now, Ben. I want you to go out and find my money and bring it back here to me. You want the job?"

I shifted, gnawed my cigar, rubbed the back of my neck, squinted. Yes, I wanted the job. Business was slow. But, as sometimes happens, my insatiable desire to maintain a regular eating schedule went into hand-to-hand combat with an inbred compulsion to level with my client. It shouldn't come as a great shock to learn that this had been known to cost me business.

"Seven years," I said. "And nobody knows where he was all that time. Long cold trail."

"You're a professional," she replied evenly.

"And, as far as you know, there's not a hint of where he might have hidden the money."

"I know you thrive on challenge," she said with uncharacteristic patience, figuratively leaning back in the fighting chair with her rod bending double. "It's in Detroit somewhere, that's all anybody knows."

I sighed, took a reinforcing toke on my cigar, and tapped off the gray ash in the heavy glass ashtray in front of me. Into the breach, as the fella said. "Case you haven't heard, Mrs. Sturtevant, you're world-class rich. A hundred fifty G's is chump change to you. You probably spent that on living expenses alone—"

"More," she interrupted. Not bragging, just giving information. Given a choice, which she always is, believe me, Joann Sturtevant prefers that people get their facts straight, right down to the damn "e" that isn't on the end of her name.

" 'Kay," I waved my hand. "You probably dropped a chunk on your lawyer already. Now you want to hire me to work on it, and to be honest with you, there's not a lot to go on. How much more money you want to pour into this thing?"

I was setting the stage in the event of failure. She can buy anything she wants, but she wasn't buying this. "It's not the money, it's the principle."

"With me," I grinned, "it's never the principle, it's the money."

Her first smile. "Don't try to con me, Perkins. I know you better than that."

"Then for God's sake keep it to yourself. I got a reputation to maintain." I took a deep drag on my cigar, pretending to consider. "Okay, I'll look into it. Have to do some traveling, I'll need an advance on expenses."

"Naturally," she said coolly. Her elegant hands went out and opened a plain manila file folder before her. She picked up a shiny piece of gold plastic and tossed it over to me. I fielded it, and stared.

It was an American Express Gold Card with BEN PERKINS embossed in black in the lower left-hand corner. Maybe I could do TV commercials now. If I played my cards right, heh-heh. "Do you know me? Well, I unplug toilets and track down runaways and fix broken windows and collect overdue bills. . . . " Well, no sense in dreaming; watching commercials are about as close as guys like me ever get to cards like this, usually.

Mrs. Sturtevant was talking. "It's in your name, but the account is billed directly to me."

I was still staring at the card. "What's the credit line on it?" I asked faintly.

"Adequate."

"Yup. Well fine then." I breathed deeply.

Mrs. Sturtevant went on, "I've also arranged a cover for you." Her hands went back into the file folder and came out with a couple of typed letters on heavy bond letterhead. Personalized "To Whom It May Concern" letters from the editor and publisher of a major national news magazine. Informing the reader that I was on assignment to do a feature story on Arthur Barton, and requesting the reader to render me all the courtesy and cooperation due to a member of the press. Very impressive and official.

I said to her, "Won't cut any ice with the FBI. I've tangled with them before, they know me, they won't buy this. I'll just have to steer clear of them."

She closed the now-empty file folder and sat back. "As my husband would have said, don't bring me problems, bring me solutions."

A man of many qualities, her late husband: top executive, former Secretary of Defense and also, apparently, phrase-coiner. I crushed out the red-hot stub of my cigar in the ashtray. "Can I ask you something?"

Her face said our business was concluded, but Mrs. Sturtevant is nothing if not civil. "By all means."

"Why me?"

"Why *not* you?" she returned.

"Hey, let's face it." I spread my hands, palms up. "I'm small potatoes. I maintain an apartment complex to put food on the table and do this stuff for walking-around money. You could hire a platoon of the best detectives. So why me?"

For the first time since my arrival—and probably the first time in the years I'd known her—Mrs. Sturtevant's imperious, businesslike demeanor slipped just a notch. "I'll tell you why." She leaned forward on her arms, folding her fingers together, eyes direct. "Because you're about the only man I know whom I can trust to bring me a hundred fifty thousand in cash money without helping yourself to the goodies. And because you've done other jobs for me and I like the way you work. You're streetsmart, you use the rules when you can and break them when you have to. You're not a pretty face or a smooth talker; you're a back-door man, like in the old jazz song.''

"Never heard it. Musta been before my time."

"Not before mine." She straightened and stood, and what for her was a sentimental moment evaporated. "Good luck."

I know an invitation to leave when I hear one. I stood up, slipped the Gold Card into my shirt pocket, folded the reference letters into thirds, and put them in the inner pocket of my one-and-only suit jacket. The maid appeared to show me out, and Mrs. Sturtevant shook my hand firmly. "Get it back for me, Ben."

"Do my best." It was the only thing I could promise her. I turned and followed the maid toward the foyer.

When we reached the door, Mrs. Sturtevant called me and I walked back. "Did you hear that Emilio Mascara is back in Detroit?"

"No, ma'am. The union doesn't brief me on prison releases anymore."

She laughed. I went out to my car, a blue '71 Ford Mustang convertible parked in the sweeping horseshoe driveway, fired it up, and drove away.

DON'T MISS
THESE CURRENT
Bantam Bestsellers

Special Offer
Buy a Bantam Book
for only 50¢.

Now you can have an up-to-date listing of Bantam's hundreds of titles plus take advantage of our unique and exciting bonus book offer. A special offer which gives you the opportunity to purchase a Bantam book for only 50¢. Here's how!

By ordering any five books at the regular price per order, you can also choose any other single book listed (up to a $4.95 value) for just 50¢. Some restrictions do apply, but for further details why not send for Bantam's listing of titles today!

Just send us your name and address and we will send you a catalog!

RELAX!
SIT DOWN
and Catch Up On Your Reading!

THRILLERS

Gripping suspense ... explosive action ... dynamic characters ... international settings ... these are the elements that make for great thrillers. And Bantam has the best writers of thrillers today—Robert Ludlum, Frederick Forsyth, Jack Higgins, Clive Cussler—with books guaranteed to keep you riveted to your seat.

Clive Cussler:

☐ 22866	PACIFIC VORTEX	$3.95
☐ 14641	ICEBERG	$3.95
☐ 23328	MEDITERRANEAN CAPER	$3.95
☐ 25896	RAISE THE TITANIC!	$4.50
☐ 25487	VIXEN 03	$4.50
☐ 25676	NIGHT PROBE!	$4.50

Frederick Forsyth:

☐ 25113	THE FOURTH PROTOCOL	$4.50
☐ 23105	NO COMEBACKS	$3.95
☐ 25524	DAY OF THE JACKAL	$4.50
☐ 25523	THE DEVIL'S ALTERNATIVE	$4.50
☐ 25224	DOGS OF WAR	$4.50
☐ 25525	THE ODESSA FILE	$4.50

Jack Higgins:

☐ 25091	DAY OF JUDGMENT	$3.95
☐ 23345	THE EAGLE HAS LANDED	$3.95
☐ 24284	STORM WARNING	$3.95

Prices and availability subject to change without notice.

Buy them at your local bookstore or use this handy coupon for ordering:

Bantam Books. Inc.. Dept. TH. 414 East Golf Road. Des Plaines. Ill 60016

Please send me the books I have checked above. I am enclosing $_____
(please add $1.50 to cover postage and handling). Send check or money order
—no cash or C.O.D.'s please.

Mr/Mrs/Miss_____

Address _____

City _____ State/Zip _____

TH—3/86

Please allow four to six weeks for delivery. This offer expires 9/86.